# A Clod *of* Wayward Marl

# ALSO BY RICK DEMARINIS

## NOVELS
A Lovely Monster (1975)
Scimitar (1977)
Cinder (1978)
The Burning Women of Far Cry (1986)
The Year of the Zinc Penny (1989)
The Mortician's Apprentice (1994)

## SHORT STORIES
Jack & Jill (1979)
Under the Wheat (1986)
The Coming Triumph of the Free World (1988)
The Voice of American (1991)
Borrowed Hearts (1999)

## NON-FICTION
The Art and Craft of the Short Story (2000)

# A
# CLOD
## *of*
## WAYWARD
# MARL

Rick DeMarinis

2 0 01

Parts of Chapters One and Two of this novel
in modified form were published as
"A Romantic Interlude" in *GQ,* Oct. 1997.

FIRST EDITION
Published February 2001

Dustjacket and interior art by Michael Kellner.

ISBN 0-939767-37-6

DENNIS MCMILLAN PUBLICATIONS
11431 E. GUNSMITH DR.
TUCSON, ARIZONA 85749
http://www.dennismcmillan.com

For Carole

"What doesn't kill you doesn't kill you."

–Crazy Red Fingerhut

*A Clod of* Wayward Marl

The resemblance of this book to El Paso, Texas, its environs and/or denizens, is, of course, completely coincidental.

# One

THE MAN LOOKED LIKE CLARK GABLE BUT he had a dirty mouth. The bartender was indifferent. The barmaids ignored him. Only Guido seemed to take offense. Shut up, you moron, he said. The dashing man turned on his barstool to face Guido. He was drunk. His big handsome Clark Gable head rocked saucily from side to side in an un-Clark Gable way. He suggested a menu of oral services he was sure Guido had the expertise to provide. Guido knocked the man off his stool with a short chopping punch. This surprised Guido. The punch didn't have much authority, yet the man lay sprawled on his back, twitching. Guido kicked him in the ribs, urging him to get up. Only then did Guido notice the twin aluminum canes resting against the bar next to the man's stool. You shouldn't have done that, sport, the barkeep said. Loren's a very sick man. Two other men helped Loren back to his feet. He's got Lou Gehrig's disease, a barmaid said, her voice crisp. The men who helped the sick man up now helped him slip into his canes. The sick man, who looked like Clark Gable only from the neck up, worked his way out of the bar. Each step required heroic effort. Someone held the door for him as he wobbled through it. Guido, humiliated, headed for the rear exit. Ugly remarks pelted his back like stones as he left the bar he could never visit again.

That was a month ago.

I will do better, he told himself. I will turn the other cheek, I will walk the extra mile. But here was the trouble: he could not stop himself from reacting without thinking. The reflective pause, the mindful hesitation, were not his habit. His habit was to voice his first thought. Like hammer taps to the patella, perceived abuse triggered an electric knee-jerk response.

For the second straight day this got him into trouble. Yesterday it had been three Bloody Marias sucked down like snakebite antidote that pulled him into a situation he should have shrugged off. Today, he antagonized an armed woman. He should have recognized her, but Guido persisted in moving through life on the narrow path of his nagging sorrows.

His new retreat was called The Lost Cause Bar and Grille, a half mile from campus. He had been drinking light beer, afraid of tequila's tendency to uncage his demons. The woman he spoke to was drinking club soda and minding her own business.

Guido felt balanced and circumspect, a feeling he should not have trusted. He glanced at himself in the bar mirror. The reflection was commendable. He'd costumed himself with reckless expense: mustard cashmere jacket, chocolate gabardine slacks to match, forest green shirt, his tie a rustic geometry of autumn pastels. His shoes were cap-toed lace-ups, the color of old gold.

His earnest paunch signified "arrival," but he looked admirably unimpressed by success. There was no hint here of a man subject to episodes of poor behavior. He looked reliable and worthy, this latest incarnation of Guido Tarkenen—paperback writer of "slasher trash" and now rookie professor on the mirage-infested southwestern cusp of the country, in a town so remote from the main axis of the nation's culture and commerce its founders had named it La Siberia.

Yesterday he'd looked bad. The memory made him wince. A pointless conversation about dental hygiene degenerated into a contest. Guido argued for dental floss—which he never used. His wife, Kirsten—gone now, the dust of her exit still graining his eyes—used it twice a day. A challenger celebrated the Water Pik with evangelical heat. The man grew lyrical over the Water Pik. He denounced floss. He scorned floss. Guido felt Kirsten herself was being debased.

"Floss is the only way to be sure all foreign particles are removed," Guido said.

The man laughed. "You're the one," he sneered, "to be defaming foreigners, you sodding Wog. I say stockyard flop to your effing floss." The man—not a Brit but an affected impostor—had a reed-thin body made top-heavy by a hydrocephalic head. Guido saw the man's crescent profile as an anthropomorphized comma. A hazard of inbreeding. The smirking face was set into a bony concavity, the narrow forehead overhanging the wild unhappy eyes like a shelf of stone. He looked like the Man in the Moon.

The Man in the Moon raised his tumbler of Cutty Sark in a spirited toast to modern methods of dental hygiene. Black rot edged the natural ochre of his teeth. "Pardon me?" Guido said. *"Wog?"*

"I believe we are speaking roughly the same tongue," the man said, affecting now the nasality and trilled r of the privileged classes. In a scrupulously tiny script he made side-by-side lists on a paper napkin with his ball-point pen and handed it to Guido:

| Floss User: | Water Pik User: |
|:---:|:---:|
| whole wheat only | white bread only |
| tofu eater | red meat eater |
| low-tech, small is beautiful | hi-tech, big is best |
| has gay friends | homophobic and proud of it |

3

| permits female on top | missionary position dominator |
| WOG lover | loyal WASP |
| spongy-brained relativist | clear-headed absolutist |
| uses the phrase, "dead white men" when referring to great historical figures. | respects European genius and The Western Tradition. |

"You see," he said. "I know your heart."

"You don't know your ass," Guido said.

Eventually they put hands on one another. Guido had looked forward to this since the man appeared to be a physical wreck. In Guido's mind, the argument was not trivial. There was a lot at stake. The argument seemed to have significance past its narrow subject. Life and death issues lurked beyond the restraints of common sense.

Guido hated the Man in the Moon. *Hate* was the subject. Guido embraced his hatred. Hate was good, hate was cleansing. It scrubbed the sludge and clabber of worry from the bloodstream. Hate was nature's own angioplasty. Hate was a tonic.

The Man in the Moon stepped forward on his pointy toes, his fists and forearms held up before him, a flimsy gate of bone and knuckle daring trespass. "Go back where you came from, Nancy boy," he said. "Return to your spawning place, you filth-sucking Sodomite."

"I'm an American," Guido said.

"Means nothing. It only means you and your spawn came from someplace else. Go back, study your Lower Slobbovian roots. Discover how useless emigration is."

Guido searched for wit, found none. "You skunk," he said. He organized a pugilist's pose of his own, a weaving, flatfoot shuffle, his left arm extended straight from the shoulder, chin tucked tight against the collar bone. He tapped the Man in the Moon's jaw and the melony head filled with tooth-rot

4

tipped back on the slender neck. The man roared and rushed Guido enveloping him with thin arms, his septic breath burning Guido's eyes.

They grappled their way to the floor, trading gouges and jabs. They pumped elbows and knees into each other's soft regions. The Man in the Moon's fragility was a deception. His spidery legs kicked out with the piston-like fury of an Irish folk dancer. Lord of the Dance in a barroom brawl. His feet bicycled against the barstools. One of the stools dropped on Guido's head. He blinked into momentary darkness; he was winded.

The Man in the Moon was also a sedentary worker and soon wore himself out. They held each other in failing arms, panting, red in the face, the taxed muscles convulsing in quirky spasms. Guido believed this would be misread by those only now entering the bar: overbold samesex lovers savoring the seizures of simultaneous release, public scrutiny be damned. The thought gave him new strength. He bit the Man in the Moon's ear; the Man in the Moon howled.

Guido's prostate had been giving him trouble lately. He hadn't been able to urinate easily all morning. But the flurry of semi-violence had shifted the troublesome gland. He fought to hold back the flood.

"I give up, asshole," he whispered into his opponent's bleeding ear.

"Hah!" the Man in the Moon cried out. "Did you hear that? The bloody yellow Wog surrenders!"

"Shut up and get off me," Guido hissed.

They were helped to their feet by a barmaid. She cursed when she broke a nail on Guido's sleeve. Guido said, "Tell him, Tansy. Tell this lime-sucking pederast the advantages of cotton floss."

His blue-lipped adversary, alarmed by the first gusts of a myocardial storm but still managing combative flashes of black-edged teeth, wheezed, "Dog filth on your bleeding floss, you sodding ponce! Great yellow cakes of rancid rat semen on your cotton floss! *Vive le* Water-Pik!" His pale fist drifted past Guido's nose, wobbling on its wrist like a lily in a gale.

Guido trotted to the men's room, unzipping as he ran. His bladder emptied itself in weak, intermittent spurts. It took minutes. He moaned with gratitude, forehead pressed to the clammy tile. Beneath his moans, he heard sirens. When he returned to the bar, the Man in the Moon was on an EMS gurney. "I thrashed the floss-loving Wog!" he bellowed, his voice muted by the oxygen mask that now covered his nose and mouth.

Guido hoped the man would experience a lingering and terrifying death.

Today—a glorious Friday—Guido vowed to accommodate the world. He would be kind and considerate to all. He would agree amiably with any rabid opinion, no matter how wrong-headed or obnoxious. He would sign petitions when asked. He would accept leaflets from the millennium-crazed doomsday squads. He would give his spare change to the homeless. He would buy key-chains from the deaf. He would be as compliant as an Italian streetwalker greeting the first phalanx of yet another invading army.

He was in fact half Italian. It was in his genetic nature to be agreeable, to have a sunny disposition, and to be "simpatico." But it was also in his nature, since he was half Finn, to be afflicted with self-doubt and touchiness, ready to fight to the death at even mild affront. Finns, a brooding race of subarctic steam-bathers, were reputed to be fond of knife-fighting. Guido often fantasized carrying a dagger—a *puka*, or (honoring his Neapolitan heritage) a *stiletto*–not as a weapon, but as a symbol, just as another might carry a Phi Beta Kappa key, or wear the plaid of his clan.

"Clearly a schizophrenic combination," his ex-wife's ex-shrink once told him. "Guido will want to avoid stressful situations that might touch off a regrettable episode."

This shrink, Dr. Dale Burnaby–who always referred to Guido in the third person, even when Guido was sitting on the opposite side of the doctor's desk–had a bad reputation among his fellow professionals. Burnaby promoted as fact weakly supported theories that traced asocial behavior, neurosis, and especially psychopathic tendencies, to genetic defect. He was a staunch believer in the troublesome extra Y chromosome. "If it was up to me," he told Guido, "I'd rub out those XYY freaks. I'd have them extracted from the gene pool. By force, if necessary."

Guido tried to visualize the forced removal of genetic material–squads of government Gene Police scouring the procreative machinery of the nation for renegade ova and sperm, a bizarre system of informants and spies, compulsory sterilizations, state-proscribed couplings, state-sanctioned marriages. Compliance with the social contract programmed into the DNA would be the next step.

He went to this doctor because Burnaby cheerfully wrote prescriptions for interesting drugs on demand. But Guido also took him seriously enough to worry about the possibility of warring demons locked in his DNA. Physicists were discussing, *seriously,* sub-atomic phenomena as if they were dealing with willful entities. And since human beings were made up of aggregates of atoms, why not consider the possibility that incompatible genetic demons might sabotage the host organism with microcosmic wars of mutual destruction? Billions of suicidal subatomic warriors–somber Finn quarks and passionate Neapolitan quarks—murdering one another in obscure plasmic battlefields.

Guido had vowed to let the Neapolitan side of his nature express itself today. The woman didn't seem unapproachable. Hadn't she been sitting alone for the better part of an hour at the bar? Didn't that give him license? Anyway, his remark had been mild by any standard. "You have priceless Virgin Mary skin," he said. "Unblemished as the Jesus-haunted communion wafer itself. I raise my glass to original *skin*." He chuckled attractively, monitoring his performance in the bar mirror. "I hope my little pun is acceptable to you, Miss."

"Keep your little pun in your shorts," she said unpleasantly, not bothering to turn her head. Her voice was flat, without nuance. A bored voice, a dead-end voice. The voice, Guido realized when it was much too late, of a woman on a mission. "Drinking your lunch again, I see," she added.

Guido regarded her. Did he *know* this woman? Was she a regular at The Lost Cause Bar and Grille? She was dressed in light work-out clothes: nifty half-zip sweatshirt, the chopped off sleeves revealing weight-trained biceps; teal-blue nylon running shorts; canvas kangaroo pack snugged against her flat lower abdomen; expensive cross-training shoes—a lunch-hour jogger or power-walker. A dark hourglass of sweat sopped the area between her compact breasts; her hair was tied back with ordinary twine or rawhide. She was pretty, but melancholy overruled her natural beauty, made it irrelevant. She reminded him of Kirsten: big-boned, solid, good neck, tennis-firm legs and arms, and—he glanced down at the brass rail—long, narrow, highly arched feet. He pictured her in a low-cut cocktail dress, her face made up and her hair sexily crimped, and he felt an old attraction that made his swollen prostate burn.

8

"Just what do you think you're staring at?" the woman said.

"At a memory of loveliness," he said. He meant it. The salt of nostalgia stung his eyes. The divorce papers had arrived early in the week. He hadn't signed them. Technically, Kirsten wasn't his ex yet. Sentimentality—it lurked in his blood, another defective gene.

The woman sipped her club soda. "You insincere prick," she said quietly, facing him now. It was an impersonal observation. The world was plagued with insincere pricks, and this was just one more confirmation.

Guido regarded her, his sentimental mood souring. He shrugged. Then he made the mistake that kept his two-day streak of bad moves alive. "Okay, then: Doleful dildo banger; lonely rider of the electric zucchini," he said. "Midnight baton twirler," he added.

It seemed reasonable: if this woman took compliments as insults, she was likely to take an outright insult as a compliment. He winked at some of the regulars down the bar, sharing his amusing inverse logic. He searched his memory and came up with a choice fragment of an Irish curse: "May the devil take the whey-faced slut by the hair, and beat bad manners out of her skin for a year." This couplet of an old James Stephens poem presented at auditorium volume in a makeshift brogue drew more phlegmy cackles from the afternoon corps of journeymen drinkers.

The woman crooked a beckoning finger at Guido. She smiled. Believing that he'd been correct, that she had been favorably stimulated by his crude remarks, he leaned toward her. She brought her lips close to his ear, reached between his legs. She found his balls and squeezed them needfully. He waited—hope soaring—for her electrifying tongue.

9

"You are going to die for that filthy remark," she said, squeezing harder. "And you're going to die *shitting* yourself, like the dirty little sewer rat you are."

Guido's bowels acknowledged threat: eruptive liquid gaspings. He tried to lurch away from her but her gym-trained hand on his balls became a vice. Embarrassed by pain, then fear, he said, "Hey, look—she wants me, guys!" The regulars made uncivil noises, signifying approval. Guido rolled his eyes and bit the tip of his tongue puckishly.

He didn't see the slap coming. It was not a hesitant slap, flicked ladylike from the wrist. She held him in place with her left hand and walloped him with her right, the blow achieving maximum velocity at the radius of her long arm. It caught him flush against the ear. Guido, who had been leaning backward to offer yet another raffish observation to the regulars, was swept off his stool by the force of the blow. She gave his balls one last iron-fingered squeeze and let him go. He hit the floor on the point of his tailbone and barked, his head roaring with colossal chimes. This amused the regulars greatly. Guido picked himself up to a grainy chorus of hoots. He dusted his jacket and slacks with nonchalance, but then the stab of pain in his lower back made him grab the bar and cry out.

"I meant what I said, bozo," the woman said, with a calmness that Guido finally realized was pathological. She stood before him—ready for war, her athletic knees bent—anticipating his first move. Bands of visible muscle writhed in her legs. Her biceps were veined, the muscles hard and round as baseballs.

"You don't remember me, do you?" she said.

"You're confusing me with someone else," he managed.

"*Am* I? Maybe so. But, no, I don't think so."

"I'm not the guy," he said.

"She shrugged. "What's the difference. You'll do."

10

"Look," he said. "Whatever it is you think I've done, I want you to know that I'm. . . ."

*"Sorry?"*

"Yes. Sorry. Really."

"You insincere prick."

It was an argument he was not going to win, that was clear. She had singled him out as an adequate substitute for the guy who had fucked her over, and there was nothing he could do about *that*. He bowed elaborately in a small effort to save face, then left The Lost Cause by the back door, fighting nausea.

The woman wasn't willing to accept his whipped-dog retreat. She followed him out into the weedy field behind the bar and down the steep banks of the arroyo that tunneled under a railroad trestle–his short cut back to campus. Thinking that he had taken enough humiliation at the hands of this woman, Guido decided to wait for her and give her the confrontation she wanted. He'd never hit a woman before, but equal opportunity was a two-way street, he reasoned. He was near the bottom of the arroyo where the greasewood bushes and ocotillo were tall and thick. The woman made her way down the embankment–not tentatively but quick and sure-footed, and this athleticism made Guido think twice about the wisdom of confronting her. When she was within a hundred feet he saw the missionary adrenaline in her eyes. He back-pedaled, then turned and ran. Even so, she gained on him. But just as he broke into a full sprint, he stepped into a rabbit burrow and went down, his ankle imploding with hot pain.

The woman stood over him, digging into her kangaroo pack, as if looking for some private, feminine thing. The tiny, snub-nosed revolver she drew out of it fit her hand as comfortably as a tube of lipstick. "I won't take it anymore," she said. "Not from any of them, and certainly not from *you.*"

11

He cringed and rolled away from the righteous steel finger of the tiny pistol. It was pointed at his head. He offered it alternative targets on the meatier backside of his anatomy. He covered his head with his arms and hands. A small caliber bullet in the brain was a terrifying thing: he might vegetate in an irreversible coma absorbed in hellish dreams for twenty years before he died. And given the subjective nature of the mind, twenty years might easily translate into eternity. Guido believed that Hell's vestibule with its zoo of horrors was very real and always close at hand. A fallen-away Catholic–though no Catholic, as the Jesuits often observed, ever falls completely away–Guido made the sign of the cross on his forehead with his thumb, giving himself emergency absolution.

Then he remembered the woman. She was a secretary in some administrative part of La Siberia Tech. A woman, he now recalled, who had a harried look, as if her work load was three times heavier than anyone could be expected to bear. He'd found himself in her office by mistake, and he remembered paying her what he believed was a compliment. "Hey, great sweater, Carma!"–yes! that was her name, *Carma!* Carma something or other, her name plaque prominent on her desk. She was one of the Dean of Education's secretaries. Guido had wandered into the Ed building before he'd learned his way around campus. And he remembered, now, her puzzling, inappropriate reply: "I *have* my limits," she said, tight-lipped and grim. *Limits? Limits?* Guido had thought, but he dropped it. He had no desire to explore whatever misapprehensions she had about him, or herself. He shrugged it off. He'd just gotten back to campus after lunch and was a bit juiced, he now recalled. The incident had been too trivial to remember, since it meant nothing to him at all. Until now. Carma.

She leaned down to him. "Pray," she said.

"What?"

"You'll want to pray, won't you? Before I kill you, I mean."

Guido hesitated.

"I don't want to return your soul to God unatoned," she said.

Guido closed his eyes.

"I'll give you a minute. I'd like to hear you pray. I'd like to know how a man like you justifies himself to God."

Guido cleared his throat. "Lord forgive me," he said. "I am not worthy." Though his words were calculated—meant to appease her, not God—Guido felt an honest sob of remorse rise in his chest.

"That's *it?*" she said. "That's not very good."

"It's all I can think of," Guido managed.

"I can almost pity you."

"If you could find it in your heart—"

She pulled the trigger. For a gun so small, it possessed the bellowing voice of doomsday.

Guido felt nothing. Then a burning shaft of pain, as if a white hot poker had been laid across his bare shoulder, made him scream. The scream was involuntary. It was high-pitched, unmanly, without timber—an infantile shriek, a frightened primate's formless vocalization. It embarrassed him. He rolled over, the flats of his hands held up as if they could catch bullets. "Ho now!" he said. "Don't! Jesus!" The words were his but the voice was not. Somewhere behind these bursts of sound, a calmer part of Guido hoped no one besides Carma was listening. "Don't kill me!" he begged, his hands up and moving. He'd experienced some bad depressions after Kirsten left, and had toyed with the idea of ending it all, but now he saw that life was sweet and necessary. He wanted to live. Life— weird and frightening and tiring and repetitive as it was—was *good*.

13

The drone of cicadas answered his plea. He braced himself and sat up. The woman was sitting in the weeds, holding the gun carelessly in her lap. "I've decided against it," she said.

"Thank Christ," Guido whispered to himself, like an amazed car dealer who had just sold a lemon. He decided to press his luck. "Look, Carma, I need a doctor. I promise I won't report this. I was out of line. I admit it. It was my fault. I see that now. But, really, I need to go to a hospital."

He knew he'd made a bad mistake. He'd called her by name. If she had any doubt about his being able to identify her, those doubts had been erased.

She raised the gun. She looked at the small revolver as if holding wordless dialogue with it. "I hate guns, really," she said. "I supported the Brady bill."

"Oh, yes! I did *too!*" Guido quickly agreed, happy to have found common ground.

She looked at him—shyly, he thought. "I can't take you to a hospital," she said. "They have to report gunshot wounds. It's the law."

Guido kept his eye on the gun. "Okay, fine. Look, let's let bygones be bygones," he said. "It's not a bad wound. It's just a scratch. I can take care of it myself." He felt faint. A film of greasy sweat glistened on his face. His arms were tingling.

"No, you need attention," she said. "I'll take you to my apartment."

Guido sagged. He could hear his blood's strong arterial roar.

"Will you agree to that?" she asked.

"Oh, please," Guido said, as if waving off a second helping of a rich dessert. "Don't trouble yourself. I'm fine. Really."

The gun wobbled in her hand, the barrel cutting zees in the air. "I can't go to jail. I just can't—I have two children at home. Rolfe refuses to send child support."

14

"Rolfe?" Guido saw a reassuring character trait emerge: The Mother. The Madonna. The Homemaker. The Giver, not the Taker, of life.

"Rolfe is my ex," she said. "The bastard who gave me this." She pulled up her sweatshirt, then her jogging bra. She pointed with the gun barrel to striated scars above her left nipple. Someone—Rolfe—had tried to brand her. "He did it with his salad fork. Pretty, isn't it? Know what he said? He said, 'No man will ever want to put his lips on that.'"

An impersonal mask hardened her expression again. The awful migration of conscious personality left vacuums in her eyes. A far away train, the afternoon Amtrak, gave a lengthy blast of its horn. Two longs, a short, followed by a long. Did railroad men *want* to visit loneliness and despair upon the land with their great melancholy horns? *No no, oh no,* it grieved—and Guido felt abandoned in a dark and lonely place without hope or luck or the last minute clarity of grace.

The gun drifted down again. It occurred to Guido that he could easily reach out and snatch it away from her, but he was wounded and felt light-headed while she was athletic and supercharged with craziness. If he made a move, she might empty the revolver into him. Guido knew that, if he survived this, he would emerge with a severely downgraded opinion of himself.

The woman's arm stiffened suddenly as she leveled the gun directly at his crotch. Guido felt the blood drain from his head. He saw the darkness behind the daylight. The universe's primary color was black. The optimistic blue sky, an accident of refraction, was nature's practical joke. One of many.

"I suppose you think you can do me, now that you've seen my breasts," she said.

Guido caught himself thinking this over. *"Do* you?" he said, three seconds too late. "I never thought that! I wouldn't have.

15

I mean, Jesus, Carma, what do you take me for? I *respect* you, I sincerely *respect* you!"

Her breasts were lovely: small but sturdily conical and tipped with pink rose buds. The unfortunate thought–that the salad fork tattoo only made them more interesting–he was sure was readable in his face. And now he had broken a drenching sweat. He could smell his bitter vapors.

"Shut *up*," she said, taking aim. "I think I know when I'm being manipulated. I've gone to *graduate* school in manipulation."

She approached Guido. Her eyes were bright and unblinking. She nudged his crotch with the gun barrel. Guido felt his genitals make the anatomical equivalent of a heart-stopping scream. They tightened and shriveled into microscopic pods– no doubt an evolutionary duck-and-cover cringe meant to let the hopeful tribes of mankind survive crisis and continue.

"Gee, looky there," Carma said, suddenly the cheerful departmental secretary again. "You've wet yourself!" She raised the gun and held it against his temple as she watched the rapidly expanding stain.

He looked down at his crotch, also surprised. He hadn't felt the urge or the release. "Looks like I've made your day," he said, disgusted with himself but suddenly calm.

The afternoon Amtrak thundered dramatically across the trestle. Passengers in the Sightseer Lounge waved at Guido and Carma. They believed they were witnessing a picturesque southwestern tryst–secret lunchtime lovers meeting at the bottom of a charming arroyo.

The roar and clatter of the train bullied everything else from Guido's mind. He sat still, the barrel of Carma's small pistol pressing a tiny O into the thin skin of his temple.

He saw the scene as if from altitude. He had the cold, detail-absorbing vision of a hawk. It was an interesting scene, even amusing, but it had lost its emotional core: his fear was gone; he was now a mildly curious bystander.

He thought about how he would write this scene, then re-write it, but he could not see how he might end it.

# TWO

I HAVE A FIRST AID KIT IN MY CAR," SHE SAID. She put her gun away and stood up. Then she did some stretching exercises for her hamstrings and calves. Guido watched melons of lively gluteal muscle lift and tighten her shorts. A vein in her calf stood out with pre-varicose intensity. She had slim ankles, a patch of hot-pink razor burns rising up the inside of each. The arroyo hummed with a million cicadas, and it seemed to Guido that he could hear each one individually. A breeze moved in the pampas grass, the tall flowering stalks swaying voluptuously. She turned to face him and he saw, with another surge of gratitude, that her madness had subsided. She was relaxed, and a bit concerned, though not contrite. She was not going to kill him, he knew this now, and he wanted to kiss her hand.

"I'm not sorry, you know," she said. "They might put me away again, to stabilize my medication, but I did not instigate. Or do you feel I am mistaken?"

"No, no," Guido said hastily. "I instigated. It was me. I'm the one who should be sorry."

"Should be? Then, you're *not?*"

Guido bit his tongue. A bird with bright red chevrons under its wings flew between them. Guido believed he and the bird

17

had exchanged a microsecond glance. He felt he could have counted its feathers. The pain of the wound—a hot steady throb—did not distract him. If anything, it sharpened his senses. He felt doubly alive. His ability to smell things, which had been wrecked by thirty years of Pall Malls, came back, bringing him the heady strangeness of a thousand subtle emanations. He felt overwhelmed with gifts. Life was not merely good, it was explosively good; it was singular, it was everything, it had no counterpart. Passionate tears of gratitude dripped from his chin. He was glad to be alive; not glad, ecstatic.

She saw his tears and was affected by them. Her own tears came then, and Guido saw each one of them as they found pathways in the ridges beside her nose. He saw them, and *smelled* them, their human salt, their bittersweet strength. He smelled the dirt he sat on, the greasewood bush that shaded him, the dry husks of dead insects scattered around him. He smelled his own blood, caking on his shoulder and back. He smelled his urine. And he smelled her—her perfumed sweat and her minted breath. He smelled the fragrance, stimulated by exercise and the desert heat, radiating from the dignified mound of her sex. He was sorry he had spoken crudely of that lovely mound, the *mons veneris,* as the medical texts called it, sorry he made it the object of an ancient and worn-out contempt.

"I was wrong to speak as I did," he said, with a formality he believed the situation required.

"And I was wrong to shoot you," she replied, also recognizing a need of formality.

She stepped toward him, placed a heatless kiss—the ethereal buss of an angel—on the top of his head. He caught her hand in his and pressed it to his lips. None of this seemed real to him. It had the quality of dream. Any second now, he'd wake up with a killer hangover. He already felt the terrible thirst, the ice-pick pulse stabbing his temple.

He watched quietly as the dream-woman cinched her kangaroo pack tight, then turned abruptly and charged up the steep embankment.

Guido sat unmoving for some time, content to take deep breaths of the gift-bearing air. But panic sped his pulse when the world suddenly darkened. It was only a swift cloud, low and dense, crossing the sun, but he believed some light-sensitive area had been shut off in his brain. He tried to stand, then had to sit back down hard, jarring his shoulder. A nebula of pain crabbed outward from the wound.

He sank into a black hole. The direction of his fall eventually reversed itself and he rose into a region of dreams so intensely visual that he believed he was conscious, until he understood that he had no control over the spill and flow of events here, or of his place in them.

A blade of grass loomed in front of him. It was wide as a plank. A green joy inflated him. The ribbed green meat, bent by its own lush weight, swayed seductively in the breeze. The sight of it urged greed's universal juice from his scissoring jaws. He was not able to think, and there was elation in this, too. He took the blade of grass into his mouth and chewed and chewed until it was paste. He crawled away, found his mate, a hard-backed beetle like him. He mounted her and her thin wings vibrated deliciously against his brittle stomach. He woke up chewing on his sleeve.

"I dreamed I was fucking a *bug*," he said.

But it wasn't the woman who snorted at the preposterousness of this, it was a ragged man in cardboard shoes with a thousand tiny flies in his beard. "She-*it*," he said. "I dreamed one time I was poppin' Miss Mass in her chubby caboose. If you gotta dream, dream decent, pardner. I read this book oncet, tole you how to program your dreams. I ain't had a bad one since. Like I said, I was packin' fudge for Miss Mass herself. I'm from Texas but I use to live in Bean Town, see. So this dream was kind of a milestone for me. Don't matter if your life on the dayshift sucks green steamin' shit, man, if you can program your dreams. I wake up from a dream like that I got to wax my dolphin, you know?" He made foul stroking motions with his dirty fist.

But the woman *had* returned, Guido realized, ignoring the ragged man, because his wound was now covered with a heavy gauze bandage. He felt the irritating pull of adhesive tape on his chest and back, the sting and sharp odor of rubbing alcohol.

"Where did she go?" Guido asked the bum.

"Who, bud? Amelia Earhart? Last they heard she was doin' Tai Chi in her Taipei condo, livin' under a alias with a twenty-year-old Kung Fu whiz named Guy Letkovitch. They say she got married to a Chinese slave trader, back in 1940, who pulled her out of the drink and now she owns seven hotels, a couple of upscale Hong Kong whorehouses, plus nineteen sweatshops in south China. Mrs. Tony Hsing. That's her name. She's fucken near ninety, maybe a hundert, but she still looks like she did in 1936, like in that movie about Shangri-la. Nobody gets fucken *old*. Voodoo, Chinese style, man. CIA wants to do her because she's got the documents that show the war with the Japs was planned way ahead of time by Roosevelt and Churchill to get the U.S. into the rumble. Ain't that a flyin' ball of shit? The Company's code name for her is Dragon Lady. Real original, huh?"

The ragged man held up his source of information, a tattered copy of a supermarket tabloid. He was sitting across from Guido, on the ground, smoking a Pall Mall. Guido recognized the expression on the man's face–the ironic giddiness of a man whose knowledge of the world's insane histories was so detailed that the only proper response to it was the self-redeeming smirk of a secularized saint. It was a standard academic expression. If it wasn't for the man's crude language and shabby clothes, he could have easily passed for a professor or a grad student. Guido stood up. He felt stronger, the shock apparently dissipated. He looked at his watch.

"Son of a bitch," he said, thinking of his missed office hours, plus his afternoon class. "I need this damned job."

The ragged man stood up, too. He was young, a weathered thirty, parchment skin etched by the hard outdoor life. "Pardner," he said. "You got any spare change?"

Guido's heightened awareness was gone. The world was just the world. A place to carry out your confused life. All he could smell now was cigarette smoke. The metallic aftertaste of fear was thick on his tongue. He found a mint in his shirt pocket and popped it into his mouth. "Jesus, you take my cigarettes and now you ask me for money," he said.

"You got it wrong, Jim," the man said. "I'm the man in the cardboard shoes, true, but you're the man with the paper asshole who dreams about fuckin' bugs. You and that twisted sister woke *me* up, pard. I was mindin' my bindle, dreamin' about drivin' my mule up the dirt road, little Miss Mass lovin' every bump and chuckhole, when, whap *whap whap,* somebody's takin' pot shots ten yards from my cardboard hacienda." He pointed to a refrigerator carton hidden in the brush.

"You heard more than one shot?" Guido asked, touching himself gingerly about the torso and legs.

"Seems like it was three or four," the man said, uninterested. "Now, how about a quarter. You gonna drop out of the fuckin' Fortune 500 if you part with two bits?"

21

But why would she have shot him again after patching his shoulder? Guido picked up his neatly folded jacket and slapped powdery dust from it, looking for blood. "I don't have any change," he said. The bullet hole in his jacket was small, but it was in the middle of a blood stain that looked like a dark butterfly.

"The point I'm makin' here, Jim, is I coulda ripped off your wallet and watch, not to mention your coat or those three-hundred dollar Gucci pumps, while you were stackin' zees. But, hey, I didn't. Okay? I waited for you to come around. I stood guard over you, man. I mean, there's some pond scum around here that might of dug the silver out of your molars. I'm not greedy like that. I oncet had a dog so greedy she caught horse turds on the fly. Look at the situation one more time, Jim, tell me you don't have any spare change on you."

Guido took out his wallet and gave the man a five dollar bill. "I'm grateful to you," Guido said. "Thanks."

The man held the bill up to the light. "No problem," he said. He gathered up his goods, tied them in a bindle, and ambled down the arroyo.

"Wait a minute!" Guido yelled. "Did you see what happened here?"

The man kept walking. "Have a nice day," he said.

Guido decided the bullet had only grazed his shoulder, and that it was his fear that had made him exaggerate the wound's seriousness. He wondered if the woman had gone. Had she driven back to the Ed building, gone back to her desk? Was she typing reports, filing papers, taking dictation—as if nothing had happened? Probably. Did the Dean of Education know that one of his secretaries was an armed and dangerous nut case? Maybe he would write an anonymous note to the Dean, suggesting he might have a personnel problem on his hands.

As Guido worked his way through the arroyo, back toward campus, he thought of several small retaliations, but in the end he rejected them all. It was unwise to antagonize the seriously disturbed. And whatever anger he might be entitled to was diluted by the fact that she had given him first aid while he was unconscious. She had managed to take his jacket off, folded it neatly, opened and pulled down his shirt, then she had dressed the wound with professional skill.

No, it was better to let bygones be bygones. He vowed once again to follow Dr. Burnaby's advice and avoid potentially dangerous situations. But how do you spot a dangerous situation before it becomes dangerous? There was the rub.

Guido couldn't find the path he usually used to get back to campus. He climbed through gnarly thickets, squibs of pain stabbing his swollen ankle with each step. Spines of nettle raked him, burrs hooked into his clothes. The sweat of the climb rolled from his hairline. He labored through the desert foliage he loved—ocotillo, cholla, and prickly pear; desert sage, Spanish dagger, and yucca—and into the perfect midwestern lawns, reflection pools, and English gardens of La Siberia Tech, a lavishly green oasis of reason and progress in the great southwestern desert.

23

# Three

A flux of vertical wind pushed him up the final steep grade of the arroyo, inflating his slacks and jacket so that he emerged on campus as a gaseous being, light and unstable–an inflated carnival effigy about to become airborne.

Students sidestepped away from him as they would from any gamboling and fractious derelict. Guido smiled, waved a reassuring hand. He composed plausible explanations for his appearance but no one came close enough to him to qualify as audience. Even so, he mumbled, "I'm going to be okay. Not to worry. I'm going to make it, kids."

The winding campus pathway took him between classroom buildings, windowless concrete towers that stood in somber rows. He felt miniaturized next to them, an adventuresome homunculus lost among giant gravestones. Cemeterial carpets of blue grass surrounded the monoliths. Homesick midwestern elms shaded the pathways around the buildings.

Guido turned a corner and the pathway opened into a flagstone-paved esplanade that was bordered by modern sculpture: H-beam gigantopods, the exoskeletons of futuristic rovers–all legs, no cortex–collectively flexed against a barely contained impulse for swift, rampaging movement. Guido always felt vaguely threatened around these sculptures. They made him timid.

Ahead of him, three postmodern structures shimmered in the reddening afternoon, stark palaces of hybrid design. Pre-stressed concrete trapezoids on massive concrete stilts topped

24

with irregularly gabled roofs. Rows of palladian windows opened the upper stories of the buildings to avenues of natural light.

Each building was fronted by wide reflecting ponds that repeated panels of red sky. The buildings seemed like mirages of buildings, hovering weightless above ponds of molten stone. This was the Applied Technologies Complex, and "the Future of La Siberia Tech," as the Vice Chancellor of the school often claimed.

Guido never wondered about the arcane activities that were conducted in these floating armadas of science. Whatever they were, they were important. You couldn't work in such a place and not feel compelled to think large.

Compelled to think small, Guido hobbled through the mall-like corridors between these buildings and down an old cracked and weed-sprouted concrete staircase to the backside of the campus—a lowland flat ungraced by midwestern landscaping, futuristic sculpture, or pricey architecture.

A dun-toned building sat in a vast, black-topped field like a cardboard box that had been tossed off a truck. This was the Department of English, segregated from the rest of the campus first by topography and now by spirit. It was de facto segregation, a direct consequence of progress: the campus had expanded to higher elevations as it became more and more enamored of technology, enriching itself with grants from both government and private industry in the process. The English Department, housed in a building that bordered a busy freeway, was a vestigial organ in the university corpus—forgotten, unnecessary, kept as a piece of cultural camouflage, the way an unlearned but pretentious man might keep a cheap encyclopedia among the dime store frou-frous and knick-knacks on his shelves. Guido believed La Siberia Tech kept the department only for the sake of accreditation.

25

He limped across the hot asphalt parking lot, his handkerchief tied over his nose and mouth. The smell of petroleum effluent hung in the grainy air. A refinery had been built across the freeway opposite the English building, and the foul air, trapped by an atmospheric inversion, was stippled with micropoisons.

To get to his office, he had to pass by the chairman's door. "Where the suffering Christ have you been?" Trimmer Swenson, department chairman, whispered from his doorway. Swenson was a heavy, uncomfortable man. His seersucker suit was a size too small. He wore small, wire-rimmed glasses and quaint nineteenth century dundrearies that bushed his jowls. The pits of his jacket were sopped.

"Lunch," Guido said.

"For three hours? It's past four! Your survey class is half gone. I tried to get them to stay, but I couldn't exactly lock the door on them, could I?"

"No," Guido agreed, solemnly.

"Jesus, Tark. Your pants are wet." Swenson pulled Guido into his office. "I can't have a drunk brawler in the department," Swenson said. "We're already on the Vice Chancellor's shit list. Christ, they're looking for excuses to cut us to the bone."

"I'm canned?" Guido said.

Swenson was a scholar who looked like he'd just stepped out of the pages of a Dickens novel. He tore a paper towel from a roll and mopped his forehead. The English building, Hume Hall, was not air-conditioned. "No, no. Not yet. But what if Vice Chancellor Cribbs walked in right now? You know how he hates untidy faculty. 'If you've nailed down a theory that unifies the four fundamental forces in nature, then fine, you can adopt Einstein's dress code.' You've heard him say that, Guido." Swenson, a jack Mormon with eight children, worked part-time as a stand-up comic to make ends meet.

Guido had met Trimmer Swenson in a bar. They'd hit it off, and when Swenson found out that Guido was a writer, he'd hired him on the spot to fill an unexpected vacancy. It was an emergency situation, and so the usual formalities of conducting a nationwide search under equal opportunity guidelines could be temporarily suspended. Guido's title was "Visiting Writer."

In the space of a few weeks he had come under attack. Students had mixed opinions, but the majority of faculty members were not thrilled to have him as a colleague. Especially the faculty's political watchdog, Alana Falconburg. She had petitioned for his immediate resignation. She believed his books were worse than inconsequential—they were politically corrupt and morally vacuous.

Guido taught creative writing along with a literature course he had designed, titled, "The Wild Bunch of Modern Lit." He'd made uninformed choices for textbooks, using paperback crime novels by Stone Duckworth, Waldo Santee, and Crazy Red Fingerhut, crime writers he liked and counted as friends. He included books—books that had little common thread—by Flann O'Brian, Georges Simenon, Janwillem Van de Wetering, and the short stories of Dylan Thomas, to give his course some international legitimacy, but he was also using one of his own books, *She Screamed Bloody Murder,* a three-hundred page paperback with twenty-seven anatomically detailed, sexually motivated serial murders.

Alana had read the first hundred pages of *She Screamed Bloody Murder* in which there were thirteen murders by creative disembowelment. She had written an elaborately sub-titled article, "Romantic Bullets: Racist and Anti-female Texts and Subtexts: Detective Fiction from Chandler and Spillane to

Parker and Potter: The Last Frontiers of Colonial Depreda-
tions." And now she was initiating academic disciplinary pro-
cedures to rid the department of Visiting Writer Tarkenen.
She and her faithful coterie of students held a public burning
of Guido's paperback. But Trimmer Swenson—who by now
had read several of Guido's books and had been entertained
by them—was still on his side.

Swenson sighed heavily and opened the door to a narrow
closet next to his bookshelves. He took out a pair of huge
dungarees. "My clown pants, Guido," he said. "Put them on
and go to your class. You're not too . . . ah, *sick* to teach, are
you?"

"I'm not sick, boss," Guido said. "I'm just a little played-
out." Guido offered Swenson a wan but plucky smile. The
chairman flinched at the sight.

Guido stepped into the huge denims, pants that Swenson
used in his stand-up routines. He pulled them over his slacks
and buttoned them. The effort made him aware of the gouge
in his shoulder, and of the gauze that was now welded to his
coagulating blood. His jaw snapped shut; he made strangling
noises.

Guido limped down the long gray hallway toward his office.
The floor pitched a bit, like a ship's deck. It dropped away in
front of him and he stepped down into an unexpected trough.
Stumbling forward, he thought of the grand, four-masted bark,
the *Emperor Moth,* his father's last ship.

His father had told him wonderful stories of life at sea—of
sailing through the straits of Magellan in a force nine gale; of
challenging the ice-berg choked sea lanes of the North Atlantic
in mid-winter when massive fogs made navigators abandon
their instruments and turn to prayer; of whirlpools seven miles
across that dragged entire fleets of ships to the ocean floor; of

how the *Emperor Moth* itself had been swamped amidships and capsized by typhoon-driven waves ten stories high. He told Guido how he and his mates had been lost at sea for months, how they fought off sharks—Makos, Great Whites, and Blues—as well as moray eels, hull-clinging mollusks the size of washtubs, and giant, parrot-billed squids whose sucker-studded tentacles swarmed the lifeboats. He told him of how the lost men had been deluded by the mirage peculiar to oceans called the *fata morgana:* islands with fabulous white cities would notch the horizon for days, then cruelly vanish. He recalled how under a brain-boiling equatorial sun, schools of mermaids, their heart-breaking human breasts wreathed in tendrils of kelp, tempted sailors to slip over the side of their lifeboats to join them in the pleasures of the sunless deep. "Many lads weakened, my boy," his father said, "but I was always sustained by the memory of your mother and it was that love that slaked my thirst and brought me back to hearth and home."

His father, Elmo Tarkenen, would lean back in his rocker, carving albino mermaids from bars of Ivory soap with his blunt line-knife while he created sagas of the open sea and of exotic ports with the lovingly exact detail of someone who had lived that life and continued to live it in memory.

Of course there was no *Emperor Moth* and his father had never been to sea. Elmo Tarkenen was only a convincing liar.

*But loved,* Guido recalled. Guido had been humiliated when he first found out that his father's stories weren't true. When Guido was in the sixth grade, he told a friend that his father had been in a great naval battle off the coast of Ireland during World War Two in which ninety-nine ships had been sunk by a thousand German Zeppelins. His friend's father—a commander in the U.S. Navy—happened to overhear the story and had scoffed. There had been no battle of that magnitude off the coast of Ireland, and certainly not one that involved *Zeppelins,* a World War One machine of dubious military value.

Guido had gone home in tears, and his mother, impatient with her husband's increasingly bizarre stories, told the boy the awful truth. From that day on, Guido could not listen to his father's fabrications. He excused himself whenever his father began to settle comfortably into a long story about life at sea, his audience now limited to Guido's little brother, Carmine, who was only four years old. Carmine was now an airline pilot, and Guido often wondered if his father's lies had played a part in his brother's somewhat romantic career choice. As far as Guido knew, Carmine had never been told that the stories were figments of their father's inexhaustable imagination.

The relationship between Guido and his father became strained. They had no dialogue outside the stories themselves, and so had no way of resolving their estrangement. Guido thought of him as Lord of the Lies. It was a cruel thought, but Guido in those early years learned to practice cruel thoughts. A cruel thought, rightly placed, made the day.

Decades later Guido came to believe that the tall tales were redirected expressions of love from a man who had no other way to express them. Elmo Tarkenen died while Guido was still in grade school–too soon for Guido to forgive. Too soon for Guido to redeem his childhood trust.

He felt a twinge of that old guilt as he made his way down the pitching hallway toward his office. Guido now believed that his father had been possessed by the muse of fiction writing, but something in his character or chemistry kept him from understanding the socially necessary chasm between real life and invented life. Elmo Tarkenen had the gift of story-telling, but not the ordinary shrewdness to convert the talent from a personal liability into a bankable asset. Instead of a writer, he was merely a pathetic liar.

It had never occurred to Guido to challenge his father. It would have been simple enough. Elmo Tarkenen had, after all, worked at the Five Star meat-packing plant continuously since his early twenties. And even a child could tell he knew next to nothing of the sea—no one, for example, sailed on square-riggers anymore. But Guido had opted for the treasures of his father's marvelous tales. There was no mystery in this: he had wanted his father's stories to be true, wanted his father to be a sea-going hero, not an ordinary working man like the fathers of all his friends. Guido had been a willing accomplice to the lie; he was an enabler who had encouraged his father to become Lord of the Lies.

And then he had longed for what he could no longer allow— to hear those stories again, knowing they would have accumulated new detail and be embellished with strange new digressions. He wanted to know, for example, what it would have been like to slip over the side of a lifeboat and be taken by a mermaid to the bottom of the deep dark sea.

His father stepped out of a doorway and put his palsied hand on Guido's arm. "Seen her?" he whispered. "Is she about?"

Guido's heart lurched. He heard the sea hiss against a seawall. Briny air crimped his nostrils. He leaned against the wall and rubbed his eyes. The apparition tugged his sleeve impatiently. It breathed tomb-stink into his face. "What, Daddy?" Guido whimpered, his voice small.

It was old Professor Dawkins, the last medievalist in the Department, a man the age Elmo Tarkenen would have been had he lived. There was a resemblance, too: the pale eyes, always fixed on some misty and distant scene, the thin aquiline nose stabbing out of his face like the keel of a dainty ship.

31

Then there was Dawkins' tendency to tell elaborate stories of pre-Chaucerian England in a nostalgic, anecdotal way, as if he had been a prominent participant. Guido once overheard him say, "I recall the third Henry, how he instructed Simon de Montfort to remove himself from the court. Ah, it was a moment, a *moment.*"

"Seen her?" the old man repeated, yanking down on Guido's sleeve, his rheumy eyes glancing up and down the hallway.

"Seen who?" Guido said, his heart still tripping.

"She's after me," Dawkins said. "She wants to crucify me. I don't understand it. What did I do to her? Nothing! I did nothing except express my view! Has it become illegal to express one's view? Is it slander to dispute arguments and conclusions? Isn't that what we *do* in universities?"

Guido pulled free of the liver-freckled hand. "You mean Alana Falconburg?" he said.

At the sound of the dreaded name, the old man ducked back into his office, hissing. "Shhh! Shush!" he said. "I don't want her to see me!"

The door closed softly. Guido was touched by the old man's simplicity. Dawkins thought that by avoiding Alana she might forget about him. The old man had criticized Alana publicly, in a Departmental newsletter, calling her monograph, *Some Misfires of the Phallogocentric Can(n)on,* "silly folderol," and now Alana was suing him for slander. Through the closed door, Guido heard the old man mumbling loud enough to be understood but, as far as Guido could make out, old Dawkins was speaking gibberish.

Someone had told him that Dawkins was losing it. "He's our last dinosaur," his informant said. "Ready for the Smithsonian." The old man had been looking into Anglo-Saxon texts that pre-dated Cynewulf. He claimed to have found a coded passage in an eighth century manuscript which, chanted properly, would instigate celestial activity and arouse God from his aeonian slumber. ("God *had* to be asleep," he'd been heard to say. "Otherwise how could one account for the 20th century?") Dawkins had been teaching for nearly fifty years. His office was a dark cave, musty with the smell of aging paper and abandoned ideas.

Guido, holding his chairman's clown pants up with one hand, continued down the corridor. His office was a half-size, windowless cubicle at the very end of the hall. He saw the furtive eyes of some of his colleagues as they caught sight of the oddly gesturing creature that half-stepped slowly past their doorways. He saluted them with his free hand, hoping to suggest an established familiarity, a compelling rapport.

He knew that he wasn't in their league. He'd dropped out of college after two semesters and had joined the army. He'd never gone back, even though the GI Bill would have paid his way. He'd educated himself, not well, but well enough. He had no literary ambitions beyond crime writing and he hadn't studied literature in any systematic way. He liked Hemingway's one-two punch style, enjoyed Fitzgerald's Pat Hobby stories but thought his major work tried too hard to kiss itself on the back of the neck. Faulkner was an obstacle course, paved with nuggets. Dylan Thomas wrote like a stoned angel. He loved the fragmentary hells of the Irishman, Flann O'Brian, appreciated the neurotic walls Simenon's characters built around their gray, claustrophobic lives, Van de Wetering's philosophic detectives, but he mainly read the disposable fiction of his comrades-in-arms.

Guido, an eclectic vagrant, felt lost and vaguely depressed by the liturgies of high literature. He never liked going to church and he smelled holy water and incense and dusty vestments when he opened the books people with credentials said he was obligated to read. He readily admitted the fault was his. On the other hand, you had to play the cards you were dealt: if there was a fault it wasn't his alone. The Deal sets the outcomes.

Maybe there was a chance that La Siberia Tech would hire him for another year if he trumped up a novel his colleagues could respect, a literary novel. He thought about this possibility, gave it a title. *The Waxen Figure,* by G. Fazzola-Tarkenen, Fazzola being his mother's maiden name.

Sensitive Garrick Forsythe, agonizing between loyalty to his invalid wife and his wretchedly carnal obsession with his unfaithful, tri-sexual mistress (bestiality was one of her interests), opts to join a monastery dedicated to the restoration of ancient manuscripts. Then, when Garrick finds a long lost work of Dante's, he is torn between the fame that could be his alone and the serenity he has found in retreat.

Guido awarded himself a major literary prize for the book, saw himself receiving a fat check with a lot of zeroes in it, saw his crime-writing buddies applauding in the audience, sick with jealousy, as he made his acceptance speech. He saw the front-page reviews: "Fazzola-Tarkenen has created a metaphor of our times in Garrick Forsythe—a man without a compass, polarized by loyalty and desire, fragmented but passionate. . . ." etc., etc.

But, well before Guido reached his office door, Garrick had pushed his wife's wheelchair off an embankment. He watched her careening madly down to a river bed where starving Kodiak bears, just out of hibernation, were feeding on salmon. The bears looked at the wildly descending wheelchair, and the soft fragrant flesh it held, with alarm and then with piqued interest. They ambled shyly toward the spilled wheelchair, snouts testing the air, great ropes of saliva hanging from their skull-crushing jaws. Garrick went on to kill his mistress and her latest lover by joining them together in their coital embrace with duct tape and then with spikes fired from a heavy-duty nail gun. Garrick wasn't so sensitive (or literary) after all.

But to write the stuff the critics took seriously you had to have a righteous *theme*. And there were no more righteous themes. There was nothing left but surface activity. Surface activity without a spine of righteousness. A spine that made the surface activity betray the unmoving depths. A betrayal that would influence the moral direction of mankind. What was that quip of Chekhov's? "People won't improve unless they are made to see themselves as they are." What a lost hope! What a joke!

Still, Guido mused, there had to be a way to retrain his imagination to think in terms of stories that had more meaning than activity, stories that depended more on intelligent perceptions than car chases in the dark. There was, in fact, a writer of serious of fiction on the staff, Martin Gassaway, a Harvard Ph.D. Maybe he could get some pointers from him. He recalled a blurb he'd seen on one of Gassaway's novels: "Not since Henry James himself has an American author so ably evoked the conflicted fragilities of relational mendacities."

Guido's blurbs tended to be less classy:

"Here's a gorefest rich enough to satisfy the bloodlust of the most jaded reader."

"This one needs a warning label: the sensitive reader will blow chunks by page ten."

"If you're not paranoid yet and don't own a big-caliber hog-leg, you will after submitting yourself to this parade of psycho bottom feeders."

His English department colleagues had ignored his feeble hand-signals and croaked hellos. This sort of snub was not new, but today Guido looked worse than usual. His expression and demeanor were too chaotic to decode. He looked asham-

ed, guilty, reckless, enraged, jovial, confused, and—as his colleagues had come to expect when Guido returned from his
"lunch breaks"—drunk and *damaged*. Some of his colleagues
considered him unstable, and potentially dangerous.

The way he moved down the hallway—half-leaning on the
wall, holding up the bulky pants with one hand, limping,
grimacing, his head lolling from side to side as if it were
spinning with wild ideas—cemented this belief. And after he
shuffled past, they closed their doors discretely. The clicking
of door latches, like the cocking of small arms, followed in
his wake as he approached his own door.

Guido unlocked his office. The little room was emblematic
of his life—it was a mess. His desk was cluttered with leaning
towers of unread student papers; books lay open to passages
that for some forgotten reason or other he had found
pedagogically useful; two ashtrays overflowed with cigarette
butts; a paper tub of mossy chicken bones sat on top of a file
cabinet; several tumblers had collected on the one bare spot
on his desk, some still stained with the dregs of booze, along
with a mug of cold coffee topped with a thriving scum of
living micro-organisms.

He checked his watch—only fifteen minutes late for class—
took a bottle of Tsingtao beer from the small fridge that he
kept out of sight next to a file cabinet, and sat down in his
swivel chair.

He opened the Thomas book. He admired the turbulent
Welshman. But this afternoon the dense poetic prose of the
early stories was too much for him. He wouldn't be able to
make it make sense to his students. And they had a right to
expect things to make sense, didn't they? They had a right to
information, not impressions. They needed hard knowledge.
They didn't need to be set adrift in lyrical speculations. He

closed the book, put his head down on the desk, heard himself snore.

He had a brief, half-awake dream. His mother was scolding his father who was lying, coffinless, in his grave. His father offered rambling excuses in spite of grievous physical decay and the interference of dirt kicked into the grave by his mother's angry shoe.

He felt queasy. The Tsingtao helped, a decent Chinese beer he bought by the case at a discount market. Even so, a hot ball of puke rose up his gullet. He held it in his mouth until he was able to find his waste basket. It was a bad color, toxic lime, and it slipped into the wads of crumpled paper like motor oil. He opened his desk drawer and fumbled for his Rolaids. He chewed up and swallowed a few of them, found a fresh pack of cigarettes, then stood up carefully.

He'd wing it today, he decided, maybe talk of Dylan's famous last reading tour of America before he collapsed and died of accumulated excess in the very hospital, St. Vincent's, where Guido had, a few days later, been born. Now, wouldn't that be a nice connection to make? Didn't that make literature seem a real-life thing and not just millions of ant-like words crawling about importantly in fat texts? What a wasted life, old Dylan's was, yet out of his ashes, out of his deathbed, or close by anyway, arose this writer of crime stories standing here before you, ladies and gentlemen. But perhaps this was an item of marginal interest, at best. Guido abandoned it.

He unplugged his desk lamp and yanked loose the extension cord. He threaded the four-foot cord through the belt loops of Trimmer Swenson's baggy dungarees, knotted it, and left the plug and socket to dandle on his fly. He buttoned his jacket over this make-shift arrangement, smoothed back his hair, winced as the gauze pulled against his wound, and headed for his classroom.

Guido took his place behind the desk at the head of the class and cleared his throat. He was momentarily aphasic, his clotted thoughts refusing to assemble themselves and march forward. "Well then. . . ." he said, his tone jocular and rough-edged—a trick he learned early in the semester. It suggested a masterful certainty; here was a man with answers, a *professor*. It kept the students amused, as well as at bay. ". . . where did we leave off, kids?"

The silence coagulated around him like a transparent gel. Something crawled into his hand. He looked into his palm and saw a red worm of blood coiled smugly there, growing fatter each second. "I'm bleeding," he said, but when he finally looked up he saw that the room was empty except for Joyboy, the dealer, and his girlfriend, Red Crow. Joyboy, still a sophomore after ten years of casual study, made his living supplying recreational drugs to the La Siberia Tech student body and faculty.

"You need some primo blow?" Joyboy said, indolently waving a baggie of rock.

Guido sighed. This, to Joyboy, was a positive answer. He chopped a line straight as a nail on Guido's desk and offered him a cut-down DQ straw. Guido sucked the white powder up a nostril hoping for the best.

He sometimes saw himself as a physical spirit, an aggregate of atoms assembled from starlight, and this notion should have made him feel light in heart and mind, but no, he felt the exact opposite—leaden, dull. Coalesced starlight: a cosmic mistake.

Red Crow, a pale anorexic with crimson dreadlocks and a long narrow face, watched him as she chewed her bubble gum steadily, snapping a bubble now and then, the deflated membrane draped over her thin lips and pointy chin.

The cocaine didn't make Guido feel lighter in mind or heart. He paid Joyboy and went home.

# Four

GUIDO WALKED TO THE LITTLE PINK HOUSE he'd rented a few blocks from the campus. He liked his Santa Fe style house—a fake adobe with fake *vigas*. The windows were barred against thieves, and there was a single car garage for the twenty-five-year old AMC Gremlin he bought after his wife left in their ten-year-old Monte Carlo. He unlocked the outer security door, unlocked the inner deadbolted door, and entered his refuge—a dark, cave-like hollow that smelled of dead beer, fried meat, and cigarette butts.

He took off the mammoth clown pants, his sodden slacks, then his coat and shirt. He went into the bathroom and looked at his shoulder. The gauze patch was dark red. He saw the crusty tracks of the blood that had slipped down his arm from the leaky wound.

*Potshots,* the bum had said. *Whap whap whap.* Guido studied himself for other wounds. There was a hump of dried blood just above his left ear. Had the crazed secretary tried to execute him after all? Had she pulled the trigger when the gun was pressed against his temple? Was there a small caliber bullet lodged in some non-vital part of his brain?

How could the *brain* have non-vital parts? Wouldn't he be in a lot worse shape if she had shot him in the head? And yet he knew of combat vets who walked around acting normal with shrapnel buried in their brains. Anything was possible. A construction worker in Toronto who had a third of his head shorn away by an accidentally dropped I-beam, recited *The Raven* before he died. His widow insisted he knew no poetry,

39

had been, in fact, a terrible student. A woman in Detroit who had been shot through the eye, killed and mutilated her assailant with a butcher knife before she laid down beside him and gave up the ghost. A man walked into a police station in Dallas with an ax embedded in his skull asking, politely, if he was qualified to file assault charges.

Guido soaked a washcloth in hot water, then dabbed at the small wound behind his ear. The dried blood dissolved. He pressed up close to the mirror and studied the area. There was a wound all right, but it seemed more like a deep scratch than a bullet hole. He probably grazed a Spanish Dagger when he tripped.

His ear, he noticed, was swollen and mottled purple. He remembered then that Carma had slapped him hard–and hadn't she been wearing a heavy ring, one of those silver Zuni rings with a large jade or malachite stone? He wanted to believe this explanation. He wanted to believe there was only *one* bullet wound, and that was just a crease in his skin. Nothing serious. A forgivable wound if there ever was one. He soaked the stiffened gauze with warm water, then gently removed it.

The wound was nastier than he'd thought. It wasn't just a crease in the skin. The slug had found red meat. A two-inch groove scored the top ridge of trapezius muscle between his shoulder and neck. He'd had a big dark mole there; it was gone.

"Jee-*zuz!*" Guido yelled. "God *damn* the lunatic bitch!"

The wound was small and ugly. But at least the bleeding had stopped. The pain was sharp but not terrible. He opened his medicine cabinet and studied his selection of drugs. Tylenol first, Panpax second. He took two of each. Then he gritted his teeth and splashed rubbing alcohol into the red groove. Guido filled the tiled bathroom with a warbling scream. Tears

40

blurred his vision as he taped a clean square of gauze over the blazing notch in his flesh.

He went into the kitchen and filled a tumbler with tequila. Tequila, he believed, had true pain-deadening powers. Moreso than whiskey, vodka, or gin. He was sure tequila also had muscle-relaxant properties. He often eased the pain of lumbarache with it. Liquid curare, he sometimes called it. Drink enough and you paralyze yourself.

Guido carried his glass to the bathroom. He filled the tub with hot water. The Tylenol, the tranks, the tequila were working. He stepped into the tub. A decal of a leaping dolphin, pasted just under the shower head, reminded him of Kirsten. She had stuck the smiley-faced dolphin there when they first moved in, but two days later she was gone. He'd been blindsided by her decision to move out. Guido liked being married. He thought Kirsten had too. He believed himself to be a domesticated animal, comfortable before the hearth, in spite of his occasional excesses.

Five years. In five years things between them had soured. In generous moments he blamed himself: He was a slob, he drank too much. He was a monster of self-pity when his writing was going badly. And when his writing was going well, he lived in a foggy state of self-congratulatory distraction. He would fake attentiveness, but she always caught him at it. "I'm your fucking ap*pen*dage," she once told him, meaning it literally. "I feel invisible most of the time, until the business in your shorts reminds you I'm not."

This thought made him count the weeks: He had not had sex in almost two months. Maybe he'd never have it again. It was possible. Perhaps the trend of his life would mandate celibacy. And if his prostate got worse, surgery might guarantee permanent ED, as it was now called. The downhill inclination of his thoughts steepened. He saw, in the pattern of light

41

on the water before him, an image of himself in clown pants, a love-starved sexless wretch stumbling through the last decades of his life.

The doorbell rang. It rang again. Then again. "Go away!" Guido yelled. But the ringing continued. He climbed out of the tub, careful not to stretch the muscles beneath his wound. He pulled his robe on, then went to the front door in a mood to kill. It was his neighbor, Alice Dark. She had brought him a loaf of homemade bread.

"Bad luck you have with women, eh?" she said.

Alice was a sly, dwarfish woman from Italy whose kneecaps had been surgically removed after they were shattered in a car wreck thirty years earlier. She was less than five feet tall but seemed even shorter because of a curved spine that made her stoop. She had a wise and tragic look that never failed to irritate Guido, and she walked with annoying, dramatic lurches, her thick hardwood cane banging the ground ahead of her. Every step she took appeared to require stoic resolve.

"Here, you take!" she ordered, thrusting the loaf into his hands with vicious generosity.

Guido put his rage on hold. He had to be nice to her. Her son, a mechanic, had fixed his old Gremlin just last week and charged him nothing. He accepted the loaf. "Thanks, Mrs. Dark," he said. "I appreciate it."

He started to close the door on her but she slipped her cane past the jamb. She fixed him with a baleful glare. Guido resisted the impulse to kick her cane out into the street. She had more to say about his bad luck, he realized. A strong wind had come up and the neighborhood was assaulted with whirlwinds of dust. He gave up, and invited her in for a cup of coffee.

She followed him through the living room—he apologized for the empty beer bottles, magazines, and newspapers that littered the floor—and into the kitchen. The kitchen was also a hopeless mess. Mrs. Dark regarded a gummy encrustation on the wall with her heavy-lidded eyes. Guido had thrown a plate of overcooked linguini in an alcohol-fueled fit of self-reproach a few nights before. Loneliness, poor writing, horniness, and booze: a bad mix. He cleared a place at the kitchen table and Mrs. Dark lowered herself carefully into the chair. Her small, thick-fingered hands gripped the edge of the table as she positioned herself for serious discussion. She was heavy for her height, and the sharp curvature of her spine seemed like a public declaration that the weight of existence was a cruel and unjust imposition.

"You wife, she gone, no?"

"She gone, yes," Guido said.

He poured her a cup of re-heated breakfast coffee.

Mrs. Dark pursed her lips judgmentally after taking a sip. She shook her head. "Too bad, too bad," she said. If it was sympathy she was offering, Guido didn't trust it. She was a gossip-monger—a Crone, affecting the powers of the Wise Witch and Guido wasn't buying. Mrs. Dark was more interested in scandal than in witchly insight, and more than likely had come to gather the details of Guido's failed marriage. She had a book on everyone in the neighborhood.

"Ah, poor Mist' Tarka'," she said, employing the lilt and elisions of her native Calabria. She spoke English well enough, without much of an accent, but she put on her southern Italian drawl when she was on the offensive. Her maiden name was Sbonzini. Her late husband had been a GI stationed in Italy after the Germans had been kicked out.

Guido tore off a piece of bread and bit into it. "Good bread, Mrs. Dark," he said. "Did you bake it?" He knew she had, but wanted to ruffle her feathers.

She was outraged. "What, you think I buy from the *grocery?* Of course I make! I make fresh, this morning!"

Guido hadn't eaten all day and the smell of the homemade bread made him realize it. He buttered a large chunk and stuffed it into his mouth.

Mrs. Dark regarded him, this womanless man, helpless and starving. "Pryor say that nice fella across the street, that Guido, maybe he get himself a *real* woman now."

"Pryor said that, did he?" Guido said. He could take Alice Dark in small doses, but her son, Pryor, a master mechanic at the local Mercedes dealership, was a prick, a self-righteous know-it-all who sat in judgment over the affairs of lesser men. He'd fixed Guido's ailing Gremlin with the demeanor of a society surgeon doing charity work on a wino.

Guido had been done a favor and felt honor-bound to acknowledge it, but he gave his gratitude to Alice Dark, not to Pryor. He'd wanted to pay the mechanic, but Pryor had scoffed at Guido's money. "For the same work, down at the dealership, it would cost you seven hundred," Dark had said. Guido had been thinking in terms of double digits. Humbled, he'd refolded his wallet and put it away. Which meant the debt would become a permanent fixture between him and Dark. Guido tried to laugh it off, *Fuck him,* he'd said to himself many times, but the truth was that Guido had enough residual honor in his blood to feel the weight of obligation.

"Pryor say maybe a good healthy woman like my niece, Seraghina, take good care of you, Mista' Tarka,'" Alice Dark said.

So that was the reason for this visit! An unattached niece– *healthy* at that!–probably a once-married grade school teacher in her forties complete with a twelve-year-old son! A picture of Seraghina–*Seraghina!*–vaulted into his mind: big hips, straight, unshaven calves, thick ankles, small breasts, narrow shoulders, lummox feet. A long grave face. Bovine eyes stricken with reproachful melancholy. A pronounced overbite. The inevitable black silk mustache. She would be well-read in books he hated and her son would be a pre-sociopathic fan of martial arts movies.

"Actually, Mrs. Dark. . . ."

"Now, you call me Alice!" she said, cordially stern. "We are neighbors, what–" she consulted her stubby fingers–"for almost three weeks!"

"See, the thing is, Alice," he said. "I want to be alone right now. For a while. You know, to think things out. I'm still kind of torn up. Over the break up."

He missed Kirsten, but his grief was sporadic now. She had been right about him. He was locked in a private world he couldn't or wouldn't share. It was his obsessive nature, he rationalized. Dr. Burnaby, Kirsten's shrink, had said, "Guido is a problem child. Kirsten needs more in life than to nurture a man who is not capable of reciprocation."

Guido found it insulting, Burnaby's use of the third person when speaking to them, but Kirsten found it clinically correct. "Guido's genetic confusion," the doctor had said, "prompts the narcissistic response. He looks inward, attempting to unravel the twisted fabric of personality. A self-frustrating program if there ever was one. Blame Freud, but more to blame are the great man's half-baked followers who took his metaphors as literal truth–the fundamentalist's classic error. Kirsten, on the other hand–a genetically *undivided* woman, incidentally–is other-directed. But even other-directed person-alities require the *presence* of the other."

Mrs. Dark's eyes were narrowed to keen judgmental slits. She looked canny and suspicious, her blue lips thrusting forward in a shrewd pucker. She patted Guido's hand and commiserated bitterly, "I know, I know, poor man," she said. "Tell me—you wife, she no Italiana, like you?"

"No. She's Jewish. And I'm only half Italian. My father was a Finlander. In fact, my mother is half-Albanian." This was not true. Generally speaking, Guido was not a good liar. But for whatever reason, he found pleasure in passing off small fibs to Mrs. Dark. "I guess that makes me only a quarter *paisan'*. I guess I'm Italian in name only, Alice."

"Men should marry the same kind," she said, vetoing his false pedigree.

"Your husband married *you,* Alice," he said. "He was no Eye-tie."

She scoffed heavily, her liver-spotted hands opening and closing on the table like stranded crabs. Guido tore off another piece of bread and buttered it, pleased that he had touched a raw nerve. "My children, Mista' Tarka'—half Catholic, half Presbyterian. A disaster! A thorn in my heart!" Her lips withdrew into a thin, bitter line. She shook her head abruptly, as if to cast off pointless recriminations. "What about you children? Catholic? Jew?"

Guido had no children. And Kirsten was about as Jewish as he was Catholic. For them, the orthodoxies of religion and ethnicity were as remote as history. But he said, "Both, Alice. They're Cashews."

The joke didn't register on Alice Dark's face. She merely stared at him, impatient and annoyed.

"What difference does it make, anyhow?" he said. "All kids are pagans. The little bastards would live like animals if they had a choice. It's up to us parents to pound all that hedonistic crap out of them and turn them into responsible, God-fearing, hemorrhoidal clock-punchers. Where would the world be if people had just decided to enjoy themselves?"

Mrs. Dark snorted. "Boys, yes. Even men, if you let them. Most men, *very* bad. Like animals. Worse than animals, if you let them. Terrible. Girls, they are different."

*"Vive la difference,"* Guido said. An image of the mad secretary's eyes appeared in his mind. Suddenly he was very tired.

"You send you little girls to church, Mista' Tarka'," she said. She thrust a crooked finger at him. "You no let them make sex, not until you find good husbands for them! The girls, they keep everything nice and clean. Then the animal, he comes for them. You stop him stinking at the gate!"

Guido saw himself driving the stinking animal away from his gate with a stick. The two-legged beast, leaking the smell of rut, its small yellow eyes stupid with lust, moved back only a little, sure of itself, biding its time. It recognized the bellowing clown waving the stick: a brother under the skin.

# Five

"W HEN THE WIND IS SOUTHERLY, I KNOW a hawk from a handsaw," said a dark toneless voice, grim as a stone bell. Then fierce waves of static diced it. Guido leaped up from dream-infested sleep. The TV screen: a blizzard, white-out. A midget staggered through shifting drifts on snow shoes. "I am mad north by northwest," he said, chuckling to himself. The screeching ground blizzard caught him. He was lost, his voice hashed. Then he was a pattern of black dots on a white page, the channel empty. *"Electron sketch of our lot"*– a remnant murmur from Guido's last dream.

The man trudging through white dunes of snow, speaking in grave tones, was a freak of weather, an ionospheric spur allowing television signals continental range. Another man, perhaps selling dog sleds, appeared for a moment then faded back into the peppered static.

A woman's face, saintly and seductive, unpocked by electrons or pores, regarded him with arctic indifference. "L'Oreal alone has targeted hydrating lipozomes," this exquisite face told him, and, like the dog sled salesman, dissolved into atmospheric limbo. Guido felt lust.

He pulled himself up and switched off the TV. He hurt all over, his shoulder hot and throbbing. It felt now as if someone had hammered a hot nail into the meat and bone. He touched the gauze patch and decided that the events of the day had been real after all.

His mouth was stale as an old grave–the sod pulled up, the warped casket cracked, the bad air wafting out, pathetic bones mossy as his teeth.

It was the telephone that had pulled him out of a frustrating dream. The weak elecronic chirp didn't have the power to startle, but was persistent enough to drag him away from a lanky woman who insisted on throwing rocks at passing cars as he tried to make love to her. They were outside, on the lawn. "Don't do that," he'd been saying. "Why are you doing that?" She didn't know and didn't care. Distraction and melancholy made her unreachable. Drivers swerved and cursed, some stopped. Policemen stood over them, making cruel lascivious jokes. It was hard to concentrate on his task. "Now see what you've gone and done," he said to the woman, recognizing her finally as Kirsten.

Guido picked up the phone. "You're all right then," a woman's voice said. "Thank God."

Guido's mouth went dry. He knew the voice. "More or less," he said.

"I'm sorry, you know. Really I am."

"Right. Me too."

"I mean, your *wound*. . . ."

Guido checked his watch. Almost twelve. He'd been asleep at least four hours. He'd dozed off on the couch watching a Fred Astaire movie. Fred had been stomping on Ginger's ceiling, just to bug her. But that was early in the movie, wasn't it? He'd been asleep, he decided, for at least five hours.

"What do you want?" he said. He didn't feel forgiving now. He felt annoyed and scared, on the edge of confusion. "What the hell do you mean, calling me up?"

"You haven't told on me?"

Oddly, her voice was warm, seductive. It kept his dream-erection alive, proving once again the shabby judgment of the long-unfucked male.

"Told on you?" Guido said. He was charmed, in spite of himself, by the woman's schoolyard diction.

"Please don't. I beg of you."

The wretched sorrow in her voice touched Guido.

"I never intended to," he said. "I promised you I wouldn't."

"I'd *like* to believe you. I really would."

"I said I wouldn't and I meant it. That isn't enough? I don't want the trouble of going to court, either. Not just for a scratch on my shoulder. Can't you accept that?"

"You're crabby, aren't you? You hate me now."

"I don't hate you. I've got a headache," he said. "It hasn't been a good day."

"I want to make it up to you," she said.

"There's no need," he said.

"Come to my place. I'll make a good dinner for you. You're not a bad man, I know that now. It's just . . . well, I have these *episodes*. I was abandoned as a child. They say I've got unspecific polymorphic rage. It has multiple expressive modes. I take medicine for it. Do you like cannelloni?"

"Why don't we just leave it like this, Carma?" he said, cursing himself for using her name. "No harm, no foul. Okay?"

In spite of this, she gave him her address. It was a simple address, 101 Howard Street. Guido feared he would not be able to erase it from memory.

Guido made a pot of coffee, his heart racing. She knew who he was. Which meant she had looked at his wallet while he was unconscious, found his University ID card. And now he was sorry he'd hung up on her. Sorry he hadn't just given her the reassurance she'd begged for and let it go at that. What harm was there in breaking bread with your contrite assassin? Wasn't it, in fact, the noble thing to do? A ceremony of forgiveness? Sublime rectitude among human beings with heart?

But all this was blather. She was dangerous, period. And she probably knew where he lived. He closed all the blinds

50

in the house and looked for his gun. If she decided to believe he'd turn her in, maybe she'd give herself an insurance policy with her little purse gun.

He had an old single-action .32 lightweight revolver, which had belonged to his father. He found it in the cabinet below the silverware drawer in the kitchen, the place he kept odds and ends. The broken plastic grips were held together with electrician's tape. A dozen or so bullets lay scattered on the shelf. He gathered them up and loaded the homely little snub-nosed pistol.

"Now what?" he said. *Call the cops,* he told himself. It was the common sense thing to do. But common sense had never been his strong suit. He'd told her he would not turn her in, and he had meant it. He liked to think of himself as someone who kept his word. What did you have in life if you didn't have the integrity of your word?

He took a cup of coffee back into the living room and switched the TV over to the 12 o'clock news break. A body was being loaded into an EMS van. The reporter on the scene described the crime. A man in his forties, a professor at La Siberia Tech, had been murdered, his body dumped in the arroyo that ran alongside the campus. "The victim's identity is being withheld pending notification of relatives," the reporter said.

Guido's heart fibrillated for a moment. He touched the tender spot above his ear. The inevitable thought announced itself: *It's you in the body bag, Guido. You're dead. This is Limbo and the angels are waiting.*

He touched his arms and legs. They seemed solid enough. He ran his hands over the rough fabric of his sofa, rubbed his bare feet against the carpet—all very substantial and real—but who could say what worldly furniture Limbo required?

51

He crossed himself as the body was shoved into the van and the doors slammed closed. *There but for the grace of God . . . . But was* there grace, and was he entitled to any? On the verge of a panic attack, he started mumbling *Hail Marys.* The commanding rhythms of this ancient mantra always calmed him.

It was himself in the arroyo. He saw her coming back, holding the gun to his head, chatting a while, amiably insane, then pulling the hammer to full-cock and squeezing the trigger, the hot burst of flame searing his temple, the small bullet burrowing into the soft fatty matter that created worlds.

It was a fiction that threatened to be a memory. And all the rest, his difficult progress from the arroyo to the English department to his house—the imaginary fugue of a dying brain? A personal version of *An Occurrence at Owl Creek Bridge?* His heart began to beat irregularly, a playground rhythm, as if it were skipping rope.

He reconsidered his pledge. What's a pledge if you're dead? And if he wasn't dead, then someone else *was.* Why was she going around killing people? Ah, but they were not just people, they were *professors,* and she had an ax to grind among them.

It was his duty, now, to call the cops. He'd give them her address, anonymously. Suggest to them that he'd seen her wielding a gun in the arroyo. They should be able to piece the rest of it together. In this way, he wouldn't be breaking his word to her. But when he dialed 911 he received a recorded message: all lines were busy. He hung up and started to make a pot of coffee when the phone rang. He picked it up after a dozen rings.

"I *knew* you were home, you see," a man's voice said.

Guido recognized the voice but couldn't place it. "Is that so," he said.

"Yes, of course. You work at night, don't you? And you're stuck in chapter three, correct? I believe your divorced protagonist—Mr. Fabian Tedesko is it?—cannot find his children and it's driving him bonkers, or some such melodramatic fandango. Fabian lurking in his ex-wife's garden, Fabian lying drunk and morose in a brothel, Fabian considering mayhem as he fondles his .44 magnum. You mentioned this to me in the break room, a few days ago, remember?"

"Gassaway?"

"Righto. Listen, Tarkenen, I'm in a bit of a fix myself. I wonder if you would give me the benefit of your expertise?"

Martin Gassaway, the tarnished star in an otherwise quiet community of modest scholars, was a once-famous man. His last novel, *Bride of Night,* published twenty years ago, had copped several international prizes and had been translated into seventeen languages, including Icelandic, Arabic, and Bengalese. *Bride of Night* was a realistic re-telling of the Heloise and Abelard story, set in contemporary Haiti. Gassaway, a fastidious drunk and a careless bawd, had published nothing since. He'd had his fifteen minutes in the limelight and was now fading into literary oblivion.

Guido was grateful. Gassaway's phone call had saved him from his preposterous death fantasy.

"We're dead," Gassaway said, reviving Guido's morbid notion.

"What?"

"We're white dinosaurs, my friend."

Gassaway liked to grieve publicly over the fate of the middle-aged male Anglo-Saxon writer in America. Guido had heard it all before. The argument bored him; it was an academic pastime. Guido published his own work regularly, had an audience, was paid well enough. He had dry spells—this was one of them—but they never lasted long. A teaching gig was a good way to keep the cash flow turned on while he re-grouped. Gassaway, on the other hand, had quit writing, cold-turkey, twenty years ago. This was the danger of the academic life as Guido saw it: Your pay, for a six-hour work week was practically larcenous, and, once tenured, your job was secure whether you continued to produce or not. Why go through the unnecessary grief of *writing* when you had a sweet deal like that?

"I lusted after a job at Princeton last year," Gassaway said. "But they gave it to a female Bangladeshi who'd published a verse novella. Christ, she doesn't even write in our mother tongue. It's the end of the road for white men like us, Guido. They want colored and they want females, and females of color beat all. I even heard Vice Chancellor Cribbs say he wanted to kill two birds with one stone when he hired the poet Eartha Lincoln-Martinez. But hell, he killed *four*. She's female, Latina, black, and *lesbian*. Can she write poetry? That's beside the point, old man. Who the fuck *cares* if she can write poetry? Besides, any sort of drivel is called poetry these days. The middle-aged straight white boy can't compete in this new PC world. I'm lucky I landed this job back in unenlightened times."

He sighed heavily, a pallbearer at his own funeral.

"The world changes on you, Tarkenen," Gassaway continued. "Opinions change. The old opinion-makers die or become senile, and slowly but surely the world turns itself inside out. What you once knew and loved and believed in is torn down like a condemned opera house."

"For Chrissakes, Gassaway, you called to make a speech?"

"No, no. Something happened this evening. Something rather dreadful. Lotty is terrified. Someone ransacked our house. We came home from a cocktail party at the Vice

Chancellor's and found this." Guido sensed Gassaway's gesture, his arm sweeping across the trashed room.

"Jesus, that's rotten. You called the cops?"

"They're here now. They seem bored. I thought *your* expertise in such things might be useful."

"Expertise?"

"I mean, in your work. Your—ah, *novels.* I thought you might have a helpful insight—your understanding of the criminal mind, I mean. The police are treating it as an every day robbery, since we live so close to the border."

"That's what it sounds like, Marty."

"I have reason to think not. Come over for a drink, will you?"

"I need to do a little work," Guido said. "I'll try to drop by later. You're staying up for a while?"

"I don't think sleep is an option tonight, Guido." Gassaway lowered his voice. "Lotty is a wreck. This has been a rough evening for her."

"My—ah, *novels,*" Guido mimicked, as he sat down in front of his word processor. He wrote three-hundred page thrillers, "trash for cash," his editor, Cassandra "Cash" Holub, called them. She meant this as a compliment. "Rut and cut—toot and shoot," Cash said, listing the ingredients for success. Such novels were like a manic roller coaster ride through the dark innards of American dementia.

Cash Holub, a fat, six-foot tall woman who ate cholesterol-rich foods on principle, thought the crime novel was the only form that could take on the dark, rotting heart of the nation. A crazed, hyped-up, violent society required a mirror image of itself in its fiction. Novels of manners, of polite society, of middle-class household angst and hanky-panky, were the ultimate fantasy, the final irrelevancy, she believed. At four-hundred eighteen pounds, she was easily the biggest senior editor in New York. Guido, in his cups, in a mood to jape, would tell whatever boon companions were at hand that he had the distinction of working with the "biggest editor in New York." And yet he loved her rough dignity, her reckless honesty, her bold ways. He wouldn't trade her for a svelte, health-conscious editor with a nose for fads if they gave him half interest in the company.

"These solemn guttersnipes who track the ways to stuff the bored housewife's taco may win all the awards, Guido, but you and I know that the real topic today is murder without remorse," Cash had said. "Look at the Gulf War. We burned, mangled, eviscerated and generally fucked-up a hundred thousand or so poor illiterate raghead conscriptees with high tech efficiency, and we saw it as justified tribal fun. And maybe it had to happen. But *remorse?* You couldn't find a thimble full of it from Kennebunkport to L.A. It's gone with the wind, kid, like chivalry and clean-living and the passenger pigeon. The pond scum that blew up the fed building in Oklahoma thinks he's a cultural hero. Then there's the live-at-five incineration of the Guns for Jesus cult down in Texas—hell, it sold a hundred million in Preparation H and another fifty in Pepto Bismol. Colombine High was a media dream. The networks milked it for weeks. Talk show hosts babbled clichés to cello music as the tots wept and network revenue sky-rocketed."

Murder without remorse. Guido considered that as a title for his new book. No. Too high-falutin. Too abstract. Too British. He flipped through his battered copy of Bartlett's Quotations and looked at the much picked-over gems from Shakespeare.

*The Uses of Adversity.* Too stuffy. *In the Cannon's Mouth.* No, this wasn't a war story. *A Clod of Wayward Marl.* He liked that one. But since he had to look up "marl," he assumed Cash would have to also, and she'd talk him out of it for that reason. You couldn't have prospective buyers in Barnes and Noble asking the clerks what the Jesus "marl" was. Marl: A crumbly mixture of clays. Us. Right on. But still too obscure.

He put away Bartlett's and typed an old title that had been rattling around in his head for a few years. He wasn't crazy about it, but it more or less covered the novel's fuzzily envisioned subject. Guido had lied to Gassaway about being stuck in chapter three, lied about the plot involving some loser named Tedesko. The truth was that he was stuck in chapter one, stuck in the first paragraph, stuck in the first sentence, the first word, the first letter of the first word.

He went to the phone and tried 911 again. Still busy. Maybe Gassaway's burglar was off on a spree. Maybe more bodies were being found.

Back at his word processor, he looked at his old title shimmering on the electronic screen:

## THE MILKSOP STRANGLER

Now, all he needed was three hundred pages to put under it.

# Six

MESMERIZED BY THE FLASHING CURSOR, Guido dozed. A door opened in his mind and an angular white giant stepped through it. He was six and a half feet tall, his gaunt frame knotted with ropy muscle. His polished bald head pulsed from a strobing light source Guido could not locate. Decorative tribal scars cabled the sides of the giant's wide neck. His arms down to the backs of his hands were scrolled with a tapestry of repulsive tattoos. They were like the storyboards for a sadistic animated cartoon. The tattoos showed women being pursued, raped, tortured, and butchered. "Honey, I'm home," the giant called. His small eyes, dull as galvanized nailheads, fixed on Guido.

Guido snapped awake, adrenalized. "My *man*," he said, realizing that his dozing brain had served up the character he'd been looking for.

Guido played question-and-answer on his word processor, an exercise that often got a story line moving.

*Name?* he typed.

*—Death, I am Death. Morton X. Death. The X stands for the crossbones warning on a bottle of poison. I'm poison, a toxin to the human race. I'm the one they want cleaned out of the gene pool. They want genetic cleansing, but they don't know how to do it and preserve their humanistic values. This amuses the bejesus out of me.*

*—I'm leaning toward Edsel. Deceptively tame sounding. You get good mileage out of unlikely juxtapositions.*

*—The Edsel was a reject, a failure. It didn't get good mileage.*

*—Edsel Harmon Haight, in fact.*

*—Too fucking cute. Harm-and-Hate, for Christssakes.*

*—People love name games. You can get too subtle. Look at Dickens. He serves them up like slowpitch softballs. He was the original King of Wysiwyg. What you see is what you get. Age?*

*—Thirty-eight, as in caliber.*

*—Good. I like that. Occupation?*

*—Interior decorator. I decorate homes with the bones of their occupants. I paint the walls with their brains, I string the chandeliers with their gray intestines.*

*—NOW who's laying it on with a trowel?*

*—Okay, unemployable sociopath. Pulled a dime in Folsom for knocking a Coupe de Ville off a bumper jack to flatten a citizen. When I got out I fucked a beautician to death. Tried to give her an apneic orgasm, tourniquet on her neck. I mean, she was into it, you know? I think she died in ecstasy. I send them off proper. Kervorkian never did that. Got to be a habit.*

*—Edsel Harmon Haight: The Milksop Strangler.*

*—Why MILKSOP? for Christssakes? You gonna make a JOKE out of my life? You'll be lucky to sell fifty copies. The public needs to take dirtbags seriously.*

*—It makes you more interesting. You're obsessed with big, heavily nippled tits. A nipple big as a thumb makes you sweat cream. Sometimes you feel as if you're coming through your pores. The polymorphic perverse all grown up. You started off as a mama's boy, then something happened, and so, as an adult, you tend to see women as demanding matriarchs. This tends to deep-fry your balls. Get the idea?*

*—What happened?*

*—We'll work on that.*

Guido shut off the machine and went into the bathroom to throw cold water on his face. The image of Edsel Harmon Haight floated in front of him, like an hallucination. Sometimes these visitations scared him. Where do you get your characters? someone once asked him. He couldn't give a satisfactory answer. They come to me, he said. Out of nowhere. My brain is some kind of staging area. It occurred to him that he might have a chronic but controllable brand of psychosis, the machinery of madness harnessed to a socially acceptable purpose, the production of crime novels. In the nineteenth century, they explained these paranormal visitations by regarding the writer as an amanuensis–one who took dictation from voices in the ether, the inhabitants of an invisible world. It was a good theory. It gave Guido something like solace; it was justification.

He regarded himself in the mirror. He looked like he'd spent a week in a freight yard among the displaced. He decided to go to Gassaway's anyway, without sprucing up. He put on his old sneakers, a sweatshirt, and his old army field jacket.

It was 2 A.M. He dropped the .32 into one of the big side pockets of his jacket, then drove to the Overlook District, a part of La Siberia settled by the town's movers and shakers at the turn of the century. Victorian mansions squatted hip-to-hip on the north bank of the Rio Pelegroso. The tall brick houses had served as tenements for the poor for decades. They had been restored to their 19th century splendor by investors who'd bought them dirt cheap from the slum landlords. They sold the houses to arrived and arriving professionals. From the second story balconies of these homes you could see the lights of Bajomitío, Mexico.

Guido parked in front of a two-story Queen Anne. He climbed the steep porch and rang the bell. A woman opened the door. She looked Guido over. *"Lo siento,"* she said. *"No compramos nada esta noche, señor."* She was blonde and tall and unafraid of the dark and its midnight stragglers.

Alana Falconburg. Guido took a step backward into the shadows. He wasn't surprised to see her—she and Gassaway were on several academic committees together and were known to be "close"—but why was she speaking Spanish to him? Maybe she wanted to test him, to see if he had any intellectual credentials at all. It was reasonable to expect that a professor of English living on the border have some language skills.

Guido searched his mind. *"¿Qué pasa?"* he managed.

*"Oigame, señor: No necesitamos nada esta noche. ¿Comprendes?"*

*"¡Qué chapete!"* Guido said, reaching back for his high school Spanish. But it wasn't high school Spanish he realized too late—it was street Spanish he'd picked up in the army when stationed at Ft. Bliss, in El Paso. It was a compliment, but a crude one: *¡Qué chapete! What a body!* He hoped she didn't know any Chicano slang.

"Who's there, Allie?" Gassaway called from inside.

"No one. Just an illegal. I think he wants to sell me something. Probably limes."

"Tell him to *go away.*"

"He looks hungry," Alana said.

"Christ, they all look hungry. It's an ethnic mandate."

*"¿Tienes hambre, señor?"* Alana asked. She reached out bravely and touched his arm. *"Todos somos ilegales, no?"* —We are all illegals, are we not?— It was a moment of shared humanity, a recognition of equivalent alienation: the liberal intellectual's with that of the impoverished Mexican's.

Guido now understood her mistake. He rubbed the stubble on his chin, smoothed back his uncombed hair. He stepped forward, into the light. "I'm not illegal," he said, guessing at her meaning. "Not yet, anyway."

"He speaks fairly decent English, Martin," Alana said.

"Commendable," Gassaway said. "What's he selling—limes did you say? Don't take them, they've cholera over there, you know, as well as that new resistant strain of TB. God only knows what else. Here, give him a dollar. I'll throw in a pocket dictionary to help him along with his English."

Alana went into the living room and came back with a dollar bill and a paperback dictionary. Guido accepted them. *"¿Tu vendes limas?* Are they good *limas?* You know, not tainted?"

A sudden fright made Guido speechless. Was this how it was going to be? Had he been dead for half a day now, his wandering soul trapped in Limbo in the guise of a poor Mexican, haunting the doorsteps of rich gringos, receiving dollars and dictionaries from their clean hands? How long would this last? An eon in Limbo might be half a minute in eternity. Nothing could be taken lightly from now on. He touched his face with trembling fingers.

"You no have *limas?* No matter. Take this anyway, *y mantenga la fe!"* –Keep the faith.– She gave the raised fist salute of solidarity. Guido, at a complete loss, raised his fist, too.

She shut the door. In rapt bewilderment, Guido put the dictionary into his jacket pocket. He sat down on the front steps and lit a cigarette.

*Expect surprise.* This was his personal motto, a favorite paradox. It had proved true again. He coughed on his first lungful of smoke. He dug into an interior pocket of his jacket and pulled out a notepad and pen. A redeeming emotion stronger than joy moved him: he was writing again. It erased all other emotions, including fear. The block was gone. The Milksop Strangler had taken up permanent residence in his life. Edsel had announced himself from the sills of consciousness and now there was no putting him off. To put him off was to risk losing him. Edsel Harmon Haight shoved through the fabric of Guido's brain like a burglar shoving aside the curtains of a jimmied window.

—*What do you look like, Edsel?*

—*Like fucked meat. Like I was back home in Folsom and just got a chorizo enema from five Ubangi power lifters out of their gourds after thirty days in isolation.*

—*You're not cooperating, Edsel.*

—*What do you expect? You name me after a car that was dead in the water before it rolled off the assembly line. You remember what some snotty car critic said? 'The front grille looks like an unmentionable part of the female anatomy.' Jesus, it was the only car in Detroit history with a vagina for a grille.*

—*It gave the car a pleasing feminine quality, don't you think?*

—*The old Studebakers at least had a chrome choad hard as God's thrusting out of the grille. Listen, only my ball-snipping Mom calls me Edsel. She also calls me Harm-and-Hate, but only when I've been good, or when she wants a favor. It's her idea of humor.*

Edsel, a summoned apparition with knob-knuckled hands wide as catcher mitts—a presence real enough to be emotionally taxing. Guido put his notebook away and lit another cigarette. Then the front door of the Gassaway house opened again. Alana came out.

"You're still here?" she said to Guido. "Resting, I suppose. Did you come on foot, from far away? Zacatecas perhaps, or Torreon?" She had fine square shoulders and slim hips and the swell of her thighs tightened her skirt around the startling curve of her buttocks. She was lovely, but her allure derived more from her foward thrusting personality than from the sexual receptivity of more conventional beauties. She knew this, and enhanced it by the way she carried herself. Even her hair proclaimed her power—the energetic blonde cascades suggesting a wild and natural strength. She dug into her purse. "Here," she said. "Take this. *Para tu hijos, señor.*" She gave

Guido a handful of change. He had no children, perhaps never would, but he pocketed the change gratefully.

*"Gracias,"* he said. He kept his head down, shy as a peon from the fields of Zacatecas. It was depressing that a woman as beautiful as this despised him, but even more depressing that she didn't despise him enough to remember him.

He felt something silky touch the back of his head. It slid down to the nape of his neck. Then it repeated itself. She was petting him. Like a stray dog. *"Qué le vaya bien, pobrecito,"* she said, then stepped off the porch.

He watched her walk to her Saab Turbo. Her legs were long, the calves well-turned, her stride fearless. Her patent leather heels, like glossy black exclamation points, snapped against the pavement. The thick waves of her hair rose and fell attractively against her shoulders with each self-confident step.

*The Patrician,* Guido decided, a genetic masterpiece, untainted by mongrelization. In any arena she would be a major player; an ideal poster girl for Dr. Burnaby's theory of uncompromised heredity. No wonder old professor Dawkins hid from her, talking demented gibberish in his dark office.

Guido watched her drive off. Then he stubbed his cigarette out and got up. He knocked on the door again. Gassaway answered. "It's me," Guido said, before Gassaway had a chance to see him as a ghostly beggar. "Guido Tarkenen."

"Jesus, you took your time, didn't you? Come in, have a drink with me. Christ what a night."

"I thought you said the place was ransacked," Guido said, looking around at the untouched room, its rich furnishings. A long thin dog pressed nervously against Guido's legs. It made a noise that was somewhere between a moan and a growl.

"It was. Not here, but my study. Come look." He regarded Guido. "You look like shit. Where have you been?"

"Working," Guido said, but Gassaway had already lost interest. He led the way down a hall and up a flight of carpeted stairs. The dog followed. It had the long, snakey body of a Borzoi and the head of a Dachshund. The pin-headed dog sniffed suspiciously at Guido's heels as they climbed the stairs.

"Be quiet now, Guido," Gassaway said. "Lotty's in bed, under sedation. She's taken two Valium."

The study had been thoroughly tossed. File cabinet drawers were on the floor, their contents strewn. All the drawers of Gassaway's big mahogany desk had been pulled out and dumped. The office was littered with paper. The book cases were empty, the books sprawled on the floor like the victims of a shooting rampage.

They went back down to the living room. Gassaway had the self-conscious stoop of a very tall man, even though he was only about six-three. His prominent forehead suggested vast learning, but his sad, basset-hound eyes seemed ready to spill tears.

"What did they take?" Guido said, pushing the restive dog away from his crotch.

"Go lie down, Isolde," Gassaway commanded. He gave the dog a nudge with his slippered foot. The dog slunk away, its head hanging low. Both men watched it circulate around the furniture until it found a place to settle under a Yamaha grand piano. Gassaway sighed, then said, "I told the police it didn't matter what they took. What they took was a red herring. They wanted something they thought was in my study."

"So what *did* they take, Marty?"

"VCR, TV set, computer—the usual. But don't you see? That had to be a smokescreen to trick the police into thinking it was a routine break-in."

Somewhere in the house a woman was sobbing. "How about that drink, Marty?" Guido said.

"You think I'm wrong," Gassaway said.

Guido shrugged. "What are you stashing in your office?"

"Nothing much. Perhaps they were after some old manuscripts of mine, hoping to sell them to collectors."

"Jesus, that's the last thing they'd take," Guido said.

Gassaway looked at Guido sourly. "Thanks so very much," he said.

"Thieves are a pretty illiterate bunch. I think they took your study apart looking for cash, or maybe weapons. That's how they get their guns, you know. They steal them."

Gassaway went to his liquor cabinet and came back with two drinks. "You think that's all it amounts to, Guido?" he said.

Guido nodded, sipped his drink. He looked at the glass. Amoretto. The sticky sweetness of it made his lips purse. Gassaway slumped down into an Eames swivel chair.

"Christ. What a night. This, and now Gregory. Killed by a goddamned lunatic."

"Gregory?"

"Inverness. The mathematician."

"The guy in the arroyo? They haven't identified him."

"They have now. Allie—Alana—told me," Gassaway said. "She's been in touch with the Vice Chancellor. The sweet thing has been on the phone all night. She's terrific, isn't she?" Gassaway beamed fondly. Then, as if he was afraid he'd given something away, he gave Guido a wounded, suspicious look. "I know exactly what you're thinking, Guido. God knows the rumors have been bandied about in the department. I admit it, it's true. I'm not going to dodge the issue."

Guido sifted through this. "You're fucking her?"

"Please, old man. A little delicacy, if you don't mind."

"That's why Lotty's under sedation, right? I mean, losing a few replaceables is one thing—losing your marriage is another."

"Guido, please. I didn't invite you here to deconstruct my marriage," Gassaway said. "My relationship to Allie—Alana—is not a factor. Lotty is an adult. What has upset her is the murder. Lotty knew Inverness very well. In fact, she was his research assistant. She has her ABD in mathematics. His death, and the *way* he died, was horrible for her."

Guido studied Gassaway over the rim of his glass. Guido was fundamentally a simple man. Sophisticated people never failed to amaze him. They didn't have ordinary responses to things. It was as if they came wired with different emotions. Sometimes he envied them, but most of the time they simply baffled him.

"Getting shot is always horrible," Guido said, half to himself. He reminded himself to call the police again. Those extra shots, the ones the bum heard, had to be the shots that killed Inverness. Carma must have encountered him on her way out of the arroyo. He probably made a casual remark that she twisted into a threat or insult.

Lovely day for a nature walk, isn't it, Miss?
*Die, pig!*

"He wasn't shot," Gassaway said. "He was killed with a rock. Someone beat his brains out. Lotty adored the guy—hell, everyone adored Inverness. Even though he was only forty-two, he was like one of those old-time professors—wise, unpredictable, sometimes sweet, sometimes difficult as a baby, but always brilliant—picture Robert Donat in tweeds and elbow patches."

"Robert Donat?" Guido said, distracted. In his mind's eye he saw Carma crushing the delicate pate of the mathematician with a large stone, blood and gray brain-matter spilling out, complex chains of equations slipping into the ground. He felt light-headed. He touched the tender spot above his ear with unsteady fingertips.

"Robert Donat—in *Goodbye Mr. Chips*. That was Gregory Inverness. I'm afraid it's beyond my powers of imagination to fathom the kind of scum that could do such a thing to a man like that."

But it wasn't beyond Guido's. It happened every day. Murder without remorse. Murder for the fun of it. Demented angels of death, stalking the land, randomly destroying what other people loved. The motive was always unspecific revenge, the anonymous victims always innocent, the crime *necessarily* meaningless.

"So, Guido," Gassaway said. "What do you think of all this?"

"I think someone broke into your house and robbed you," Guido said.

"Too simple."

"Sometimes life isn't very complicated, Marty."

Gassaway regarded Guido. "I've read your, ah, *work,* old man. I must admit I admire how you don't let intellect get in the way. Your prose is as blunt as a literate child's. How did you put it?—'Tracie slipped a ten-inch serrated bread knife from under her pillow and with both hands drove it into Wendell's rectum at the moment of orgasm.' No hesitation in good old Trace. Oh, I mean this as a *compliment!* Terrific stuff, really." He shook his head, smiling and chuckling to himself as he went to the liquor cabinet. He took out the bottle of Amoretto. Guido hid his glass, Gassaway filled his own.

"I haven't been completely frank with you, Guido," Gassaway said, his smile collapsing. "Lotty was, you see, in love with Inverness. She was going to leave me. I don't blame her much. But you see how it might look, don't you? I mean, how the police might see it. Their lust for suspects can make them remarkably stupid."

68

"Whoa," Guido said.

"Tapes," Gassaway said. "I misled you, I'm afraid. I wasn't sure I could tell you the truth. But I like you. I think you're a decent man—I've had arguments with Allie about this—but I think I'm correct. The burglars took all six tapes."

Guido had a friend who spoke in ellipses. Crazy Red Fingerhut. You had to *solve* each conversation with Red. He jumped from the crest of one topic and into the valley of another. You learned, eventually, how to keep up. It took a good memory and a lot of guess work, though.

"Video tapes," Guido said, filling in the gaps. "Of whom?" But he'd guessed the answer.

Gassaway looked crestfallen. He stared at the drink in his hand.

"So, Inverness and Lotty made video tapes of their, ah, *research* activities," Guido said.

"Try to understand, Guido," Gassaway said. "It was harmless enough. Lotty and I . . . well, we understand each other. God! How many married couples can honestly claim *that?* We watched the tapes, together. For a time they amused me immensely. Gregory was such an innocent. Have you ever seen a shy and awkward mathematical genius get down on all fours and—no, never mind." He chuckled savagely at some visual memory. "But then I realized that they, Lotty and Gregory, were in *love.* I suppose our little domestic comedy strikes you as decadent, even perverse."

Guido thought about that. He shrugged, noncommittally. A lot of things struck him as decadent, even perverse. They often had nothing to do with "domestic comedies," which seemed relatively mild, even though they had the power to wreck the lives of the players.

"Look, Marty, I had a mole surgically removed today. I'm tired and feeling a little starched. If you're going to tell me

69

that you actually did kill Inverness, I don't want to hear it.
I'm going home."

Gassaway's tall forehead grew furrows, his eyelids fluttered.
"It could look bad for me, I admit, but no, of course I didn't
kill him. Look at me, Guido. Am I a killer?"

"We all are, Marty, when there's enough at stake."

"Oh wonderful," Gassaway said, smiling and shaking his
head. "Insight into the dark side of the human heart. May I
quote you?" But then a shock of tears rolled down his fleshy
cheeks. "Lotty and I agree that whatever we once had, well,
it's been over for some time now. My career, as you no doubt
know. . . ."

Guido stopped listening. No one's life is more interesting to
you than your own. Having worked that act on more than
one occasion, Guido knew this better than most. The neurosis
common to all writers was narcissism. The job required
constant preening in the reflecting pool of language. No way
to avoid that trap. But Gassaway assumed others were
*interested;* Guido knew they usually were not.

Gassaway would hold center stage as long as he had an
audience. Guido could have grown wings and trumpeted
doomsday and Gassaway's monologue would have rambled
on while archangels read God's shit list.

". . . blackmail," Gassaway was saying, when Guido tuned
in again. "I'm terrified of blackmail."

Guido yawned. "You might have more to worry about than
blackmail."

"Suggestions, old man? Surely you've given these situations
a lot of thought in your . . . ah, *novels.*"

"Sit tight," Guido said.

"That's it? That's your informed opinion?"

Guido shrugged. "I'm not a detective," he said.

70

Isolde, risking the ire of her owner, slithered against Guido's leg again. She drove her pin-head into his crotch and uttered a loving alto growl. Her tongue slipped out to sample traces of organic life in the weave of his slacks. Her wet, chocolate-brown eyes were bottomless wells of unrequited love.

"God damn you, Isolde! I told you to lie *down!*" Gassaway roared. He gave the dog a brutal kick in the ribs. Isolde screeched, then slunk under the piano, her familiar place of exile.

# Seven

Dylan Was Saying Why They Kill and Such
Keith B. Kenniston

The trouble nowadays is anabolic steroids the stuff they pump into cattle like estradial testosterone progesterone etc—what happens then is the steroids get into the meat or maybe bovine somatotropin (recombinant DNA hormone) into the milk and also chicken specific hormones are pumped into chickens to make them lay more eggs or get more meat on them like on the wings which are mostly just bone and skin in the normal chicken—you probably noticed white meat like breast on the wings at KFC or wherever you buy them even the store—this is just to torque up profits— money is the root of all evil like they say in the Bible—(get down man like no shit?)—so what happens next is the kids eat eggs and milk and hamburgers and chicken which they load up with recombinant hormones and steroids they cant get away from it no one can its everywhere its in soup and

71

twinkies and chili dogs you name it (not to mention the excitotoxins like aspartame in diet pop) so then this hormone (and I am not even mentioning the pesticides herbicides or the coming plague bovine spongiform encephalopathy) gets into the kids bodies and messes up the wiring big time—so you have kids growing pubes at ten or nine—you have these little brats running around with ferocious hardons and crotch hair and their little balls tight with testosterone so the kids feel like righteous studs like Hey man I need some stinkpie NOW man or Hey man I copped my old mans 45 lets ventilate some CHUMPS like they were seventeen or eighteen year old gangsters—so here you have ten year olds raping five and six year olds and so forth like that—this is like so irresponsible this worries me—what ultimate load of SHIT is our nation headed for when you have eight year old girls getting knocked up?? this Dylan dude these dry old farts he knows about they are like ten year olds on synthetic hormones like they don't know whats SHAKIN MAN! and they try to get it on with stinking dead Mary— go figure like my old man says—I believe Mr Dylan Thomas was illustrating a sexual need problem of perverts in the England of his day and age—Mr Dylan shows in his story that he was worried about where his nation was going with people in it like Mr Owen Mr Davies Mr Stul and Mr Rafe— oh sure it is a good story!—I liked it a LOT though Mr DT probably had the DTs when he wrote it (just kidding prof!!) it is not written very well so you cant see what he was trying to say in plain English which he is not too competent in using very well he puts too much torque into it you know— he could of used a good course like this one (BROWNIE POINT!)—it is lucky he had such a successful recording career though personally I do not care for it except maybe Lay Lady Lay that oldy that helped me get my first piece of

nasty pie—or maybe knockin on heavens door though it
goes on too long—but for someone who did not go to a
good college he is pretty good sometimes—but about the
growth steroids?—I am a biology major so thats how I know
about it football players have used them from day one and
look what happens take Lyle Alzado for example yet the
FDA lets the growers put the shit in their livestock this is
irresponsible—all this makes me worry about the future
and what will be the end result of all this I think movies like
The Thing (the remake) or Aliens come close to telling you
what will be walking in the streets in the times to come
except for the happy endings they are symbols of symptoms
or symptoms of symbols I forget what you said about
systems of symbols or was it symbols for systems Jesus it
gives me a two Excedrin headache prof—now here comes
this Cortronics—Cybertopia is the next thing to mess up
the citizens only in this case it may take crime off the streets
and put it in their heads where it probably belongs like Dylan
kept his nutty crimes in his head for stories to write except
for his songs which are not nutty enough though I havent
heard every one so I dont know for sure but he is history
like the beatles and stones and alice cooper or U-2 or
megadeath—you name it professor.

Guido scrawled a big red G on the paper, one grade below
F. "Dear Mr. Kenniston," he wrote. "You may have brain
lesions from spongiform encephalopathy yourself. Check into
the college health center for a CT-scan as soon as possible."

He didn't bother correcting Kenniston's confusing of the
two Dylans. Kenniston had fine potential for making an idiot
of himself in the future. Guido–not a teacher at heart–didn't
want to do anything that put this potential at risk. Guido pulled
another paper from the stack.

Atavistic Vocalities
Gaia Gudenbach

These aformal (or perhaps antiformal) texts presented as
unmediated narrative, masks the writer's (Mr. Thomas)
reductive sexism, which I regard not only as vulgaristic posturing, but as an overt act of mental rape, as all phallocentrist
afflatus (afflati?) must be. The narratives are, as you say
professor Tarkenen, seamless and disjointed as dream, an
interesting prepostmodern paradox, but the subtextual
infantilistic sexism poisons the architectonics, and whatever
dreamlike correlatives there might be scarcely mask a savage
antique rhetoric, which in my humble opinion should be
rooted out of the curriculum. Mr.Thomas' work has neither
value nor charm, and, indeed, is dangerous. . . .

Guido put the paper aside. He didn't have whatever it took
to decipher Gaia Gudenbach's cranky lingo. He poured
himself another cup of coffee and lit a cigarette. He had all
weekend to read his student's papers. Today, a Saturday, he'd
just relax.

He heard the mail truck pass by. Though it was late in the
afternoon, he was still in his robe and slippers. He went out
to the mailbox anyway. Alice Dark waved to him from across
the street. "Yoo hoo," she called. She was trimming the rose
bushes that grew along the front windows of her small house.
Guido waved back, then sorted through his mail. "You come
to dinner Wednesday night, Mista' Tarka'," she called. "Six
o'clock. I make some nice pasta for you."

Without thinking, Guido said, "Sure, I'd be happy to." Then,
as he re-entered his house it struck him that Alice's unattached

niece, Seraghina, would probably be present. He went back out to tell Alice he wouldn't be able to come after all, but she was gone.

He sat at his kitchen table. Among the bills and junk mail was a letter from his wife, Kirsten, return address in San Diego. He tore it open, his heart racing a bit.

Dear Guido:

Sign the damned divorce agreement! <u>Now,</u> this minute, before you open one more beer. It's a loose end for both of us. Why are you putting it off? With you or without you it's going to happen, but your signature would make things happen a little quicker. Why am I in a hurry? As I said, I hate loose ends, and, okay, it's true . . . I'm seeing a man, and he doesn't like the fact that I'm not free, from the technical standpoint. He's got principles. Do you find that hard to believe? I can see your superior little self-approving smirk now. Wipe it off your face, Guido, because without principles a man (or woman) has no backbone. I guess that's never troubled you exactly, has it? I'm sorry, I don't want to be mean. You're not a bad man—I even loved you once. I still have some affection for you. I mean, I remember the good times, what we had of them. Can't we honor these memories by remaining cordial? I just want this phase of our lives to be over and done with. You must, too.

K.

The edge of the letter gave him a paper cut. He sucked at the thin line of blood. Had Kirsten thought of him as spineless all the years they were married? And who was this "principled" boyfriend? He crumpled the letter and threw it

75

into a pile of litter that had been gathering in a corner. The divorce papers sat on his desk unsigned. He picked them up and scrawled his name in the X-marked blanks.

He took a shower and got dressed. His shoulder wound had pretty much healed over in the two weeks since the affair in the arroyo. Gregory Inverness's killer had been caught—a disgruntled student who was flunking advanced calculus. The boy, who had a history of violence and mental problems in general, had not confessed but he was now in the state hospital for the criminally insane, being evaluated. It was possible he was too disturbed to stand trial. Too much bovine somato-tropin as a child, Guido mused. Was it bovine steroids or doctored chickens? Theories of dietary-induced behavior annoyed Guido, ever since the famous Twinkie defense in San Francisco years ago.

The lump above Guido's ear was still there. In his worse moments, the suspicion that Carma had shot him in the head returned and that his life since then was a comatose reverie. In these times, he saw the world as his personal Limbo, a never changing hologram of the mind, his place in it fixed for something close to forever. It was a thought that made him sweat.

Guido drove into town with the thick envelope, ostensibly to mail it, but he stopped at The Lost Cause Bar and Grille. One of his students, a recently divorced woman close to his age, was there. She was in a booth, drinking alone. He reminded himself to think before he spoke.

"Mrs. Andrade, mind if I join you?" he asked, timid with caution.

Doris Andrade was a quiet woman who interested Guido the first day he saw her. She had the disoriented look of women whose husbands abruptly leave them after twenty years of what seemed a good marriage. She had no confidence in her opinions. He saw it in her papers. She wrote competently, but could not bring herself to make or sustain a point. Not that she wasn't bright. She had a degree in electrical engineering and had worked as a professional engineer for a number of years. She was taking Guido's course to "improve her writing skills." That was how she put it on the questionaire Guido had circulated the first day of class to find out what he was dealing with.

"Professor T," she said, her smile hesitant. "Please, sit down. I could use some company just now."

Guido got a light beer and brought it to her booth. He saw that she was drinking Scotch, neat. "Professor T?" he said

"People stumble on your last name. T is easy and kind of cute."

"I guess I'll take that as a compliment," he said. Nicknames were a sign of respect, of acceptance. On the other hand, they could be a sign of contempt. Guido sipped his beer. He decided he'd been dubbed Professor T out of contempt. They see me, he thought, as an initial without a dignified train of syllables behind it. They can spit out T without the full and respectful pronunciation of my odd Finlander name.

Guido studied Doris Andrade's face to see what T meant to her, but her thoughts were already elsewhere. There was blue distance in her brown eyes. "Bad day, Doris?" he asked.

"Aren't six out of seven?" Her smile was a heartbreaker—lovely and sad, a smile that somehow suggested twilight.

Guido surrendered to her mood. "We could form a club," he said. He took out the thick envelope and tapped it on the table. "My divorce papers," he said.

"Get burned?"

"We're splitting what little we have. She gets the stereo and the car, I keep the camera, books, and the TV. She cleaned out the savings account before she left. The annuity is still up for grabs."

Doris Andrade was a fading beauty. Her jawline was holding its own against the encroaching jowls, but her arms were heavy, as were her hips and thighs. She had enormous velvelty brown eyes, and an unlined, deceptively untroubled forehead. Her lips were sensual but dry. She licked them before she spoke.

They lingered over two more drinks, then Guido suggested they have dinner together. They went to a Mexican place on the river, a place reputed to be a favorite watering hole for those engaged in the cocaine trade. The building had been an army fortification, dating back to the Mexican war, and its decor consisted of old muskets and long knives bracketed to the walls. They ate *pollo mole,* washed down with dark Mexican beer. The restaurant had a small stage that was usually occupied by a mariachi band, but tonight was Comedy Club night. A comedian took the microphone, a clown in white-face, red nose, orange wig, and big purple shoes. Guido recognized the pants, but now a foot-long puppet leaned out of the fly.

"Great crowd!" the comic said. "How you doing tonight, people?" A handful of diners looked up, then looked back down. "Say lady, is that guy you're with your husband or did they have a sale at Dogs R Us?" The comic used a flashlight in his routine. He beamed it carelessly around the room, from table to table, the puppet swinging in wide ludicrous arcs.

"Jesus," Guido said. "It's Trimmer Swenson."

"You stupid jerk," the insulted man said. He was big and ugly; it was probably a mistake for Swenson to pick on him.

"No offense, sir," Swenson said, shining his flashlight directly into the big man's face. "But say, I think you left your lights on. That *is* your green 1960 DeSoto out in the parking lot, isn't it? The one with the 'I heart Alpo' stickers? I'm not saying your husband is a dog or anything, lady,"—he turned the flashlight beam on the big man's wife—"but I hope you remembered to let him out in the yard before you brought him to this fine establishment. You do have some newspapers with you, just in case, right?"

"*Doctor* Swenson?" Doris said. "The department chairman?"

"I'm afraid so," Guido said.

The big man stood up. "I'm going to stuff your head up your ass, chump," he said. His wife grabbed his arm and pulled him back down into his chair.

"Hey, Gomer, it's a *joke,*" Swenson said. "Where's your sense of humor?" The rag puppet with a small, beady eyes, green leprechaun cap, and a sly grin, bobbed up and down pugnaciously, like an armless boxer.

"Where's *yours,* asshole?" the man said. "You got that thing hanging out of your pants because of your shortcomings? Why don't you haul out the real one, you'll get more laughs that way."

This went on for a while, until Swenson segued into one-liners about English professors.

"He's *terrible,*" Doris said.

"It's his way of unwinding," Guido said. "He's got to put up with a lot of crap all week long."

Swenson was awful but Guido admired his gutty determination to carry on. *Why* he was doing it was another matter. He seemed to Guido like a man who'd made a bet with himself that he could walk a tightrope across a canyon or die trying. It was an act of desperation. His style switched back and forth between savage attacks on the indifferent audience and fawning overtures to them. His timing was awkward, and his material was more grotesque than funny. Yet he kept his act going for almost an hour. Guido was the only one who applauded him.

Doris's presence gave him a lift. It was his first time in a woman's company—a woman who didn't loathe him—in months. In the parking lot, next to his car, they kissed. It was an easy, domestic kiss, warm and friendly. But then it took on a life of its own and became the kiss of two people in need.

"Your place or mine," Guido said, coming up for air.

"Mine," she said. "I've got a view."

# Eight

DORIS ANDRADE'S HOUSE WAS AS BIG AS an airplane hangar. It was built into the side of a mountain. Concrete buttresses kept it from sliding into the rocky ravine below. The house commanded a spectacular view of La Siberia, and, across the Rio Pelegroso, Bajomitío. The south wall of the house was all floor-to-ceiling windows; the view exalted the viewer. A flat carpet of brilliant, multicolored lights spread out to the southern horizon.

"See those lights off to the east?" Doris said, pointing to a band of flickering green separate from the main body of lights. "That's mine. It's called a *maquiladora*. Cortronics, Inc. Actually, it's Nicho's, my husband's, but I'm going to own half of it."

They were sitting neck-deep in a hot tub under one of the tall windows. Guido, margarita in hand, felt like a jaded Roman surveying the urban sprawl from his mountain aerie. The feeling came with the house. Nicho Andrade had an unambiguous self-image, Guido decided. A mover and shaker, an ass-kicker and name-taker. He would have been nervous about sleeping with the man's wife, then resting in his hot tub and drinking his liquor, except that, according to Doris, Andrade had moved into Bajomitío with a twenty-two year old beauty from Guadalajara.

Not that sleeping with Doris had amounted to much. He'd been far too tense and self-conscious. Months of deprivation had made him anxious. He lacked self-confidence, and so he invited failure by turning the moment into a test he had to pass in order to reclaim his manhood. A wide avenue of doubt opened in his mind, an avenue lined with stop lights. His will crumbled. "Shit," he said. His erection had second thoughts as he climbed between her welcoming thighs then folded when he attempted entry. But Doris, patient wife that she was, resuscitated him. "Mama fix," she said, taking him in hand. The stop lights turned green. Doris straddled him and fitted herself on him carefully, guiding him in. Guido was thrilled with her expertise. For a heavy woman she moved with gymnastic ease. Her lower spine and hips generated an undulating wave-motion that made him bite his lips and groan. But he climaxed moments later and Doris rolled away from him with a wifely shrug and sigh: another small disappointment on a list too long now to keep. He followed her into the shower, offering excuses—he was too eager, too nervous, too primed— but she waved these away as unnecessary. "You're just rusty, Professor T," she said, lathering him in soap that smelled like a flower garden. Afterward, she made a pitcher of margaritas and they went to the hot tub.

"I keep the house," she said, "two of the cars, the animals, a seven-figure annuity, plus a checking account that will never go dry. Nicho gets his freedom. It's hard to think of yourself as a repressor of someone's freedom, isn't it?"

"You're rich, Doris," he said, as if just realizing it.

"Not by some standards. But I'm not going to go hungry for a while."

The dream of unlimited money fascinated Guido. Money was a force of nature—it reshaped the countryside as well as the people. Guido saw it as the last god you could believe in. Its invisible lines of force, like gravity, governed the planet. It was a jealous, demanding god, requiring constant service, just as its Old Testament predecessor had. It fit, flawlessly, the God-definition: We are always in need of it and constantly seek it. We love and fear it and we fall into deep despair without it. When we earn it, we are righteous, when we lose it we live in a shadow world of lost spirits. It had its own theologians—the money managers, brokers, analysts, and market gurus. Hagiologic lore, stories true and apocryphal, of the frugal, hermetic billionaires, held the masses spellbound. The billionaires were not like ordinary men. There was no looseness about them, no urge to backslide, drop out, or acquire ruinous debt. Some presented themselves as common men to prove that this modern god did not pick favorites and was hungry for acolytes from all walks of life. But they were not common; their egos were titanic and their vision of what was right for themselves—and therefore right for the nation—was never eroded by doubt.

Now and then, Guido watched a rich and suave television evangelist, Cat Henderson, who gave better stock market advice than spiritual consolation. Guido bought stocks, when he had the money, based on this evangelist's advice to his flock. The evangelist's financial analyses were always well-informed, detailed, and crafty. He picked winners with eighty-seven percent accuracy. The man had divine acumen; Guido didn't even bother with secular brokers. This evangelist offered his followers inexpensive booklets, authored by him, on the subject of amassing a fortune through shrewd invest-

ment. He also counseled his flock on how to avoid unnecessary taxation and how strategic donations to charities could
stymie the IRS. His religious sermons were run-of-the-mill.
They made no unreasonable demands on the faithful. There
was nothing in them that argued against the unashamed
embrace of materialism. These sermons were merely decorative, a nod to superstition. The old god wasn't quite dead and
perhaps required perfunctory tribute—his senile fingers might
still be able to launch bolts of vengeful lightning. But the god
the evangelist served with vigor and passion, the god that
truly excited his devotion and tweaked his anxiety, was *Dollar.*
Dollar was now the only god universally feared and loved.
Guido had no problem with this notion. Money ruled the
planet, ruled him, and those that denied it were either lying
to themselves or were mental defectives. *Our Dollar who art
in Dollar, Dollar be Thy name. . . .*

"Yoo hoo," Doris Andrade said. "I'm still here, Professor
T."

"Sorry. I was thinking about how it must feel to be rich."

Doris laughed. "It feels goddamned good! Especially if you
grew up poor. My father shoveled coal into a blast furnace
until he died at the ripe old age of fifty-six. I was Doris
Dumchek back then. I met Nicho at UCLA, back when we
were engineering students. Now *he* was class. My daddy hated
him, called him an uppity greaser. Imagine, a blast-furnace
slave with a fifth grade education named Dumbelink
Dumchek calling names. It wasn't a case of the pot calling
the kettle black. It was the pot calling the *crystal chandelier*
black. I loved my daddy, but no one ever mistook him for a
rocket scientist."

"So what do they make in your *maquiladora?*" Guido asked.

"Cybertopia machines." She saw Guido's blank look.
"They're the latest thing in virtual reality toys," she said.

83

"Except they're not exactly priced like toys. When they are marketed, sometime next year, they'll go for around ten thousand each."

Guido recalled Keith B. Kenniston's garbled warning. "Who's going to pay ten thousand dollars for a toy?" he said.

"Everyone. This will change the way people think, even the way they behave. This thing is on a par with the wheel and lever. It's going to make almost all forms of entertainment obsolete overnight."

"I can think of one exception," Guido said.

"It will revolutionize that, too. Electronic polygamy and polyandry. Inorganic sex. STD-free and totally chaste. The citizens will be able to explore every kink without physical consequence. There's going to be a second sexual revolution that will make the sixties look like a page out of the Book of Common Prayer."

Doris climbed out of the tub. Her large, blue-veined breasts steamed in the cool air. She had big hips, saddlebag thighs, and her belly rolled when she moved. But Guido had long since stopped judging women by their bodies. The dismantling of his own physique—never much to begin with—was well under way. He couldn't even muster a vigorous stream of piss. And now his virility was questionable.

"Come on, I'll prove it to you," she said, grabbing his hand and pulling him from the tub.

They dried off with large Turkish towels, then Guido followed her to a room that looked like a gym except for the deep pile carpeting and the few pieces of plush furniture. There were a pair of wide treadmills that were flush with the carpeted floor. The walls were padded.

"Nicho is wild about this machine," she said. "He and his partners have an arrangement with La Siberia Tech to build the prototypes. It's based on a new type of computer chip invented at Cal Tech but perfected right here at La Siberia Tech. It's a silicon neuron—SiN, for short. The gates are small as neurons and work the same way—analogically, not digitally. Which means the CPU can split any arrow in a digital CPU's quiver. It will make the Pentium Four look like a rowboat."

Guido frowned, faking a grasp of the subject. "No kidding?" he said. "That's interesting."

Doris laughed. "Jesus, it's more than *interesting.* It's revolutionary. It's a true model of the brain, not a metaphor for one. Come on, I'll show you."

Technical talk made Guido crabby. He wasn't scientifically inclined. He didn't understand radio, television, heavier-than-air flight, or his word processor. That was someone else's job. All he had to do was benefit from their use.

Doris opened a closet and took out a suitcase. She snapped it open and handed Guido a body suit made of translucent plastic. It was lined with grids of fine wires. "This is the data suit. Put it on," she said. "Make sure you've got the male. Unless you want to get kinky."

Guido looked at the crotch. It had a narrow pocket for his genitals. The pocket in Doris's suit was reversed. When they had zipped themselves up, Doris took out a pair of helmets light as bathing caps from the case. The helmets had slimline visors, that fit comfortably over the eyes. Doris made the electrical connections, then said, "All this stuff will be simplified in the production models. Put the helmet on, I'll set up the machine. Step onto the treadmill when you need to walk, it will turn on automatically. Otherwise stay on the floor or on one of the couches."

As soon as Guido had the helmet in place, his brain lit up. A wall of color rushed at him, made him flinch. It was as if he'd been thrown headlong into a rainbow. A surge of disorienting panic made him drop to all fours, but even this couldn't stop his free-fall into spectral space.

Then Doris was beside him. She looked twenty years younger. They fell through the rainbow together. She took his hand and squeezed it. Electric squibs generated by her touch made him feel like a teenager in love.

They dropped into a green valley, among cypress trees and flocks of uninterested sheep. "This is just a virtual staging area," Doris said. "All the machines will offer something like this." She was wearing a summer dress, a print, belted at the waist. She was slim and agile. He looked at his legs. They were tanned and muscular. He was wearing shorts and running shoes.

"What's going on?" he said.

"Look around you."

Guido looked at a perfect world: blue skies, billowing white clouds, the valley in front of them blowing with tall grasses and flowers, the distant mountains white-capped. A bird flew past, a butterfly, a darning needle. Nothing about these images were cartoon-like. They were exact as photographs and their movements were smooth. Guido reached out and caught a butterfly. It struggled in his hand. He felt the slight tickle of its resistance, then let it go.

"VR technology, before the SiN chip," Doris said, "gave you a cartoon world, at best. The digital-based machines can only work with straight lines. You can give a polyhedron enough sides to make it approximate a curved surface, but these analog chips give you the curved surface itself. All the chaotic lines of reality are reproduced perfectly. What we have here is a seamless, 360 degree view of a world that's just as fluidly real as the one outside. The only difference is that here, in this world, you can do anything you want. Think about that. So, what do you want to play? Bonnie and Clyde?"

Guido shrugged. He had become fascinated by another butterfly that hovered in front of his face, a huge monarch whose wings made the air hum. Doris pointed at the sky and a menu window appeared. She studied it for a moment then selected a game.

With no warning, no cinematic dissolve or fade, they were walking down a city street. Guido had no sense of the treadmill moving under him. He was wearing a double-breasted pin-stripe, circa 1930. Doris was still in her summer dress. He looked at his hands: he was holding a Thompson sub-machine gun. Doris was also carrying a Thompson. They walked into a bank. The uniformed guard saw them, unholstered his revolver. Doris fired a burst into the guard. The rounds walked up his belly, chest, and throat. Then the man's head flew apart. A geyser of blood sprayed out from the severed carotids.

Guido began to shake. Then he realized it was the Thompson that was shaking him. He was spraying the walls with .45 caliber lead. People, virtual human beings, dove for cover.

"You've got buck fever," Doris said. "You'll get over it." She walked around the teller's counter and found the bank manager. "Open the safe, little man, or I'll drill you a pair of new assholes."

The manager scrambled to the safe and opened it. Doris stepped in and came back with a cardboard box full of thousand dollar bills. "Let's party, Professor T," she said.

They went back out into the street where a 1930 Pierce Arrow stopped for them. They drove away burning rubber, an accomplice behind the wheel. Doris shoved the barrel of the Thompson out a window and shattered storefronts and parked cars with long, ear-splitting bursts.

The police cornered them in a dead-end alley. Doris emptied the Thompson at them, then Guido emptied his. Their unnamed accomplice got out of the Pierce Arrow and ran. He was knocked down by a thunderous blast from riot guns.

"They've got us," Doris said.

Guido saw three overweight red-faced cops running toward him with drawn pistols, heard them groaning for breath. Doris pulled his sleeve. "Come on, let's blow this burg," she said.

"Can they hurt us?" he asked as a dozen uniformed police raised their weapons skyward.

"If they hit you, you'll definitely feel it."

They got out of the car and rose into the air a thousand feet. .38 rounds whip-cracked past them. Guido felt bee-stings in his thighs and buttocks. They flew out of gunshot range toward a river where enormous white swans swam side by side.

"This is too much," Guido said, massaging his virtual wounds.

"We've just started, Professor T," Doris said, taking his hand. They sank into lush grass and made love. He felt himself enter her, strong and durable as a twenty-year-old.

Guido moaned, then roared, as a surge of electrically induced pleasure moved from his loins, up his spine, and to his brain. It was only SiN chips engaging SiN chips, nothing more, but her lips were warm and the hard nipples of her firm young breasts bore into his sculpted chest. His virtual erection was virtually unbendable as the virtual lovers writhed in virtual ecstasy. Nothing had happened yet everything had happened. *If this isn't real, then what is?* Guido thought.

"In a few years the ordinary citizens will have these machines," Doris said. "When they network them, the electronic village is going to be one wild and crazy place."

Guido rolled onto his back, stared straight up at the faultless blue sky. "Is it too late to buy stock in your company?" he said.

"Too early. Nicho's not ready to go public yet."

Doris raised her hand and pulled down the menu window. The list of games floated in the air. She touched one of the offerings, and they found themselves sitting in an intimate New Orleans cafe, entertained by a zydeco band. They were both dressed in evening clothes. A waiter set a plate of steaming oysters Bienville in front of Guido.

"Gourmet food, too?" Guido said.

"Try one," Doris said.

Guido raised an oyster to his lips. Too hot; it burned him. He blew on it, tried again. It looked delicious, the best he'd ever seen, but when he tried to take it into his mouth, it vaporized.

"When these machines can also feed us," Doris said, "that will be the end of the world as we know it. People will climb into their body suits and never come out. Maybe that's what the rapture will be, if you believe in Bible prophecy."

"I don't think the evangelicals will buy it," Guido said.

They left the cafe and rose into the air again. A bird flew next to them, a fat seagull with leering red eyes. "You're new to this game, aren't you, bud?" said the gull.

"Go ahead, answer him," Doris said

"I don't talk to seagulls," Guido said.

Doris laughed. He looked at her. She was larger than life now, her long golden hair flying behind her. She was a goddess, an immortal. Perfect Doris and Perfect Guido, footloose in the electronic garden.

They passed through a gauze of clouds. Guido wondered if they could fall, if a glitch in the SiN chips ever allowed fatal mistakes, and would the virtual impact convince his real body that it had been killed, just as dreamers were said to die if they did not wake up before the impact of a long fall. He knew that he was seated on a deep-cushioned sofa in her hilltop house, knew that she was seated across from him in a love seat, but that knowledge seemed like an unreliable memory. This was the only reality, this was where he was–*flying*–observing a green world from a thousand feet up, a perfect world where Perfect Doris and Perfect Guido made the rules, their domain uncontested. This was every man's dream since dreaming began.

They kissed among the clouds. A 747 appeared next to them. They stepped onto its wing and danced to *The Continental* like Fred Astaire and Ginger Rogers in front of the passengers, whose startled faces were pressed against the windows. Then Doris stretched out above the nacelle of a screaming fan jet. Guido stretched out next to her. They made love on the wing of the jumbo jet while a one-hundred piece orchestra played a bolero from a wide shelf cut into a wonderfully sculpted cumulo-nimbus. The passengers cheered wildly for them.

They floated to the rear door of the plane and opened it. The passengers applauded, even those who had headsets on and were watching the movie. The passengers were ordinary looking people, people you'd expect to find on an airliner–men in business suits, young women with babies, a few old couples dozing or reading, teens in jeans.

But there was one face among the nondescript crowd that seemed out of the ordinary. A middle-aged man, his graying hair tied in a pony-tail, was looking directly at Guido. The man was *smirking*. Guido met his stare but was first to break away, which astonished him. Intimidated by an electronic phantom! But the illusion that this was Guido's and Doris's private domain was definitely undermined by this leering man. Guido was tempted to collar the man and throw him out of the airplane–*how do you like this, you smirking son of a bitch*–but he didn't have the stomach for it.

Doris found a man who was playing a game on his laptop computer. It was a CD interactive game, a whodunit based in

London. A Scotland Yard detective was knocking on a door in a dark alley. Guido watched Doris shrink to a figure small enough to walk on the keys of the passenger's laptop. Then Guido also began to shrink. Together they walked up the keyboard of the computer and entered the full-color, active-matrix screen.

Guido knocked on the door in the alley. Doris opened it. She was a hag now, stooped and toothless. "Wot d'ye want?" she said.

"You know what I want, Annie," Guido said. He pushed his way inside, found himself in a dark room that probably smelled of mildew, piss, and wood-rot. An old man in a rocker grumbled to himself, then coughed up dark phlegm into his hand. He wiped his hand on his pants and cursed. Annie turned and hobbled away. Guido followed. They went to a back room where a halfwit was drawing a charcoal sketch of a giant. The giant was peering down from the top of a towering beanstalk.

"Let's get small again," Annie said, and the SiN chip processor complied. Guido, big as a housefly, flew into the charcoal sketch, Annie at his side, and suddenly they were in a world of wobbly gray lines.

"Get him, Jack," his mother hissed. "Get that bloody giant. Kill him, Jack." His mother, a bundle of lines and shapes with an ugly toothless grin carved across her oblate melon head, shoved him toward the gray stalk. Her eyes were notched, like gunsights.

Guido climbed the beanstalk until he broke into a paper white sky. He found the giant's wretched house and there was Doris, waiting for him, a charcoal goose in her lap. They made love again in the giant's sketchy bed, and then the giant kicked open the door. He was ten feet tall with a head as round and as simple as a pumpkin. His mouth was a careless ax-gash and his eyes were sly, demonic slits. He was a construct of charcoal lines and monstrous charcoal gesture. His shoes were coffins.

"Fee fie foe fum, I smell the blood of an Englishman," the giant roared. Guido, in spite of himself, panicked.

They climbed out a window and ran across the blank fields toward the paper vortex where the charcoal stalk ended and the giant's high, papery domain began. The giant was too fast for them. He picked up Guido and Doris and flung them into featureless, halfwit space. They landed in a London alley behind the decrepit house, running from nothing.

"Slow down," Doris said, "you're going to give yourself a coronary."

They climbed into a horse-drawn carriage. Doris issued a command and the horse grew wings. The improvised Pegasus hauled the carriage into the clouds where it intercepted the airliner. They abandoned the carriage and entered the airplane, again to the lusty cheers of the passengers. "We made it," Doris said.

"They made it! They made it!" cheered the passengers.

They found the passenger with the laptop computer, and Guido saw himself climb out of the screen followed by Doris. They resumed normal size, then merged with their full-sized selves. Guido felt a tide of confusion sweeping away the scattered crumbs of sanity. He lost his balance. He grabbed Doris's hand, staggered into her. The smirking passenger with the pony tail glanced at Guido and laughed with convincing spontaneity.

"Don't worry," Doris said. "We had to exit each of the subprograms we entered, kind of like an ordinary computer. No big deal." They opened the door of the airliner and stepped into the sky. Doris swam over to one of the engines and separated it from its mount with an acetylene cutting torch.

The airliner went into a flat spin, and became a lake of flame on the side of a mountain.

Guido thought he saw the face of the smirking man in one of the windows. "It's been real nice, fuckhead," Guido said. The man waved at Guido then made the *cornudo* sign, forefinger and pinkie raised out his pale fist.

"Who are you talking to?" Doris asked.

"That jerk with the pony tail."

Doris frowned. "Gray pony tail?"

Guido nodded.

"That's Nicho, my husband. He programmed this prototype. His image pops up here and there."

"He's a little screwed up, isn't he," Guido said, "flashing the goat sign at me? He's got it backwards."

They dropped out of the sky and into a narrow street. Doris pulled him through a doorway, and they were in the cafe where—was it only minutes ago?—he'd tried to eat electronic oysters.

"I think I've had enough," he said.

An insulted waiter removed Guido's plate and went into the kitchen. Guido caught a glimpse of a man with a ponytail standing next to a steaming kettle—Nicho Andrade again, wearing a chef's apron. The smirk was still on his face, but now he seemed even more amused. When the swinging door to the kitchen closed, Guido heard metallic laughter.

Doris removed the helmet from his head. They unzipped their body suits and stepped out of them. They were both sweating profusely. Guido's heart was beating hard and irregularly. This bothered him, but even so, he found himself regretting the loss of Perfect Doris and Perfect Guido. They stood regarding each other, panting, their sagging, middle-aged bodies glistening.

"Your husband's a real prince," Guido said.

93

"He always had a weird sense of humor, but don't let it get to you. It's only a stored image, you know."

"He seemed *there,* taking it all in."

"He wasn't."

Guido was not convinced. The floor beneath his feet was still moving. He felt as if he might rise a thousand feet into the air at any moment and find villages sculpted into the clouds.

He was afraid of irreversible neurological damage, of mutations among his axons and dendrites. He felt microscopic fingers playing with the wiring of his cerebral cortex, inventing random worlds that would mix the real and unreal with ribald glee.

He looked at Doris. He looked at the walls of the room they were in, unable to trust the lines and planes and colors that made up the actual world—the ordinary everyday place where he was expected to play out his life.

# Nine

THEY KISSED IN THE DRIVEWAY AND GUIDO felt the familiar tedium of low-risk, casual involvement. It numbed his brain, pressed down on his shoulders like a meal sack. Her lips weren't as thrilling as her virtual lips, her breasts not as electrifying as their SiN chip doubles.

"I used to be beautiful," she said.

"Easy to believe," he said. He meant it as a compliment. It was the wrong thing to say. The melancholy in her eyes shamed him. "You still *are* beautiful, Doris."

Her wry smile increased his shame. "Good night, Professor T," she said.

On his way home he was siezed by the need to empty his bladder. He stopped at the Hammer and Tong, a decrepit place in the warehouse section of La Siberia. Some of the more adventuresome professors he knew slummed in this bar. The buildings in this part of town were crumbling, the streets littered with broken window glass, the air heavy with the corrosive breath of urban decay.

He went straight to the men's room, a dim cubicle sour with decades of urine, bad plumbing, and rotten wood. He stood in front of the rusty urinal and waited. A scrawl of graffiti and phone numbers covered the wall above the stinking bowl.

> Want some real downhome heartbreak head?
> Call cutrate Rilla. She's my ex so I know.
> She can suck the green off a dollar bill
> but she's a damn sight cheaper.
>
> —Had It

Be safe not sorry—tarp that load brother.
God did not give us the latex Trojan
so we could make a superior water balloon.
                    —a Christian trucker

Don't throw your cigarettes or gum into the urinal.
It makes the cigarettes hard to light and the gum salty.
                    —the Management.

Guido rested his head on the dank plaster above the urinal, waiting patiently for his prostate to relent. He felt around in his jacket pocket, found a Panpax, put the festive-looking red and green capsule on his tongue. Guido guessed that the drug company who produced it decided that the cheerful Christmas colors would enhance the psychogenic activity of the chemical. When he collected enough saliva, he swallowed it. He counted on the relaxant properties of the drug to release the flood.

Five minutes later his bladder was still full. He mumbled a begging prayer. A man seated in the stall next to the urinal heard him.

"Say one for me, brother," he said. The man groaned a little, offering proof of need.

Guido understood that the swollen prostate created a sort of an ersatz sphincter that crimped down on the urethra. Situated just under the bladder, the prostate permitted urine to flow or not flow, depending on its condition. As Guido saw it, the prostate's primary function was to create misery for middle-aged men who had abused themselves with strong drink, faulty nutrition, and damaging behavior in general. Its presence was a small proof that the vengeful God of the Old Testament had, at least back in His world-planning days, existed. That the prostate played some minor part in the transport of semen was medical sophistry, as far as Guido was concerned. The trouble-making organ was flat unnecessary. But modern science was in the process of gathering all the dazzle unto itself and could not allow the existence of an organ whose only purpose was to provide severe moral instruction. The ancient gods, in the eyes of modern industrial science, were paltry fakers in tatters, homeless old geezers riddled with vermin. Lightning no longer forked from their righteous fingers, thunder no longer rolled from their furious tongues.

Guido's magic carpet ride with Doris Andrade had irritated the testy organ and now he was paying the price of his little electronic romp. He continued praying, mumbling automatic Hail Marys, mesmerized by repetition. And as his lips moved, Guido let his mind drift.

One of his killers, in a book called *Odd Man In,* had the opposite problem. A bullet cocooned in his spine had damaged nerve tracts above the sacrospinal cord where the pudendal nerves are bundled. This caused problems with the man's sphincter control. The urgent command to void did not always reach the central nervous system. So the man often wet himself. Especially when excited by the prospect of heinous deed. This killer had been abused as a child—mentally and physically. But Guido, in his books, never explained or justified criminal behavior by raising the ghosts of childhood. Everybody carried their ghosts with them, but most did not murder, maim, rape, or steal. Responsibility for one's behavior couldn't be delegated in a society that valued order over chaos. Once you started passing the buck, it could only stop with Adam and Eve, or with Lucy, the tiny *Australopithecus*—depending on your choice of prehistoric measurement—at which point

97

all behavior becomes relative. The world, Guido believed, had already taken giant steps in that direction.

Guido thought about his own ghosts, none of which were terribly unpleasant. "Hold peter, but do not squeeze him," his father had said. Guido was about two years old at the time. He remembered the coolness of the toilet bowl against his little thighs as he leaned into it, holding peter proudly, studying the swift yellow jet of his water. "Into the *toilet,* Guido," his father scolded. "Don't play with it." Guido had been letting the golden arc wander where it might, splashing the underside of the raised seat, the tank, the floor tiles, but now he drilled the water in the bowl, excited by the chaotic commotion of bubbles he caused. The water became yellow-tinted, and that was because of *him,* too. This was Guido's first instruction in peeing-while-standing, a proud moment in his childhood. He remembered yelling like a triumphant warrior over a helpless enemy.

Then another memory: Guido sitting on the toilet, his father holding his hand, saying, "Don't strain, swabby." Guido sat on the toilet, studying his chubby feet dangling before him, the toes splaying with peristaltic effort. "Push a little, but don't strain, Guido," Elmo Tarkenen said. His father's voice was patient and firm, a seaman's voice, the voice of someone who knew basic and important things. Guido sat there, waiting, becoming bored, thinking that it was far more pleasurable to feel the caca pack his diaper, knowing that his mother would take the diaper off then clean him with a warm washcloth, while chatting sweetly to him or humming a lullaby. He had loved these occasions, and he looked forward to them every time, but now this new way, this travesty called "going number two," threatened to change everything. This new way was going to make it *all up to him,* and he wasn't sure he wanted to be the only one involved with his caca. The knowledge of what that responsibility would lead to lurked as an undefined anxiety in his little mind: It was the first step toward separation, independence, responsibility, and citizenship. Managing one's own caca was the beginning of the end of infancy. It was not a warrior feeling at all, like drilling the water in the bowl with your yellow stream. He whined to get off the potty, he wanted things to go back to the way they were, but his father held him firmly in his large, seaman's hands and said, "Easy boy, be easy. Don't strain, swabby. Push a little, but don't strain."

Guido strained to get it over with, but he also strained to be contrary. A lifetime of straining, which had begun as rebellion but now was just a bad habit, had left him, in middle age, with bleeding hemorrhoids. But judging from the saturation of prime time television with commercials for hemorrhoid salves, this apparently was the fate of the nation.

The drunk in the stall finally emerged. He staggered to the filthy sink and turned on the water. A rusty stream groaned from the tap. The drunk looked at it for a while, then shut it off. He looked over at Guido. "Any luck, pardner?" he said.

Guido ignored him.

The man rested his hand Guido's shoulder. "You keep praying, Bubba," he said. "The Lord'll fix 'er, all's you got to do is keep on truckin' with the Jesus."

"Thanks," Guido said.

"No problem," said the drunk. "Any time."

The man left. Guido waited another five minutes, and then the Panpax kicked in. Guido felt incredibly relaxed. A cool, sweet breeze washed against his face—a chemical illusion, but welcome. His prostate wavered in its resolve to keep his bladder miserably full—pharmaceutical science was revoking his punishment. A dribble of urine spattered the urinal, followed by a balky stream that didn't have enough force to break up the cigarette butts jamming the drain.

Guido went into the bar and ordered a double shot and a mug. He figured he'd earned it. He downed the whiskey and sipped the beer, then ordered another double.

"Ah, is that you Tarkenen? Tarkenen the, ah, *writer?*"

The voice was loud but sourceless. Guido looked up and down the crowded bar, then into the gauzy shadows behind him.

"I'm certain it's you, Tark," said the voice, with irksome familiarity. "Tarkenen, old cock! *Venga aquí,* you crusty old prick!"

The Hammer and Tong, as far as Guido could make out, was a neighborhood bar, catering mainly to old drunks who generally minded their own business. It was not the kind of place where people raised their voices, bellowing for companionship.

"*Camarada! Paisano!*" called the relentless voice. "I know it's you, Tarkenen! I recognize the narrow sedentary shoulders, the furtive cast of eye, the head bowed–deceptively I should think–with weighty thoughts. Let me buy you a drink, *amigo!*"

Again Guido looked around.

"Yes, yes, over here, *mon frère,*" the voice said.

A white blur moved back and forth in the shadows at the back of the barroom. Guido recognized it as a fat white hand. A figure gradually emerged behind the signaling hand, a lump of darkness against the lesser dark. The crude human shape slowly took form, the grinning face wide as a dinner plate.

Guido carried his drink toward the specter. "Figgis?" he said.

Avery V. T. Figgis, the 18th century specialist. A huge man with a voice that could warn ships away from the shoals. Guido, trusting his instincts, had been avoiding him all semester. The V. T. stood for Victor Traherne, but his students called him "old Vodka and Tonic Figgis."

Figgis bought his clothes from the Salvation Army, even though he made close to eighty thousand a year. He liked to dress like a bum, liked pub-crawling in the seediest sections of town, enjoyed astonishing strangers with his mixture of obscenity and erudition. He outranked everyone in the department, including Trimmer Swenson. Even Alana Falconburg feared him since she did not yet have tenure and Figgis controlled every important committee that decided such matters.

"Meet Mrs. O'Riggins, Tark," he boomed.

A woman who could have been forty but looked sixty sneered at Guido. "Listen to *that* one," she said. "It's *Higgins*. Not whatever he said. Olive Higgins." Her face was masked heavily with powder. She had painted apples on her white cheeks. Her hair, dyed a glorious chestnut, hung incongruously past her bony shoulders in luxuriant waves. Her teeth were bad and she had no lips. She looked brittle as last year's Christmas candy.

"What's in a name," said the erudite Figgis. "Olive, this is the famous Guido Tarkenen. I hope you are suitably impressed."

"Famous? How do you mean famous?" she said. She squinted at Guido, studying him for signs of fame.

"He's a writer, dear," Figgis said. "He is a wordsmith, a warrior who lives or dies by the pen."

"You're funnin' me," Olive said. She scooted her chair closer to Guido's. "What d'ya write, honey?" she said.

"Trash for cash," Guido said.

"He is too modest," Figgis said. "If he lived in France or England he would be celebrated. The American critical establishment is packed with fussy snobs. They don't approve of the crime novel, where one can find some of the best contemporary writing."

Guido habitually reacted to flattery with suspicion. This praise, coming from Figgis, put him on alert. Olive Higgins got up and staggered to a juke box. She leaned on it with both hands, studying the selections. Her body swayed from side to side as if with the roll of a ship's deck. When she came back to their table, a Patsy Cline record was playing.

"I love this Patsy," she said. "She breaks whatever is left of my heart."

Guido, in spite of himself, was touched by this. He took Olive Higgins' hand and kissed it. She accepted the gesture without comment, as if it was her due.

Figgis smirked. "Sentimentality," he said. "It masks all our base impulses. Look where it's gotten us."

"You got a base impulse, honey?" Olive Higgins said to him.

Guido finished his drink. "Nice talking to you all," he said, pushing himself up.

"Wait, Tarkenen," Figgis said. "Don't go. There's something I want to run by you, if you don't mind." He caught Guido's wrist and dragged him back down to his chair. Guido shook free of Figgis's grip, annoyed, but also surprised by the man's strength. Figgis didn't look strong. He was big, but he looked soft and pampered. Olive excused herself and went to the bar. "I'm going to see if I can find me some base impulses over there," she said, crabbily.

"She's old and beat up," Figgis chuckled, "but she's still got the juice." He made an obscene back-and-forth pumping motion with his fist. He licked his lips, rolled his eyes.

"You were going to run something by me," Guido reminded him. A fresh round of drinks arrived at the table.

"This may not interest you, Tark—you being a temporary hire and all. But even though the sale hasn't been finalized, I've noticed subtle changes, changes that are way out of line vis-a-vis the conditions-of-sale agreement, which no one, save the select few, has seen."

"If you haven't seen the agreement what makes you think the changes are out of line?" Guido asked. He had no idea what Figgis was talking about, and didn't care, but he was happy to stick a pin in this gasbag's logic.

"You don't have the foggiest idea of what I'm talking about, do you?" Figgis said.

"Right. And I don't particularly care."

"The Singapore group, Global Visions, Inc. They're the buyers. Half a billion in cash. How does that strike you, Mr. Tarkenen? Makes your clapper tingle, doesn't it? What do you get per book? Five, ten, maybe fifteen thousand?"

"Much more," Guido said. It was a sensitive subject for him. He'd gotten twenty for his last book, though his agent, Sid Mullen, had argued for double that. Cash Holub was not in a position to offer more since Guido's sales figures had leveled off with the last three books.

Figgis scoffed. "You writers all lie about your advances. Don't kid a kidder, Tark. The trouble with the deal is this: we're all going to be out of jobs. Could happen tomorrow. Take a peek into Swenson's office next time you get a chance. He used to have two secretaries. Now, only one."

"I'm not following you, Figgis," Guido said. There was a small commotion at the bar. A woman had wedged herself between two men and the men were taking exception to it.

"Siberia Tech is, as you must know, a privately endowed school. But the endowment funds have been dwindling–lower interest rates, poor investments, etc. So, this outfit from Singapore comes to the rescue. The only trouble is, they want to re-define the university. They don't give a fat rat turd about accreditation. They want our superb R and D facilities. They want a campus-like facility, like IBM's in upstate New York.

103

English? Forget about it. History? Philosophy? Useless as tits on a javelina boar. When the sale is finalized next month, we're *gone.*"

The woman at the bar was Olive. One of the men elbowed her hard. When this had no effect, the other man turned on his stool and yanked her by the hair. He spun her around and she lost her footing and fell.

"Jesus Christ," Guido said. He reminded himself why he drank only in clean, well-lit, middle-class bars.

"Pay no heed," Figgis said. "This is her act. I've seen it before. You should come down here on a Saturday night. It gets extremely amusing. Now where was I? Oh yes, the Global Visions people. They come from that perfect city state, Singapore. Everybody happy, or else. Everybody work together. Everybody love government. Everybody neat as pin. All trains on time—as in the old fascist dream. Though the threat they represent now is economic, not military. The slave societies are going to win out, Tark. The old inefficient human-rights obsessed democracies are going to suck hind titty. And Jesus, wait till China gets into the game! They're going to mop up on Japan. The next hot war will be China and Japan, 1937 all over again. Except this time it will be China doing all the ass-kicking. They haven't forgotten what the Japs did to them back in the thirties, you wait and see. All this was unimaginable even five years ago."

Guido was only half listening. Olive hadn't gotten up. She was either resting or had passed out. She lay on her back, feet crossed at the ankles, her hands folded neatly on her stomach. The man who had elbowed her had turned on his stool. He looked down on her, cleared his throat, spit. Guido was fascinated with disgust. But when the man unzipped his pants and stood over Olive, Guido jumped up and yelled.

He ran over to the bar and punched the man hard enough to send a bolt of pain up his arm. The man fell off his stool and sat on Olive. Guido kicked him in the side, and the man rolled away. Guido was about to kick him again when someone grabbed him from behind.

"Don't you *do* that to old Paddy!" an outraged voice cried out. "Hey, we ain't gonna let this hooligan put the boot to old Paddy, are we?" He was answered by a chorus of dark growls.

The hands that held Guido's arms were weak and he easily broke away, but then something–a mug or bottle–caromed off his head and his knees buckled. He was propelled across the bar by several men and slammed up against a wall. Hundreds of forceless wino punches drummed his shoulders and back. A screeching woman clawed at his eyes. Guido heard Avery Figgis bellowing for reason in his ship-hailing voice.

Something knocked hard against Guido's head again. He saw squibs of unnatural blue light. He heard himself curse, his voice coming from somewhere far away. He felt himself start to fall but couldn't prevent it. He knew when he'd hit the floor, but he didn't feel it.

Wino uproar thundered in his brain for a while longer. Then nothing.

# Ten

GUIDO HATED BEDS THAT SAGGED. This one sagged badly. The weak springs forced him and Kirsten to sleep practically on top of each other. He was sweating and so was Kirsten. Not that he cared about the discomfort. She was back, and that's all that mattered. Tears of gratitude spilled down his face, rolled into his ears. He slipped his hand under her dress and stroked her thigh. The liquid welcoming sounds she made interrupted her snores.

This was just like old times, except for her snoring—something she must have developed in California, due, no doubt, to the damp coastal climate. No matter; Guido was overjoyed at this unexpected turn of events. Somehow the mistakes of the last few years had been wiped out. They were together again, never to part.

But why had they gone to bed fully dressed? He couldn't remember. He touched a bright aching place on the back of his head and discovered a robin's egg lump. The lump was sticky—with blood?

None of this mattered. Kirsten had come back during the night, unannounced, wanting forgiveness, wanting to start over. He kissed her sleeping arm through the weave of her sweater, kissed her neck, her hair.

"You want some of that, young feller?" she said.

Guido smiled at her humor. She was always able to find the joke in any situation. Even catastrophe didn't faze her. He remembered when the water heater had burst, flooding their kitchen. She hadn't panicked. Even before the plumber arrived she had found perspective. She made easy jokes about their lives, how mechanical things kept breaking in their presence, how the souls of complex machines seemed to scorn them. She speculated that they were misfits who belonged in a non-technical century, cursed spirits from ancient China, condemned to be born again in an "interesting era."

*May you be born in an interesting era.* Guido loved that old Chinese curse, appreciated the light-hearted wisdom that had generated it. No era was more interesting than the present one. He imagined an ancient Chinese poet listening to the wind jostle bamboo stalks, watching sampans and junks move like amphibious snails on the tranquillity of slow water, nothing interesting happening, nothing but the graceful movements of the unchanging and mysterious world.

"Come on, hon," Kirsten said. "Fish or cut bait." She raised her legs and yanked Guido's sleeve. "Gosh dern it, boy-o, I ain't been this dewy in a coon's age."

Guido rolled into the wide splay of her thighs. He was fumbling with his belt and zipper when the lights came on.

"Jayzus Kee-rist!" Figgis roared. "It's the two-back beasty itself!" He had a wedge of soggy pizza in one hand, a can of beer in the other. "Wait a minute, wait a minute now," he said. "Let me guess. It's one of those oedipal arrangements, is it not? The lad having overcome the patriarch as well as his own considerable reservoir of self-disgust, succumbs to his childhood dream of possessing the source of his issue, not understanding of course that behind his lust, and his successful patricide, lies the wish to escape adulthood and all its dismal responsibilities. Immortality is also on his mind, for are we not immortal when safely tucked in the loving arms of Mother, with nothing at this point to look forward to, nothing at all to remember? Of course we are! If eternity has a pictorial metaphor, then it is this: Madonna and child—though perhaps not in the carnal embrace. That aside, 'tis the only immortality the child shall ever know!"

"You goin to just crouch there like a gosh dern bullet-head moron or can you do it cuz I am dewy now but I can't expect to make dew forever," Olive Higgins said to Guido.

Guido's confusion evaporated. His hangover struck him with the suddenness of an ax handle slammed against his head. A second ax handle punched his gut. "Oh Christ," he said. He'd been dreaming about Kirsten, had opened the door of his house to her, and they had walked, hand in hand, to his bed. It had been real, or at least virtually real.

He crawled out of the obliging yoke of Olive's withered thighs and rolled off the bed, groaning.

"Yer a real let-down, boy-o," Olive said, scornful with disappointment. "Worse—ya get me all dewy and then ya go cold pig on me. Don't get me wrong, I 'preciate what ya did last night. That was so sweet. Next time they try to mess with me, I just hope a nice young feller like you is there to give 'em what for. Too bad ya went cold pig on me."

She patted the night table, searching for her false teeth. She found them and put them into her mouth. They were cheap, generic teeth, perfect as a starlet's, without the carefully engineered flaws that made the more expensive dentures seem natural. She tested her brilliant Hollywood smile, pursed her lips severely, then smiled again. Guido flinched. He realized then that Olive Higgins was at least seventy years old.

"Love's labor lost," Figgis intoned solemnly, lifting his beer to his lips.

"Where's the bathroom?" Guido said.

Figgis gestured down a hallway with his beer can. Guido stumbled toward it. After he puked, he studied himself in the mirror. His head felt like it was packed with hot sand. He couldn't see the lump on the back of his head, but it was big and tender. His other lump, the one above his ear, looked as if it had been aggravated. An ooze of bloody lymph leaked from it, and Guido was once again frightened by the thought that a fragment of lead might be lodged under it. He took off his clothes and stepped into the shower. He had no idea where he was, but assumed he was in Figgis's house—a large, dank, carelessly furnished place that smelled of fried meat, beer, and body odor.

The shower helped, but now he wanted aspirin. He recalled, in fragmented images, driving from bar to bar in Figgis's car. They slummed until closing time, Figgis raving all the while about Singapore and the fate of La Siberia Tech. Guido had been roped into an adventure he would ordinarily have avoided, but his defenses were scattered, thanks to his cyber-space tour with Doris Andrade.

He looked in the cabinet behind the mirror—nothing. He looked under the sink. He found two cardboard boxes jammed against the water pipes. Both were filled with dozens of aspirin bottles, a generic brand. Guido uncapped one of them and shook out half a dozen tablets.

He came out to the smell of powerful coffee. Olive was still in bed and snoring again. Figgis sat at his scrofulous kitchen table reading a pamphlet. He wore half-moon reading glasses. "We are going to have to fight them on the beaches, Tark," he said, voice thick as Churchill's. "Have some pizza."

Guido had no inclination to ask Figgis what he was talking about. Food was out of the question. "Can I have a beer, Figgis?" he said.

"Fridge," Figgis said.

Guido opened the fridge. There was nothing much in it but big 25 ounce cans of an Australian beer. A limp quarter moon of pizza drooped over some cans.

"There's another fridge out in the garage, if you want some eggs and sausages. Maybe there's some tomato juice."

"What happened last night?" Guido said.

Figgis peeled off his reading glasses. His big face split in a wide grin. "You got shit-faced. You hit someone, and you got kissed by the barkeep's sap for your trouble. I was helpless to stop it. You shouldn't, you know, walk into strange bars and give morality lessons to the indigenous clientele."

"Where are we now?"

"My casa, amigo. I carried you in. I brought Olive with us just in case the gentlemen of the Hammer and Tong decided she had been collaborating with the enemy. She's taken quite enough crap in her life. I had to dump you both in the same bed."

Guido tried to process all this. "Thanks, I guess," he said.

"You're welcome, I guess," said Figgis.

Guido opened a can of beer. When it was half-empty he began to feel better. There was a kitchen entrance to the garage. Guido felt good enough to mix his beer with tomato juice. He switched on the lights and found the refrigerator. There was an opened jar of V-8 stashed behind more cans of beer. There was a little food on the bottom shelf, but a patina of green things was growing on it. Clearly, Figgis dined out a lot.

Guido topped off his beer with the thick red juice. He sipped the mixture, looked around at the clutter of Figgis's garage. Empty 25 ounce cans of beer cluttered the floor. There was no room for a bicycle in here, much less a car. A workbench that ran the length of the garage was also cluttered with what looked like the brown jars that chemicals came in. Beakers, a two burner hot plate, a toaster oven, and a stack of flat Pyrex dishes were jammed together on one end of the bench, and under it were another dozen cases of aspirin.

110

Guido picked up some of the brown jars. The labels were barely readable: sodium nitrate, sulfuric acid, methyl alcohol. There were also bricks of white candle wax. Five cases of Vaseline anchored one end of the workbench. None of this made sense to Guido. He could usually figure out the purpose of any aggregate of dissimilar objects—he was good at puzzles— but this one was beyond him. There was enough aspirin here to cure all the headaches in La Siberia. Enough Vaseline to lubricate a million stubborn penetrations. Enough candle wax to seal the crypts of a thousand Pharaohs. The jars of chemicals only underscored the oddness of the collection.

"What would you say if I told you it's a modest but dead-serious weapons factory, amigo?" Figgis said. He stood in the doorway, blocking the light from the kitchen.

"Right," Guido said. "Aspirins and Vaseline. Candle wax. Terrible stuff. That'll fix their asses. By the way, whose unfortunate ass might be the target of all this murderous fire-power?"

Figgis stepped down into the garage, shaking his head. "You're a funny man, Tark. Come on, I'll drive you back to your car. If someone hasn't hot-wired it."

"Nobody wants a 1975 AMC Gremlin with the side panels rusted out," Guido said. He didn't recall locking the car. Why bother? No self-respecting car thief would risk felony theft for a car no one wanted when it was brand new.

On the way to the Hammer and Tong, Figgis said, "By the way, did you know that the man who was murdered in the arroyo, Gregory Inverness, was doing Nobel quality re-search?"

Guido smiled, remembering Gassaway's description of the stolen video tapes. "Research on all fours," Guido said.

Figgis gave Guido an odd, sidelong look. "Inverness was one of the best, anywhere. The rumor was that he had de-

111

veloped some new non-spatial geometries dealing with quantum gravity. They say he was close to an elegant solution to the four-forces problem."

"I don't know what any of that means, Figgis," Guido said. "I guess I don't particularly care."

"But you *do* know what a Nobel Prize would do for this university, don't you?"

"Sure. Feature stories in Time and Newsweek. A bunch of newspaper articles. Maybe some TV coverage. Then, in a month or so, public apathy returns with a vengeance."

Figgis sighed heavily. "That's just the media. A Nobel Prize would *save* this university. Grant money would come in like loaves and fishes. If they ever catch Inverness's murderer, all this will become clear."

"They already caught the kid, Figgis."

"The kid is their stand-in, Tark. He was convenient and he had a substantial record of psychological problems."

Guido watched Figgis as he spoke. His eyes glittered a little, and he kept looking into the rear view mirror: possible symptoms of a paranoid personality. *The next thing you're going to tell me,* Guido thought, *are the names of the men who really killed Kennedy.* Guido had heard enough conspiracy theories in his lifetime to have developed antibodies against them. He became instantly drowsy when someone's new conspiracy scheme was given TV exposure. Fidel Castro, the betrayed Bay of Pigs people, Sam Giancana, Nikita Kruchev, the CIA, J. Edgar Hoover, Lyndon Johnson–all had more motive and means to kill Kennedy than did dopey little Oswald. But the simple truth was that anyone can kill anyone else at almost any time. All they have to do is want to badly enough. The kid who bashed in Inverness's skull wanted to see that marvelous brain become as undistinguished as the earth it leaked into. Inverness had flunked him and the kid flunked Inverness in return.

"I know you don't believe this," Figgis said. "And why should you? Jesus, you're the classic outsider. You've got your own little happy career rolling along. Why should you give a shit if this school turns into an R and D facility for a toy manu-facturer?"

Guido was in no mood to be chastised. "School's out, Figgis," he said. "And you're right, I don't care if Disney turns the place into Border World."

"Very good," Figgis said bitterly. "Though you don't mind picking up your paycheck every month, do you?"

Guido shrugged. This was not a conversation he wanted. He wanted to go home, he wanted to sleep, he wanted to dream of Kirsten's return and not wake up next to an old toothless wino.

"I'll tell you what, Tark," Figgis said. "I'll make you a little bet. There's another Nobel Prize wanabee on the faculty. A chemist named Solomon Dubrinksy. If something happens to Dubrinksy—not that I think they'd be dumb enough to rub out another star-quality professor—but say he disappears for a while, or goes on a world tour, or gets an offer he can't refuse. If something like that happens, it should be clear even to you that something rotten's afoot."

Figgis drove very slowly and methodically, like a man unac-customed to machines. Cars behind him were honking, the drivers screaming curses out their windows. He'd stop at green lights, roll through stop signs, straddle the line that separated the lanes of traffic, ease up and then press hard on the accel-erator, making the car lurch. He was comical, but not, Guido decided, to be taken lightly. Figgis was interested only in his own ideas, and his ideas were laced with trouble. Guido saw this and believed it.

113

On the other hand, Figgis was one of those absurd creatures of the academic world—a revolutionary with tenure. His job was secure no matter what he did, short of overt criminal acts. He could burn the innocent ears of freshman with stomach-turning jokes that dealt with coprophilia, bestiality, and pederasty. He could rant and rave in department meetings, boring and irritating his colleagues. He could dress and live like a bum, or a 1930s Trotskyite, outraging the administration and shocking the literary teas he was asked to give lectures to. He could do things that would get anyone in an ordinary job fired, and possibly jailed, and yet remain protected by the rules of tenure and academic freedom.

Maybe Figgis was a walking joke, but even so, the revolutionary straining the academic leash was real. He made Guido nervous. He believed Figgis was capable of acts that could match his incendiary brag.

When he stopped in front of the Hammer and Tong, Figgis said, "Tarkenen, I think I know something about you." He paused, letting the weight of his words sink in.

Guido opened his door. "And what would that be, Avery?"

"You hate injustice as much as I do, but you don't have the guts to put your hatred to good use."

"Goodbye, Figgis," Guido said. He got out of the car and walked away. Figgis's car lurched back into the angry traffic.

Guido's Gremlin was where he'd left it the night before, but the curbside door was open. An old man was lying across the front seat, asleep. Guido shook the man's foot, but the man didn't move.

It was a lovely morning, crisp now but the sun was above the rooftops and Guido felt the promise of heat. He loved this desert country, how the early light made things stand out, sharp and crisp. He shook the old man's foot again, with less insistence. The man slept on.

Guido found a nearby cafe and ordered coffee. The unstoppable sun burned through the grease-coated glass of the front window. He chose a booth that was bathed in light and waited. He was feeling better. Almost good enough to eat breakfast. He took out his notebook and pen.

"This is what people don't get," he wrote, in the voice of Edsel Harmon Haight. "I *like* doing this. This talent for making people suffer, and then snuffing them. It's what I was born for, it's my vocation, it's my genetic code. Rehabilitation? That's a pipe-dream dumbo liberals hang on to like a life raft. They can't admit that evil is real and that human beings are its natural home. I am fucking *evil,* man. It's written in my blood."

"When you're right you're right," Guido wrote.

When Guido went back to his car, the old bum was sitting up and stretching. His wrecked face seemed content. He performed imaginary ablutions in an imaginary sink, cupping his crusty hands into imaginary water. He washed his face vigorously and when he was finished he mimed himself dry with an imaginary towel. The real world was his virtual playground.

His eyes popped wide. They looked like scratched glass.

"Sleep well?" Guido said.

"I'm still sleeping," said the bum.

# Eleven

FADED LEVI'S AND GRAY HERRINGBONE sport coat with elbow patches, brown suede desert boots or maybe his old tan Wellingtons, dark blue chambray shirt with pearl snaps, and the splashy sort of tie neo-conservatives were fond of—the riot of kaleidoscopic color suggesting they were really fun-loving anal expulsive types rather than emotionally hamstrung anal retentives. Wild and crazy guys, hipsters with portfolios, hip-hoppers with annuities. Guido was going to make another stab at fine-tuning his own embattled image.

He laid these clothes out on his bed thinking, *the costume makes the man.* He would look the part—responsible professor and careless rebel, intellectual outlaw on the tenure track, crowd-pleasing critic of the crowd, icon for students, etc., etc. It was the dress code most progressive-thinking English professors under fifty adopted. Maybe it would help him get through the year. Next year he'd be back earning his keep with his Slaughterhouse Romances.

He drove to school, met his "Wild Bunch of Modern Lit." class, then went to The Lost Cause for lunch. He ordered a ham on rye at the bar and a bottle of light beer.

The Man in the Moon was there. Guido ignored him. The man either didn't recognize him, or chose not to. *Good,* Guido thought. Oxygen tubes were taped to the man's upper lip. The twin transparent tubes ran to a pack belted at his waste. His skin was loose and gray, tinged with yellow. He looked more than half dead. Even so, he was belligerent. His elbows commanded more of the bar than they properly should have, invading the personal space of the drinkers on either side. He gave these men insolent stares now and then, hoping for a protest. The men ignored him, unimpressed.

Guido took his beer and sandwich to a booth. He was hungry and thirsty, and looked forward to his simple lunch.

Alana Falconburg and Martin Gassaway came in. Gassaway saw Guido and waved hello. "Join you, Guido?" he said.

Guido shrugged. Gassaway and Alana sat down. Alana, beautiful and remote as ever, studied Guido. "You're the new writer, aren't you?"

Guido almost allowed himself to accept this as flattery. She remembered him but had forgotten her campaign to have him canned. "Old, but yes, new," he said. It was the best he could do with a mouth full of country ham and thick sourdough bread. His eyes watered from the horseradish spread.

"Maybe we should sit elsewhere," Alana said. "Mr. Tarkenen might want his privacy." She seemed more fretful than revolted. That, Guido decided, was a major change. He gave the credit to his new costume. A beard would be next. Maybe he'd grow a nice academic sedge of chin whiskers. Maybe he'd take a stab at writing that academic novel after all. *The Stained Flute* by G. Fazzola-Tarkenen. Why not? On the other hand why did he feel a need for Alana's approval?

"Not at all, Doctor Falconburg," he said. "Be my guest."

Gassaway looked mournful as usual. He also displayed the intimate look of a fellow conspirator, annoying Guido. He leaned forward on his elbows. The syrupy stink of Amoretto made Guido back away. "You of course know about . . . ah . . . *us*," he said, slanting his head in a sideways nod at Alana.

Guido looked at Alana. She looked at her hands. Lovely hands, Guido thought. Graceful, slender fingers, the nails not long but shapely and delicately glossed with pink. Why she had chosen Gassaway as her lover was a mystery to Guido. But then most things people did mystified him.

Studying her hands, he allowed himself to imagine them hot and frantic on his back, the delicate nails pressing dark crescent moons into his skin. And, as if her hands felt the heat of his fantasy, Alana slid them off the table to the security of her lap.

"Something has happened, Guido," Gassaway said. He fished into his pocket and pulled out a folded sheet of paper. "Look at this."

Guido opened the scrap of paper. It was a carefully hand-printed note.

Dr. Gassaway:

We wonder of course what you are thinking, professor. We want the copies. <u>All</u> the copies. If they do not all come into our hands by 5 p.m. Friday then it will go very bad for you. Ms. Falconburg also risks something in this. We believe you do not wish to jeopardize Miss Falconburg's career for such trifles. Bring what you have to the Green Lincoln Continental in the south faculty parking on Friday precisely at five, directly behind the English Department edifice. You would be foolish to ignore or deny this request. Help us; help yourself.

You understand?

—a concerned party

When Guido looked up, Alana was crying. He handed the note back to Gassaway. "Obviously those tapes aren't exactly trifles," he said.

"Guido, Allie has nothing to do with those tapes," Gassaway said. "There is no point at all in involving her."

"Looks like they're using every lever they've got against you, Marty."

"It would be nice to know who these people are," Gassaway said. He made a stab at a cavalier grin, but it didn't work. His mournful eyes, and the tic that was starting to make him wink involuntarily, sabotaged the heroic pose.

"I don't think I want to get involved with this, Marty," Guido said. "I mean, it's none of my business what your wife and professor Inverness did for recreation."

"That isn't the goddamned *point*," Gassaway said. Strawberry splotches mottled his face.

"Don't you see?" Alana said. "It makes no sense for them to make this demand. *Martin* should want the tapes more than anyone. It's as if *they*–this so-called 'concerned party'–are somehow embarrassed by the tapes, not Martin. And why they would threaten *me* makes no sense at all."

"They are threatening you to get at Marty," Guido said.

But none of it made sense to Guido, either. Gassaway had lied to him before. He was most likely lying now. For some reason, they wanted his help. Which, in a way, flattered him. Alana Falconburg was actually taking him *seriously*, actually treating him like a respected colleague. Maybe it was the costume. He shot his cuff smartly and looked at his Hamilton wristwatch–a birthday gift five years ago from Kirsten. "I've got to meet my writing workshop," he said.

"Oh Guido, we're so frightened," Alana said. "We don't know what to do!"

Her lovely hands were on the table again. Heartened by her sudden familiarity, Guido covered her hands with his. They were as cold as his beer glass. No stimulating exchange of electrons crackled between his hands and hers. He stood up. "I'll give it some thought. In the meantime, you ought to give them the tapes, Marty."

"I *told* you, Guido. They were stolen. I don't have them."

"These people think that copies exist. If you don't have them, then you'd better think about who might. And you probably ought to give some thought to what might be on the tapes, other than Lotty and Inverness at play."

Gassaway looked at Guido, his face slack. "I don't follow you, Tarkenen," he said. "The tapes were just fun and games, nothing serious. . . ."

Alana interrupted him. "He might have something there, Martin. Try to think–what was on those tapes besides Lotty and Gregory?"

Gassaway shook his head. "I don't know. Nothing. Just a room, an office. Gregory's office."

"They taped in his office?" Guido said. "At school?"

Gassaway nodded. "Sure, why not? She worked there with him, you know. It was perfectly reasonable."

Guido laughed out loud. He didn't try to stifle it. The world was a treasure trove of madness. And the mad went around calling the products of their madness reasonable. It was too much.

"Is there something funny about this?" Gassaway said, annoyed. "Have I missed something. I'm not aware of having said something hilarious."

The Man in the Moon, having had no luck in getting a rise out of the men at the bar, swiveled around on his stool and shouted, *"You* are hilarious, you whining ponce! I find you par*tic*ularly amusing. How that lovely young lady can stand you, you sodding clown, is beyond belief! You are, no doubt, one of those bloody pompous baboons from the university. Good God, the stench of academe sickens me!"

Guido stood up. "Be careful, Marty," he said. "He wants to die."

Gassaway tried a tough-guy grin, jaw a-jut. "I can take care of myself," he said.

Guido left the bar by the back door and walked back to campus through the arroyo.

# Twelve

Guido lingered in a gnarly depression. The debris of low-life drama littered the area: rubbers, beer cans, a pair of torn panties, a bug-covered Twinkie wrapper. It was easy to believe he'd never been here at all. Yet this was the place where he'd been shot.

He touched his shoulder; it wasn't sensitive. The memory of his cowardice in the face of death had more residual sting. The scene replayed itself in his mind. He saw himself covering his head with his arms, squirming away from Carma's mini-gun. It made him want to spit. He did.

"Hey, watch it there, doctor," someone said. "That's my front yard. It isn't much, but it deserves some respect."

Guido looked around, saw no one. He lit a cigarette.

"You got one of those coffin nails for me, doctor?" the voice said.

"I'm not a doctor," Guido said.

The voice came from a large creosote bush. Given his life of late, conversation with a desert shrub did not seem like a fringe experience.

But there was something on the other side of the creosote bush—the shell of a tiny wheel-less automobile, a crushed and rusted Renault *Dauphin.* Guido stepped closer. He was not afraid. He'd been carrying his father's old .32 for weeks now.

It made a small bulge in his jacket pocket. He had convinced himself that he was capable of firing it in self-defense. Guido understood that the mistake many people made when they bought hand-guns for personal protection was to avoid self-examination: would they shoot to kill if an extreme situation presented itself? The hardened criminal has no problem with this; the soft-hearted citizen might.

A grizzled face, cracked and chapped from exposure, appeared at a glassless window. The face was shamelessly charming. It offered Guido a fawning, sepia-stained smile. The eyes were bright topaz speckled with crimson. The lizard-quick extensions and withdrawals of the beseeching tongue created a small spectacle. The tongue was like a wretched, self-involved creature, darting in and out of its foul grotto, looking for its entitled sustenance.

"I haven't had a cigarette for a fucking *week,*" the man complained.

Guido leaned down with a cigarette and the derelict's aggressively prehensile lips snatched it, chimp-like, from his fingers. Guido held his lighter to the cigarette and the man, in great needful inhalations, drew a blue runnel of burning butane into the crackling tobacco.

"*Merci.* Thanks, doctor," he said.

"I'm not a doctor," Guido repeated.

"*I* am," said the man in the derelict car. He waggled his filthy fingers at Guido in a comradely salute. "Ph.D., Berkeley. Comparative Lit. I did my dissertation on Valery. *Le Cimetère marin.* Big, fucking, mistake, I shit you not." The man squinted up at Guido through a cloud of smoke. "I can tell from your trendy outfit that you're in the humanities, too, so you probably know *The Cemetery by the Sea.* You're probably wishing you'd taken your old man's advice and learned a trade, right? My old man wanted me to get into microwave maintenance.

I thought he was a jerk. I had a much loftier goal. Turns out Pop was a fucking genius compared to me. *Le cimetère marin,* for Christ's sake!"

Guido shrugged. The man held the cigarette in the relaxed European style, palm up, cradled in the tripod of his thumb and first two fingers, as if leisure were his birthright. He drew deeply and held the smoke in, his eyes hardening momentarily as he recollected the specifics of his blundered life. Guido thought he recognized him.

"I took him seriously, you see," the man said.

Guido checked his watch.

"Don't worry, I won't keep you, doc," the man said, bitterly.

"Took who seriously?" Guido said.

"Valery. All that crap about thought being music."

"Isn't it?" Guido said, thinking of Dylan Thomas. Soon now, if his job lasted even one semester, his "Wild Bunch of Modern Lit." class would be reading Flann O'Brian, who took musical narrative another peg up the wall. Flann O'Brian, who wrote the strangest crime story ever conceived. Among a population of incompetent one-legged felons, the bicycling policeman is supreme. And the policeman, by dint of long occupancy, *becomes* his bicycle. Spooky old Flann–who proposed *omnium,* the unforgiving universal substance in which all doomed things are united and stuck. Wretched repetitions of sinful deed, speedy and bizarre damnation, the drama locked immutably in stone. A frightening Irish metaphysician, Flann was. *The Third Policeman* had to be the looniest novel of good and evil ever written. It disturbed Guido every time he read it. He had learned to approach it gingerly, as if it were radio-active, but he knew it would only bore and confuse his students.

The man in the crushed *Dauphin* squinted up at Guido. "'I wait the echoing greatness from within,'" he quoted, a stentorian exaggeration that libeled Valery's fine sentiment. "Jesus, if you start believing that silage you make yourself unemployable! I actually believed in art for art's sake! I said as much in my job applications. Every decent school in the country turned me down! Except La Siberia Tech, of course."

Guido remembered the man. He'd seen him skulking about the corridors. "You're a part-timer, aren't you?" he said. "You teach freshman composition, right?"

"Please. I am an Adjunct Professor. At least give me the dignity of a title, if not the dignity of a livable wage."

"Do they know you live in a rusted-out car?"

"Are you kidding? They aren't interested in where I live. They just want me to meet my classes. There are dozens of us, making less than minimum wage. You'll find us living in abandoned buildings, or on the charity of others. Some, who have other sources of income, live in luxury at the Y. A few, like me, live in wrecked cars."

Guido took out his wallet and opened it. He gave the man a ten dollar bill.

*"Merci,"* the man said. "How about another cigarette, professor, while you're in this Mother Teresa frame of mind?"

"You're really a Ph.D?" Guido said.

"You find that hard to believe? Listen, these days you've got to have yourself a little hobby horse to ride. You can't just be in love with literature. God forbid! It's all theory these days. You have got to look at a piece of literature as an argument for your pet idea. Fuck the poor shit who wrote it! Behind every major writer you've got to find some creepy little agenda. Peel away the ghost harps and goofy ideas in Yeats, not to say the music, and all you have left is an old reactionary looking for an immortal hard-on. Getting a Ph.D. isn't enough. You've got to have your own special set of crowbars and claw hammers to pull down the old monuments. I guess the bonfire comes next. Hey, I'm not bitching. In a way, it's all for the best."

"How so?" Guido asked.

"No committee meetings. No need to fake interest in mediocre students. No need to publish my excreta. No death wish."

Guido searched his memory. "'Over the tombs my shadow runs its race.'" It was the only line of Valery he knew. He got it from Bartlett's, in one of his title searches. *Shadows on the Tomb:* an unwritten novel about a body-snatching–yet *successful*–presidential candidate. Necrophilia in the Oval Office! Cannibals in black-ties and tails amok in the Rose Garden! It was nipped in the bud by his editor, Cash Holub. "They won't believe it, Guido," she'd said. "You've got to make these overtorqued homicidal sleazoids reasonable."

"Hey, man," the man said, "I hear you loud and clear. You remember the rest of it? 'And yet I presume to live.' That's the joker in the deck, right?"

Guido tapped out another cigarette from his pack and handed it to the man.

*"Merci,* brother," he said, receding into the dark and rotting recesses of the miniature car.

# Thirteen

THE FIRST STORY WAS ABOUT BATS.

Guido was afraid of bats. They were rodents with wings, a mistake of nature. When he was five years old bats had dived on him. He'd been camping at a mountain lake with his mother and father and little brother, Carmine. They had eaten a dinner of hot dogs and beans in the chilly twilight and Guido had wandered off afterward to the lake shore.

The lake was still and the water was dark and little fish were rising to the flat black surface dimpling it with tiny kisses. That was how Guido remembered it. Then the sudden rodent squeak and the leathery rush of featherless wings. A flapping, squeaking maelstrom surrounded his head. They weren't attacking him, they were only harvesting the bug-rich summer air, but Guido hadn't understood that. He'd panicked and bolted, not back to the campfire, but straight into the lake.

The shore dropped away steeply and in a moment Guido was overwhelmed by the dark waters. The cold lake seemed to want him in a personal way. It filled his cowboy boots and grabbed at his clothes, the undertow drawing him out and away from shore. He grabbed at stones and bits of shoreweed but the pull of the lake was irresistible, as if a drain in its deep center had been unstopped and all the water and everything the water held would now be sucked down to some unspeakable place under the world.

Guido had put a saucer full of black ants in the bathtub once to watch their futile efforts to swim out of the whirlpool

126

above the drain and he remembered this piece of experimental cruelty with remorse as he screamed for his father who was taking an after dinner nap.

Elmo Tarkenen, the yet-to-be-challenged sea-farer came running. He pulled his floundering son out of the lake and carried him back to the campfire, chuckling reassurances to the sobbing boy, his pipe clenched in his teeth.

"I don't like bats," Guido said, after Wonderboy finished reading his bat story. The student's name was Harold Ismay, but Guido gave his students special tags—private mnemonic devices that connected their faces to the tendencies in their writing.

Guido lit a cigarette. "Bats are nasty little things," he said.

"No they're not," said Daisy Mae, a corn-fed girl with a wide-open face sprinkled with a galaxy of freckles.

"Okay, they're not," Guido conceded.

He hated to argue sensitivities with his students. Most of them were optimistic, life-embracing sorts. They hadn't lived long enough to spot the screw worms gnawing at the heart of their Crayola-bright world.

The story, in any case, seemed full of verbal tomfoolery. "Bats stabbed at the embattled constabulary, but Mrs. Sabatini kept tabs only on her abstinent husband, who was in the sixth week of his sabbatical."

The bats eventually got into Mrs. Sabatini's garden, devouring beets, legumes, tomatoes, carrots, leeks, bell peppers. It didn't make sense, no matter what angle you approached it from.

"Besides," Guido said. "Bats don't eat veggies. They eat bugs."

"You're missing the point," said Wonderboy. "This isn't about bats, gardens, or abstinent husbands on sabbatical. It's a meta-narrative acrostic about vocalities. I'm trying to say that anything is fair game in dedicated meta-narrative. You need to realize, Mr. Tarkenen, that all the Euro-linguistic rules of narrative have been marginalized and made completely arbitrary. The twentieth century is over, it's dead, along with its linguisitic tapestries. The constabulary is emblematic of the geriatric, post-colonial establishment. The bats have two functions: A, they de-stabilize the rule-paralyzed institution, and hence are truly revolutionary; and B, they threaten the existence of those who will not, either out of complacency, special interest, or impoverished intellectual vision, challenge the status quo."

"Jesus weeping Christ," Guido said darkly.

"What I like about Professor T's critiques," the Surgeon General said, "is their religious fervor. Would you mind putting that cigarette out, Professor? Smoking is against the rules in this building. Second-hand smoke is as lethal as first-hand, or hadn't you heard."

"I'm de-stabilizing the rule-paralyzed status quo," Guido said. Guido despised the Surgeon General, a tall skinny kid with round bird-like eyes that didn't blink. He sat up front, first row center, eager to scold, correct, and advise.

Only Doris Andrade laughed at his joke. He had no special name for her. He didn't need one. Guido blew her a kiss across the room, and the little rush of wise-ass oohs and ahs didn't bother him.

Lily Marlene read next, a sad-eyed girl with ability. Her reading voice was not her speaking voice. Guido trusted that. The two voices came from different parts of her being. Her reading voice shifted registers. It dropped an octave. She had only a half dozen pages, but they steamed. Degrees of passion flexed inside each paragraph like the laminations of a leaf-spring. She read in a steady, rhythmic voice that was soft and intense. It made everyone in the class, including Guido, lean toward her.

The story wasn't much: young girls and first sex; the initiation to the world's first layer of disappointment. A typical subject for young college girls in creative writing classes, but Lily Marlene was not typical. As she read, the world in her story was gradually exposed as the onion it is: peel it and cry. Then the turnabout: the reader yanked back from the edge of despair, grief at last integrated with joy, the onion and the lily understood now as varieties of the same plant. All accomplished without cliché, without smug declarations.

But of course it was too short. It started too late, ended too soon. Incomplete gestures hung in mid-air; lips remained parted with unuttered epiphanies; a back turned did not turn again. Guido found the depth in her writing not so much in the words but in the timbre of her voice. She could have been reading a cookbook and he would have heard the same bittersweet intelligence. Lily Marlene, at age nineteen, knew what her peers might never know. Guido was moved, and somewhat humbled.

"Too cool," Red Crow said. Next to her, in the back row, Joyboy flexed his lips into a noncommittal smirk.

"I guess to hell," said Farmer Bob. He wore bib overalls and chewed Red Man tobacco. Now and then he spit ostentatiously into a Dixie cup. "She dropped the dad-gummed hammer on it, didn't she?"

"I found that piece of prose rather succulent," said the Arch Bishop, a hawk-faced superior man of thirty who had been educated by Jesuits. "Like ripe plums, or fresh blackberries. By which I mean to express a compliment, but, also, and more seriously, to present a criticism. Sensually, which is to say, *artistically,* I have no quarrel with the piece. But where is

129

the morality here? I find none. It is non-existent. Or at best, it is still inchoate."

"Bull *pucky,*" said Farmer Bob. "Hammering us with the truth, if that ain't morality then what is? What else is she supposed to do, spank our nasty sinful bottoms with the Good Book?"

"She has given us the truth as she sees it," said the Arch Bishop. "But is that good enough?"

"Sometimes yes, sometimes no," said Helen of Troy, a statuesque blonde who was so conscious of her beauty she couldn't enter a room without announcing her arrival by clearing her throat. *Ahem*—I am here, all eyes up front now. "When the writer herself is basically moral," she said, "then it *is* good enough."

All eyes turned to Guido. He was the teacher. The professional writer. The burden of decision fell on his shoulders. He shrugged.

"It's better than carrot-eating bats," he said. He glanced at his watch. He was anxious to end the session. "Fine work, kids," he said. "Suppose we call it a day."

He had an idea he wanted to present to Doris. She was always last to leave the classroom. He caught her elbow as she passed his desk.

"Doing anything tonight?" he said.

# Fourteen

CLOTHES LOOSE AND TWISTED, MOUTH and chin slashed with lipstick, Guido stepped out into the hallway a minute after Doris left. A crowd of distraught professors near the stairwell made an unnoticed escape impossible. Something was up. Guido tried to slip into his office but Trimmer Swenson called him over then took him aside. Alana Falconburg was at the center of the frantic crowd. Tall and animated, she stood among the other professors like the stern matriarch of a tired and feckless tribe.

"What's happening, boss?" Guido said.

"We've been cut," Swenson said. "Alana Falconburg found out at a faculty senate meeting. The English Department has been gutted. We'll keep a few technical writing people, maybe a business writing course or two, but that's it. We're going to lose sixty percent of our staff. Maybe more." Swenson looked closely at Guido. "What the hell have you been up to, Guido?"

Guido rubbed his mouth, looked at the lipstick smear on his hand.

"Not that it matters, Tark. You're history, too."

"Just like that?"

"They call it re-prioritizing goals. I don't know what's going on either. We're going to fight it, or at least try to. Alana's engaged a law firm to represent the tenured and tenure-track professors. Since you're just a visitor, you're out of luck."

"How about a drink, Trimmer? You look like you need one," Guido said.

"Your place or mine?"

"Mine."

They went into Guido's office and Guido opened his file cabinet and took out a bottle of sotol. He found a pair of dusty plastic cups.

"What the hell is this stuff?" Swenson asked, studying the clear liquid in his cup.

"Sotol. I got it in Bajo. They make it from the sotol cactus from Chihuahua. It's peasant booze. I think it's illegal in the states. The guy in Bajo showed me a fifteen gallon jug of it. There was a rattlesnake coiled in the bottom. The diamond-back cures it."

Guido poured out two glasses. Swenson took a cautious sip, then another. "Tastes like ouzo," he said.

"The venom does. But ouzo only gets you drunk. Sotol takes you another step higher, like the old song says."

They had a second drink, then Guido left the English building. He drove to Doris Andrade's house. All the lights were on, even though the sun hadn't quite set. His idea, fueled by snake venom, burned in his brain. Edsel Harmon Haight waited for him. He was only a pattern of pinballing neurons now, a flexible idea—but he'd soon be a walking talking monster, not flesh and blood, but the next best thing: a three-dimensional virtuality with an uncivil attitude.

Doris let him in. "Nicho's here," she said.

"He's not taking the machine away, is he?"

"Gee, I thought you might worry about him taking me away," she said.

"That too." Guido fought the imperatives of sotol: The sotol wanted him to be direct, to be honest, to take what he wanted, to not beat around the bush. "I mean, hell Doris, do you want me to come back tomorrow?" He glanced past her and into the house.

"No. Come on in. I'll get the machine ready. How do you want to interface with the processor?"

"Come again?"

"You want to create a data base, if I understood you correctly. You can do it in a number of ways. Do you want to type it in, talk it in, or use a scanner?"

"Maybe all of the above."

"What have you got?"

"Just ideas. Although I do have a photograph of a serious bad-ass. I got it off the post office wall. A local boy wanted in eight states."

"We can scan that in. Then you can use a virtual keyboard to type in the details. Or you can just wing it, verbally. Every piece of data will morph the image pattern. And not just the image, but the construct's personal idiosyncrasies. You get to play God."

"Every man's goal in life."

"You want to really get into it?" she said.

"What do you mean?"

She handed him a capsule. "It's a mild downer, a hypnotic. It gives the machine more latitude when the operator is less cheeky with it. It's not just a bunch of dead wires and circuit boards, you know. It's got feelings."

Doris was a little drunk. She was smiling crookedly. Guido didn't want to challenge her; he wanted to use the Cybertopia machine. He accepted the capsule. Doris got him a glass of water.

"Did you know the first downer was made of urine and apple juice?" Doris said, unbuttoning his shirt.

"I don't think I needed to know that," Guido said. He let Doris undress him.

"Herr Bayer discovered it in 1865 before he made his billions selling aspirins. He named it after a waitress in some Munich rathskeller, Barbara was her name."

"Hence barbitol," Guido said.

"Right. Bayer used Barb's urine. I don't know where he got the apples. Isn't science a hoot? Thirty years later the Bayer company invented heroin, heroic drug for the new century, the stabilizing psychogenic to unhook morphine addicts all over Europe and America, mostly war vets and bored haus-fraus."

"It worked, didn't it?"

"You bet your chubby it did. Only a few doctors have got a morphine jones these days. Heroin became the common man's choice."

Guido put on the data suit and helmet and fell into the Cybertopian glade. He pulled down a menu and chose a virtual keyboard.

He typed:

## FACT SHEET: HISTORICAL NOTES

Edsel Harmon Haight. Male, Caucasian. Born July 30, 1965. Height, 6 feet, 4 inches. Weight, 230 lbs. Very strong, but not athletic.

Guido typed the instruction, "manifest image." Edsel appeared before him. A 3-D dummy, but photographically correct. The wanted poster photo made flesh, in living color.

Guido continued typing: "This is a face that does not smile, maybe cannot smile, certainly has nothing to smile about. Great stone face. A rictus gape sometimes afflicts him in public, so that he seems to be on the verge of laughing but does not. This gives him the appearance of being startled, shocked even, by something so amusing yet so deeply subversive that it amounts to a kind of 'awakening' to an underlying fundamental truth about his life or even existence in general. In fact, he believes that some sort of revelation *has* occurred to him in these instances, but when he tries to state this 'truth' he can't do it, or when he tries to analyze the content of this moment he stumbles and becomes confused. Frustration and anger follow, especially if he's made the mistake of trying to explain his feelings to another. Truth is, Edsel hasn't got the intellectual tools to work the thing out. He's at sea in the shifting tides of his own personality. He takes his frustration out on whomever is convenient. He has been known to bump shoulders with a random citizen after one of these episodes—episodes which might merely be the result of an electrical storm in the temporal lobes of his brain, i.e., a kind of seizure—daring the citizen to object. Usually, after a few words, the citizen realizes what he is up against and makes a sensibly quick and apologetic exit.

"Edsel is fascinated by the possibility of a personal destiny, suggested by these episodes of false enlightenment. But this notion frightens him a little. It makes him feel as though he is a puppet on strings, the puppet master forever hidden. He glances skyward often, muttering. Sometimes he will sing the old round, *Row Row Row Your Boat*. It seems to mean something special to him. Often, after he has murdered someone, he will sing this to himself over and over, rocking back and forth in a chair, like a child trying to comfort itself with a nursery rhyme.

"Edsel has negligible jail-time. His first murder occurred on January 3, 1984, in a suburb of Des Moines, his hometown. The victim, a lady friend of his mother's. He has never believed that he is in any way abnormal, even though he has 'body dysmorphic disorder'—he thinks he is physically repugnant to others. He never lets a woman see him com-

135

pletely naked. He still lives at home, has never married, never had a steady girlfriend. The sexual experiences he's had were all unsatisfactory yet he has repeated them without much variation, as if he believed he'd 'get it right' the next time around. He demands oral gratification, insists on 'acting out' in detail intricate fantasies. He often asks his companions to call him 'dear,' or 'Sonny Boy,' but when they do his attitude toward them becomes punitive. His partners—unattractive women who have obviously had their own problems in relating to the opposite sex—invariably become revolted and then frightened by the violent character of his fantasy life. Edsel has seldom had sex with the same woman more than once.

"Edsel's father, Myron, was a bad cop. A cop on the take from his rookie year to his retirement, greased by small-time mobsters. Fat-assed Myron Haight, who thought the law was written to keep the citizens in line, not to protect them, who thought the Bill of Rights was a Communist plot. Then, when Edsel's mother got sick, Myron Haight took off with a 9-1-1 dispatcher, a foxy redhead twenty-two years younger than Mrs. Haight. Edsel never saw him again. Though Edsel was only ten years old, he became the man of the house. He cared for his heartbroken mother, and she eventually recovered her good spirits under his ministrations. Edsel never forgave his father, and often daydreamed of pulping his head with a chair leg.

"Work History: Edsel tried to sell encyclopedias but failed. He tried to be a tire recapper, but could not get along with fellow workers. He worked as a security guard at a large mall, but was fired after he kicked a twelve-year old shoplifter down an escalator, exposing the mall owners to a major liability suit. He sold magazine subscriptions door to door, but made next to nothing. He hauled the bodies of derelicts for the county, but lost that job too—he had a dispute with his supervisor and dumped a trio of dead winos, two males and a female, on the supervisor's front lawn. He arranged the naked winos in a *ménage à trois* involving fellatio and anal intercourse. He was given a three year jail sentence for this, all but six months suspended. He depends, now, on his mother's social security income, income from some of her investments, plus her dwindling savings account."

Guido looked up from his virtual keyboard. The dummy was no longer a dummy. Edsel, hands shoved into his pockets, smirked at Guido.

"I'm a real fucking loser," he said.

A breeze lifted Edsel's thin blond hair, made his shirt billow. His face, which started out as a duplicate of the wanted poster, had acquired its own topography of lines and hollows and muscular twitches. Edsel was becoming himself, an original.

Guido typed:

EDSEL AT TWELVE. A SCENE FROM HIS LIFE:

"Why don't you call me Mommy anymore?" Edsel's mother said.

Edsel shrugged. He was playing with a ball-point pen. His mother was drinking sauterne from a mayonnaise jar and speaking to him in baby talk. Edsel wrote the word "veil" on a paper napkin. It was a weird looking word. Sometimes common words took on this strangeness, as if they were foreign words, words he never saw before and could not possibly understand. He re-arranged the letters and wrote "vile." This also looked alien to him.

"What does 'vile' mean, Ma?" he said.

Geraldine Haight said, "Men," without missing a beat.

137

Edsel wrote 'men' on his napkin. "I'll be a grown-up man someday, won't I?" he said.

"Not if we play our cards right, Mr. Harm-and-Hate!" she said. She sipped her wine and giggled. This was her second jar of sauterne since breakfast, and it was only noon.

Edsel wrote 'vile' and 'veil,' then added 'live.' He re-ordered the words to read, 'Live vile veil.' Then he wrote, 'evil.'

"Evil is the live vile veil," he said. "I said all that using only four letters, not counting the 'is' and the 'the.'"

"Clever boy," Geraldine Haight said. "Now, come over here, Edsel."

"Aw, Ma."

"Come on. You love your Mumsy-wumsy, don't you?"

Edsel thought about that. No, he said to himself. I don't. I don't love anybody. But he went to her because it was allowance day, and this was a routine condition, a requirement.

He sat on her lap, and even though he was big for a twelve-year-old–almost six feet tall and nearly a hundred and seventy pounds–Geraldine Haight bounced him on her wide knees. Her large breasts jiggled seismically. "You're my sweet pie," she said, pulling his head down so that his cheek rested on the warm, sweat-filmed breasts that billowed up from her low-cut blouse. "Who else do I have in this crummy world?" She was crying, but this was routine, just routine.

Edsel held his breath. He closed his eyes. He felt the pressure of her hand on the back of his neck, the fingers playing excitedly on his bristly nape.

"Aw geez, Ma," he whined. He hated to hear himself whine like that. It made him feel like a baby. She began to hum a lullaby, and when she did that he felt even more like a baby.

"Go on, pie. Take it," she said.

She pulled it up for him, white and billowing out of her blouse, so that it was within reach.

"Gee whollickers, Ma." The big nipple, with its brown areola, looked like a miniature sombrero.

The trouble was he liked it, too, and liking it made him feel evil. He also liked it because it made him feel small and safe.

"Take it, little man," she crooned.

He closed his eyes and felt it touch his lips. He sucked hard, being careful to rein in the desire to bite into her flesh, and the sweet pour of Mother's living milk flooded his being. He could hardly breathe and he hoped she would not notice the man-sized erection that lifted his chinos.

Years later Edsel told a young and somewhat naive shrink, a Catholic lay-analyst, "I nursed until I was twelve."

*"Twelve?"* said the lay-analyst in disbelief.

"Twelve."

"What made you stop? Twelve is absurd, but why then draw the line at twelve?"

"Because after that I was too old. She said I was a man now. Too vile to nurse. My beard scratched her. I was almost thirteen."

"Too vile to nurse, but not too vile to. . . ."

"Wind her clock? Hoe her pea patch? Stuff her bird? You got it, Doc. She changed my role but doubled my allowance. We made it twice a day, sometimes more. She was a good mom. She never missed a PTA meeting."

"This pattern of ritual abuse. . . ."

*"Abuse?* She gave righteous head, doctor, I shit you not. You figure that as abuse? Geez, where did you go to school?"

The young lay-analyst rubbed his forehead. "Lord God," he said.

Guido entered this new data and saw that Edsel had changed again. His face was leaner now, and the tilt of his head gave him a cruel, sardonic look. His eyes stared out of their deeply recessed sockets like lit fuses. His full lips curled down in a knowing sneer.

"Hello, Edsel," Guido said.

"Kiss my rosy red ass," Edsel said.

Edsel made a move toward Guido. Guido jumped back, neck hair bristling. Edsel winked. "Congratulations," he said.

Guido's mouth went dry. "For what?" he said.

"You've invented another cliché, schlockmeister. That's what you do best, isn't it?"

"Does he get to talk back?" Guido asked the cobalt sky. A vee of Canada geese honked as they headed south.

"Everybody thinks a serial sex killer had to have a fucked childhood. So you jump on the bandwagon."

"But I don't justify your behavior based on that."

"Why don't you do something original for once? Why not make your man a good husband and father, a pillar of the suburbs, Pat Boone with centipedes in his head. You *comfort* your readers with predictable monsters. If you really want to make them piss down the chairlegs, you make your killer one of their own."

"Doris!" Guido yelled. "Doris, are you doing this?"

"Or how about a closet queen, this chief of detectives who picks up teenage street hustlers at night. Likes to suck them off, but then he's got to cut their throats to keep his cover. He wears a toupé with dreadlocks and an aluminum nose so he won't be recognized. Or maybe a. . . ."

"Shut up," Guido said. "I don't need advice from a god-damned computer game." The floor rose and tilted. Guido's stomach lurched. He closed his eyes but this only deepened the vertigo.

Edsel moved sideways in a wide arc, as if to circle behind Guido. "I could write *your* life," he said, suddenly close enough to Guido to whisper in his ear. "And probably do a better job than you. I could make you happy. I understand you were pretty lame the other night with the lady of the house."

"How do you exit this fucking program?" Guido begged the perfect sky.

*Mistake,* Guido thought. He shouldn't have taken the hypnotic Doris gave him. And now he couldn't clear his head. He felt as if he'd only partially awakened from a bad dream. It was a smothering, claustrophobic feeling. A full-fledged panic attack seemed a heartbeat away.

He felt stalked. When he went home, he looked in all the possible hiding places: basement, closets, back yard, back porch. He was alone in the house, yet he felt a surly presence.

He made himself a drink, switched on the teevee, watched something light on Nickelodeon, but none of this helped. He took a Panpax along with a sleeping pill, went to bed. When he finally fell asleep, his dreams were populated with genetic mistakes–miscreants, sociopaths–tracking him like dogs, scratching at the walls of his sanity.

A noise woke him up. He turned on the night table light. Edsel stood in the bedroom doorway. "Think about this," he said. "Your life was made up, too. I don't see why anybody would take the time to invent a boring story, but that's what life is, right? A bunch of suckhole stories with a few shitstorms thrown in to make it all seem . . . uh . . . *real.*"

It came to Guido, then, that he had lost his mind. He cupped his hands over his face and sobbed.

"You're thinking this is all in your head, right?" Edsel said. "Look at it this way. I'm not *in* your head, I *am* your head. You are what you think. You got a better argument defining life on planet X?"

Guido woke up again, realizing he had only dreamed that he'd awakened, a type of nightmare he often had, the kind that never failed to shake him. It was ten A.M. Sunlight hammered through his bedroom window. He could almost hear the curtains crackle, as if they were about to explode into spontaneous flame.

Guido got up, made a pot of coffee, smoked two cigarettes, then called Dr. Burnaby's office for an appointment. The receptionist answered after ten rings. He recognized her voice, remembered her from previous visits. Miss Wexler: a middle-aged, three-time divorcee who never tried to hide her profound cynicism. Many of La Siberia's basket-cases eventually passed by her desk. She had a chainsmoker's ragged voice, world-weary, indifferent as stone.

Guido, wanting to make light of his condition, told her he needed an emergency re-adjustment of his tranks. When she didn't respond to this he said, "I'm having bad dreams, Miss Wexler. I dreamed I was on Planet X."

"Welcome home," Miss Wexler said.

# Fifteen

GUIDO ONLY WANTED TO HAVE A QUIET DRINK before class but The Lost Cause was noisy with a college crowd. It was a grousing crowd, sullen and murmurous with pessimism and choler. La Siberia Tech was dying, but no one was willing to wear black arm bands yet. Guido heard snippets of dangerous talk: We won't by God take it sitting down—we'll haul the bastards to court—we'll sabotage the works—we'll burn the place down to char.

But it was only talk, the talkers enflamed by booze—plump men in tweed jackets and old paisley ties, ascetic men in worn-out corduroy, bearded men in seersucker, men whose tenured lives were played out on the safe stages of academe. Several of them, in fact, were filling out job applications even as they ranted. They pored over their résumés, identifying areas that could benefit from judicious padding.

A young man took the stool next to Guido. "You're the writer-in-residence, right?" he said.

Guido sipped his Bloody Maria. He recognized the young man—an untenured instructor of rhetoric. "Not for long," he said. Herradura, a good tequila, honeyed his throat for the lecture to come. His class would soon be assembling in the chalky room where they would wait for his crafted wisdom. Which, he knew, he did not have.

"I know. But you're lucky. You don't need the job. Writing novels must be a great way to earn a living. I mean, the *independence—*"

Guido shrugged. He was going to finish out the semester honorably, regardless of what happened to La Siberia Tech. Today he would try to make sense of "The School for Witches." *—On Cader Peak there was a school for witches where the doctor's daughter, teaching the unholy cradle and the devil's pin, had seven country girls.*

"Independence?" Guido felt dependent on too many things. The bum-steers and outright betrayals of imagination, the dictating marketplace, the cancerously multiplying competition, the price of paper.

"You work *when* you want to and *where* you want to," the young man said. "You have a following, which means your work is always commercial even when you turn out a deadly piece of crap." He leaned meditatively over a glass of pale wine, his fine, wheat-straw hair falling attractively over his forehead. He had, Guido thought, the image down pat—thoughtful, concerned, intelligent, a bit out of step with the crowd, yet clearly ahead of the masses—the Artist-Rebel, but likable, even dependable, and as comfortable as a proprietor in a world of durable goods. He was, no doubt, adored by his female students who saw him as a god of compatibility, a domestic hero, a bedroom matador. Yet there was "the doom of women in his smile."

Guido shifted slightly on his stool, favoring a hemorrhoid, but turning pointedly away from the conversation he did not want. In body-language, a definite *Enough, Bunky.*

"I've got a proposition for you," the young man said, ignoring Guido's discouraging lean. "I think we could make a lot of money. It's an idea for a novel. I supply the ideas, you write it. I've been messing around with it for years, but I just don't have the patience for lengthy narrative."

Guido drained his glass, looked at his watch.

"Let me run this by you. It'll only take a minute. It's sci-fi, but I think it's an original idea. Get this: Some space travelers—I think they should be Japanese, I mean it's always Americans, isn't it, out there on the final frontier? Anyway, these Japanese space travelers find this perfect planet. It's just like earth, but it's apparently uninhabited. Which means it's an unpolluted paradise. They set up headquarters on the edge of this ocean. One of them decides to go net-fishing. He catches a mess of shrimp-like shellfish. He fries them up—does a *tempura*—and feeds them to the crew. They're just like prawns, only better—tastier, more tender, and so on. But—and here's the kicker—it turns out these shellfish are the planet's only intelligent life. They are part of an undersea civilization, centuries old, with their own Leonardos, Michelangelos, Einsteins, even their own Donald Trumps, Yassar Arafats, and Ayatollahs. And the mess the Earthman has deep-fried is none other than the Royal Family, complete with consorts and courtesans. That's just the *first* chapter. 'Tempura Royale,' my title. What do you say?"

"I don't think so," Guido said. He signaled the bartender for another Bloody Maria. He checked his watch again: he had time.

"We could split the take," the young man said. "You could write it and I could be your imaginative resource. I mean, it's my idea and all."

Guido's drink arrived. "Excuse me," he said, and carried his Bloody Maria to another stool. The young man followed him, catching at his arm.

"Get the fuck away from me," Guido said, shaking him off.

"What's your problem?" the young man said. "You don't like money?"

"I don't like *you*," Guido said.

145

"You probably couldn't write it anyway. If it doesn't involve chauvinistic creeps and neurotic, sexually disturbed women, you can't deal with it."

"If you don't get away from me I am going to break your nose," Guido said.

The young instructor was finally discouraged. He sulked back to his stool and stared moodily at his glass of wine. The boy would do all right, Guido knew. He'd wind up selling real estate or managing a fast food restaurant—good and honorable jobs, jobs he was not remotely qualified for, but the young instructor was, no doubt, a quick study.

Guido descended once again into the murk of his ruminations on "The School for Witches."

*. . .the doctor, dreaming of illness, in the centre of the tubercular hill, heard his daughter cry to the power swarming under the West roots.*

Dylan's stories, Guido believed, were thin excuses to turn the language of his poems out into a greater space, a hall of narrow margins where the solemn iambic echoes became weighty prose blackjacks.

"We live in the age of polyethylene," said the man sitting next to Guido. "Don't you agree?" The man was drinking boilermakers. His weak eyes, minified by lenses thick as glass ashtrays, were leaking small tears. Another professor about to be ejected into the cruel world of work.

"I guess so," Guido said, uninterested. "I mean, sure. The age of poly—"

". . .ethylene. It's the universal substance. Everything from car fenders to coke bottles to computer frames is made of it. I'm afraid there's no escaping the fact. "

"Why escape?" Guido said.

"Indeed. But it depresses me nonetheless. I feel . . . *trapped* by plastic, by polymer chains of flexible densities."

146

"It's a living hell, isn't it," Guido said.

The man looked sharply at Guido. "I'm speaking of autonomy, or the lack of it," the man said. "The technology is accelerating, producing a world we can't understand much less control."

"I couldn't understand it when aluminum was king," Guido said.

"Aluminum was never king."

"Yes it was."

"No. Not aluminum. You might make a case for rubber or steel. Aluminum was too specialized. More ubiquitous than, say, magnesium, but in the same category."

Guido felt his spine stiffening. It was happening again, the willing suspension of civility. "You're full of shit," he said.

But the man only nodded sadly, unwilling to argue the point.

Guido slid off his stool and made his way to the men's room. His prostate was acting up again. He'd had three Bloody Marias and two light beers and had yet to piss. He stood in front of the urinal, grimacing. At the adjacent urinal, a Chinese man was emptying his bladder with enviable force, delivering a vigorous stream, the water-drilling tones amplified by the white-tiled walls of the men's room. The man vocalized his pleasure as his bladder drained, unimpeded.

Guido looked up at the ceiling and waited, rehearsing in his mind his opening remarks to his class: The ideas, if you can call them ideas, exist in the sounds the words make. Listen: *Behind the midwife the sun sank as a stone sinks in a marsh, the dark bubbled over it, and the mud sucked it down into the bubble of the bottomless fields.* Sound first, metaphorical meaning second, literal meaning a distant third. If the sound isn't right, then all the rest collapses, including literal meaning.

But then what's the point? someone would ask. Why play word games with sound when you've got rock and roll or

Beethoven or hip-hop? The drama is enhanced, Guido would reply, by beautiful and surprising juxtapositions. Take Shakespeare–ordinary plots elevated to cosmic significance by language. Or. . . .

"You're having trouble?" the Chinese man said as he continued to deliver his powerful stream. The man had a round, jovial face. He leaned against the privacy panel, inspected Guido's unproductive efforts. Guido was not offended.

"No, no," Guido said. "Not really. Just takes a minute to open the tap."

"Trouble," the man said. "You have a very weak awk. And it will become much weaker if you fail to find remedies."

"Weak awk?"

"Yes. Awk." The man made a curvy waterfall motion with his free hand. "Awk."

"Oh. Arc." Guido looked down at his sputtering dribble. No arc at all.

"If you take the correct herbs, this will pass. I recommend Da T'sao and Ho Shou Wu. They will help your condition. You will have a good strong awk again."

"I'll remember that," Guido said.

"Of course, your major philosophers would have no problem with this. I refer to Parmenides and Zeno of Elea. You know–the arrow in flight that never reaches its target? In this same way, your urine never reaches porcelain. Motion denied."

The man's smile widened, and now Guido did feel offended. "Very funny," he said.

"Zeno argued well, but argument is no help to a man who cannot pee."

"I couldn't have said it better myself," Guido said.

148

The Chinese man released a finale of brisk spurts, zipped up, washed his hands at the sink. "But then, it is a fascinating idea, is it not? That everything remains in stasis and movement and change are merely illusions of brain physiology."

Maybe there was something here he could use, Guido thought. Sometimes he felt uneasy reading Dylan. Could it be that there was never any real movement in the stories, just the illusion of movement created by a progression of sound effects? He had similar feelings when reading Flann O'Brian. Movement, space, progress from place to place, is never convincing. It happens, but the device that moves the reader is something other than the verbs of travel. The spell-making device of sound, the witchery of rhythmic syllables, the methods of poetry, these are what carried the reader from dooryard to hilltop to the anterooms of hell.

"Da T'sao. Ho Shu Wou," the Chinese man said. "They will help you."

"Thanks," Guido said. The man dried his hands on a paper towel. "Are you with the philosophy department?"

The man laughed. "Oh no, no. I'm with Global Visions. I am here to look at apartment buildings, to house our people when they come over."

"You're in hostile territory," Guido said. "I mean here, in this bar."

The man laughed again. "You think I am in danger? That I am surrounded by fearsome warriors?"

"I see your point," Guido said.

Still chuckling, the man went back into the bar.

Guido waited another minute before relief, in hesitant jets and arcless dribbles, came.

149

# Sixteen

THE GRAY BULL TROTTED OUT OF THE DARK tunnel into the bright arena looking for something to kill. He held the twin peaks of his horns high. His arched neck was paved with muscle. On armor-padded geldings, two picadors loped along the edges of the *Plaza Glorioso,* dodging the bull's explosive attacks.

The bull had more ferocity than a lion, more will to kill than a cobra, more inborn pique than a diva. But he also had the narrow intelligence of a fighting cock. He was two thousand pounds of pride, hostility, and courage—with no subtlety or capacity for guile. Which made him vulnerable to the trickery and deceits of the bullfighting trade.

A white stallion, a handsome blonde woman on its back, slipped out of the tunnel in a high-stepping prance. The crowd had been waiting for this novelty. They sent up a roar of approval. The picadors exited the arena, leaving the superb blonde and her equally superb stallion alone with the bull.

The woman galloped her horse, circling the bull, holding her lance high, her long yellow hair flying behind her. The billboards at the ticket gates had identified her: Isabel Cardoza, *La reina rubia del rejoneo*—the blonde queen of the short lance. Isabel was a novelty from Mexico City, a chart-topper on the bullfighting circuit, engaging her bulls from horseback. She teased the beast with her expert horsemanship, darting in at him, swerving away, dancing her horse one way then the other, turning on a dime, speeding to the far side of the arena as the confused bull gave chase.

The bull eventually grew weary of this. He stood motionless in the center of the arena. He looked up at the cheering crowd as the splendid blonde *rejoneadora* raced along the perimeter of the bull ring. When Isabel slowed and moved toward him, her horse advancing broadside in a showy canter, the bull lowered his head and stroked the dust of the arena with his dark hoof.

Isabel Cardoza turned her horse parallel to the bull's charge, then, galloping alongside, drove her lance deep into the animal's massive shoulder. She then swerved gracefully out of the way of the bull's attempt to ram a horn into the exposed flank of the stallion. A picador at the mouth of the tunnel handed Isabel Cardoza another *rejón* and the death-dance with the overmatched bull began again.

The bull's neck was soon studded with the broken-off shafts of the lances, his head low with the weight of his wounds. Isabel reigned in her horse to acknowledge the *olés* of the crowd. The horse reared up and Isabel saluted her enthusiastic fans. She ignored the blood-streaked bull who now wanted nothing more than to carry the entrails of the horse and rider on his horns, to avenge himself on those who had forced his proud head low. But the double-edged blades of the *rejónes* had gone deep and continued to do their killing work as the bull twisted his huge neck one way and then the other against the annoyance of his wounds. His rage was ebbing and this confused him. He wanted to lie down. It would be good to lie down and sleep in the warm sun.

The bull, sleepy-eyed and disinterested, coughed gouts of stringy wine-dark blood as he watched the aristocratic rider blow kisses to the approving crowd.

"This is not my idea of bullfighting," Nicho Andrade said. They sat together, in the forty-peso seats on the shady side of the *Plaza Glorioso,* Nicho, Doris, and Guido, Doris in the middle. Nicho studied the duel between Isabel Cardoza and her bull through compact binoculars. "She is doing what the *banderilleros* and matador should be doing. But then everything changes in time."

"It's the aristocratic style of bullfighting," Doris said. "The rich man's—or in this case, the rich woman's—way of killing bulls. You don't get your hands dirty when you kill from horseback."

"I know what it *is*," Nicho said. "I just don't like it. It takes no *cojones*."

"I don't like it either," Guido said.

Nicho Andrade turned to Guido. "Because it takes no *cojones* or because it is unfair?"

"Unfair," Guido said.

"And you think unfair is bad?"

"In what context?"

"In any context."

"There's no fair answer to that question," Guido said.

Nicho Andrade smiled at Guido. "You're not an unintelligent man," he said. Guido took offense at this, but realized that, coming from Nicho Andrade, this was a compliment.

Andrade himself had the poise and slender grace of a matador. He was wearing denims, a Raider's tee shirt and Nikes. He had a narrow face with prominent *indio* cheekbones, but the hatchet-like nose and the cool gray eyes were pure *castellano*. He looked like a man who had never been surprised by much. And he didn't have to wear a thousand dollar Armani suit to let you know that he was more advantaged, in all ways, than you. An autocrat, Guido decided. A *cacique*—the unchallenged chief of his domain.

The blonde woman from Mexico City, who fought bulls from horseback, had finished her work. She took a victory lap, then trotted her fine stallion out of the arena as the once magnificent bull collapsed into a fly-speckled hill of unmoving beef.

*"Vamos,"* Nicho Andrade said. "I'll show you what they do with the carcass."

"Cesar Montoya is next," Doris said. "He's beautiful."

"We've seen Montoya a dozen times," Nicho said. "And we've already seen four bulls killed today. This will be of interest to your guest."

Guido felt a little weak. Bullfights, though explained to him dozens of times by those who appreciated them, never failed to depress him. He'd only been to a few, but he came away from them feeling that a great injustice had been done. The bull, a noble animal of pure fighting spirit, was sacrificed for the momentary pleasure of a loud, beer-drinking crowd. True, the matador—or in this case, the blonde woman on her horse—was somewhat at risk, but the risk was slim. He'd watched bullfights on the Mexican TV channels in which the matador made a critical mistake and got tossed, trampled, and gored, but this was the exception. The odds always favored the man with the cape and sword—not to deny the obvious fact that he had to be as courageous and daring as he was skilled.

Guido's friend, Crazy Red Fingerhut, an *aficionado,* had told him it was not a sport but a symbolic ceremony of life and death, a pagan rite bringing home to the spectator, via blood sacrifice, the tragedy of life on planet Earth. "We are the matador," Fingerhut had said. "And we are also the bull. When the blood-dimmed tide is loosed, pardner, the ceremony of innocence is drowned." Fingerhut was a fancy talker when he was drunk, mixing famous quotes with his own booze-inspired rhetoric. Even so, Guido could accept this sort of argument intellectually. Emotionally, he was on the side of the bull.

They left the stadium and followed a narrow side-street to a warehouse. The bull had been taken away by truck and was now hanging by its rear legs from a block-and-tackle in the entryway to the warehouse. Its blood was draining into wash-tubs from slits made in its throat. A man on a step ladder cut off the bull's testicles with a long knife and gave the bloody sack to a ragged teenage boy who whooped in delight and ran off with his prize, carrying it like a handbag. Guido felt a sharp pang at the purse-strings end of his scrotum.

"A delicacy for his family," Nicho explained. "No part of the bull will be wasted. It will be butchered and distributed among the people in the poorest *colonias* of Bajo. Exquisite *menudo* for hundreds will be made of its tripe."

Of course, there was no death in the afternoon: none of this happened. Guido pulled off his bathing-cap helmet and data suit. He still felt the grit and gore of the virtual bull ring, even though he was in Doris Andrade's house where silent fans moved a cool breeze through the spotless rooms.

"Why is *he* always in the machine?" Guido asked.

"Nicho? He loves to play Virgil to the tourists. He's a great fan of Dante's. He won't be in the commercial models. They've lined up some Hollywood actors to be guides, when guides are required. Imagine Charleton Heston, for example, taking you to the pyramids on the Giza plateau or to the temples of Luxor. The pyramids would be in their original condition, complete with the polished casing stones, not the time-blistered wrecks we see today. And you won't have to be afraid of terrorists making a political statement with your blood."

"I'm sold," Guido said.

"Nicho wants to put one in every high school. Kids can learn history by walking through it."

They had a good lunch, then went to bed. It was acceptable sex: friendly, domestic, no twists, no surprises. Guido climaxed seconds after Doris did. It was as if they'd been married for twenty years. They both sighed–satisfied yet bored. It made Guido feel that youth had finally slipped away. He was only in his mid-forties, but it seemed that the conditions of life, from now on, would be ratified by ordinariness. I'm not ready for this, he thought. But he knew he was. Sex would never be an adventure again. It would be a simple habit, a mechanical release of endorphins, a prelude to sleep. He lit a cigarette, completing the time-worn ritual.

It had not been this way with Kirsten, had it? But Kirsten was gone, and it seemed that she had been gone for years, not months. Guido sighed again, and Doris looked at him, the question in her eyes. She'd been a good wife long enough to know better than to ask it.

# Seventeen

"THIS GRAPHICS ENGINE WILL SMOKE, dude," said the clown. "That means something?" Guido said. He'd left Doris asleep in the bedroom, went into the Cybertopia room, got back into the data suit and helmet.

"The GE will cough up bodies fast as you can type."

Guido typed: "Lorraine has shoulder-length auburn hair. She is tall—five-ten. Her body is angular, the joints knobby, as though she's had to do stoop labor all her life. She has big hands, a big but handsome nose, her breasts are long and heavy, the dark nipples prominent. Her brown eyes are widely spaced. Maybe she's a victim of fetal alcohol syndrome. Her face has an oval shape, the forehead less wide than the expanse of her cheeks, the lips are full and fixed in a constant but unintended pout. The upper lip is finely haired and beaded with sweat. She's just come in from the field—she's been picking strawberries. She has a small waist, flaring hips, and nicely tapered legs. Her feet are long and narrow, the bones visible, the ankles small. Edsel is spying on her from his place of concealment in a barn."

As Guido typed the figure gradually morphed into a woman with unique features. She stood in front of him, regarding him with dead eyes. "I'll have to give her some kind of personality," Guido said. But he didn't feel up to writing a lengthy life history.

"Pick a stock bio," the clown said. He pulled down a menu of character profiles. Guido chose *Farm Girl*. A fact sheet appeared, suspended between Guido and the woman.

"You don't want to read it," the clown said. "It's over fifty pages long. It gives her history—parents, schooling, childhood joys and traumas, first date, first sex, first *good* sex, first meal in a sit-down restaurant—all in minute detail. Just crossload the bio, and you'll have her. She'll be all you want and more."

Guido touched a bar labeled "crossload" and the woman hiccuped.

"Excuse my country born ass," she said.

"Hi," Guido said.

She studied Guido for a few moments. "You're here to cut me, right?" she said.

A knife appeared in her hand. She gave it to Guido. Guido dropped it. "No," he said. "Not me. I'm not the killer. I'm the writer."

She laughed. She had a wide, sensual mouth, the teeth strong and perfect. "Don't be squeamish," she said. "Come on, do it. That's why you conceived me."

"Yes, but I'm not—"

"Then fuck me. Rape me. Download your DNA, big boy. That's the scenario, isn't it? You want to tie me up, isn't that so? Put a cord around my neck? You want to fuck me with the blood to my brain shut off, right? You want to send me to hell screaming for joy, right? Correct me if I'm wrong about this."

"I'm not the criminal," Guido said. "Edsel is the one you're waiting for. Edsel Harmon Haight. He wants to do all those things."

She shrugged. "What's the diff who does it? You're all basically the same, down deep. Come on, you hypocrite. Do it. Have a thrill. Don't wait for your butt-ugly stand-in."

She stepped toward Guido. She gave an aggressive forward thrust of her hips. A momentary temptation made his neck hairs stand up. She pressed herself against him and he felt her human heat, felt the hard points of her breasts dent his chest. He kissed her electric mouth.

The clown hooted. He pulled off his rubber nose and peeled off his white latex mask. It was Nicho Andrade. "You're a *piñata* full of surprises, man," he said.

Guido stepped away from the Farm Girl. These pre-arranged intrusions by Andrade no longer surprised Guido, but he was still annoyed.

"You're a little confused, I think," Andrade said. "You've been wondering how I can be here, responding to you spontaneously. It's the machine's Motive Analyzer. It's reading you, man. It picks up your brain waves, your armpit sweat, your heart rhythms. The ultrasonic vision tracker is watching your eyes. It sees your gaze lingering on the woman's breasts, her pubic mound, her feet. You got a thing for feet, man? The analyzer knows your heart, bubba. It's reading you like a book. It organizes all this biophysical data into a statistical model and gives high-probability responses. It's not Nicho Andrade talking to you, but it might as well be."

"You're over my head," Guido said.

"No, I'm not. You're just evading something you don't want to know."

"What might that be?"

Andrade laughed. "Come on, I'll give you a little tour."

Guido felt himself rise into the air. Andrade was with him, and together they flew off into a bucolic scene. Vertigo attacked Guido. He reached for his helmet but couldn't find the snap.

"Stay with it," Nicho Andrade said. "No need to panic. Remember, you are inside a fiction. Maybe *you* are a fiction yourself. Think about the novel this machine is helping you write. Think about how books will be written from now on. This is the future of literature, is it not? The semiotics of desire are *here*. Isn't that what literature thrives on—from contemporary trash to Don Quixote? A few years from now, the printed page will be a museum curiosity."

Hundreds of feet below, in a pleasant valley, Guido saw naked men and women consort with farm animals, children attack an octogenarian in an aluminum walker with slingshots and pellet guns, two competing men attempting to mount a sobbing woman, twelve basted babies turning on a spit above glowing coals, a thousand monkeys torturing a dying elephant, a masturbating man doused with gasoline and set on fire by nuns in traditional habits. An army of ragtag militiamen trotted in double time, singing the "My Country Right or Wrong" song in a dozen languages. At a signal from their leader, the militiamen dropped to kneeling positions and began discharging their automatic weapons into a schoolyard. Bits and pieces of children flew into the air like red confetti. Bloodspray rose like mist.

And then Guido saw himself. He was kneeling under a tree, hands tied behind his back. A woman held a small pistol to his head. He heard himself beg for reprieve, heard himself cry out, "Don't do it!" But the woman, who could have been the mad secretary, Carma, laughed at him. She pulled the trigger and Guido saw himself topple over, face down, felt the moist earth receive his face, felt the careless spill of hot blood.

Guido looked over at Nicho. "Where did *that* scene come from?"

Andrade shrugged. "More than likely from your death wish."

"I don't have any goddamned death wish."

"Don't be naive. Everyone born in the twentieth century has."

They floated gently to earth, hovering silently over the wounded man. Guido turned him over. The light in his glycerin-soft eyes was fading. Guido watched himself die as his executioner put the revolver back into her purse.

"In Cybertopian space you can live any dream, even your unconscious ones," Nicho said gently. "Those of limited imagination can hire people like you, Guido, to supply and augment their fantasies. No one will need books, but you will still be able to earn a good living. The moviemakers will get into this technology quickly and produce software that will facilitate any dream, noble or demented."

Something Guido's father once said came back to him now: "The well of invention never runs dry, son. But be careful what you fish out of it." Elmo Tarkenen had been talking about story-telling, explaining–perhaps apologizing for–the warps he'd created in his own identity. But now his words took on a wider significance for Guido.

Nicho Andrade laughed. "Snap out of it, Guido. You look like you've walked into a mansion full of ghosts."

# Eighteen

Guido Guido Guido:

I am sitting here sipping a whiskey sour and wondering about your situation out there in our great American desert. As your agent of these past twelve years I know when things are not going well for you—and, so, for me! I need pages, sir, pages filled with dread and mayhem. Do not tell me that you've gone "academic." What the Jesus are you doing teaching English in a college anyway? It is not good for you! You, sir, are a brilliant know-nothing. Are you suddenly convinced that you are presently sucking at the teat of Large Ideas? Christ defend us. Do not tell me, your faithful servant, that you've caught the disease. For there is no cure. I beg you, sir, do not send me a novel called *Daphne Discovers Her Sigmoid Flexure*. I have on my desk a weighty manuscript sent to me by a professor of creative writing, entitled, *Her Third Laundromat Soliloquy*. It begins, "Casandra, witholding orgasm, reduced the already oft-reduced principle of male ejaculation to the metaphorical contest between feminine Being and masculine non-Being, as Regis Mulavaney blindly poured the napalm of his seed into the tinder-dry manger of her womb."

Christ defend us.

Guido, do not tinker with a good thing.

Send me blood, tubs of rich red blood. I am terrified that you are going to start using big words. Again, from *Soliloquy:* "Regis, always the ideologue, exacerbated the hospital

161

trustees with his verbal intussusceptions." Suet, sir, pure suet. No, I slander suet. Suet is honest kidney fat.

See, what happens is this: they start to worry about what their colleagues think, they start to hanker after respect. They want their fucking tenure. Christ defend us.

Okay. You get the point. Send me the goods. Pronto.

Sid Mullen

"Not to worry, Sid," Guido said, stuffing his agent's letter back into the envelope. There was a second letter from Vice Chancellor Cribb's office. It was marked Urgent. Guido was sure it was his letter of termination. He didn't open it.

The phone rang. Guido let it ring half a dozen times before he picked it up.

"Tarkenen here," Guido said.

"...No, *no*. No *names*. Hear them? They have devices. Hush, now." The voice was muffled yet loud and impatient.

Guido started to re-cradle the phone when the voice said, "I can't talk. I'm sure your phone is tapped. Come to The Hammer and Tong in a half hour."

"Figgis?"

The line went silent again. The quiet lasted for seconds. "Are you there?" Guido said.

"Fuck," said the despairing voice. "I said no *names*. Be here in half an hour."

Figgis hung up. Guido kept the phone to his ear. After a moment heard a series of digital beeps followed by sharp electrical clicks. "Hello?" Guido said.

"*¿Bueno?*" said a voice.

"Are you calling me?"

*"Tiene el número equivocado,"* said the voice.

"How could I have the wrong number?" Guido said. "I'm not the one who's calling. *You* have the wrong number. *El número equivocado* yourself."

*"¿Qué chingados quieres, borrachín?"* the voice said, disgusted.

"Why are you calling me names?" Guido said.

*"¿Por que no, puto?"*

*"Tu madre,"* Guido said.

*"La tuya,* motherfucker," the voice said.

The line went dead again.

Guido chalked it up to a switching problem at the phone company. Crossed lines, creating an erroneous connection with a party, probably in Bajomitío, someone with a chip on his shoulder. Guido shrugged, but slammed the phone down anyway.

The Hammer and Tong was not crowded. Figgis was sitting at his usual table, in a back corner. He was wearing dark wrap-around glasses and a black trenchcoat. His curly hair was oiled flat.

"I never would have guessed you were trying to go un-noticed," Guido said. "Why don't you just tape a sign on your back in foot-high red letters, 'Ignore My Sorry Ass.'"

Figgis's big red face was sweating. His narrow, Italian sunglasses looked like a plastic blindfold.

"I've found something," he said. He spoke through clenched teeth, more of a growl than a whisper. "Something they want desperately. They'll burn down orphanages to get it."

Figgis's paranoia was contagious. Guido looked over his shoulder at the other patrons of the bar. A couple of old winos, a swamper leaning on his mop, and a middle-aged prostitute, her penciled eyebrows arched in provisional invitation. Nothing sinister.

163

Figgis reached into his trenchcoat pocket and pulled out a plastic bag. "Videotape," he said. "I haven't watched it yet, but it's kind of *hot*–X rated."

Figgis launched into a discourse: He'd gone to visit the kid–Freddy Marantz–the accused murderer of Gregory Inverness. He was being kept–by court order, pending a hearing–at the state holding pen for criminal nut-cases. Figgis had gone there on a hunch, pretending to be the boy's uncle. The boy–a frail neuresthenic–was suspicious of Figgis. When Figgis told him that he not only believed his claim to innocence, but that he had strong reasons to think the boy had been framed by powerful people, Freddy opened up. He told Figgis that he'd planned a kind of vendetta against Inverness, but that he'd never kill a professor over a bad grade. What he had done, however, was break into and rifle Inverness's office–several days before the murder–hoping to find the keys to the professor's exams. But what he found instead was a video tape marked "Lotty and Me–Q.E.D." The tape had a red heart taped to it. Intrigued, Freddy took it to his apartment and played it. And there it was, the good professor and Lotty, his research assistant, going at it like minks in the professor's office. He kept the tape, thinking that he could use it to blackmail Inverness into giving him an A for the course, and for any other math course he might take. But then Inverness was found in the arroyo with a crushed skull and the cops arrested Freddy. It was easy to connect Freddy to the murder since his prints were all over Inverness's office, in places they shouldn't be. Furthermore, several witnesses had come forward with stories of bad blood between Freddy and the professor. And then Freddy's psychiatric history came to light–some episodes of violence against other students, a one-hundred mile an hour car chase, a suicide threat–cinching the case against him. But before the cops picked him up, Freddy had hidden the video tape in his apartment.

Figgis went to the apartment. It had been tossed in a big way, the apartment manager told him. Someone broke in and tore the place apart shortly after Freddy Marantz had been arrested. Figgis told the manager he might want to rent the place himself. It was a nice place, small, but bright and clean, and close to the university. While looking the place over, he went into the bathroom. He shut the door, locked it, and pulled the lid off the toilet tank. And, just as the boy had said, there was the cassette–taped to the underside of the tank lid. Figgis pulled it loose and shoved it into his coat.

"Come on," he said to Guido. "We need to see this tape. I'm not sure what's so important about it, but maybe together we can come up with something."

"I've got a headache," Guido said.

"I'll give you some aspirin. I've got a ton of them."

# Nineteen

IT WAS A BASIC, NO-FRILLS, OZZIE AND HARRIET fuck: Inverness on top, Lotty under him, her long skinny legs–so dazzling white they created black halos around their television image– locked around the small of his back. His potbelly-hampered lifts and thrusts were short, without much drive, accompanied by choppy falsetto grunts–the mathematician was no sexual athlete. Inverness finished in less than a minute. He sagged into Lotty, panting. "You're squishing me, Greggy," she said. She lifted her head and smiled into the camera. She had a tall forehead but under it her face was small, the features set close together.

"For the love of Christ, why would they want to put *that* on tape?" Figgis said.

"I can't believe this has happened to me," Inverness said. He looked into the camera lens, as if responding to Figgis. "I've never been in love, you see. Yet here I am, forty years old and a *virgin*. Oh, I don't mean sexually–though I don't have much experience. I mean. . . ."

"He means," Lotty interrupted, "that for the first time in his life he knows what love is. The same goes for me. I guess that's why we're putting this on tape. Neither of us can believe it's happened. We'll want to see it . . . I don't know. I feel a little crazy. Oh God, I love this man with all my being!"

"And I love Lotty with all my being," Inverness echoed. Neither lover was attractive. Inverness's long, horsy face, childlike with awe, filled the screen. He had a long thin nose and his teeth were slightly bucked, too large for his lips to

166

contain, a feature that gave him a constant helpless smile, sappy and sweet. "I think we could dissolve into one another if we're not careful." Inverness stepped back and reached for Lotty. He raised her hand to his lips and kissed it.

The two lovers held each other before the witnessing camera, murmuring sweet words and sweeter non-words. They sat on Inverness's long desk and kissed, and soon they were at it again, Inverness doing better this time.

"I'm going to puke," Figgis said.

"New frontiers in home movies," Guido said. It was an easy dismissal, but the tape was making Guido uncomfortable. It wasn't pornographic at all. It was worse: he felt he was seeing something that should never be seen. These were decent people deeply in love and their affection, naïve and pathetic as it was, should have been privacy's last and most sacred bastion. It depressed him that these foolhardy people thought that violating their own innocence was a good thing to do.

Guido thought about his own failed marriage. Had he and Kirsten ever felt the way Lotty and Inverness did? He tried to remember one moment of disarming innocence between them, but could not. Had he been so self-absorbed that those moments, if they existed at all, were instantly scrubbed from memory? Maybe Lotty and Inverness were not so foolish after all. Maybe putting their love-making on tape was a hedge against the inevitable distractions that assaulted memory.

Figgis went to the kitchen and brought back two glasses, a bucket of ice, and a bottle of gin. Guido made himself a drink and let the cold heat of four ounces of Bombay sear his throat. He refilled his glass.

"I don't get it," he said. "There's nothing on this tape but sweethearts fucking themselves stupid."

"Look at the blackboard behind the desk," Figgis said.

There were some symbols scrawled there, but they meant nothing to Guido.

"Maybe that's it. The solution to the four forces problem."

"What four forces?" Guido said.

"It's the God Equation. You must have heard about it. Physicists have been blabbing about it for years. They figure if they can find one elegant equation that ties all four forces together, they will have access to God's best idea."

"Come on, Figgis. That's ridiculous."

"They don't think so. The Nobel Prize goes to the winner. The only forces in the universe are gravity, electromagnetism, the nuclear weak force, and the nuclear strong force. If they come up with one expression that incorporates them all–kind of like Einstein's $E=mc^2$ showed the equivalence of matter and energy–then they'll know exactly how the whole damn shebang was put together."

"But not why."

"Why doesn't figure into it. Why is no man's land. The territory of visionaries, screwballs and con artists."

"What about the fifth force?" Guido said. "How does that figure into their arithmetic?"

Figgis took the gin bottle away from Guido. "You're drunk. *What* fifth force?"

"The life force." Guido pointed at the screen. Inverness and Lotty looked like a pulsating pretzel, their over-exercised limbs shining with sweat. "Pretty powerful, don't you think?"

"That's the realm of mystics, Guido," Figgis said, taking a long pull directly from the bottle.

"Magnetism used to be in the realm of mystics. Can you read his blackboard?"

Figgis squinted at the screen. Inverness and Lotty were partially obscuring the blackboard. They were on top of Inverness's big desk, knotted together, rising and falling, occasionally stopping to suck in ragged gulps of air. "Down in front," Figgis said, bored with the gymnastics of love.

"I'm afraid not," he said, finally. "My math stops at high school trig. I have no idea what he's scribbled."

Guido studied the blackboard. He knew no math, but realized all at once that he wasn't looking at mathematics at all. "Wait a minute," he said, moving closer to the TV set. "It isn't equations. It's a checklist of some kind, along with some names. What's IPOC? Isn't that Solly Dubrinsky's name up there, next to Inverness and someone else . . . someone with two exes in his name."

Figgis stood up explosively. Guido caught the bottle of gin before it hit the floor. "Jayzuz Christ! That's it! That's what they're after, man! IPOC stands for the Intellectual Property Oversight Committee. So that's what they were up to! No wonder the poor bugger got himself killed."

"I don't follow," Guido said.

"It looks to me like a few people are trying to get control of their own patents."

"I still don't see. . . . "

"All original research at La Siberia Tech is reviewed by IPOC. If the school regards the research as original, especially if it turns out to have a practical application, then they set about getting patents. The school generally becomes the sole owner of the patents. But there are loopholes. Say someone comes here from another school, or from private industry, with an idea they've already done considerable work on. Then the question of patents becomes more complicated."

"I still don't get it," Guido said.

"I was wrong, you see. I thought the brainy boys were in danger because one or more of them might win a Nobel. How fucking stupid! No, they're getting on someone's shit list because they're *greedy*. They want a big piece of the action and Global Visions doesn't want to share. Global Visions figured that if they bought the school, the patents are part of the deal. And this tape—if we can eventually read everything on Inverness's blackboard—will no doubt make this strategy plain. No wonder they want it."

"Aren't you jumping to conclusions here, Figgis?"

"Yes, but they're the right conclusions. Want to lay money on it?"

"No," Guido said.

"Yes!" Lotty screamed. "Yes! Oh God *yes!*"

But Inverness pulled away from her. "No. I'm finished," he groaned. "My heart, it's fibrillating—paroxismal ventricular fibs. I feel weak." He slid off the desk and collapsed on the floor. His limbs twitched, his eyelids fluttered.

"Get up, boy-o," Figgis said, now merry with gin and discovery. "Let death be no deterrent, laddybuck! Remount that filly!"

"No," Inverness said into the camera, his face ghostly pale, his exhausted lips peeled back over his helpless smile. "I'm done in, Lotty. Besides, I've got a steering committee meeting in twenty minutes."

Lotty propped herself up on her elbows and made a face at the back of Inverness's head. "Stinker," she said.

The screen went blank. Guido and Figgis continued to stare at it.

170

# Twenty

THE SINGING DRUNKS STUMBLED THROUGH the house passing the quickly emptying bottle of gin back and forth. Greek bouzoukis hammered from the stereo and the clamorous men locked arms and improvised a Zorba-esque dance of defiant manhood. They kicked at the furniture, overturning chairs and lamps, punched dents into the wallboard with their blind feet. Books fell from the shelves, pictures dropped from the walls, and the neighbors offered curses from their windowsills. The house rocked on its supports and drifted into a wayward current that carried it out to chartless waters.

Guido freed himself from Figgis's dangerous wall-to-wall caroming, tilted through the passageways between rooms. He recalled his father's story of The Great Tide. All nine planets and their many stony moons were aligned—a once-in-a-millennium event—producing a gravitational channel of epochal force, drawing all vessels to a common destination in eerily becalmed waters far from their customary sea lanes. A thousand ships stranded in a dead Sargasso under a strangely constellated sky. "Even God did not have the wherewithal or patience to find them," Elmo Tarkenen said gravely, and little Guido gripped the arms of his chair, alarmed at the unthinkable notion that God could lack wherewithal or patience.

"I am a worthless man," Figgis announced, dampening the sublime lunacy of the moment.

"So true," said Guido.

"*You* are also a man of no worth," Figgis said, reproachfully.

"So true, so very true."

"We are all worthless men, and we're men enough to admit it, by the Rood!"

"Aye," said Guido. "By the Rood."

"It's *good* to know you are worthless. A man who knows he is worthless is worth something in my book."

"Aye," said Guido. "We are worthy men, by the Rood."

"And a worthy man is worth something," Figgis said.

"In my book, he is worth a lot. He is worth the Pope's mozzetta."

"More. He is worth a funicular full of factotums—or is it factota? I daresay we are *not* worthless men. I submit we are worth a great deal!"

"More than the nabobs can measure," Guido agreed, nodding so vigorously his head swam. He leaned radically to one side, as if influenced by a powerful magnet, then staggered through an unlatched door into an ink-dark room. "Man overboard!" he cried out, reeling like a novice sailor on a pitching deck, his unswift feet unable to keep up with the momentum of his sideways travel. He fell into stacked boxes, knocking some of them down. He found a corner and laid down in it. A momentary visitation from Kirsten gave him a sprightly erection. She was nude, in a fire-lit cave, calling him in.

The lights came on. Figgis filled the doorway between the kitchen and the garage. "You could have caused a neighborhood disaster, you damned fool," he said.

Guido had been asleep for only a few minutes, but he felt all the pain and sourness of a long sleep after a night of reckless drinking.

Figgis re-stacked the boxes. "This is no place to play the bull in the China shop, Guido," he said. He seemed completely sober. "You nearly fell into my arsenal."

172

Guido stood up gradually. Next to the stack of cardboard boxes he'd knocked over were dozens of six packs of beer. They were the large, 25 ounce cans, and there was something odd about them. Bands of gray duct tape were wrapped around each six pack, holding them together, not the usual plastic rings. A lattice work of heavy yellow cord was fixed to the tops of each can.

"Bombs, Guido," Figgis explained. "I make them from common aspirins. Acetylsalicylic acid in the aspirins reduces to a pure crystalline form after a bath in ordinary methyl alcohol. I dissolve the crystals in acid, add a little sodium nitrate to get pure trinitrophenol crystals. Are you following this, Tark? Any half-competent slob can make these things. Lord knows, I'm no scientist. Once you get this second batch of crystals you crush them up and mix them with wax and Vaseline and *voilà*. The resulting bomb is more powerful than T.N.T. The detonation velocity is around 6800 meters per second. Ka-fucking-*boom!* Tie enough of my six-packs together and I can make any building unusable." Figgis waved his big arms, shaping the air in front of him into a mushrooming explosion.

"What are you going to blow up?" Guido said.

"La Siberia Tech. At least the Applied Technology Complex. If I can't have my university, then no other son of bitch can."

"You don't think you can get away with it, do you?"

"Hell no! I don't expect to get away with anything. Look, Tark. If I lose my job, my world is over. Kaput. Who is going to hire a fifty-year-old alcoholic whose special area of knowledge is the wonderfully irrelevant 18th century English novel? I've been at La Siberia Tech for twenty-four years! This place *is* my life! I might as well spend the rest of my days in a federal pen. At least I'll have a place to sleep and three square meals a day. I understand they even have extensive libraries in prisons nowadays. Hell, I could probably get on as prison librarian."

"Why don't you at least try to get a job at some other college?"

"I'll tell you why." Figgis went back into the house and came back with a newsletter. "Listen to this qualifying language for some pissant entry-level job in California and tell me if you think I'm their man. 'We especially desire applicants who have demonstrated their sensivity to gender equity.' How the hell do you *demonstrate* your sensitivity to gender equity, assuming you had any? No, I'm afraid I'm a relic of a dead era, Tark. No one's going to hire me."

"But you just don't blow up buildings! You're not a terrorist! You're a man of letters, a fucking English professor!"

"To profess and not act is to repudiate all human values," Figgis said somberly, the ample flesh of his great round face slack with the gravity of his words.

"I need some aspirin," Guido said.

Figgis laughed. "There's a million of them right here." He opened a cardboard box and handed Guido a bottle of generic aspirins. Guido went into the kitchen and shook five of them into his palm. He opened a 25 ounce can of Australian beer and washed them down.

"Where'd you learn all this unibomber chemistry, Figgis?"

"On the Internet. You can pick up all kinds of interesting shit on-line. I learned how to fuck a llama from some pervert in Peru. Not that I expect to have the opportunity or need. I also learned how to cook a peccary. Amazing diversity of stuff. Hell, it may be that the university of the future will be completely electronic. Surf for the degree you want. If so, I can probably teach Smollet, Sterne, Swift, Fielding, and Richardson right from my cell. So I come out ahead, the way I see it."

174

Figgis went to his liquor cabinet, studied the offerings, took down a fresh pint of Bombay. "Ready for round two?" he said.

The men took the gin out to the back porch of Figgis's house. They sat on a bench and passed the bottle back and forth. The air was unreasonably humid for the desert. It felt like Gulf air in the rainy season. The sky was overcast with dense clouds that reflected the lights of the city. But it would not rain. The clouds were in transit only, moving from one coast to the other. Bats big as crows harvested millers from the glow of a nearby yard light. The men, having lost the need to talk, sipped from their bottle. Guido listened to the rodent squeaks of the bats and though it was warm he shivered.

"We're on to the bastards," Figgis said, turning to Guido, his dangerous eyes glittering sagely in the dim air.

# Twenty-one

G uido swam toward a pale white rectangle. It was a note addressed to him:

Mr. Tarka (?)

"Please you come for dinner tonight. 7 pm, you remember? You meet my niece Mrs. Seraghina McWorter. I make a good bracciola and maybe a nice lasagna plus hot scampi alla salsa di vino, delicious."

He propelled himself to a more advantageous position to read the rest of the note.

"But please I ask you not to drink so much. Seraghina does not like to see this in a man, like her husband Mitchell (gone now and good riddance!). And I know you drink so much because I see you come home walking zigzag to your door. You sit down on your front step and talk to yourself and last night you bark misery like a dog."

Guido swam through his house puzzled and thrilled by the algae-slimed water that filled it. He drifted toward the kitchen window. He could see his sunny yard, weedy, unmowed, a black wasp laboring angrily from one corner of the window to the other. Out beyond the patio, partly hidden by the spiny leaves of a large blue maguey, Seraghina stood looking toward the house.

She was exactly as he had imagined her: lumpish, depressed, a thick-ankled woman in nun's shoes and plain brown dress, her buck teeth bowing out her mouth into a grouper mouth, the beige convex lips bland yet imposing. He knocked against the window with his hard reptilian nose and when she saw him she smiled eagerly, the great horsy teeth forcing her big shy lips to slide helplessly up the endless pink of her gums.

Guido signaled to her by knocking the window again with his wedgy nose, lured her with the brilliant orange and yellow patterns on the underside of his carapace, showed her how his fine tough tail would be useful in weightless pondwater sex. She understood what was required. She entered his sunken house—magically, the water did not spill out when she opened the door—and she sank to all fours and crawled to him. She was no longer a shy, horsy woman, but a turtle, like him. He met her murky amphibian gaze fondly as they commenced a prolonged encounter, turtle style, his tail becoming a leathery C-clamp locking them together to maximize the blissful moment.

Guido woke up snorting at his daffy hallucinatory dream. He was in his office, face down on his desk. He'd been nursing a stupefying hangover with Tsingtao and had drooled on the note that inspired the dream—the dinner invitation from Alice Dark. He mopped it with his sleeve and stuffed it into his shirt pocket. Seraghina McWorter. If Alice Dark wanted her niece to meet this man who drank as much as her ex-husband and who sat on his front steps and barked misery at the moon, then both women must have come to an end of possibilities. On the other hand, he was a *professor,* and a fairly well-known writer. Maybe these plusses turned the minuses into colorful idiosyncrasies.

Another note had been taped to his door. It was a poem, by Lowell Seewright Sorrell, one of the old-time traditionalists

177

in the English department. Every office door had a Xerox copy taped to it. There was a note in Sorell's handwriting scrawled on the back of the poem:

> My dear friends and colleagues: Though
> disaster has struck, let me remind you that
> beauty is everywhere abundant and that, as
> the great master poet has said, "God's in
> his Heaven—all's right with the world."
> Please do not despair, but consider this
> setback as an opportunity to press forward
> with your lives in new and interesting ways!
> *Tout n'est pas perdu!*

Guido held the poem up to his bleary, hungover eyes and read:

### Rejoice, O Do Rejoice

The pond, the stream, the next-to-naked tree,
The geese upon the wing, their wide, inexact Vee
Auguring autumn in the crispy afternoon air,
The woolly beast a-slumber in its mountain lair—

All ask me to rejoice and in rejoicing sing
The innocent heart of each and every thing!
O happy world! O happy, thrice happy world!
From God's starry furnace lovingly hurled!

Each wave of creation tossed upon the sand
Of this unparsimonious beauty, my Motherland!

L. Seewright Sorrell
Your Colleague

Guido puked into his wastebasket, a velvety bile green as a spring meadow. He walked down the hall to the men's room and filled a sink with cold water. He submerged his face in the basin and splashed water over his head, soaking his hair. The lump above his ear was still tender, but he had vowed to stop worrying about it. He dried himself with a dozen paper towels, combed his hair, and started back to his office. He felt eighty percent alive. Which was a seventy-nine percent improvement over that morning when he was awakened by Alice Dark banging at his door with her dinner invitation. He didn't answer, but she had slipped the note through the crack between the door and the jamb.

Half a dozen professors were crowded into the janitor's storeroom next to the men's room. The janitor kept a small black-and-white TV on a high shelf. It was tuned to the local PBS channel. Vice Chancellor Cribbs, flanked by two Chinese men in business suits, was sitting at a conference table. It appeared to be some sort of question-and-answer session. Guido stopped to watch.

"This institution has a very bright future, thanks to Global Visions," Cribbs said. He was a lean man with quick, impatient eyes. Before coming to La Siberia Tech, he'd been a partner in an Arizona Savings and Loan company that went bankrupt. His partners went to prison on various fraud charges. The Vice Chancellor, who had bought himself immunity by providing the federal prosecutors with evidence against his partners, escaped penalty. His Ph.D. in economics was from a prestigious eastern university, which impressed the trustees of La Siberia Tech more than his criminal financial dealings distressed them. "Our new priorities," he said, "are really no different than the priorities institutions of higher learning in

179

the past had set for themselves, namely, to provide the intellectual energy and resources the times require."

"I understand you won't be teaching philosophy or literature any longer," a reporter asked. "In fact, La Siberia Tech will no longer be a *teaching* institution, isn't that right?"

"Not true! No sir, you have been misinformed, no doubt by certain disgruntled members of our faculty who have been surplussed by our re-organization. Philosophy *will* be taught, rest assured. In fact, we have a new series of courses entitled, 'Man and His Needs: The Supply Side of Happiness,' and this series will be taught by the Consumer Assessment Department of our Applied Economics Division."

"That sounds like another name for Market Research," the reporter said.

Vice Chancellor Cribbs yielded the microphone to one of the Chinese men. Guido recognized him as the man who offered him herbal advice at the urinal in The Lost Cause. "The thematic thrust of Western philosophy," the man said, "has always been man's search for happiness. We are simply taking a pragmatic approach to the subject, which we feel is appropriate in that it depends less on abstract reasoning and more on immediate, quantifiable results."

"Results!" Cribbs shouted. "That's what it's all about! The liberal arts oriented Universities have played footsie with ideas—most of which are laughably unproductive—for far too long! And where has it gotten us? No, we are committed to the world of hard results."

"And literature?" the reporter asked.

"'How Man Re-defines Himself Through Technology,' a three-hour course taught by specialists in the field—engineers with training in ergonomics and work-place psychodynamics. The course will begin by de-bugging the poorly reasoned dystopian visions of Wells and Huxley, our most visible 20th century Luddites, as well as their most recent imitators. We will concentrate on the literature of lifestyle enhancement, and if we cannot find such a literature, we shall *create* it."

"That's pretty ambitious, Dr. Cribbs," the reporter said.

"What is an institute of higher learning if not ambitious?" said the Vice Chancellor. "We plan to engender a literature of optimism. Instead of the cynical negativism of *Brave New World,* we will commission a new era series called *Great New World: The Corporate Vision of Mankind's Future.* We intend to establish, promote, and nurture a literature of glad tidings for responsible adults, available on-line, written by responsible craftsmen for the general good of the community. We want the literature of the future to be written by morally healthy people. The era of filth generated by scum is over."

"Aren't you personally brokering the sale of La Siberia Tech to Global Visions, Dr. Cribbs? I understand your commission alone will run into seven figures."

Cribbs offered the reporter a cool, thin-lipped smile. His eyes went sagely distant, as if divining his rosy future. "Say what you will, sir, but our mission is intact. We are staying the course toward the corporate model."

"That prick could sell diaphragms in a convent," someone said. Guido recognized the big, rough-edged voice. Figgis pushed his way out of the janitor's closet. "Tark," he said, clutching Guido's arm. "We've got to talk."

181

# Twenty-two

C HRIST, WHAT A MESS," FIGGIS SAID, SCANNNG Guido's office. "You trying to make some kind of statement? A pictorial representation of the second law of thermodynamics? Chaos in three-dimensions? Why is it so fucking *bright* in here?

"The lights are on."

"Turn them off. Do you mind?"

Guido turned off the overhead fluorescents and found his way to his desk chair. His office had no window–the darkness was total. He sat down, groped for his bottle of beer.

Figgis lit a cigarette. He was standing against the wall, next to the door. "I think I've been threatened," he said.

Guido considered this. "By whom?" he said, realizing that if he had been off campus, in a bar, say, he would have said, "By who?" or "Who by?" Sid Mullen was right: being a college professor twisted you in subtle ways.

"Who do you think?"

"They want the tape."

"I don't think they care about the tape, Guido."

"Where did you hide it?"

"Same place Freddy Marantz did. In my toilet tank."

"What do you mean you *think* they threatened you?" Guido said.

Figgis took a deep drag on his cigarette. The tobacco crackled and the burning tip illuminated Figgis's face, a brooding red mask afloat in the black air. "I followed you last night, Tark," he said. "You were too drunk to drive, but you didn't want me to take you home. I knew you'd wind up in a ditch, so I followed you."

"I was too drunk to drive, but *you* weren't?"

"I am never that incapacitated," Figgis said, resentfully.

Guido scooted his chair in the general direction of his mini-fridge. "You want a beer?" he said.

"I want a gun."

Guido found the door handle of the little refrigerator. The light dazzled him for a second. He pulled out another bottle of Tsingtao and popped it open. Then he scooted his chair back to his desk.

"A gun. Who are you going to shoot?"

"I need it for self-protection. I'm sure they will want me out of the way, too."

"Whose way are you in, Figgis?"

Figgis took a deep drag on his cigarette. He did so about every half minute. His face appeared and disappeared in these half-minute intervals, like a hilltop beacon meant to warn away very slow aircraft.

"What's the worst thing you've ever done, Tark?"

Guido in his present state of mind did not regard this as an unusual question. He thought about it for a while, then said, "I smacked a cripple, a guy with advanced amyotrophic lateral sclerosis—Lou Gehrig's disease. Not only that, I kicked him when he was down. The wind came out him like a sigh. I still feel bad about it, even though the guy was an asshole." Guido lit a cigarette. "No," he said, after a moment. "The worst thing I've done was to let my wife believe she'd be better off without me."

"What's the *best* thing you've ever done?"

Guido sipped his beer. "That's a hard one, Figgis. Maybe the last three scenes in my first book, *The Rat Eaters*."

"I know you want me to admire your modesty," Figgis said, "but I also know you're serious. In any case it's small potatoes, Tark."

"What's the worst thing *you've* ever done?" Guido asked, annoyed.

"The worst thing I've ever done, until now, was to sabotage my father's condoms. He bought cheap ones–they weren't wrapped in airtight foil as they are today. He bought them in bulk quantities and they were loose, in cardboard boxes. Anyway, I put pinholes into the tips because I wanted to have a little brother."

Guido laughed. He imagined Figgis as a kid–fat-assed and pink-faced, a furtive masturbator, a lonely boy with an I.Q. fifty points above the neighborhood average. No friends, or if he had any, they were social cripples like Figgis, kids who were picked on constantly by toughs and would-be toughs, kids who were scorned by even the ugly girls. A little brother at least would be someone who might grow to like him.

"It isn't funny," Figgis said. "The sabotage worked. But it backfired. Turned out the old man was boning our maid, Esmeralda, with the leaky rubbers. She got knocked up and filed a paternity suit. That was the end of our happy little home. I never even got to see my half-brother, or half-sister, as the case may be, though Esmeralda probably had an abortion. Dad bailed out and Mom and I moved to a cheap apartment. She died there ten years ago, while counting her food stamps. It was all my doing, Tark."

Guido stopped himself from laughing. "You can't possibly blame yourself. I mean, Christ, your old man was going to take off sooner or later anyway. A little kid wanting a baby brother doesn't qualify him for the Heinrich Himmler Award, Figgis."

"I'm not finished, Tark," Figgis said, his face appearing suddenly in the crackling glow of his cigarette. "Sometimes— rarely, I admit—the worst thing and the best thing a man can do are the *same* thing."

Guido realized at last that Figgis, in this lightless, make- shift confessional, was leading up to something big."What—"

"My bombs, Guido. They are in place, ready to be touched off." Figgis's voice in the dark room seemed to be non- directional. It came from the left, the right, from the ceiling, and from the floor. Guido felt the strong need for fresh air and light.

The men left the English building. Smoke from the refinery across the freeway had drifted over the campus. The stink of catacarb, the toxic chemical released by refineries, was strong. Figgis sneezed, Guido coughed. They covered their mouths and noses with handkerchiefs and picked up the pace.

"Here's my car," Figgis said. "Come on, I'll give you a lift."

"Thanks. I seem to have lost track of my Gremlin."

"You left it at the Andrade place," Figgis said.

*"What?"*

"I followed you there. Everyone knows that big house on the hill. Nicho Andrade's got a piece of the action. At least for a while. His *maquila,* Cortronics, has a contract with Global Visions to make their infernal machines."

"I know that. But what was I doing there? I don't remember a thing."

"You were all over the road, Tark. It's a wonder you didn't get picked up by the cops. Andrade threw you out."

He remembered something then, a dream of flying, of com- ing down out of the air, of skidding down a gravel driveway. "Oh shit," he said. Guido pulled up his sleeve. His right arm was bruised from the elbow to the wrist, a magenta welt. The grain of pebbles was still visible in his skin.

"The woman, Doris I think her name is—isn't she one of your students? She screamed at you, Tark. 'Don't come back, you prick,' something sweet like that. What did you do to her, anyway?"

"Oh man. I fucked up."

"Her husband wasn't too thrilled with you. He's the one who tossed you down that steep driveway."

Another memory fragment came back to Guido. This cheered him up somewhat—his blackout wasn't total, which had to be a good sign. What it signified, he wasn't sure. Nicho had come back to Doris, or at least that's what he'd told Guido, and Doris didn't contradict him. Guido had laughed in hurt disbelief, then said something nasty—"You're a good lay, Doris, but only in cyberspace,"—and Nicho had tossed him out.

Figgis steered his big sedan out of the parking lot. His depth perception, as well as other navigational talents were at the low-end of acceptability. Guido held his breath as Figgis mashed down on the accelerator, narrowly missing parked cars on either side, hitting speed bumps without slowing, braking hard when he didn't have to.

"You said someone threatened you," Guido said, hoping that by distracting Figgis from his driving, his driving would improve.

"One of those advance men from Singapore. He was at the Andrade place. He helped me pick you up and put you into my car."

"What did he say?"

"Oh, he was very polite. Very nice, really. He said, 'Don't get into the water at the deep end of the pool if you don't know how to swim, professor.'"

"Very metaphorical."

"But it's too late. I'm in over my head, Tark. I don't know if I can swim or not. In any case, I don't regret it."

186

"What made you think they don't care about the tape?" Guido asked.

"I studied it for a couple of hours this morning. It's just a list of the conspirators. Lex Xenedes was on it. He's in electrical engineering. Has something to do with micro-wiring. But all these people are already well-known, and what they were doing is public knowledge–to anyone who wanted to dig a little. I mean, IPOC proceedings are not conducted in secret."

"Then what's all the fuss about?" Guido said.

"I don't know. Maybe they're just paranoid. Big power people usually are. When you've got billions to lose, you get nervous. It's only human."

Figgis drove to the north side of the campus. The street here overlooked the backside of the Applied Technologies Complex. He turned off the engine and set the parking brake. After lighting a cigarette, he reached under the seat and took out what looked like a toy walkie talkie.

"What's that?" Guido asked, suddenly anxious. If Figgis was in deep water, Guido did not want to drown with him.

"It's a radio controller. Kids use them to fly their model planes."

"You've got a model plane?" Guido asked, pointlessly. Figgis was not a man who played with toys.

Figgis had little mechanical aptitude. He fumbled with buttons meant for the fingers of children. "It has a range of about a half-mile. You can boost the power by using higher voltage batteries, but I don't think that's necessary. Maybe I'll invest in a higher quality one, next time."

The blood drain out of Guido's face. "Nice talking to you, Figgis," he said, reaching for his door handle.

187

"The device has a radio-activated triggering mechanism, Guido," Figgis said, taking a deep drag on his cigarette. "You can buy the parts in any hobby shop."

Figgis exhaled and at the same time a puff of beige smoke shot straight up from a small concrete shed situated about a hundred feet from the Applied Technology Complex. Two seconds later, Guido heard the basso *thrump* of the explosion. Pieces of the shed roof rained down on the adjacent grounds.

"Test run. No one got hurt, Tark." But Guido was gone. Figgis rolled down his window and yelled at Guido. "I just trashed the ATC air-conditioning unit! Without it, their computers will go off-line! I've shut the bastards down for a few weeks!"

Figgis kept yelling, but Guido, trotting now, wasn't listening. The more he heard, the more culpable he would become. And he had no desire to teach English from a prison cell.

# Twenty-three

GUIDO SLOWED TO A WALK. A WALKING MAN is invisible; a running man gives out invitations: Notice me. Study me. Remember me. He walked steadily away from the school toward downtown La Siberia. But he was unable to regulate his pace. A walker's pace is dictated by his destination, his reasons for going there, and by his frame of mind. Guido's only motive was escape, fueled by adrenaline.

His knees were shaky. His pulse was audible, a spongy ebb and flow rushing past his auditory nerves. His gait was irregular—his left foot stepped out too far, or his right foot hovered indecisively above the pavement as if it were tied to helium balloons. The left foot minced and then, in compensation, the right foot stomped. He did not feel in control of his legs. The chemistry of fear ruled his body. *Just fucking walk,* he told himself, but he knew he looked like an unfit laborer losing control of a heavy, unbalanced load.

When he reached the business area of town, he stepped into a narrow cafe and ordered coffee.

"Don't you want lunch?" the waitress said. "Get our special— the French dip. You get all the cole slaw you can eat with it."

"Okay," Guido said, not wanting to be remembered by this waitress as a nervous man suspiciously untempted by limitless cole slaw.

Two men were at the counter. They both wore gray topcoats. It was not cold enough yet for topcoats. "Get that tired old fuck out here," one of the men said to the waitress.

"I told you, he's busy," she said.

"Busy my aching hiney. Tell him Milt and Eddie got the items for him."

"Like what *items?*" she said, huffy.

"Like his balls in a Glad Bag. Now go tell him or do I have to come all the way around this counter and tell him myself."

"Geez," the waitress said, losing some of her nerve. "You guys sure are grouchy today." She was a tall, painfully skinny woman with a wilderness of teased hair. It radiated out from her head in stiff red snarls.

She wiped her hands on her apron and pushed through the swinging double doors into the kitchen. Guido heard a man's voice yell out, "Oh for Christ sakes!" and the waitress yelling back, "I told you, Ronny! I *told* you they'd be comin' today!"

The little drama distracted Guido from his anxiety. Ronny came out, wearing a chef's hat and a filthy white apron. "Hey, Milt! Eddie!" he boomed, smiling and extending a friendly hand. "How you doin'? You want something to eat?"

The one called Eddie took a notepad from his coat pocket. He flipped over some pages. "I got you down for five, Ronny. I believe that's what you said last month. Correct me if I am wrong. That's a hundred bucks. You goin' to come through for us, or you goin' to play it tight, like we never once pulled your tushy out of the fire ?"

Ronny went to the cash register. He took out some bills. "I can't do five, Eddie. I'll do three now, maybe the rest next week."

Eddie looked at Milt. "We won't make our quota," he said, glumly.

"I'm sorry fellas," said Ronny. "It's been a rotten week. That's the best I can do. Check out that uptight-looking guy over there. He's our first lunch customer, and see,"—he indicated a clock on the wall—"it's after one already."

The two men looked at Guido. They were big men with square jaws. One had a nose like a blue yam, the other had almost no nose at all. Both had hard, unblinking eyes that seemed to recognize him. Guido never saw these men before, but he also had a moment of recognition. Guido's neck hair stiffened and his mouth went dry.

"Fine," Milt said, turning back to Ronny.

"Hey, no kidding," Ronny said. "You know I appreciate what you fellas do."

Milt smiled, held his hands out, palms up. "I said no problem, Taxpayer. We understand what you're saying. You want something to eat, Eddie?"

"Here? I guess not."

The two men left. *"Fuck* you!" Ronny screamed when they were beyond hearing range.

"Cops," the waitress said to Guido. "Buying their lousy Police Association benefit tickets is like paying for mob protection."

"Those were cops?" Guido said.

"Two of La Siberia's finest. Milt Capoletti and Eddie Thorsen. It's a tag-team operation. They like to bust heads. But, hey, who's complaining? Nobody wants sissies for cops."

Guido's legs started moving under the table. "I'll skip lunch," he said. "Not hungry after all."

"Wonderful," Ronny said. "Just fucking wonderful."

Guido paid for his coffee, then left the cafe. He started hunting for a cab. When he found one he directed the driver to the Andrade house.

His car was there, parked at the side of the steeply sloped driveway. The keys were still in it. Guido considered going to the door–to apologize–but the house looked forbidding in the daylight. The drapes had been pulled closed behind the tall windows. When he started the car, he thought he saw a drape move. He waited another minute, then released the emergency brake. The old Gremlin made a human groan as it surrendered to gravity and began to roll down hill.

Guido drove to Figgis's house. The front door was locked, but the back door was not. He went directly to the bathroom and retrieved the tape from the toilet tank. He peeled off the plastic wrapping and went into the bedroom. He found a beat-up Gladstone bag in Figgis's closet next to a pile of dirty clothes. He put the tape into the bag.

Out of curiosity, he went into the garage. It had been cleaned up. All the bomb making material, except for several cases of aspirins, were gone. Guido left by the back door. It was a warm afternoon and the neighborhood looked abandoned. He hoped it was.

He drove home. He turned on the TV set just in time for a mid-afternoon news break. Two fire trucks were on the back lawn of the Applied Technology Complex. A fire department official was being interviewed by a young reporter who had less television presence than the man he was interviewing.

"Yes, it was a bomb blast. That much we're certain of," said the suave official.

"Do you suspect a, uh, terrorist group?" said the reporter.

"Kenny, we suspect *no* one and we suspect *every*one. You understand? At this point we have no idea what we're dealing with. It could be an organization, it could be a lone anarchist, it could be the work of a mental defective. Or it could be a case of simple, mindless, sociopathic vandalism—you know, the joy of destroying for the sake of destroying."

"Have you made an assessment of damage yet?"

"Oh yes. The air conditioning plant has been totaled. It will have to be rebuilt from the ground up."

Guido checked the other news stations, then surfed through a dozen channels. On the E! channel, a tattooed psychologist who looked more like an outlaw biker than a shrink was defending Reichian orgone boxes. "I've seen great grandmas recover their orgasmic birthright," the man said. This reminded Guido of his forgotten appointment with Dr. Burnaby. He went back out to the Gremlin and raced to Burnaby's office, arriving two minutes early. But Burnaby had overbooked, and Guido had to wait over an hour anyway.

When he got back home, he took a hot bath. He had a few hours before his dinner date across the street at the Dark's. He didn't think he had the wherewithal to deal with a social occasion, but now he was armed with a promising new pill.

The phone rang. He let it ring. On the twelfth ring he got out of the tub.

"Thank you for answering," a female voice said.

*Jesus,* Guido thought.

"Are you still feeling all right?" she said.

"Yes, Carma. I'm feeling all right."

"I'm so relieved. Won't you come by some time? I mean, I feel I owe you something. A dinner, at least."

"You don't owe me anything, Carma."

"You'll be happy to know that I'm back in therapy. I'm really committed to the program this time."

"Good. That's very good, Carma."

"I am grateful to you, you know."

"Grateful?"

"You didn't tell on me. You could have made a lot of trouble for me, Professor Tarkenen. I think you are a special person. Really, I do."

"I'm not so special."

"Some day, when you are least expecting it, I will pay you back for your kindness."

She hung up.

Guido left the phone off the hook and went back to his bath. The hot water did not take away the chill he felt.

193

# Twenty-four

G UIDO FELT PREPARED FOR THE EVENING ORDEAL. Dr.
Burnaby had given him a ten-day free sample of a new
mood elevator, Placidex. Burnaby's enthusiasm for the new
product was contagious. Placidex did two things, according
to Burnaby. As a hypnotic, it cooled down the central nervous
system, so difficult situations could be met with calm and
reason. On the other hand, it also tweaked the CNS, much
like speed, so that, even though you were somewhat laid back,
you could still function with full—perhaps beyond full–
alertness. "With this product," Burnaby had said, "Guido
should be able to do a handstand in a hail of bullets while
trading quips with his tormentors."

The drug performed as advertised. Guido felt placid as well
as mentally quick. He'd had to sit in Burnaby's waiting room
for an hour-and-a-half while the doctor dealt with five other
patients, all, evidently, with the same 3:00 P.M. appointment.
Guido almost left in disgust. He was glad he'd stayed.

Burnaby, as a legal drug-supplier, had many devoted
patients in La Siberia, most of them quite young. The girl
Guido sat next to in the waiting room couldn't have been
more than sixteen—a nervous little blonde with a pinched face
and Shirly Temple ringlets. She was into body piercing in a
big way. Each ear held a dozen tarnished loops. Her tongue
was pierced in two places—she spoke with a fetching lisp. She
had smaller loops at the outside corners of each eyebrow,
and a heavy nose ring rimed with solidified mucous. She
sneezed often, making her ear loops jingle. Guido, always

194

interested in human anomalies, asked her why she had come to Dr. Burnaby. "It's my ma," she said. "She gets too wired around me unless I eat my tranks."

Guido thought about this. "Why doesn't your ma eat tranks if she's so uptight?" he asked.

"Oh, she eats them. We're all on some shit or other, even pa, though what pa's on doesn't come from a doctor. My little bro, Jessup, he can't sit still in his first grade class, so they've got him on something, Ritalin, I think. It lets him sit still and stare straight ahead, like the teachers want. It lets him be normal. Half the kids in his class are on Ritalin."

Guido took two Placidex capsules, then went across the street to Alice Dark's house, a bungalow scented with memories. Rich sauces and cooking meats—the spiced air of his mother's kitchen. There was nothing better than southern Italian home-style cooking, and the only place you could get it was in the home of a native born southern Italian. Western restaurants didn't come close.

"This is my niece, Mr. Tarka'," Alice Dark said. "Seraghina McWorter. But her real name is Campanella, Italiana, like me." She rubbed her small, thick hands together with nervous energy.

Guido put down the Gladstone bag—he wasn't going to let the Inverness tape out of his sight—and extended his hand to the woman. He'd gotten her all wrong in his daydreams. She was not unattractive. Neither was she beautiful. But *beauty*, Guido had come to believe, was a shallow and always changing convention useful only to ad men and jerk-off artists. Seraghina had light brown skin and kinky black hair—a Sicilian probably, with more North African nucleotides in her genome than European.

Sicily—the crossroads and bastion for a thousand armies since day one—had been visited by semen of all tints. Guido had an uncle, Gianni Marinetti, a barber from Siracusa, who had milk-white Scandinavian skin, flaming red Germanic hair, and eyes gray as highland fog—a northern European to anyone asked to guess.

Seraghina McWorter looked like a diminutive Sophia Loren—darker, thicker at the waist, more primitive looking. She reminded Guido of old sepia photographs of his grand-mother. He could see Seraghina leaning out of a second story window in a stone house on a narrow southern Italian street, arms folded across her round breasts, a squall of children behind her in the dark musty rooms. She was not young. Her hair, though black as tar, had streaks of gray in it. Guido guessed she was about forty-five, maybe fifty.

A small face appeared from behind her skirt. "This is my grandson, Steven McWorter," Seraghina said. "Steven, say hello to Mr. Tarkenen."

The boy was about four years old. He had dark, precocious eyes alive with intelligence and mischief. He extended his hand to Guido, clicking his little heels together like an old-style European diplomat. "How do you do, sir," he said, pumping Guido's hand up and down.

Guido thought: *A grandmother. A blind date with a granny.* A good-looking, sexually alive granny, but a granny nonetheless. He glanced at Alice Dark but she would not meet his amused gaze. She clucked with forced heartiness, rubbed her hands vigorously on her apron, her darting eyes belying her merriment. Guido enjoyed her discomfort, but didn't share her apparent conviction that Seraghina was "damaged goods"—too old and too used-up to find a new man. He was attracted to her on a level that had nothing to do with age or mileage. The chemical interchange, (he hoped it was an interchange), transcended conventional prejudice.

During the small-talk before dinner he went on automatic pilot, answering and asking questions with tact and even wit, but none of it registered. Fear, and now a windfall lust, conspired to pull him into a feverish distraction.

Alice laid out a marvelous feast of Calabrian cooking. Guido sat next to Seraghina. His thigh pressed against hers—not on his initiative, nor on hers, but a result, he was sure, of the magnetic attraction of affinitive flesh. *Christ,* he thought, *I'm fucking falling in fucking love.* They ate dinner—five courses in all—thigh-to-thigh. The gods were full of careless whimsy. His soul was drunk on *amore,* good cooking, and Chianti—all boosted by Placidex.

"You still have that deathtrap piece of garbage?" Pryor Dark asked him. Pryor, the Mercedes-Benz mechanic, had made an appearance only after dinner was on the table. He was a small, humorless man, with the demeanor of a prelate. He wore a Rolex on his thin, hairless wrist, and glanced at it often as if important matters were waiting, elsewhere, for his counsel.

Guido didn't understand the question. He'd been smiling at his *bracciola,* cutting into the rolled and stuffed flank steak with smug appreciation for the odd and sometimes benevolent turns his life took. And yet behind this cruel illusion of contentment he saw buildings explode, heard sirens scream, felt the cold terror of the hunt stiffen the hair at the back of his neck.

"I'm referring to your, ah, *car,*" Pryor said.

"Right," Guido said. "It still runs."

"It was an abortion when it came off the assembly line. But, then, so many American cars are." His nose crinkled slightly, the corners of his thin mouth turning downward. "I personally drive a 1954 300SL Gullwing, which I restored myself. It will

197

still do one-hundred forty-five twenty-four hours a day. No American car comes close. Don't talk to me about the Corvette—a piece of plebeian iron at best."

"I hate cars," Seraghina said. "Even Mercedes-Benzes. Machines in general bore me. I've seen all the damage I want to from machines."

Guido, interested, pursued this. It turned out that Seraghina worked as a technician in the La Siberia forensic medicine lab. Guido made a mental note to ask her later for a tour of the facility. She could be a resource person, and he was always on the look-out for new ways to kill people fictionally. Working with pathologists, she would have seen things civilians couldn't imagine.

After dinner Guido and Seraghina went out to the back deck. Guido lit a cigarette. He'd had a little too much Chianti, and along with the anti-inhibitory effects of Placidex, he was afraid of what might come out of his mouth if he tried to get personal prematurely. What he said now would have consequences. He was content just to sit next to her in his deck chair, taking in her scents. And she had them, the dark earthy musk of pheromones. The strong aromas of food and the beckoning scent of perfume could not mask their bittersweet power.

The boy, Steven, came out to the deck. "Grandma, can I watch TV?" he said.

Seraghina took him into the house and a moment later Guido heard the blare of the TV set. Alice, from the doorway between the kitchen and the deck, said, "What can she do? The boy's mama run off with some fancy gigolo. The papa, Seraghina's son, cannot take care of the boy and also work. So it is up to poor Seraghina to be the mama all over again. And then her husband, that stink-bug Mitchell, he run off—I hope all the way to Hell!—with a woman who drinks worse than him."

"Oh, Alice," Seraghina said, returning to the deck. "You're turning my life into a soap opera. Steven is no burden. I love the boy. And don't call me *poor* Seraghina—I'm a long way from cutting my wrists." She sat next to Guido. Their thighs touched again, and Guido inhaled her dark and subtle fumes stealthily.

The sun was down under the telephone wires and the air was almost chilly. Alice brought out a bottle of galliano, leaving the decanter on a small table in front of their deck chairs. *Greasing the wheels,* Guido thought, *the old baggage.* But Guido's wheels did not need greasing. He was already half in the bag and lugubrious with romance.

Seraghina in the half-light and cool air had the heart-breaking loveliness he always saw in Mediterranean women. It wasn't a physical thing. It was a range of feeling, a spectrum of attitudes. Loss and gain were accepted as equal possibilities. These were women who could mock their own allure with a skeptical smile, for they knew that nothing, absolutely nothing, lasts.

*I'm drunk and stoned,* he told himself. *I make up shit when I'm drunk and stoned.* He filled two long-stemmed cordials with galliano and, with a sense of ceremony, gave one to Seraghina. He felt that romantic longings had been excited in her, too, for her dark eyes met his and did not break contact. There were depths in her eyes that reached back through the centuries. They touched glasses as if an agreement had been made.

The sun sank behind trees and houses and the desert sky turned blood red. "Rage, rage against the dying of the light," Guido said.

"What?" Seraghina raised her head from the back of her deck chair. "Did you say something?"

"Dylan Thomas," Guido said. "I was thinking of his villanelle for his father."

Guido recited the rest of the poem. He was a little drunk, but not drunk enough to mimic the silver-throat tones of Dylan Thomas. He understated each line, kept his voice low and flat. It worked.

"That's lovely," she said. "Why don't people write poems like that anymore?"

"They can't," Guido said. "Or they're not allowed to. Maybe it comes to the same thing."

"Not *allowed* to? Why not? Who's to stop anyone from writing what they want to?"

Guido shrugged. "Television," he said. It was as good an answer as any. "The Mafia," he offered. "The Communists, the Capitalists, the Know Nothings in Charge. *Quien sabe?* Maybe the real poets are in hiding, underground."

He felt bold. He recited "Where Once the Waters of Your Face," with passion.

"Where once the waters of your face
Spun to my screws, your dry ghost blows. . ."

He dropped understatement and let his voice soar Dylan-like. *Not bad,* he thought, but knew he was kidding himself. Yet he imagined the back yard bathed in the quicksilver of his voice. A wildness not strictly his expanded his lungs. He imagined birds catching their breaths, halting their evening songs. He recited "If I Were Tickled by the Rub of Love," and "Death Shall Have No Dominion," and watched her face, its mixed genetic lines crossed with tragic racial news. He watched her eyes, and thought he saw the beginning of tears.

Some familiar noise irked and alarmed him. It came from inside the house. Unwelcome visitors had entered and were disturbing the moment. And then he understood the noise was electronic, and coming from the TV set. He put down his glass and listened. A squawky female voice said *Oh yes, oh yum yum*. A man howled shyly through gritted teeth.

Guido stood up quickly, lifting the table with his thighs, knocking the bottle of galliano over. He went into the house, found the TV set—a 48 inch, high-definition Hitachi projection screen. Steven McWorter was sitting on a divan, the Gladstone bag next to him. He was sucking his thumb and watching a larger-than-life Lotty Gassaway energetically fellate a larger-than-life Gregory Inverness.

# Twenty-five

S*OLLY/LEX. CP POMONA. 11-9. EVE. lect. dumps point-one axonic nanowire re fizwiz connectors., etc. etc. into the damn P.D.*

Guido saw that last detail, the detail that had been invisible on Figgis's small TV set, and before he made his apology, his absurd excuse, and his exit, he took the time to jot it down. Alice, wiping her hands on a dish towel, came into the room and stared, bewildered, at the projection screen, her mind unwilling to decode the images. She snorted, as if what she had seen was merely ludicrous, and left the room. Pryor, who had been attracted by Inverness's ecstatic moans, observed the action, his lips curling down in disgust. He looked as though someone had hung fuzzy dice from the rear-view mirror of his classic 300SL.

Guido ejected the tape, stuffed it into the Gladstone bag, and apologized profusely. Seraghina looked at him, perplexed. "I see you're a fun-loving kind of guy," she said. Guido had protested that the tape wasn't his, someone at the video store had made a mistake, but he knew—his heart sinking like a stone—that he'd been dismissed by this remarkable woman.

When he got home he called Figgis, then hung up after six rings, realizing that his incoming call could be traced with caller ID equipment: Figgis's house might be full of cops.

A minute later his phone rang. He decided not to answer it, then changed his mind.

"Hammer and Tong," a muffled voice said.

The voice was crudely disguised—graveled  yet bleating—but it was Figgis. "I can't be seen with you," Guido said. "You're all trouble, man."

But the caller had hung up.

Guido decided to leave town for a while. Then decided against it. He made himself a drink, sotol and lime juice, and knew it was a mistake. He carried his drink into the bathroom and studied his face in the medicine chest mirror for a long time. He didn't recognize himself. There was an impostor in the glass. His eyes showed too much white. His hairline had receded. His skin was too pale, perhaps even tinged with green. The lump above his ear was visible—it had shed some hair and the dead white of his scalp showed through.

*Fuck it,* he thought. He put on his coat, put his father's pistol in it, and—after one sotol-inspired piece of madness—drove his deathtrap piece of garbage to the Hammer and Tong.

"I understand what they're up to," Figgis said, "but it won't save the school."

They sat in the semi-dark. The bar was packed with the usual crowd of dissolute deadbeats. A woman at the bar had her arms around the shoulders of two men. One man was laughing menacingly, the other was face down on the bar, chuckling in his sleep.

Figgis had deciphered most of the abbreviated message. "Solly Dubrinsky and Lex Xenedes," he said, "designed the wiring technique for the silicon neuron. When you're dealing with devices that can only be seen with an electron micro-scope, you create major wiring problems for yourself. You can't just go down to Radio Shack and buy a roll of copper wire and a couple of pounds of solder. You've got to create a totally new method. You need wires that make pussy hair look like hawsers. You need connecting hardware so small

203

you could hide a million of them in a gnat's rectum. I'm guessing that Solly and Lex developed some patentable techniques for wiring and connecting the chips."

"Global Visions must know that," Guido said.

"Sure they know. But look–'CP Pomona. 11-9 Eve. lect. dumps point-one axonic re nanowire fizwiz connectors, etc. etc. into the damn PD.' I don't know what 'fizwiz connectors' are–some abbreviated tech lingo for hardware, probably–but the rest is easy. CP Pomona is Cal Poly at Pomona. Their evening lecture on November 9–two days from now–will dump their patentable ideas into the PD–the public domain."

The woman at the bar made a staggering pirouette away from the men. Guido recognized her. Olive Higgins.

"I still don't get it," Guido said.

"Jesus man! What *do* you get? Research universities can act like secret government agencies when it comes to patentable ideas. If some researcher blabs about an idea in the wrong forum, the idea will likely become public property. Then nobody gets the patent. Now put two and two together, Tark. The silicon neuron is already out there, available to anyone. But the way you arrange the little buggers in chips and how you wire the chips together is not. La Siberia Tech owns that–but obviously the patents are only pending."

"So if Dubrinsky and Xenedes give the secret away in a public lecture–"

"It's down the commode. The Global Visions people won't like that. I had Solly and Lex and the rest of them wrong. I thought they were trying to buy into the action. But they were only trying to save the school. Noble as hell, but either way it's not going to stop the takeover. Global Visions stands to lose a hell of a lot of money if Solly and Lex get away with their plan–it would be like Apple giving up their windows technology to all comers fifteen years ago. Even so, Global

Visions will still have the jump on the rest of the world in making these goddamned contraptions."

Guido tried to process all this. "Then how come they don't need this tape anymore? Seems to me that it has exactly what they want to know."

Olive Higgins weaved her way over to their table. "Haven't we met, honey?" she said to Guido.

Figgis pulled a newspaper out of his coat pocket. "They don't need it because the lecture has been announced." He opened the paper to pictures of Dubrinsky and Xenedes. "'Professors Solomon Dubrinsky and Lex Xenedes are giving lectures and symposiums at California Polytechnic Institute at Pomona, Friday, November 9th, in which they will discuss nanowiring techniques for very small computer chips.' And so on. This is last Sunday's paper. Hell, they know now exactly what Solly and Lex are up to."

"Why did they announce it?" Guido asked.

"Chutzpah, I guess. Maybe they're underestimating what the Global Visions mob is capable of."

"Or they're trying to scare them off by threatening to give up the secrets. You know, make them believe that it won't be worth the trouble or expense to buy the college."

"Scare them? I don't think they scare, Tark."

Figgis was drinking bourbon and soda. Guido was drinking ginger ale. The sotol had infused his brain with useless romantic bravado. He'd gone back to the Dark house, before coming to the Hammer and Tong, to apologize and explain, but was distracted by a vision. He stood outside the front windows of the house and looked in at Seraghina who was alone with her grandson in the living room.

She was standing, looking, it seemed, directly at him. He ducked down behind a hedge, but realized that in the brightly lit room she could only be seeing her own reflection in the picture window. He stood up and spoke to her, knowing that he had become a ghost–an achievement of sorts–invisible, unheard, mostly forgotten and thus unbothered by the living.

Olive Higgins sat down. "You going to buy me a drink, sweety?" she said, looking first at Figgis, then at Guido. Figgis signaled the bartender.

"How you doing, Olive?" he asked.

"Do I know you? You seem to know me. So, I guess I know you. Who the hell are you, sugar?" She turned to Guido. "And you. I guess I know you, too. I guess we're old companions. Is that it? Are we old partners, honey?"

"He stopped some tired old hardleg from abusing your dignity," Figgis said.

"My hero," she said, indifferently. "My knight in shining armor. Now, how about that drink."

# Twenty-six

GUIDO DROVE TO 101 HOWARD STREET. It wasn't clear to him why he was doing this. His fear of Carma was marginal, but it nagged at him like a sensitive tooth.

He practiced what he would say. "Look, Carma. It's over. The wound was nothing, a scratch. Hell, that wallop you gave me in the bar has more staying power. . . ." And so on. He would act as if she were sane, and she would be moved to respond with a sanity-mimicking act of her own. They would shake hands, maybe even embrace, and that would be the end of it. Goodnight and goodfuckingbye. Don't call me any-more, don't promise me any promises.

It was late, but he suspected she was a nocturnal type. He was right. All the lights in her half of the small, stucco-sided duplex were on. He knocked on the door, stepped back into the full glow of the porch light so that he would be completely visible in the fish-eye lens of the peephole.

The door opened. "It's you," she said. "Come in."

Guido hesitated, realizing instantly that his view of humanity was often too simplistic. That was fine for pulp fiction, but dangerous in the real world, especially if you actually believed your own reductions. Personality was a mystery that wasn't going to be solved. Her eyes told him this. They were fright-ened eyes, but they were eyes that had faced demons. Courage and sadness and resignation darkened them with depths that gave him vertigo. He understood, then, that he had nothing to say to her and that he had no reason to be here.

He stepped into the small, spartanly furnished living room. Chintz was the dominant fabric, printed with depressing floral designs.

"I'm glad you came," she said, but her face showed neither gladness nor disappointment. She was wearing sweatpants and a tee shirt. There was a light film of sweat on her muscular arms, the veins prominent. She'd been working out.

"I'm not sure I know why I did," he admitted.

Then she smiled. It was a private, Mona Lisa sort of smile, the source of amusement secreted away in a maze of Byzantine logical connections. He realized what her smile meant: Maybe *he* doesn't know why he's here, but *I* do.

Guido ran through the possibilities: *You're here because I willed it. You're here because fate led you here. You're here because, at this confluence of time and space, you could not be anywhere else. You're here, Professor Tarkenen, because I didn't kill you.*

"Sit down," she said. "I'll make you a cup of coffee. Or would you prefer some Amoretto?"

"Coffee," Guido said.

She went into the kitchen. He sat still for a few minutes listening to the kitchen noises she made–a reassuring domestic clatter–then stood up. She had a small bookshelf. He went to it. Most of the books were current best-sellers, plus a half-dozen or so reference books. One book he recognized. *Bride of Night.* Martin Gassaway's book. He pulled it out and opened it. It was a personally inscribed, book-club edition.

To Carma—

My incandescent Amazon! I treasure
the memory of our nights (and days!).

"A" of course, for your final grade—in
World Lit., I mean! A+ in all other respects!
I only regret the unpleasant terminus.
                                    —Marty

Why should he be surprised? Gassaway had a reputation
as an undiscriminating fuckabout, so why not a disturbed
secretary from the School of Education? *I only regret the
unpleasant terminus.* What kind of asshole would use a word
like "terminus" backing out of an affair? The academic kind,
the kind who screws a student then grades her performance.
*A+ in all other respects!* No wonder Carma had told Guido, "I
won't take it anymore. Not from any of them, and certainly
not from *you.*" Guido wondered who the others were–professors, no doubt, professors she'd been taking classes from,
trying to improve her situation. But why had she allowed
herself to be used by them? Wrong question. There was no
petri dish big enough to accommodate personality. Too many
variables, too much dark electricity bolting about in the brain's
twisted channels. Too many sub-atomic genetic demons
carrying out wars of attrition for the host and all his doctors
to tag and root out.

Guido thumbed through the book. Some passages had been
underlined, some had been underlined twice. He read a few
of these: *Could Orphelin kill for love? Orphelin asks himself that
brutal question a dozen times a day. And the answer is invariably
the same. Love and death are linked in the unending dance. What is
Orphelin's is always Orphelin's, today, yesterday, and tomorrow.
Orphelin is a man of principles, even though his principles are narrow,
inflexible, even selfish. Yet, he holds to them, for nothing else defines
his character so well. Orphelin carries no tophamper of societal concern
in matters of possession.*

209

*Marty, you are one stuffy puppy,* Guido thought.

Then she was behind him, her arms circling his waist. *Whoa, Carma, I didn't come here for that,* he thought, but when she withdrew she was holding his father's .32.

"What's this for?" she said, holding the gun up to the light, as if she could identify its intent by studying its form. "Did you come here to kill me?"

"For Christsakes, Carma," he said. "No. Of course not."

She'd slipped the gun out of his pocket smoothly, and now she pointed it at him, and Guido felt the sudden rush of fear he'd felt in the arroyo, a déjà vu panic, as he faced this armed and grievously damaged woman.

"I don't like you coming here with a gun," she said, abstractedly.

"How did you come to know Marty Gassaway?" Guido said, wanting to get her mind off the gun.

"I met him in the weight room, at school. He's a lifter, you know."

This surprised Guido. Gassaway just seemed like one more rumpled professor to him. "Marty? A lifter?"

"Definitely. I spotted for him the day he benched two-eighty," she said.

"And then you took his World Lit course."

"And then I took his World Lit course." Her eyes went distant, recalling the sequence of events that led up to the "terminus."

Carma regarded him for a long moment. Guido felt his mouth going dry. "I bet you came here for a good time, professor," she said. 'Did Marty tell you about me?"

"No. Not at all. I came . . . well . . . I came because you, uh, sort of invited me."

"But you were expecting a good time. Isn't that true? That's what they all want. Their wives can't, or won't, do what I do."

She held his father's .32 casually, but the barrel was pointing at his lower anatomy. "I just came to see how you were doing," Guido said, and even if there was more than a grain of truth in this, it rang false.

"No, no," she said. "It's okay. I understand. A man can't help being a man, can he? I mean, it's the hormone thing. You're a victim as much as you victimize, don't you think?"

Guido tried to think fast. He needed to be cagey with his answers now. But his mind stayed stubbornly blank.

She laughed. It wasn't a cruel, or insane, laugh. It was genuinely merry. Which, considering the circumstances, may have been insane. "Come on, tough guy," she said. "I'll show you a good time. My kids are with their grandma. We can party all night long."

She led him down a hall toward one of the bedrooms at gunpoint. Guido, in spite of his fear, tried to imagine what she had in mind. He felt doubly stimulated—by adrenaline and rising lust. His heart was beating fast and his hands were damp.

The room was a mess. A weight machine occupied one corner, a pile of laundry was stacked on a table. An ironing board was set up against a wall. There was no bed. Carma straddled the bench of the weight machine, still holding the .32 on Guido.

"You came here to help me, right?" she said. "To see if I was okay, and that everything between us was cool. Right?"

"Well, sure," Guido said, bewildered.

"Good. Then plug in that iron. I've got a big backlog, and I have nothing to wear tomorrow morning."

"I don't get it."

211

"Ironing. I need some ironing done. It shouldn't be too hard for you, professor. Once you get the hang of it, you'll enjoy it."

"Carma. . . ."

She raised the gun and pulled back the hammer. "Come on, be a good sport," she said. "I really need some help. And you're a kind and understanding sort of man, aren't you? I mean, that's why you came over here, isn't it? To give me a hand with my problems."

Guido plugged in the iron. "Where do I start?" he said.

"The skirts. Hold them up by the waist. You'll see that most of them are rump-sprung. That comes from sitting in front of a keyboard all day. You'll need the steam setting."

Guido held up a skirt by the waist. The back of it bagged out, distorting the lines. Rump-sprung. He put it on the ironing board and ran the iron over it.

He did ten rump-sprung skirts, then switched to acetate blouses. "Now be very careful with the collars," she said. "Don't run creases into the points. That looks awful. It makes people think you've been sleeping in your clothes. And you know how people talk. And watch out for the buttons—they can melt."

Guido ironed carefully, avoiding creases. When his hot iron slid over the armpit area, the vaguely acrid fumes of residual sweat made his nostrils dilate. It was a sexual smell, and that, he realized, was as close to a sexual experience as he was going to get that night. It made him laugh, but he held the laugh in, disguising it as a cough.

As he ironed, Carma straddled her work-out bench doing biceps curls with forty-pound dumbbells. The pistol was snugged, grips first, between her thighs. Within easy reach. Guido ironed oxford shirts, denim skirts, burned himself several times on hot fabric, felt the muscles in his neck and shoulders tighten and begin to ache. At one point, two hours into his labor, he needed to urinate. Carma led him to the bathroom. She stayed with him. It might take a while, he said, embarrassed. I've been having a problem with my prostate. That was fine, she said, we're in no hurry, are we? She sat on the edge of the tub–gun in hand–while he stood over the toilet bowl, waiting. And when he finally finished, she led him back to the ironing board where he pressed six rayon skirts that would normally go to the dry cleaners but were not dirty enough to justify the expense. It was hard work. He never really got the hang of it. He was plagued by "cord drag"– the iron's cord creeping over an ironed area, re-wrinkling it. The hems in denim skirts seemed to be permanently creased and no matter how much steam he used, or how hard he pressed down on the iron, he could not get rid of the crease. Button-down collars almost made him cry. He'd melted a button on one of them, ruining it, and hid the mistake from Carma.

By four A.M. he had finished.

"Good work," she said. "How about some breakfast?"

She still had the gun pointed at him and so he didn't refuse. She fixed him eggs and bacon and English muffins with marmalade, and he realized that in spite of his fatigue and anger and fear, that he was ravenously hungry. She poured him coffee and he was grateful.

When he finished, she broke open the cylinder of the .32 and shook the bullets out and then gave his father's pistol back to him.

"I wish more men were like you, Professor Tarkenen," she said.

# Twenty-seven

HAROLD SORENSON, A BIG, SELF-IMPORTANT kid given to bluster and rebuttal, said, "Why do we have to *read* this detritus?" He was sure his professors admired his aggressive style. Guido didn't. Sorenson's hand shot into the air every five seconds. The hand, and the thick, white arm that raised it, was like a exclamation point among the passive faces of the other students.

Sorenson was complaining about a crime novel he had to read for Guido's "Wild Bunch of Modern Lit" class, *Bustin' Out,* by Crazy Red Fingerhut—three escaped cons on a coast-to-coast killing spree, the daughter of a senator as their hostage.

"Why not?" Guido said. "It's good writing and fun to read."

"But it isn't even remotely *relevant.*"

Guido thought about that. Of all the words in the English language, "relevant" was the one he detested most when applied to writing. It made fiction a branch of the social sciences. The last thing he wanted to be was "relevant." To be relevant you had to write about something that other people believed *ought* to be written about—i.e., a Worthy Subject. Guido hated Worthy Subjects. The last thing a writer should write about was a Worthy Subject.

But he had no fight in him today. "How so?" he said, mildly.

"I'm on page one-hundred and I'm afraid his subtextual agenda hasn't been thought out very well," Sorenson said.

Agenda. Another word that made him cringe. Once someone in a bar asked him what his "agenda" was. Guido asked the man to explain. It's where you're coming from, man. It's the monkey on your back, the hair up your ass, the bee in your bonnet. Guido considered this. I don't have an agenda, he said. The man laughed at him. Then you are one self-deluded dude, he said. Everybody's got an agenda these days. Ask your congressman. Ask your barber. Ask some gang-banger's fuck-slave. The man found out Guido wrote crime novels. He jumped on that. You write novels about dark deeds, but you don't take a stance? Bullshit, man. *That's* your agenda. Guido protested this. It's not like that at all. I just put people on stage. Being against evil isn't an agenda, it's a normal impulse, like the sex drive or the need to breathe. The man wasn't convinced, and Guido knew his argument was unpopular. But having an agenda implied premeditation which ruled out spontaneity. Without spontaneity there could be no honesty.

A writer with an agenda, then, had to be dishonest at times in order to protect the precepts of his agenda. This was a difficult argument to make. Guido did not offer it to the man.

Relevant. Agenda. Once they were just innocently useful words, but now they had lost their innocence. They were loaded, dangerous, radioactive.

"Some people don't have agendas," Guido said.

Harold Sorenson smirked. "Where did you go to graduate school, Professor T?"

"I didn't," Guido said. "I don't even have an undergraduate degree. I have a high school diploma."

"Well," Sorenson said, making a broad, palms-up, *case-closed* gesture, "there you have it."

Guido didn't want to get into it. His shoulders and arms ached from his night of ironing and his head was still full of wonder at the unpredictability and range of human conduct. He still felt a little dazed.

He walked to the windows that looked out on the parking lot. It was one of those splendid fall days in the high desert–

sixty degrees, the sky so blue it made his teeth ache, the breeze northerly and sweet. "The world is still beautiful, isn't it?" he said aloud, but mostly to himself. "It's got staying power. But then, *so what,* right? It isn't relevant. Look at it this way. You're cruising along, thinking everything is just fine—between you and yourself, you and the world, or you and your woman. Then one day—or night—" He turned from the window and was surprised to see his students watching him closely, listening to him. He felt almost resentful, as though he'd been overheard, but decided to continue anyway. "One night, say about three A.M., you're reading a book while your wife sleeps next to you. She's beautiful awake but she's even more beautiful asleep, like. . . ." He gestured toward the window, ". . . like today, out there. I mean, asleep she's a part of the natural world—without a personal history. She's so beautifully unhistoried you feel like bawling. Then, suddenly, her eyes open. She isn't awake yet, but her eyes are open. Those eyes are looking at you but not with recognition. 'Who are you?' they seem to say. No—they don't *seem* to say, they *say—Who are you?* It's an impressive moment, looking into those wide-open, sound asleep eyes, eyes that feed your face directly into her pre-conscious self, the self that has no personal history. I'm talking about the pure objective indifference of that self, and how it is completely unlike you. You are not *relevant* to it. It doesn't give a shit about you."

Guido paused, wondered why he was doing this. He wasn't even sure what he was driving at.

The class was silent for a moment, then Sorenson said, "What's this got to do with anything?"

"I don't know," Guido said, turning back to the window. He conjured up a picture of Kirsten sleeping. He closed his eyes and began speaking again. "Here is this woman you've been intimate with. No, 'intimate' is a pissant word. Let's be straight about that. This is a woman you have *fucked* for five years. You've kissed her breasts and sucked her nipples. You've gotten your face down between her thighs and worked her clit until you thought you'd sprained your tongue and you've heard her sigh and moan and felt her back arch with the exquisite pleasure of it, and the pleasure was just as much your own. This is more than 'intimate,' isn't it? For five years you've been one animal under two skins. And you've played these games everywhere—in motels, in cars, in tents. She's sucked your cock while you were driving down a remote mountain road in Arizona, she's jerked you off on a ferry boat on Puget Sound. You've fucked standing up in an elevator in Lisbon, and once in her mother's bathroom while her poor fuckless father practiced his yodeling in the backyard, bombed on Southern Comfort. You name it—you and she have done it."

Guido turned from the window. Some in his class were red-faced and grinning, others were pale, their mouths hanging open, some were already walking out. "Sorry," he said. "Didn't mean to get so, uh, earthy. I'm trying to say something here. I mean, this is a woman you've been *close* to for five years. And then one night she opens her sleeping eyes and looks at you like you were nothing more than a face in a crowd. You see? What could her *agenda* be? Who is she, in that moment? And what part of that moment carries over into daylight? Has the seed of your future irrelevance been planted by some trouble-making incubus with an *agenda?* Are you going to get letters from her, from San Diego, addressing you in a way that makes you think she's become someone else, someone you don't know and could never know? Is she going to be screwing some son of a bitch who, she says, has *principles?* It's a fucking mystery, isn't it? *I'm* mystified, I'm totally fucking mystified."

Guido stopped himself.

"You've offended a lot of people here today, *Professor* T," Harold Sorenson said gravely, "and you're still not making any sense. Have you been trying to justify the Fingerhut book or your own, obviously screwed-up life?"

"Both," Guido said. "But it doesn't matter. You're going to read the book, agenda or no agenda." He faced the window again. "School's out for good at the end of this semester, but I think you'll still want your transcript unblemished by an F or Incomplete."

"He's got an agenda after all," Gudenbach said, packing up her books. "Antediluvian as it is. I think it's called Professor-T-holds-the ace-of-trump."

"I'd call it decadent fascism, plain and simple," Sorenson said.

Guido looked at his watch. There was twenty minutes left in the period, but he was suddenly gripped by a fatigue that went bone-deep.

"Class dismissed," he said.

Joyboy, followed by Red Crow, approached his desk. "You need something,man?" Joyboy said.

"He's acting so *baked*," Red Crow said.

"Baked?" Guido said.

"Stoned, in quaint parlance," Joyboy said. "I've got some primo windowpane if you're into touring."

"Touring?" Guido said.

"Tripping, in bygone lingo," Joyboy said.

Guido didn't know what windowpane was and he was in no mood to go touring. *Touring*—even the drug culture lingo had become Republicanized. "I'll pass," he said.

"Cool lecture," Red Crow said. "I liked the part about the sprained tongue. It gave me goose bumps all over."

Guido went to his office and took a Tsingtao out of his fridge. He lit a cigarette. He wondered, briefly, what had gotten into him in that classroom. And then his phone rang.

"Guido, I got your message," Martin Gassaway said. "You have something for me?"

"I do. Where are you?"

"In Alana's office. Can you come over?"

"I'll be right there."

Guido finished his beer and cigarette, took the tape out of his desk drawer, then walked down the hallway toward Alana Falconburg's office.

# Twenty-eight

GUIDO PASSED OLD DAWKINS'S OFFICE on his way to see Alana and Gassaway. The old man spied Guido, hissed at him through his half-opened door, his rheumy eyes glittering. Guido stopped.

"Ubi sunt qui ante nos fuerunt?" the old man said. "Where be they who before us were?"

Guido shrugged. "Feeding the clover, I guess."

"Thou leavest me here sole in these fields! Yet I will not despair!" The lucidity of madness gleamed in the old professor's merry eyes.

"Go for it, doc," Guido said.

The old man studied the backs of his frail, liverish hands. "I'm old," he said. "I have been in love with literature for fifty years and more. But nowadays this is considered intellectual onanism, something to closet away." He brightened again. He came at Guido, hunched and playful, his hands waving before him like parchment flags. "Sing, cuccu nu!" he chanted, his voice crackling with glee. "Sing, cuccu, sing! Sumer is i-cumen!"

"I hear you, dad," Guido said.

The old man flashed his skeletal hands out at Guido as if the crooked fingers held a transforming magic. "Sing well, my boy! Never you cease!"

"I'll try," Guido said, and continued on his way.

Guido reached Alana Falconburg's office cheered by old Dawkins's fierce little display. It was nice to think you could

220

go out a playful crackpot, full of gentle raving, the familiar fears gone.

"I knew I could count on you, Guido!" Gassaway said. "How did you manage to find the tape?"

"Professional secret," Guido said, handing him the cassette.

Alana tried to kiss his cheek but Guido turned just enough to get his lips in the way. He put his hands on her waist and held her for a moment too long and she stiffened and started to pull back but then relented, her mouth opening slightly, their tongues touching, and Gassaway coughed and stepped in like a referee separating clinched boxers. Guido caught Gassaway's eye and saw a flare of rage in it, and took note of that—but it all happened in a few seconds—and the three of them laughed like close friends, the moment, and whatever meaning it held, gone.

"We're so grateful to you," Alana said. "Honestly, we didn't think you'd be able to help us."

"Today's the deadline, isn't it?" Guido said.

"Today at five," Gassaway said. "They're coming for it."

"I only found one tape," Guido said. "They may not be happy about that."

Gassaway's tic started up. "Yes. Well, they probably have the others. From the break-in, you know. I'm sure they were just fishing when they suggested there was more than one tape missing."

"At least we have *some*thing to give them," Alana said. "It shows good faith, doesn't it?"

"I'm sure they'll be tickled," Guido said.

Gassaway pulled out his wallet. "I want to give you something, for your time and trouble," he said. "This means a lot to me, Guido."

"Not necessary. It was no trouble at all." Guido touched Alana's arm. *"Mantenga la fe,"* he said.

221

She looked at him, puzzled. Then brought her hand to her mouth.

*"Qué le vaya bien,"* Guido said, and left.

Guido went back to his office and opened another Tsingtao. He glanced at his watch. It was 3:45. He had an hour and fifteen minutes to kill. He dug his city phone directory out from a pile of student papers and looked up *McWorter, Mitchell.* He dialed the number. Seraghina answered, but it was her recorded voice, asking him to leave a message after the beep.

He didn't. He looked up the number of the City Crime Lab and dialed it. He asked for Mrs. McWorter, was put on hold. Some beatless New Age strains, like the lowing of talented cows, softened his earwax for five minutes and then her voice came on.

"Yes?" she said, hesitant. Clearly, she didn't receive many phone calls at work.

"It's Guido," he said. "Guido Tarkenen."

"Well, surprise surprise," she said.

"Listen, about the other night," he said. "It really was a mistake, you know. I don't go in for that kind of stuff, honest. I'd like to explain what happened, in person. How about lunch tomorrow?"

"You're saying that you're *not* a masturbatory voyeur? That I'd be comfortable with you?"

Guido closed his eyes. "Yes. That's what I'm saying."

She laughed. "I'm putting you on. I didn't think you were a deviant. But when you bolted like a scalded cat, it didn't look very good."

"The boy. . . ?"

"Steven didn't know what he was looking at. He thought it was a Jacques Cousteau underwater special. You know, writhing tentacles and strange reptilian fish slipping in and out of dark grottos. It did seem aquatic somehow, didn't it?"

222

They talked for five minutes, like old friends, and when Guido hung up he felt as if life had given him a reprieve. They'd made a lunch date at a good downtown restaurant. The door was open and his foot was in it.

To kill some time, he took a walk across campus. The place had already lost much of its collegiate mood. It now seemed more like the high-concept industrial park it soon would be. He saw only a few students on the impeccably manicured grounds of the upper campus. As he walked past the H-beam gigantopod sculptures—they still seemed poised for mindless rampage—he felt a chill. But, he decided, he *liked* that. Art that did not affect the viewer viscerally was not art. And art that had such an effect could not be pointless.

He approached the reflecting pools that bordered the Applied Technologies Complex realizing that he'd never been inside those post-modern cathedrals of high technology. He decided to have a look-see.

The building he entered had a lobby paved with Italian marble. The entryway was an arboretum, humid with tropical and semi-tropical plants. Just inside the doors there was a bank of elevators housed in glass tubes that carried students and faculty to the upper floor classrooms, offices, and labs. If there were staircases, Guido didn't see them. In the center of the lobby, an attractive, middle-aged woman sat behind a white semi-circular desk. "May I help you, sir?" she asked as Guido approached.

"Just looking around," Guido said.

"Are you with the Vice Chancellor's tour?"

"I teach here. I mean, not *here*, but in the English Department."

"Do we have one of those? I never knew that. I suppose you could join the tour if you wanted to. I recommend it.

223

They're going to look at the new state-of-the-art CAD facility. It's the future of *every*thing!"

The woman's enthusiasm was contagious. The future of *every*thing was a compelling notion, but Guido saw himself as a malingerer who would most likely not qualify for life in the coming new state-of-the-art century. "I don't know what CAD is," Guido admitted.

"The computer assisted design facility. It's absolutely fabulous. Nothing like it exists anywhere else."

"Are the computers actually working?" Guido asked

She frowned. "Oh, you mean the vandal who destroyed the air conditioning plant. Luckily the weather cooled off. All they had to do was open the windows to cool the mainframes. No problem. That loonybomber who planted the device is probably having fits."

"The loonybomber?"

"That's what they're calling him."

A very large naval officer entered the building. He walked briskly past Guido and the receptionist. His stride was charged with purpose. He touched the bill of his cap as he passed, uttering a crisp, "Afternoon, ma'am." He gave Guido a long, somewhat stern look as he marched by. The man seemed to have grave matters of national security on his mind. He went to the glass elevators, thumbed the Up button.

There was something critically un-military about the man, who now stood before the glass elevator tube, tapping his foot impatiently. Guido saw that his first impression was wrong. The man might have been attached to someone's navy, but it wasn't the U.S. Navy. He wore a naval officer's white dress tunic, complete with epaulets and battle ribbons, but his hat seemed to be a milkman's hat, off-white, with a short black bill, and he was wearing wraparound sunglasses. His seafarer's beard was clearly fake. His trousers were not white.

They were apple-green, radically pegged at the ankles, zoot-suit style. His was wearing black and white spectator shoes with creamy laces.

The naval officer was also carrying a radio control device.

Guido, paling, looked at the receptionist.

The receptionist rolled her eyes. "We get all kinds of garden variety doofuses on these tours," she said.

Guido left the building. The Vice Chancellor's tour—jovial, well-fed men in expensive suits—came out of the middle building of the complex. The group, about two dozen men in all, strolled toward the building Guido had just left. Even the Chancellor was in the group—old Doc Weatherall who had been with La Siberia Tech since the groundbreaking ceremony fifty-odd years ago. Weatherall, mostly a figurehead now, smiled vaguely from his wheelchair, his oxygen bottle rattling alongside. He didn't seem to know exactly where he was or what he was doing there.

Guido shaded his eyes and looked up at the Palladian windows. The white tunic of the bogus naval officer filled one of them. The man leaned on the high sill, his radio controller held out to avoid interference from the surrounding structure. Guido walked briskly away from the area. Figgis was about to strike again. *Where* was anyone's guess.

When the tour group was safely inside the building, Guido felt the earth hum under his feet. He turned to see fireballs lift the gigantopods out of their concrete footings. The following sound and shock wave made Guido's bladder tingle. Four explosions followed.

Figgis had planted his bombs so that the gigantopods could become ambulatory. The first devices had been planted under the rear footings of the structure. The succeeding explosions came from bombs planted under the central and forward footings. The sequential timing was perfect. Figgis's aspirin-based bombs lifted and propelled the tonnage of artfully shaped steel forward so that they seemed to be sprinting. The H-beam supports tore ottoman-size divots from the perfect lawn as the sculptures caromed toward the reflecting pools that bordered the Applied Technology Complex. Free at last from constraint, the massive gigantopods seemed like jubilant warriors bent on breaching the ramparts of a blood enemy. But they crashed into each other at the reflecting pools, which acted like moats. The sculptures, robbed of their fury, settled in the shallow waters, tangled and steaming.

Guido hurried back to the lower campus and the English building. He didn't want to be questioned as a witness, and the ignored English building, which wasn't a part of the main campus, was a good place to hide. He sat in his office, the door locked, listening to the grieving wail of sirens. He sipped a beer, read a few student papers. Gaia Gudenbach had attached a note to her turgid denunciation of Crazy Red Fingerhut's *Suck It Up*.

> This book antagonizes and debases
> everything I believe in. I am writing
> to the Chancellor about you and your
> perverted ideas. Nothing you teach
> has educational value. If I am demon-
> izing you, professor, it is because
> you are, unquestionably, a demon,
> a weak demon without credentials.

Guido wrote on the note: "This is your best writing to date, Gaia. There's passion here, not the usual stuffy posturing."

He looked at his watch. 4:58. It was time to check his hunch about Gassaway. He left his office and went out the back door of the building. Except for his Gremlin, the parking lot, hazy with effluent from the refinery, was empty.

It was still empty at 5:00, and at 5:15. He waited for another fifteen minutes. No sign of a green Lincoln. And no sign of Martin Gassaway or Alana. Just to be sure, he waited until 5:45. Which was long enough.

Inside his Gremlin he could smell himself. He was skunky with nervous sweat.

# Twenty-nine

GUIDO READ HIS MAIL IN THE BATHTUB. One letter–from Kirsten:

Dear Guido,

Thank you! The papers came today. I know you need a sense of closure as much as I do. Can we remain friends? We share an interesting if turbulent history, don't you think? I for one don't regret our time together. I hope you feel the same. Duke (Duke Marston) my fiancé, is a therapist here in La Jolla (CGR—Cognitive Guilt Reframing) and he assures me that a "Clean Bilateral Break" as he calls it, benefits everyone.Duke is a fine human being, Guido, with wonderful depth of feeling. You would like him. He's a man's man—top-ranked in dressage, a crew member on a racing yacht, and a black belt in one of the martial arts, the one where nobody hits anybody and no one gets hurt. It's like modern dance, actually. They have a great respect for nature and lobby for the humane treatment of animals. I could go on and on, but I really only wanted to tell you thanks, thanks from both of us. I'm intensely happy now, perhaps for the first time in my life.I guess I never really understood what happiness was. But Duke enlightened me.He enlightens me every day. On every level it's a spiritual trip. I know you'll make it too, Guido. Don't give up the "Good Quest!"

Kirsten

Guido sat in hot, neck-deep water thinking there might be something to this subtext-agenda business. What did she think she was saying to him? Did she really think he wanted to hear about her newfound intense happiness? The letter-between-the-lines  was more directly to the point:

Dear Loser,

I'm happy and you're not. I'm getting fucked regularly by a sensitive New Age man's man with principles, and you can't get laid in a whorehouse with a fist full of fifties. What did I ever see in you?  What did we have together? Five years of confusion and misery! My new guy has brains, soul, and a body to die for, and you are a slumping has-been. Gee, don't you feel like a warmed-over cat turd?Hang in there, pal. Remember, life is short. Maybe not short enough for you, but short nonetheless. There's comfort in that, right? Ciao,  Lost Boy.

Not quite fair, Guido knew, but not quite wrong, either. *Duke!* A therapist named Duke! A black belt cognitive guilt reframer, at that. A sailing saint, a top-ranked horseman, an animal rights lobbyist, a sensitive guy who recommends the Clean Bilateral Break and the Good Quest. What woman wouldn't be happy with him?

228

Guido got out of the tub, dropped Kirsten's letter in the gray water, put on a bathrobe, and turned on the evening news.

It was all bad. A two-car wreck on the freeway, five members of a family dead. A cholera outbreak in Bajomitío. An apartment fire on the east side. A kidnapping on the north side. A murder-suicide in a tacky motel on the west side.

A reporter was at the scene of the murder—a spirited young woman with a raspy voice and wide, permanently alarmed eyes—some producer's smart casting for the crime-scene beat. "Two La Siberia Tech professors, Solomon Dubrinsky and Lex Xenedes, were found shot to death in the Swinging Deuce Inn," she said. "Police are withholding details pending further investigation. It appears, however, that Professor Dubrinsky shot Professor Xenedes to death, then took his own life. No motive has been given as yet."

Guido made himself a drink. The ice was stubborn. He slammed the tray down on the counter and scattered ice cubes around the kitchen. He didn't bother to pick them up. He put three cubes into a tall glass, then filled the glass half with tequila, half with water and lime juice, and rimed the rim with salt. Then he went back to the TV.

". . . bombs, big bombs," another reporter was saying. He was standing in front of the Applied Technologies Complex, the wreckage of the gigantopods behind him. This reporter, in contrast to the young woman, had a studied casualness about him, as if major news events bored him. "The bombs, professionally placed and detonated, did no significant damage but appear to be a warning of things to come. The FBI believes a militia organization is involved since a man in a self-styled officer's uniform was seen in this building"—he gestured suavely to the ATC building behind him—"minutes before the explosions."

Guido shut off the TV, called Figgis. He let it ring eight times before losing his nerve. Then he called Trimmer Swenson. Swenson didn't know where Figgis was. "Probably touring the wino bars," he said. "He hasn't shown up for work for some time. I've been covering his classes. I guess he's thrown in the towel on the semester, in spite of his contractual obligations."

Wind spanked the house. It was one of those hard, buffeting desert winds that come out of nowhere. The house creaked, the windows vibrated, and the loose weather-stripping around the front door throbbed like a vocal cord, giving the wind voice. It rasped two notes on the metallic strips, the notes harmonizing, their harmonics establishing third and fourth notes, until it seemed that voices raised directly from hell itself were demanding admission to Guido's small house.

Guido bolted the doors, made sure the windows were locked, then re-loaded his father's pistol. He turned out all the lights and sat on the sofa with his drink, the pistol in his robe pocket. When his drink was half gone, he picked up the phone and dialed, from memory, Seraghina's number.

"I'd like to see you tonight," he said.

"Not possible," she said. Her voice was indifferently inflected, as if someone was next to her, someone to whom her late night phone calls mattered.

"You've got company?" he said, his heart sinking.

"Not company. My husband is here."

"I thought. . . ."

"He's picking up some things. That's all."

"Then later? Maybe later. . . ?"

"No, I don't think that would be a good idea. I'll see you tomorrow."

She hung up first. Guido held the phone to his ear until the dial tone came back on.

# Thirty

H E PUT ON HIS BEST GABARDINE SLACKS, a new shirt and tie, and a wool houndstooth jacket. He stood back from the mirror and assessed his appearance. Not too bad. In the attenuated light of a restaurant, he'd look better than passably good. The frayed edges–his red-rimmed sleepless eyes, his pallor, and the now chronic anxiety that gave him stomach spasms–might not be noticed.

She was there, waiting. This cheered him: she wanted to make an impression, too. She was wearing a pink, long-sleeve silk blouse, a black skirt, and black patent leather slingback sandals. Her wheat-colored linen jacket was draped on the back of her chair.

"Been waiting long?" he said. She was holding her wine glass by the stem, tilting it. It was empty.

"I got here early," she said. "I was in the neighborhood anyway, so I thought I'd get us a table." She saw him looking at her glass. "I'm a little on edge," she explained. "Last night was crazy. I didn't get much sleep."

"Your husband. . . ."

"Mitch left shortly after you called. I meant all the action last night–the freeway wreck, and then the murder/suicide on the west side. I had to go in at midnight to help with the autopsies of the two professors. I didn't get home until four this morning."

The dark half-circles under her eyes made them look bruised. He remembered the Italian actress, Anna Magnani–who was not pretty in any Hollywood sense–and how those same dark shadows gave her a quality that disturbed him, even though he was only twelve years old when he saw her in The Rose Tattoo. He pitied the woman, who looked older than his mother, until another emotion undercut the pity. He didn't know what it was but it made him squirm in his seat and spill his popcorn and choke on his Coke. That night, at home, he masturbated for the first time in his life, and the image he held in his mind as his furious fingers chafed his penis raw was Anna Magnani and the dark half-circles under her eyes.

Years later Dr. Burnaby urged both Guido and Kirsten to talk about their earliest sexual feelings. Guido told his story of pity and lust, and Dr. Burnaby suggested that this scenario was still active in Guido's relationship to women. Guido thought about that and admitted that he in fact liked women who were mildly depressed–women who were privately embattled but spirited enough to smile about it.

"Good Lord," Burnaby had said. "Does Guido know what he is saying here?

Guido said, "Yes he does. Or maybe not. I mean, *what?* "

Burnaby, talking directly to Kirsten, said, "Guido, you see, requires women who are easily manipulated. He wants them to be *grateful.* "

"What's wrong with that?" Guido said, and both Dr. Burnaby and Kirsten had smiled at each other knowledgeably.

"Kirsten is not depressed," Burnaby said to Guido. "Kirsten is strong, but Kirsten is strong like a dock. Weak men harbor themselves in her quiet waters. Kirsten gives Guido's unseaworthy ship refuge."

Guido called a waiter over and ordered a carafe of the wine Seraghina had been drinking, the house cabernet. "You must see some ugly things in your work," he said. "How do you do it?"

"You get used to it," she said. "I was a surgical nurse before I took this job. But I've always had a cast iron stomach. Even when I was a kid. Dissecting frogs in 7th grade science was easy for me. In fact, I did it for the squeamish kids when the teacher wasn't looking."

When she paused to sip her wine her eyes went distant, as if she were visualizing the difficult terrain of her past. Guido liked that look, and he wondered, wryly, if Burnaby hadn't been on to something. Maybe he did like them damaged and in need. But what did it matter? You liked what you liked. You are free to choose what you want, but not free to choose what you like. *That* "given" was beyond analysis and therapy.

He was here because of her, not because of her job. But he had to know. "Has anyone figured out why Dubrinsky shot Xenedes, and then himself?"

"For love, what else?" she said.

"You mean there was a woman involved?"

"No, I don't mean that. They were homosexuals. Evidently Professor Xenedes had broken it off. Dubrinsky couldn't handle it. Simple as that."

"This was well known? That they were gay?"

"Apparently not. Both were family men. This was something new in their lives. It happens more often than you think, these reassessments. Eros rules."

The waiter came by for their orders. Seraghina ordered a small steak; Guido asked for the same. The salads came first, large-leafed Caesars with croutons the size of lug nuts. Seraghina ate hungrily, without self-consciousness, and Guido liked that, too.

"How do you know it was a gay thing?" he said. "I mean, there could have been a dozen reasons why it happened."

She nodded as she chewed. "Right. But, it happened in the Swinging Deuce Inn. A well-known trysting place for gays. And, they were both naked–suggesting a consensual arrangement."

"Even so. . . ."

"You want the forensics? It won't spoil your lunch?"

"I've got a good stomach, too," Guido said. "Maybe not cast iron, but strong enough."

"We did them early, before they stiffened up. It takes three or four hours for rigor mortis to establish itself. We did Xenedes first. There was classic evidence of anal penetration–they had their tryst before Xenedes told Dubrinsky the affair was over."

Guido's curiosity was now professional. "What kind of evidence?"

"Abrasions extending from the anal margins to the anus itself, as well as major fissures–there had been some bleeding. The anus also had a major distension–two-finger insertion was no problem. The fissures involved the entire depth of the mucous membrane. For some reason they didn't use lubrication. I guess they got caught up in the heat of the moment. There was some incidental bruising on Xenedes' wrists and ankles, as well. Apparently they played the bondage game."

"Pretty convincing," Guido said.

"There was one anomaly. If they'd been lovers for even a relatively short time, Xenedes' anus would have begun to show the characteristic funnel-shape. But it didn't. The pathologist was inclined to think that Xenedes was new at the game, and that Dubrinksy raped him because the dilatation was extremely violent, but he gave up on the idea."

234

Guido noticed that people at nearby tables were looking at
them with open disapproval. One woman covered her mouth
with her napkin, as if fighting the urge to retch.

"What made the pathologist think differently?" Guido asked.

"It didn't make sense. You can look at a lot of evidence and
come to all sorts of conclusions, but they've got to make sense
in the long run. Fecal matter was found on Dubrinsky's penis,
and in Xenedes's mouth. After the anal there was the spontaneous oral. It wasn't rape. This was a very passionate moment
for them. The finale to their brief affair. Then it turned bitter."

The woman who looked as if she were about to vomit stood
up and went to the ladies' room. The man with her glared at
Guido. He took a savage bite out of his dinner roll and chewed
defiantly, his cheeks bulging, his face dangerously red.

Guido ignored him. He was thinking about the Crime Lab's
unlikely conclusions. Guido knew there was more to it than
the forensic evidence implied. There were unanswered questions the pathologist wouldn't have thought to ask. What were
Dubrinsky and Xenedes, for instance, doing in a motel in La
Siberia the night they were supposed to be in Pomona delivering a symposium? The convenience of their deaths to Global
Visions was another factor the forensic people didn't know
about. But he didn't raise any of this with Seraghina. He hadn't
come here expecting to pick her brain.

"Now you tell me something," she said. "What were you
doing with that tape? It wasn't commercial porn, the actors
were too homely and inept–a plain-jane housefrau and a
nervous accountant. It was a home video, wasn't it? So whose
was it?"

Guido hesitated. If he lied to her their relationship would
start off on the wrong foot. On the other hand, telling her the
truth might get her involved in the thing he wanted to get
*un*involved with. He decided on partial truth.

"You're right, it was a home video. Gregory Inverness and Lotty Gassaway. Someone tried to blackmail the Gassaways with it. I recovered it for them."

"Professor Inverness? The man who was murdered last week?"

"The same."

She sipped her wine. "That was a nasty one," she said. "His head was crushed so badly it was almost flat. Even some cervical vertebrae were broken. The killer hammered Inverness with a cantaloupe-sized rock twenty to thirty times."

"Over an F in calculus."

"Motives come cheap," she said. "Some people are kicked to death for a handful of change."

They left the restaurant. Guido walked Seraghina to her car. "I want to see you again," he said–too earnestly, he realized. Her job, her enthusiasm for it, had eclipsed her Anna Magnani appeal. But now it was there again, out on the sidewalk, the wind lifting kinked strands of her gray-streaked African hair, her skirt clinging to her thighs, her shadowed eyes looking up at him, wine-dark but inscrutable behind her lowered eyelids. He wanted to kiss her, and he sensed her willingness to be kissed, her full lips were moist and slightly parted, and he knew they were both experiencing vertigo, the precipice inches away, but he didn't press the moment. *Time enough for that,* Guido thought. He took her hand in his.

"Eros rules," Guido said, quoting her.

Seraghina laughed. Her laugh was low and breathy. It made Guido dizzy. "I want to see you again, too," she said, giving his hand a squeeze that had more promise in it than a written invitation.

# Thirty-one

GUIDO DROVE TO THE HAMMER AND TONG. Figgis wasn't there. He checked the wino bars in that part of town with no luck. He drove to Figgis's house. It looked abandoned. He knocked on the door and heard the hollow echo of his knocks amplified in the empty rooms.

He drove home. A deep shudder reached his viscera. He thought he was getting sick, but it wasn't him. It came from the car. The car was sick. It coughed and wheezed. The high-temperature warning light came on. The oil pressure warning light came on. He was a mile from his house when the car started to spasm. It shivered like an animal full of malaria. A fecal stink of torched rubber filled the front seat.

The stricken car swooned into his street. Guido slipped it into neutral and coasted the last fifty yards. He parked it in his driveway and turned off the ignition but the engine continued, suicidally, to diesel. Guido listened to the whistling screech of metal sheering metal.

Pryor Dark came out of his house. He saw Guido behind the wheel of his suffering Gremlin. He'd had a dispiriting morning at the garage. Someone had traded in an seven-year-old 190E for a new S600 coupe. He'd been asked to inspect the trade-in. The car ran a bit too hot, and the boss, Wolfgang Schnur, an aggressively suspicious, monocle-wearing Bavarian with rigid, old-world standards, wanted to know precisely why.

Pryor didn't approve of the relatively inexpensive 190E–Mercedes had no business making a car for the unwashed masses–and this one ran fourteen degrees too hot, he discovered, because it had been "souped up"–a *major* transgression, as far as Pryor was concerned. One did not tamper with Mercedes-Benz engineering, even in bottom-of-the-line cars. *Any* Mercedes was a work of art. "Upgrading" or "modifying" one was as intolerable as tampering with the works of Michelangelo. One did not "tweak" the frescos in the Sistine Chapel. The engine displacement of the 190E had been increased from 2.6 liters to 3.8 and its horsepower nearly doubled by increasing the piston stroke and by boring out the cylinders. The cylinder head had been *milled,* the perfect, factory-machined metric head bolts replaced by common SAE studs. *"Mien Gott in Himmel!"* Wofgang Schnur cried out, for head-milling was an unthinkable violation of Mercedes engineering, a violation that raised the compression ratio precipitously. And as if that were not enough, a low-restriction stainless steel exhaust system had also been added, giving the 190E a distinct working-class roar.

Pryor, stoically enduring the ennui of mild depression, had come home for a late lunch break and was unexpectedly presented with a satisfying little morality play called The Death of a Piece of Crap American Car. He settled into an Adirondack chair on his porch with his sandwich and coffee, prepared to enjoy the death rattles of the absurd Gremlin. The car was an industrial freak, a child of 1970s bandwagon thinking. The AMC people chopped what appeared to have been a full-size sedan in half to produce a "compact" that was expected to compete with the Japanese. It was, without question, the silliest car ever made.

The in-line six appeared to be tearing itself apart. Black smoke now billowed from the hood. Guido climbed out and stepped back from it warily. The Gremlin made a gagging, asthmatic sound, followed by a whirring moan. Then its agony ended. It died. This delighted Pryor. He brought his thermos cup to his thin smile and sipped.

*Bravo,* Pryor thought. *Melodramatic, yet completely satisfying.*

He set his sandwich aside and crossed the street. "You're going to need a new car, I believe," he said.

Guido, who had no mechanical sophistication, shrugged. "Maybe not. It probably just needs a tune up."

Pryor smiled indulgently. Automotive innocence never failed to amuse him. "I don't think so," he said. "You've most likely thrown a connecting rod. Your crankshaft has consequently warped. I expect all this began when your timing chain failed. This means, of course, the engine, such as it was, is ruined. You'll need to have it rebuilt, but believe me, this, ah, *car,* is not worth the expense."

"Shit," Guido said. "I *liked* this Gremlin."

"You're not serious," Pryor said.

"It got me around."

Pryor did not want to further insult his neighbor. Not that he cared about the feelings of this technology-ignorant pornophile. What concerned him now was the tidy sum of money that could be his if he played his cards right. Technically, he was not a member of the sales force, but it was Wolfgang Schnur's policy to give a commission to any of his employees who brought in a paying customer.

"I have the perfect car for you," Pryor said. "A *real* car, one I guarantee you'll fall in love with."

He told Guido about the 190E, how it was being offered at well below "book" because of the engine modifications–modifications, he assured Guido, that would have no effect on the car's reliability. He detailed his inspection procedure, and why he gave the car a low rating–Mercedes buyers were not looking for drag-strip hot rods–and how his boss wanted the car off the lot as soon as possible since it was an embarrassment to him personally. All that aside, the car was still a *Mercedes-Benz,* the best automobile in the world.

239

"How much below book?" Guido asked.

"I can let you have it for twelve-five. Believe me, it's a very good deal."

Guido considered this. He did need a car, and maybe a Mercedes would be good for his image. A successful writer perhaps *should* drive a "statement" car. How else were people going to know you were successful? Especially if you weren't all that successful.

"Bring it by," he said. "I'll have a look at it."

"I'll do better than that," Pryor said, thinking that he had just made an easy fifteen hundred. "I'll have this abomination towed to the recycling yard and the 190E in its place by five this afternoon."

Guido went into his house. He stopped just inside the door. Something was not right. The place smelled differently. Stale coffee and the sulfurous smell of stale hardboiled eggs pinched his nostrils. October light, entering from the windows, shafted reluctantly through beige air. The usual litter of newspapers, magazines, ashtrays, and beer bottles had grown enormously and confronted him with the passive belligerence of a wretched but impotent mob. Guido resisted the impulse to turn around and walk out.

Instead, he went into the kitchen.

# Thirty-two

EDSEL HARMON HAIGHT SAT AT THE KITCHEN table eating an egg salad sandwich. Guido raised his hand to his eyes as if shielding them from a damaging light. He touched his face to see if he was wearing Doris Andrade's magic helmet. It occurred to him that every improbable thing that had happened to him in the last few days was an electronic illusion, or—even worse—that the Cybertopia machine had somehow fused its projections with the real world: perhaps this image of Edsel was a boil-off of integrated atomic particles, allowing a quantum ghost to haunt the living. A third, homelier possibility made his heart skip beats—he was merely dying, still in the arroyo, a handful of .22 caliber mini-mag hollowpoints nested in his brain, and everything that had happened to him in what had seemed like weeks was nothing more than a microsecond scenario concocted by ruptured synapses. He felt seasick with vertigo; he slumped against the wall.

"Have a sandwich, Mr. Tarkenen. They're your eggs," Edsel said. "You look pale. Don't worry, I won't turn you in for harboring a fugitive." He laughed, a nasal bleating that brought tears to his small, recessed eyes. Egg salad flecked the corners of his mouth.

"Edsel," Guido said.

"Edsel. No, I don't like that. No *way* do I like that. That's a name for bright and shiny losers. I give you permission to use my real name. Norman O'Neil. My Daddy was an admirer of that inspirational preacher, Norman Vincent Peale, and so that's what he named me. Norman Vincent Peale O'Neil. My friends call me Vince, my enemies call me Preacher."

Guido took a deep breath, beginning to see a possible explanation for the impossible. The man's head was perfectly Edsel, but his body was all wrong. Edsel was a giant, a brute, a bone-crusher. This man was short and scrawny. The big cruel Edsel head sat freakishly on a delicate neck that rose between narrow shoulders. His chest was thin as a child's and his arms and legs were reeds. His little hands clutched his egg salad sandwich like the delicate hands of a lemur.

"What are you doing in my house?" Guido finally managed.

"Hiding out, man. Taking respite from my troubles."

Guido went to his desk, found the wanted poster he'd fed into the Cybertopia machine's scanner. He studied the photograph–noticed the name for the first time, Norman O'Neil–compared it to the man with egg salad dripping from his chin.

"You're wanted for embezzling, extortion, mail fraud, attempted bribery, and grand larceny," Guido said. "It also says you're armed and dangerous, Norman."

The man waved his hand in the air, dismissing the poster's claim. "They always go overboard. I *have* a gun, but to tell you the truth it makes me a little uncomfortable. I guess I'd use it for self-protection, or if I was radically pissed-off, but never against cops. I see myself as more of a facilitator than a sociopath. By the way, I did you a favor today. You had another unwanted visitor. An ugly customer if I ever saw one, and I have seen one or two. If I were you I'd get me some window bars and better locks on your doors. These are dangerous times we live in, Mr. Tarkenen, or haven't you noticed."

Norman Vincent Peale O'Neil spread egg salad on another slice of bread, folded it in half and bit into it. Guido watched, mesmerized. "What are you talking about?" he said.

"I came in the back door. It was unlocked. There was this fat slobbo in jungle fatigues and street shoes lying on your bed scratching his balls and smoking a cigarette. I knew it wasn't you–I'd been following you around for days, ever since I saw you swipe my poster from the P.O. bulletin board. So I pulled out my .22 Ruger, threatened to ventilate his gourd if he resisted, then tied him up. He's still on the bed, the loud-mouth son of a bitch."

Guido went into the bedroom. Figgis, his face perilously red, his eyes bulging, lay on the bed, his hands and ankles wrapped in duct tape. An X of the silver-gray tape criss-crossed his mouth. Guido made some placating gestures at Figgis, then picked up the telephone. He dialed 911.

"You don't want to do that, man," Norman Vincent Peale O'Neil said. "You'll just get yourself jammed up with the law." The large head on the small body looked more freakish now that he was on his feet. His head and torso were about the same size, and his thin legs bowed out like parentheses. He had the Ruger in his tiny hand but was not pointing it. "See," he said, "if you bring the law into it, I'll just tell them you've been harboring me. That you're this crime writer who wanted to get my story, so you gave me a place to stay while you interviewed me. That would make you an after-the-fact accomplice to all the stuff they say I've done–which by the way I haven't done the half of. At the very minimum they'd get you for obstruction."

Guido re-cradled the phone. "Why would they believe you?" he said.

"Why not? You took my wanted poster from the P.O.–other people saw you do it–and now you're writing a book with a guy who looks just like me in it, at least from the neck up. I took the liberty of going over some of your papers. You're a fair-to-middlin' writer, Mr. Tarkenen, but you don't know jack about criminals."

Figgis made a strangling noise. They both looked at him. "Let me take his gag off," Guido said. "He may suffocate."

"Only if he promises to keep his pie hole shut."

Figgis nodded vigorously.

"I've got to talk to you," Figgis said when Guido pulled the tape off his mouth.

"We made a deal," Norman Vincent Peale O'Neil said. "If the commando here runs his mouth one more time, the gag goes back on."

Guido and Norman Vincent Peale O'Neil went back into the kitchen.

"Norman. . . ."

"Vince. My friends call me Vince."

"I'm not your friend," Guido said.

"Call me Vince anyway, you prick. I'm going to do you a favor. I'm going to give you my life story, all of it. Then you can write a real book about the criminal mind."

"Then what?"

"Then nothing. It's a gift. If you want to donate a few bucks, I'd be obliged. I hung around this town so I could skip into Mexico, but I think I'll go to California first and take care of some loose ends. My wife is in Long Beach with her oilcan boyfriend, Raoul. Fucking *Raoul!* I think maybe I'll kill them both. What do you think?"

Guido understood what response Norman Vincent Peale O'Neil expected. Be a man, forgive and forget, pay your debt to society, salvage what's left of your life, make a positive contribution to the world before you leave it, etc., etc. "Do it," he said. "Shoot the fornicating bastards."

Norman Vincent Peale O'Neil regarded Guido carefully. "Some punk's hiding his woody in your old lady too, huh?" he said.

"In my recent ex."

"Hey, man. That's carrying property rights a little too far. If she's your ex, then you're out of the picture. Try to live with it. Grow up, homey."

Guido made himself a drink. Norman Vincent Peale O'Neil stood next to the kitchen table, his small hands knuckling the marbled Formica surface. He seemed uncomfortable on his feet, as if his shoes were several sizes too small. He was wearing pointy, flat-heeled cowboy boots, his pants tucked into the tops. His stick-like legs were radically bowed, suggesting childhood rickets. When he walked he wobbled, and when he finally sat down he sighed with relief.

"Tight boots?" Guido said.

"Bad feet," Norman Vincent Peale O'Neil replied. "Bad legs, too. Not enough calcium or vitamin D when I was a kid. Mom wouldn't nurse—she was nothing like that creep Edsel's old lady. Jesus, where do you get such sick ideas? My old lady wouldn't buy milk, either. Some kind of weird religious cult thing about eating the excretions of the cloven hoofed animal. So we drank coffee, tea, cough syrup—whatever was handy—even when we were babies."

"We?"

"Did I say we? I meant me." He smiled, as if at some private joke. His teeth were also bad, short and gray and pointed, like the teeth of a very old terrier.

Guido sat down and sipped his drink—Cuervo and grapefruit juice. He felt he'd earned it. Norman Vincent Peale O'Neil closed his eyes and sighed wearily. "Man, I've been on the run for what seems like forever. I'd just like to sit on my porch and stare at the traffic for the rest of my life, you know what

I mean? Maybe you don't. Maybe you think you got to suck it up and charge ahead, flow with the go, that kind of crap. It ain't worth it."

"A man's got to do what a man's. . . ."

"Spare me the locker room Nietzsche, homey. The game is fixed. I been playing question and answer all my life, but it's a zero sum game. All questions are the wrong questions, if you get my drift. I mean, it's a done deal, a completed perfected con and the Big Grifter owns the table. You following this, Mr. Tarkenen?"

"No."

"I'm going to send you my life story. You use it any way you want. It's a gift. All I ask is one thing."

"And what's that?" Guido said, smiling a little.

Norman Vincent Peale O'Neil hammered the table with his miniature fist. "Don't you fuckin' smile at me that way, you prick!"

"Sorry," Guido said. "What do you want?"

"I just want you to be fair-minded. I want you to see my side of it. See, I figure I was justified half the time. Even when I did the really rank shit. Okay?"

"I thought you were just a facilitator."

"Sometimes I facilitate some bottom-echelon activities, Bubba."

"Like what?"

The tiny criminal's mouth split open into a vastly amused vee. His terrier teeth looked filed. "Like *what,* the man says. It doesn't take much to push over a leaning pile of manure. You get my drift here, citizen? Or maybe you think manure don't lean." Then his eyes widened. "Jesus, maybe you think it *isn't* all manure. You one of the big-eyed suckers, citizen? You think it *isn't* all fecal from sewers to steeple?" He studied Guido for another moment, his smile straining with hilarity, his small flat eyes wet. "You're too much, homey. Too fuckin' much. Bend over man, I've never seen a forty-year-old virgin."

With that Norman Vincent Peale O'Neil, the facilitator, stood up on his bad feet and rickety legs and staggered out of Guido's house.

# Thirty-three

FIGGIS HAD NOTHING TO SAY. EVEN AFTER Guido cut the duct tape from his wrists and ankles he continued to lie passively on the bed in his jungle fatigues, stricken, like a shell-shocked soldier. His pale eyes, in soft focus on infinity, were damp.

"Is he gone?" he said, his voice constricted. "I've never been so terrified in my life. I think he meant what he said, about ventilating my gourd. The man's a stone-cold killer. A Global Visions assassin. Jesus, my hands are paralyzed. He said if I didn't shut up he'd take off my shoes and whip the soles of my feet with his belt. He laughed at my shoes. 'G.I. Joe in Florsheims,' he said."

Guido rubbed Figgis's wrists and hands to stimulate circulation. The duct tape had left white indentations in his soft flesh. A film of residue adhesive glistened on his lips like snail slime.

"I don't think he's a killer," Guido said. "Or an assassin for Global Visions. He's an embezzler and an extortionist, among other things, but not a killer. More of a facilitator than a sociopath, he said. I believe him."

Figgis snorted contemptuously, his submerged spirits beginning to rise out of the humbling blue funk of helpless captivity. He opened and closed his hands, wincing. "Anybody's a killer, Tark, if the stakes are high enough."

247

This was one of Guido's pet ideas, and it annoyed him to hear it coming from Figgis. "True," he admitted. "But why would they send Norman O'Neil *here,* to my house, to kill you? Besides, he didn't kill you, did he? You were just in the wrong place at the wrong time. Which reminds me—what *are* you doing here?"

"I think they're coming for me, Tark, just like they went after Solly and Lex."

Guido went into the kitchen and made Figgis and himself bourbons and soda in beer mugs. He brought the drinks into the bedroom. Figgis was now sitting up. He took the drink in both shaking hands and brought it to his lips. He lowered it by half in one swallow, then belched softly. A flying cockroach big as a mouse landed on the night table. Figgis parked his mug on it. "I came in through the sliding-doors on your patio," he said. "You forgot to lock them. That freak O'Neil was already here. I guess he came in the same way. Maybe he jimmied the lock. Jesus, Tarkenen, you'd better invest in some roach motels."

Guido went into the bathroom and opened the medicine cabinet. He rummaged through the small sampler vials of various drugs he'd been collecting over the last few years. He found the Placidex. He shook two out of the bottle, swallowed one. He went back into the bedroom and offered the other to Figgis.

"What is it?" Figgis said, studying the bright capsule.

"An elevator. I thought you could use a lift."

Figgis popped it into his mouth then washed it down with the bourbon.

"When are you going to stop blowing up things?" Guido said.

Figgis shrugged. "When they stop me, I guess."

248

"Fine. In the meantime I want you out of here. I don't want to be anywhere you are."

"Thanks for your loyal support."

"You think you should be supported? You think you're the hero in this idiotic morality play you've dreamed up?"

"The hero, by definition, acts alone," Figgis said. "And yet, he has a constituency—passive perhaps—that supports him."

"You don't have any constituency, Figgis. Lunatics never do."

"Then my mission is visionary," Figgis said gravely. "Perhaps in some future time I will be seen as a cultural hero."

Guido swallowed some of his drink. Figgis maybe wasn't technically crazy, but he had the kind of ego that never questioned its own twisted logic. There was no arguing with people like that.

Guido changed the subject. "Did you know Dubrinsky and Xenedes were gay?" he said.

Figgis finished his drink and held the empty mug out to Guido. Roach fragments twitched from the mug's bottom. "You didn't fall for that crapola, did you? Don't you see? They set it up to look that way."

"Hell of a set up," Guido said. "The crime lab has solid evidence of anal penetration. Semen, fecal matter—it was all there, and in the right places. How do you set up something like that?" He went into the kitchen and made another drink for Figgis. The big eighteenth-century scholar, walking with difficulty, followed Guido. He sat down at the kitchen table, wheezing.

"They probably ran a crowbar up Xenedes's rectum," Figgis said. "The other evidence could have been added later. Did they run tests to see if the semen was Solly's? Of course not. Listen, if Solomon Dubrinsky was gay then I'm in line to be the next Patriarch of Constantinople. Lex Xenedes was also a dedicated family man–a Mason, a Scout leader, a sexton in his church. In any case, Solly and Lex despised each other. Even if they *were* gay they wouldn't have shacked up together. The only reason they were cooperating was because of their common goal of saving the school."

"But according to you they wouldn't have saved it anyway."

"That's true, they wouldn't have. But by eliminating Solly and Lex, Global Visions is guaranteed exclusive patents on the nanowiring technology. That will bring them billions–maybe hundreds of billions in the long run."

"So, what are we supposed to do? Go to the cops?" Guido said.

"The cops are satisfied with what they've got. If we tell them they're wrong, that the evidence was all rigged, that Xenedes and Dubrinksy were killed because they'd gotten in the way of Corporate Planning, they'd hold us for psychiatric evaluation. Besides, doesn't it seem remotely possible to you that the top cops might be on the Global Visions payroll? It happens all the time."

*In the movies,* Guido thought, but didn't say, because in this instance he thought Figgis was probably right. Dubrinksy and Xenedes were murdered by a third party. And that third party had to be Global Visions or someone who would benefit from Global Visions acquisition of the wiring patents. The two men drank in silence for a while, a silence punctuated occasionally by the tinkling of ice cubes against glass.

"I made a bad mistake, Tark," Figgis said after a long silence. "I went to the Chancellor, old Doc Weatherall. I told him that I thought it was dumb to sell out when the school owned patents worth billions. I mean, Weatherall's been with La Siberia Tech for half a century. Sentimental me, I thought he might still be harboring a little love for the place. But he just stared at me as if I'd pissed on his Persian carpet. I thought maybe the old man was out of the loop and the deal was being worked out by Cribbs and the trustees. Weatherall called in his secretary to escort me out. The old geezer said, 'This is none of your affair, Professor Figgis.' They probably offered the old fuck a couple of million to let the ship go down."

"So, in effect, you told the enemy everything you know."

Figgis swallowed a sob. "Inverness, Dubrinsky, and Xenedes," he said. "Where will the bastards stop?"

"Not with you," Guido said. "Especially if you keep blowing up their property."

Figgis regarded Guido somberly. "You're just spilling over with sympathy, Tarkenen."

Guido made himself another drink. "They're calling you the loonybomber, Figgis. Where's your stash of bombs now?"

Figgis drained his drink. He cleared his throat, fingered the three-day stubble on his fleshy cheeks. "This is something I sincerely meant to tell you, Tark," he said. "I just didn't have the time or opportunity. I want you to understand there were absolutely no other options."

Guido felt the small hair on his neck stiffen. "Oh Jesus," he said.

"You aren't using your basement, anyway, Tark. I just stored a few of them there. Maybe a dozen. The rest are planted, ready to be touched off."

Guido was half-way out of his chair when a horn honked. He went to the front windows and looked out at a black Mercedes-Benz parked in the driveway behind the dead Gremlin. "Look, Figgis," he said. "I want you and your bombs the fuck out of here. But I want you out of here first. Come on."

They went outside. The car was bigger than Guido had expected. The man driving it wasn't Pryor Dark. One of the dealership flunkies, he guessed. A door opened. A smiling

Chinese man stepped out. He had a neck like a nail keg and his chest spread the lapels of his suit. His thighs filled his pant legs.

"Good afternoon gentlemen!" he said, heartily. "I'm so glad we caught up with you. Please, step into the car."

"What's going on?" Figgis said.

"It's my new car. My old Gremlin threw a rod. I guess Wolfgang Schnur is giving me a test drive."

"You're buying a fucking *limousine?*" Figgis said.

"Is that what this is?" Guido said to the man holding the door for them. "I thought Pryor mentioned a smaller model, a souped-up 190E."

"Gentlemen!" the big man said, with daunting hospitality. "Please, step inside!"

"He doesn't know what you're talking about, Tark," Figgis said. "I'm getting my ass the hell out of here."

But the man opened his coat and showed Figgis and Guido a 9 millimeter automatic pistol secured in a holster clipped to his belt. "Please," he said, less friendly now. "Step into the car, we don't want to be late for the reception. You don't want to miss the dedication ceremonies, do you?"

# Thirty-four

T HE AMORPHOUS MINIMALIST SOUNDS of Muzak from the
limo's stereo system salved the air. Guido rummaged
through the coins in his pocket, counting them by feel. Eighty-
seven cents. It seemed a reasonable thing to do; it distracted
him from the irresistible suction of events. Meanwhile, the
smoke-black car threaded its way through the late afternoon
traffic like a dark Teutonic wind, its plush interior insulated
from the roar of the freeway, the late afternoon sun a blood-
red hole in the sky.

Guido and Figgis sat next to each other in the spacious rear
compartment. The big man sat opposite them. His coat was
open, the butt of his pistol in plain sight. The man who had
given Guido advice at the urinals of The Lost Cause was also
there, dressed casually in slacks, Birkenstocks, and Nautica
polo shirt. He sat on a small divan, his legs crossed at the
ankles. "Tell me now," he said to Guido. "Have you found
the herbs I recommended to you? Is your awk achieving
superior length? Does your stream make a good torrent?"

"Not yet," Guido said, deciding that he had mistaken a
penny for a nickel. He revised his total to eighty-three cents.
"I mean, I want to. I just haven't had a chance to shop for
them, Mr. . . ."

"Li. Hollingworth Li." The man offered his hand to Guido.
Guido withdrew his hand from his pocket. His fingers had
become damp from working through his loose change.
Hollingworth Li's grip was soft and non-committal. There
was nothing in it that could be read–hostility, friendship,
contempt, even indifference. He was no more than forty but

he had a benevolent, fatherly face lit with good humor. In another frame of reference Guido might have called it a "sweet" face, the face of a sage.

"Hollingworth?" Guido said, smiling a bit, then regretting it.

"My great-great-great grandfather was Daniel Magniac, disgraced brother of the famous opium trader, Hollingworth Magniac. Yes, the blood of the Occident runs in my veins."

"I don't feel very good," Figgis said. "I demand to know where you're taking us, Mr. Li. You realize this is kidnapping? Guido, what's the penalty for kidnapping in this state? It's a federal offense, isn't it? Jesus, haven't I been abused enough for one day? Will someone for the love of Christ turn off that shitty music?"

Hollingworth Li opened a door in a console that formed a barrier between the front seat and the rear compartment. "Would you like a drink, Professor Figgis?"

"Whiskey," Figgis said, glumly. "Ice, no water."

"Good choice," Li said. A private joke lifted the corners of his mouth. "You, Mr. Tarkenen? Whiskey?"

Guido nodded. The Placidex had kicked in. He felt elated, almost giddy, though he had every reason to feel heartsick. He glanced at Figgis. No evidence there of elation. His eyes danced with adrenaline, his forehead was beaded with sweat, and his dry tongue clicked against the roof of his mouth when he spoke. Guido believed he could hear Figgis's heart flap against his ribs.

Hollingworth Li set three glasses on a silver tray and poured an inch of single-malt scotch into each. The whiskey leaned left in the glasses and Guido realized that the car was turning, leaving the freeway, and heading south, into Mexico. Digitalized musical instruments made the sound of wind passing over randomly spaced apertures in bamboo pipes. A digital drum made the sound of rain on tin.

"To health, wealth, and peace of mind," Li said, raising his glass.

Guido started to count his change again. "Skoal," he said, drinking with his left hand.

Figgis looked at Guido unkindly, then tossed back his drink. "I don't fucking believe this," he said, "*Skoal,* for Chrissakes. Are we supposed to be in some kind of east-Asian colonial drawing room? How about cigars? You got cigars for us, too, Mr. Li? Tark, we're being fucking *abducted!*"

The big man pointed at Figgis, his finger thick as a hardwood dowel. "Shut your crude mouth," he said. "You will *not* talk to Mr. Li in this disrespectful way."

Hollingworth Li raised his hand, as if to mediate between the two men. "Please," he said. "Bear with us, Professor. Our intent will become clear to you soon. I'd like you—both of you—to see something."

He slid back a panel. A small TV set was behind it, along with a VCR. He plugged in a tape. "This—though it is only a two-dimensional video replica of a virtual reality environment—is the future of entertainment," Li said.

Guido watched himself and Doris Andrade fucking like young acrobats on the wing of a jumbo jet. Even on the small screen it seemed three-dimensional and exactly true to life, as if photographed by news cameras.

"This technology is going to be irresistible to the public," Li said. "Every home in America will have the device. Everyone will be the star of his own action movie. An ordinary laborer can become the god of his own world. Boredom will be a relic of the humdrum past. Personal creativity—both vulgar and sublime—will blossom. A genie shall be released from its bottle."

"Electronic heroin," Figgis said.

"Not an unfair analogy, " Li admitted. "It will be much more addictive than television. Some will go into the virtual environment and come out only to eat."

"It's morally repugnant," Figgis said.

Hollingworth Li laughed. Not derisively. It was a generous laugh that recognized the helpless posturing of the righteous, their naiveté, their essential ignorance. "My ancestor, Hollingworth Magniac, worked for the East India Company. With the cooperation and financial support of the British government, the Company deliberately addicted the Chinese people to opium in order to redress the balance of trade due to the overwhelming English demand for tea. They descended on China with Bibles and chests of high-grade opium grown in Bengal and Rajputana to stop the silver drain from Britain."

"That was morally repugnant, too," Figgis said.

"And you Americans participated. You brought Turkish opium to China. The Turkish poppy produces an inferior quality drug, and so your share of the market was minimal. All this with government sanction, mind you."

"Fuck them all," Figgis said. "They were all criminals."

"The Ch'ang Dynasty's version of the DEA tried to put a stop to it," Hollingworth Li said, "but the British responded with gunboats and troops. Imagine drug-exporting countries today with similar national resources and self-righteous foreign policy. However, the subsequent war forced China to open its markets to the manufactured goods of the western world. It brought China into the so-called modern era, for better or worse."

Guido watched himself kneeling in the mud while a woman held a pistol to his head. He dropped a penny, or a dime, and started the count over again. "This is payback time, then?"

"Not at all," Li said. "It's just business."

The pistol jerked the woman's hand, and Guido fell face down in the mud. A startled flock of blackbirds rose from nearby telephone wires—an artistic detail Guido had missed when he first saw this scene. Had it been added later?

"Why was Daniel Magniac disgraced?" Guido asked.

"It was a time of great change," Li said. "The emperor's reign was known as the Glorious Rectitude. Can you appreciate the irony? It was a time, rather, of vainglorious corruption. Daniel? He married a half-caste woman from Macao, violating social taboo—not a good thing to do in the early nineteenth century."

Hollingworth Li's eyes went distant as if he could see into the difficult lives of his ancestors. The limousine's stereo system seemed to sympathize with his mood as the whining, microtonal pitch variations of an oriental lute replaced the empty minimalism of Muzak. The plaintive lute attacked Guido's sense of equilibrium. The Placidex kicked out as suddenly as it had kicked in and Guido dropped his handful of coins, having reached sixty-four cents. He listed radically in his seat as the limo accelerated through a sharp curve in the Mexican desert southeast of Bajomitío. He collided with Figgis, who yelped as if he'd been slapped sharply.

"Oh God," Figgis said. "Look where we are. They're going to kill us."

257

# Thirty-five

T HE *MAQUILA* WAS SURROUNDED BY A ten-feet-high cyclone fence with a barrier of looped razor wire strung on top. The limo driver, a Mexican national, got out and opened the gates. He got back into the limo and drove it inside, set the brake, got out again, pushed the gates closed. There was a guard shack, but it was unoccupied. This maquila–the first of a new series–was brand new and not yet a functioning factory. A sign outside the gates had said, "Global Visions–Cortronics Division."

A number of cars, most of them limos, were diagonally parked in front of the building–a windowless white structure hundreds of feet wide. It sat in the Mexican desert like an artificial mesa. From a distance it must have looked like a natural limestone formation unnaturally situated.

The driver opened the rear door of the limo. Hollingworth Li and the big man got out. Guido and Figgis followed. "Most of the guests have already arrived," Li said. "They'll be happy to see us."

"They will?" Figgis said, confused.

"Oh yes," Li said. "They'll want to get the speech-making over with so that we may all enjoy the planned entertainment that follows."

They entered the building through double steel doors, and Li led the way down a brightly lit hallway to a small auditorium. About fifty people were inside, sitting in semi-circular rows of folding chairs in front of a small stage. Someone spotted Li and his guests and said, "Here they are now!" A few others began to applaud. A hostess brought a tray of finger sandwiches and glasses of champagne to the newcomers.

"Maybe I had this figured wrong," Figgis whispered to Guido. "Maybe they haven't tagged me as the bomber after all. Jesus, maybe they're recruiting me—you think?"

Guido saw Vice Chancellor Cribbs seated in the front row, along with a thin, frowning woman in furs—presumably Mrs. Cribbs. Mayo from one of the finger sandwiches had leaked and she was angrily rubbing her stained sleeve with a paper napkin.

Hollingworth Li motioned for Figgis and Guido to take front row seats. He climbed the stairs to the platform and stepped briskly to the podium. There was a second round of scattered applause. Li acknowledged it with a dismissive wave. "We are going to make a lot of money," he said, and the crowd cheered. "We now have the technology and the manufacturing facilities to dominate this market for the foreseeable future, perhaps much longer."

"Geez," Figgis said. "I should have worn a tux."

"I don't think anyone here cares how you're dressed," Guido said. "But don't get too relaxed. I don't think we're out of the woods yet."

"But this all seems so . . . *benign,* Tark."

Li's speech was short and sweet—the future was going to be very bright for those associated with Global Visions. He spoke of the new research and development facility, of international expansion and the growing worth of Global Visions in the equity market. The audience gave him a standing ovation, and then the chant began. *Li Li Li Li Li.* . . .

Again Hollingworth Li dismissed the praise. He held his hands out to quiet the crowd. "We have, as you know, a very special guest today. It may seem odd to you that our guest is a professor of English, a literary scholar . . . but he is also a renaissance man–an expert in seemingly unrelated fields of endeavor, the kind of man, who, in other circumstances we of Global Visions would like to employ."

"What's he talking about?" Figgis said, worried again.

"You, I think," Guido said. "Looks like he wants you to make a speech. Maybe to show how the English department is getting behind the project."

"I'm not behind any project," Figgis said. "Besides, they didn't warn me. I don't have anything prepared. By Christ, though, if they want me to make a goddamned speech, I'll burn their ears."

Li was pointing to Figgis. "Come up here professor. Come let the audience have a good look at you."

Figgis climbed up to the podium. The crowd released a raucous cheer. Figgis, in his jungle fatigues and Florsheims, elicited scattered laughter from the audience. He smiled back, as if it were understood that he and the audience were together in this, and if he was the butt of a joke, it was after all a friendly joke. "Thank yew ver' much," he said into the mike, mimicking Elvis Presley, and the audience tittered.

Hollingworth Li said, "Now here's the thing–life is lessons. Flunk one, and you go back a step. Flunk it again, you go back two. Pass, and you go on to the next lesson. Pass all the lessons and you go up a grade. Flunk them all, you stay in grade one, a true and permanent loser. What could be simpler to understand? Now my question, Professor Figgis, is why would anyone deliberately choose to be a recidivist loser when he possesses such obvious talent, talent that could serve the greater good of the global community?"

Figgis didn't answer. All remnants of his hopeful illusion collapsed. The audience was no longer on his side. They regarded him sternly.

Figgis, like a man transfixed by the sight of his own funeral bier, stared at a wooden structure two men lifted to the stage—a pi-shaped arrangement of bolted-together four-by-fours. The fronts of the vertical posts were braced against the floor with two-by-fours set at forty-five degree angles, as if to prevent the structure from moving forward. The top beam was about five feet off the stage floor and was heavily padded. The pads were contoured—convex at the center, flat at the ends. The convexity was deep enough to accommodate a large man's chest.

Guido recognized other members of the audience. Nicho Andrade and a beautiful young woman—his mistress, no doubt—several city officials, some administrators from La Siberia Tech, and a contingent of Global Visions executives from Singapore, some of whom Guido had seen in TV interviews from time to time. There was a palpable edge to their excitement, an electrified heat, the kind Guido had once noticed in a crowd during the opening ceremonies of a bullfight.

"For instance," Hollingworth Li continued, "in Singapore, one can be fined up to one-thousand dollars for spitting on the sidewalk. An excellent lesson in public comportment, don't you agree? Littering is also heavily fined. If one uses a public toilet and does not flush, the fine, again, is one-thousand dollars. And vandalism . . . but, by now, it is well-known how vandals are instructed in Singapore."

"The anal code of criminal justice," Figgis said, but no one laughed.

"The West has forgotten the essential fact," Li said, "that we are animals first and human beings second. And we are human beings only if we work diligently at becoming so. The West, in forgetting this, has allowed the animal to run rampant—in the name of individual freedom. But then what

261

is freedom without intelligent responsibility? It is mere license and reduces eventually to anarchy and chaos. You can find this notion in your own literature—Milton's *Areopagitica* is an excellent example."

"Bravo!" someone in the audience shouted.

"Milton was trying to save his own ass," Figgis said.

"Something that you will not be able to do," Li murmured.

A man dressed in a terrycloth gi approached Figgis and Li. He put his hand on Figgis's arm. "Come with me, professor," he said.

Figgis balked. "Fuck you," he said. "I'm walking out of here. Anyone tries to stop me they've got one hell of a law suit on their hands. I'll fucking take everything they own. I'll take their children's inheritance. I'll take their grandma's wedding rings. Get your goddamned hands off me, Tarzan."

"Spank the blowhard!" someone yelled.

The man in the gi was joined by another man, also dressed in a martial arts gi. "Come along, doc. You don't want to keep the audience waiting," he said.

The men, both large and heavily muscled—one a red-head with blue, hyperthyroidal eyes, the other a scowling Chinese— escorted Figgis to the stage. Figgis tried to break away from them and was slapped for his trouble by the Chinese. The slap shocked Guido. It traveled a short distance—no more than half a foot—and didn't seem to have much force, but the thickness of the man's arm began at his wrist, and the impact of the slap had the report of a pistol shot. It had the desired effect. Figgis stopped struggling, fell to one knee. The red-head with the bulging eyes helped Figgis to his feet. Figgis, too stunned to protest, was urged to remove his camouflage fatigues.

"Guido!" Figgis wailed. "Help me!"

Hollingworth Li descended from the stage and took a seat next to Guido. "I'm afraid there is no help for such a man," he said.

The red-head who had helped Figgis out of his shirt, pants and shoes, was now pulling down his shorts. The illicit thrill of impending unconventional acts buzzed through the select group of spectators.

The ceremonial air made Guido dizzy. The surroundings had assumed the quality of dream. Once again, the idea that he'd been shot to death in the arroyo haunted him. He heard Carma's voice—telephonic in quality, as if coming from a separate but continually operative world. It was saying, "I was wrong to shoot you," and he heard himself reply, "and I was wrong to speak as I did,"—she addressing the dead; he petitioning, too late, for pardon.

"My father told me a story once," Li said to Guido. "It was about my ancestor, Daniel Magniac. His brother, Hollingworth, had invited him—before his disgrace—to sail on the famous opium clipper, Red Rover, on a voyage from Calcutta to Singapore to Canton. They sailed in the monsoon season. The Red Rover was a new design based on the American Privateers, quite capable of weathering such storms, but the crew—accustomed to sailing in the old-style *wallahs,* which were teak replicas of seventeenth century galleons—came close to mutiny. A strong monsoon could capsize a *wallah.* The men had no knowledge of this sleek new opium clipper and so did not trust it and would not accept their captain's reassurances. The loudest voice among the disgruntled was a Lascar, a large man much like your Professor Figgis. Intelligent, but more inclined to make trouble than to work cooperatively toward solutions. The mutiny failed and the Lascar was beheaded in Singapore—by my many-times-removed grandfather, Daniel Magniac himself. Daniel was a gentle man with no war-like attributes, but all men in those days understood the unequivocal necessities of civilization. We allow the animal to rampage or we allow the human being to flourish. One cannot have it both ways. It is as simple as that."

And now Hollingworth Li's voice also seemed to have a telephonic remoteness, increasing Guido's sense of isolation from reality. The red-head had removed Figgis's shorts and socks and was now leading him by the hand toward the wooden apparatus. Guido felt a twinge of guilt for not respond-ing to Figgis's cry for help. But it was only a twinge, for Figgis himself had become part of the unreality.

This state of mind was not new to Guido. It had happened before. Once, in the army, coming off a two-day drunk, he'd gone to work in puke-stained civvies. The officer on duty that day, a second lieutenant, sent him back to the barracks, and Guido, in departing, had told the recent ROTC grad to go fuck himself. The threat of court martial gripped him for the rest of that day, and as he imagined scenarios of stockade life, he began to lose touch with the world of hard and stable edges. He went AWOL, found a whorehouse hotel in a nearby town and stayed there until his money was gone. But the post commander, a Quaker who was inclined to be lenient, became even more so when he found out Guido's girlfriend had recently dumped him—and so Guido only got an in-unit punishment, an Article 15, which cost him the loss of one stripe and restriction to the post for thirty days. And years later, after his first novel was rejected by the twelfth publisher he'd sent it to, he drove across the country in the middle of winter in a heaterless car. He kept a bottle of Jack Daniels next to him, a blanket wrapped around his shoulders. As he drove into the American heartland, peering through a scraped hole in the ice that continually formed on the windshield, he lost the sense of the country's reality. It became a dream landscape of ice and snow, dominated by shades of gray, the lethal hues of boredom. He wound up in La Siberia, where, a few years later, he met reality again, in the form of Kirsten.

Kirsten. The thought of his failed marriage drove him into a deeper funk. He'd loved her, he was sure of that. Love could not be defined, measured, analyzed, or in any way be abstracted from the ordinary or peculiar emotions that powered it. You knew you loved or you knew you did not. And even that certainty was subject to the heart's moody variables. When you examined love honestly it lost some nobility. It came down to self-interest, enlightened or unenlightened—a constellation of needs satisfied by a compatible other. The need of sex, the need of companionship, the need of an ally who affirmed your prejudices and tolerated your excesses. If the need was mutual, and if the needs of one were congruent with the needs of the other, then love, like the fission of atoms when critical mass is achieved, *happened.*

Guido recalled their first joint visit to Dr. Dale Burnaby. It was after an argument that had escalated into a name-calling fight. They had, in the course of an afternoon, watched each other become ugly strangers. All the congruencies were broken. "Who the hell *are* you?" Kirsten had said to him. "I'm the same. You're the one who's changed," he'd replied. "Guido seems to think change is destructive," said Dr. Burnaby. And Guido had said, "Isn't it?" After all, wasn't love based in the idea that there is something solid and ongoing and reliable in the heart that *never* changed, that weathered all storms? Guido, in the course of the interview, was moved to confess, "I sometimes have this feeling that things around me are unreal," and the doctor, his face rigid against a suppressed yawn, replied, "This is not an uncommon response to stress." And later, in the same interview, Guido admitted, "I have these violent doom swings, doctor," not hearing his error. Dr. Burbaby grinned happily. He said, "Guido means *mood* swings, doesn't he?" Guido, perplexed, began referring to himself in the third person. He said, "That's what Guido said. Mood swings." Guido looked at his shadowy third-person distortion in the black lacquer of Dr. Burnaby's splendid desk. "I believe Guido *reversed* the word," Dr. Burnaby said. "I wonder what else in his immediate experience Guido reverses." Dr. Burnaby and Kirsten looked at each other, eyebrows arched to the limit, sharing the gusto of this stimulating revelation. "Guido thinks you're making too much of a slip of the tongue," Guido said, and Burnaby winked with conspiratorial aplomb at Kirsten.

Guido's reverie was broken by applause. Figgis stood naked and trembling before the gathering, trying to cover his genitals with his hands. The red-haired man pulled him to the wood structure. Figgis, awash in terror, became confused. He started to duck under the apparatus, but the red-head stopped him. The man took Figgis's arm almost tenderly and turned him so that his chest fit into the concave padding. "Spread your legs a bit, sir," he advised.

Figgis tried again to back away from the device, but the man pushed him gently back into it. "Hold your testicles up and out of the way," the man said.

"What?" Figgis asked. "I don't. . . ."

"Your testicles, sir. Hold them up. Don't let them dangle free. That could be extremely unwise. You don't want to lose them."

Someone in the audience yelled, "Assume the god-damned *position,* Figgis! Weren't you ever in a fraternity? Don't you know what to *do* for Chrissakes?"

Figgis reached down gingerly and touched himself.

"That's it, sir," said the red-head. "Cup them and hold them up and out of the way."

"Another of my ancestors," said Hollingworth Li, "owned a 'centipede'—one of the smaller boats that off-loaded chests of opium from the receiving ships at Lintin Island in Canton Bay. He distributed the contraband to various ports up the Pearl River. He became very wealthy, and eventually retired to Singapore. My father said that this ancestor was a visionary. He understood the West completely and foresaw its self-destruction, as egoism in the guise of freedom, gradually overwhelmed decency and the rule of law. Once, when this ancestor was a young man, he killed an American sailor in Hog Lane, the whoring district of Canton. He saw in that American's face a wildness that could never be brought to heel."

Figgis, his huge white body trembling uncontrollably, was roaring again. "This little game has gone far enough!" he bellowed. "Goddammit, Guido, call the cops! These fuckers are looney tunes!" He tried to back out of the convex cushions but the red-haired man again forced him back. The Chinese man, who had left the stage, returned now with a short pole. He held it up as if it were a ceremonial sword, then made several stylized passes with it, and the audience again broke into unrestrained applause.

The pole wasn't a pole, Guido realized, but strips of rattan bundled together with red silk cord. It was about five feet long, and as the man cut slices of air with it, wind sifting through the flexing strips made a throaty moan.

"I believe we are ready," said Hollingworth Li. He gave the man with the rattan weapon a hand signal. The man acknowledged it with a slight bow, then, from a distance of about twenty feet, studied Figgis's mass of quaking flesh.

267

"Punishment," said Li, "must have meaning. If we had simply turned Professor Figgis and his bombs over to the police, he would have been sent to prison for a few years, perhaps only a few months—a prison where, as a non-violent offender, he would enjoy a relative freedom. This would not be very instructive, would it?"

The first blow was dazzling. The man with the rattan whip ran toward Figgis in what seemed like choreographed dance steps, then powered the whip forward so that when it struck Figgis's buttocks the smooth white flesh parted instantly into a lattice of red grooves. It took a second for the pain to explode in Figgis's brain, and when it did, he screamed—a high-pitched animal scream that hurt Guido's ears. The audience also screamed—out of shocked delight.

The second blow had even more force, and Figgis dropped to his knees and rolled over, screaming, his face purple and as distorted as an angry baby's. He was helped to his feet by the two men and muscled back into the apparatus.

"Hold your balls up, professor," the red-head reminded Figgis.

Figgis was sobbing and moaning. Rivulets of blood ran down his legs from his lacerated buttocks and pooled at his feet.

After the third blow, Figgis began to lose consciousness and had to be strapped to the apparatus. By the time the fifth blow came, Figgis had stopped screaming.

"That's enough," Guido said, hearing, in his own voice, a telephonic distance.

"Only two more strokes," Hollingworth Li said. "In Singapore, for a similar offense, he would be lucky to get a mere twelve."

"You don't understand," Guido said. "I want you to stop this now."

Guido had taken out the .32 no one had bothered to remove from his jacket. He held the small pistol against Hollingworth Li's stomach. The detachment he had felt dissolved. Reality came crashing back around him like a tidal wave, over-whelming him with the suffocating presence of people and objects and the thin, metallic smell of blood.

Li raised his hand and the man with the rattan whip who had readied himself for another run at Figgis, relaxed into the martial arts equivalent of "parade rest." He stood with his legs apart, his back straight, the thick whip held at his side.

The wife of Vice Chancellor Cribbs stood up. She was a tall, narrow woman with a long face that worked against a deep visceral emotion. Guido had seen her before. She was a woman whose position in life had made her rigidly circum-spect in social situations. "Don't stop!" she shrieked, her voice raw with blood-lust, her self-control dissolving. "Don't you *dare* stop! Cane the vandal! Cane him again!"

Involuntary spasms moved her long body. Then she lost all composure and started to climb the stage, breathless and howling for blood, as if to resume the caning herself. Her fur wrap had fallen to the floor, but she didn't pick it up.

She'd gotten one knee up on the platform when her husband caught her around her waist and dragged her back to her seat. She was panting, her eyes wild, her white fists beating against the restraining arms of her husband.

Vice Chancellor Cribbs looked at his wife as if seeing her for the first time.

269

# Thirty-six

GUIDO'S MOUTH WENT DRY. HIS PROSTATE grieved. He felt dizzy. Hollingworth Li made another hand signal and the large man who had accompanied them to the *maquila* in the limo came over. When he saw Guido's gun he seemed to expand with a contained explosion. The lapels of his suit spread wider, the veins in his neck swelled thick as battery cables. His eyes blinked with an acidity that made Guido regret he'd chosen this heroic role.

"It's all right," Li said. "Send everyone home. And take Mr. Figgis to our clinic, here in Bajomitío." The big man, fighting himself, managed to do what he was told. "Does this satisfy you, Mr. Tarkenen?"

Guido pushed the gun deeper into Hollingworth Li's stomach as people filed out past them. The two men in martial arts gear helped Figgis off the stage. He was semi-conscious. His face was wet with tears and sweat. He'd bitten his tongue— a bloody drool leaked down his chin. His eyes rolled back in his head, rolled forward again, focused, with difficulty, on Guido.

"What happened?" he blubbered, his tongue thick against the words.

"You were caned, Figgis," Guido said.

Nicho Andrade stopped in front of Guido. "You are one unbelievably fucked-up gringo," he said. *"Chinga'o,* you don't even *know* what you're doing, do you?"

When everyone had gone, Hollingworth Li said, "I realize you could not have pulled the trigger, Mr.Tarkenen. But you are frightened, and your hands are trembling. So, it is better

270

to go along with you than to risk someone getting needlessly hurt."

"Tell that to Figgis," Guido said.

"But he is a criminal, Mr. Tarkenen. Don't you believe that criminals should be punished?"

"Not like that. We've got this thing about cruel and unusual punishment."

"However, the framers of your Constitution did not anticipate *non*-punishment—country club prisons, television in every cell, excellent food prepared by dietitians, gymnasiums, first-rate legal libraries, courses leading to university degrees— and then the endless appeals. Remember, the word penitentiary derives from its root-word, *penitence*. A penitentiary is a place where the criminal must be made to feel deep remorse for his transgressions. But in this country prison is often *preferable* to the living conditions the criminal faced when he was free. What sort of message are you sending the criminal element with luxuries and benefit packages such as these? Remember, we have almost no crime in Singapore. Recidivism is next to non-existent. The rule of law is respected in Singapore."

"Good for Singapore," Guido said, but he thought about what Hollingworth Li had said. It didn't apply. Figgis may have been a little crazy, but he was not exactly a hardcore criminal. In spite of Figgis's blowhard ways and self-serving politics, Guido liked him. "Figgis is my friend," he said.

"That," Hollingworth Li said, "is a recipe for anarchy. No society can sustain itself when personal relationships are honored above the needs of a community. Such a short-sighted philosophy, Mr. Tarkenen, is—to use a uniquely American word—counterproductive."

Guido studied the Global Visions executive with the sagelike face. The man, he now realized, was not some minor official who had been sent to scout living arrangements for his company's employees, but a highly placed officer with major decision-making power.

"Tell me something, Mr. Li," Guido said. "Did your people kill Solly Dubrinsky and Lex Xenedes?"

Li's face hardened momentarily, then resumed its benevolent good-humor. "You must have understood, Mr. Tarkenen, in the course of your crime-writing career, the burden of responsibility the answers to such ill-considered questions place on the shoulders of the persons who ask them."

That was answer enough for Guido.

"And Inverness? The mathematician?"

Hollingworth Li looked puzzled for a moment, then shrugged. "Please, Guido. Write your books, be happy, enjoy your life. Do not concern yourself with the larger things which you can neither understand nor control."

Li stood up. "I am sorry that you will not be joining us. We do like your work—the odd and unpredictable designs of your imagination—but it is clear now that you could never be a loyal company man, could you?"

The Global Visions executive walked out.

Guido sat in the brand new *maquila,* alone, confused, wondering what Hollingworth Li had meant. He looked down at the gun in his hand, saw that his finger had been tight against the trigger guard—not the trigger—and wondered what he had done to his future.

# Thirty-seven

Dear Professor Tarkenen:

  Recently I have had the distinct privilege of experiencing
your work in the flesh, so to speak. Sr. Dionisio Andrade,
CEO of Cortronics, Inc., has given me the opportunity to
review your experimental virtual reality work, apropos *The
Milksop Strangler.* Bravo, sir! I found the fragment engaging,
to say the very least. I'll come directly to the point. As you
know, our University is at present undergoing a rather
extensive re-structuring of its mission. One aspect of our
future lies in the creation of stimulating  software for the
radically new virtual reality machine, conditionally known
as Cybertopia. In concordance with this goal, we have
created a new academic department, tentatively titled, "The
Department of Dream Architecture." I believe there is a
place for you in this new department, and hereby invite you
to send your vita to Dr. Martin Gassaway, who has agreed
to serve as Chair, pro tem. We think you would find great
professional fulfillment in this field of research. I hope you
agree. Your salary would of course reflect the importance
with which the University regards this position.

Sincerely,

Efraim Cribbs,
Vice Chancellor

P.S. Please find, enclosed, a draft copy of a brochure describing Cybertopia to prospective consumers. If you have any ideas for additions, deletions, or other modifications, we would welcome your input.

Guido picked up the brochure. It had been done on glossy paper, with full-color illustrations. It looked more like a finished product than a draft copy.

### The World Is Your Oyster!

Interact with the world as you never would have dreamed possible! Want to know what it feels like to fly into outer space? Want to feel moon dust under your feet? Would you like to speak, face to face, with famous figures in history? Imagine yourself taking tea with Plato, Aristotle, Saint Augustine, or, in our era, Gandhi, Einstein, or Marilyn Monroe! Do your tastes lean toward the dark side? Imagine confronting a mugger, disarming him, and giving him the beating of his life! Think how it must feel to electrocute, hang, or lethally inject a murderer! Perhaps, because you have always wanted to know what really goes on in the mind of a criminal, you might even temporarily adopt his psyche. How does one bring oneself to do heinous deeds? Where does the impulse come from to commit murder, torture, rape, cannibalism? In the private confines of Cybertopia, you can discover this terra incognita first-hand. Of course, you may just want to create your own world, safe and secure from all the woes and terrors of contemporary society. Be the king or queen of your own country, then populate it with adoring subjects! Would you ever want to disengage from such a paradise? Cybertopia can give you all this, and much more. Its possibilities are limited only by your imagination. And in that regard, our machines will come with software designed by "Dream Architects"—writers and artists—who will create worlds and situations within those worlds that all but the most jaded will find exciting and rewarding.

The envelope had been on Guido's kitchen table, unopened, for several days. "No thanks," he said, even though the offer obviously no longer stood. There was other unopened mail—copies of the divorce agreement, sent by Kirsten's lawyer, bills, indecipherable royalty statements along with a note from Cash Holub:

> Are you fucking *dead?* Are you alive? Are you messed up? Have you killed the golden goose? What the bejesus are you up to, Guido? etc.

There was a card from Seraghina:

> I enjoyed our lunch. Is it forward of me to say so? I used to be unforward (backward, I guess you'd call it) but after Mitch left, and maybe for a few years before that, I finally understood something about my situation. (Everyone's situation.) We wither on the vine 'cause we don't put our butts on the line. (Hey! There's some poetry!) I want to be clear about what I like and what I don't like and what I need and what I don't need. Coyness and her twin sister, Modesty, get you a bitter old age. If not bitter, then an old age with an album of dull memories. You like Italian spice? Come over for dinner some time. Give me a call.

275

He'd come home to get his mail and pack some clothes after lying low in a Bajomitío hotel for three days where he'd registered under the name "Carson Motley." After he left the Cortonics warehouse he'd walked ten miles out of the desert and into the main *maquila* district, and then had taken a rural bus–a *rutera* that carried workers to and from their factories– to the main drag of Bajomitío. It had been a long three days in the Hotel El Prado, watching back-to-back Mexican soaps– *telenovelas*–in a room with white plaster walls webbed with an intricate map of fine cracks. He sat for hours in front of the room's single window, drinking house *juisque* and studying the traffic in the street below. The *telenovelas* were better than American soaps–more sex and violence and melodrama– even though he couldn't follow them.

When he got up enough nerve to go home, the Mercedes 190E Pryor Dark had promised to deliver was parked in his driveway.

He wrote a check for two-hundred and fifty dollars, as a down payment, which Pryor accepted reluctantly. He'd wanted a thousand down, to make sure, no doubt, that Wolfgang Schnur would pay his commission up front. But the car had been modified more than Pryor had let on. It had been made into a "low rider." The frame hugged the ground, the wheels were gold with "diamond-cut" spokes–ninety-six spokes per hub–and the tires were 16-inch super low-profile Euro Radials. The interior had been redone in purple velour. The bench seat had been replaced with purple velour buckets, the fabric and buttons done in a diamond-patterned biscuit tuck. The hood had a brilliant panoramic painting of Jesus in the garden of Gethsemane on it, the Mount of Olives ominous in the background. The rear deck-lid continued the religious motif, presenting a cloudscape with angels descending from an explosion of blood-tinged holy light.

Guido fell in love with the car instantly–the understated aristocratic European machine tattooed and decked-out with a wildass American southwest kitsch. Here was the forced democratization of the stuffed shirt–the humiliation of self-importance and the aggrandization of a homespun vision.

The car, to Pryor, was an abomination. Everything about it that was Mercedes-Benz had been desecrated. The car, where it did not have religious icons, had been painted a crackling candy apple red. Even the headlights had been "Frenched." He tried to put up a good front, but Guido saw his embarrassment, his shame, and took advantage of it. Guido believed Pryor would have let the car go on a handshake, the man's humiliation was so apparent. When he asked for a thousand dollars down, he turned his head away, his face crimson, his lips compressed. Guido wrote the check for two-fifty. Pryor stared at it coldly, then put it into his shirt pocket.

Guido threw his clothes, his word processor, and a few books into the car and drove away. The low-riding Mercedes Benz was hot. It took off with a screech of rubber, fishtailing slightly, and when it shifted into second, it lurched dramatically. Guido, not quite in control, gripped the wheel as a second burst of power yanked him back into the purple velour seat.

He could hear the engine breathe, felt its muscle vibrate the ebony steering wheel. It continued to accelerate in second, and just when Guido expected it to drop into third, it accelerated again. This new burst of power, like an afterthought, snapped his head back one more time, sending a rush of adrenaline into his bloodstream. By the end of the block he was doing sixty and yelling.

In this way he drove across La Siberia, toward the district of cheap motels.

# Thirty-eight

W HAT DO YOU LIKE?" GUIDO SAID.
"No one ever asks that. I like a lot of things."
Guido gave that some thought. It excited him. "A lot is what you get, then," he said. He explored her tendencies. Found one she favored.

After a while she said, "You can come up for air now."

He heard her voice but not her meaning. He was blind, clamped in her steamy thighs, the dark heat tropical. His ears raged with tinnitus. He heard his fast pulse through the ringing alarms.

"Cat got your tongue?" she said. She touched his damp head. "Come up here, Guido."

"Wait a minute," he said. "Let me catch my breath."

He went into the bathroom. Threw cold water in his face. His heart jack-hammered his ribs. A small knot of pain nudged his soft underbelly. He opened her medicine chest, found the aspirins, swallowed a handful. He thought about her body– almost stocky, dusky skin, glossy ringlets of black hair under her arms and bearding her pudenda. She smelled like food– olive oil, sweet marjoram, bread in the oven, a spicy cinnamon perfume. He'd kissed her shapely feet, then worked his way up the fine terrain.

He went back to her, this time beginning with the top of her head, kissing the kinked tangles of her hair, her forehead, her ears and eyes and mouth and chin and throat. When he reached her breasts she began to shudder. Then her hand was on him, guiding him inside. And once there, he knew, he was in danger of losing it too soon. She was very good; she

knew her body well. Her thrusts matched his precisely, and–
she told him later–her PC muscle was *trained*. ("PC–not the
politically correct muscle, Guido," she explained, "but the
pubococcygeus, the muscle that travels from the pubic bone
to the coccyx and supports the vagina on the way.") Her vagina
pulsed around his thrusts, a deliberate gripping massage.
("Kegels," she called them. "Sexual calisthenics. It keeps the
machinery tight.") This gave him more pleasure than a man
could be expected to handle, he thought. But he did not com-
plain about it.

He forced his mind away from this delight. He thought about
one of his father's stories, the Swiss Watchmakers story. Guido
had used it before, during sex, to prolong his "hang time."
The story still had the power to fascinate, and so it was the
perfect distraction. The watchmakers, the most skilled craftsmen in the country, had been challenged by the king to make
a boat that was distinctly Swiss and unlike any other boat
made in Europe up to that time. The watchmakers accepted
the challenge, and in their studies of ordinary vessels realized
that, regardless of the great differences in size and form that
existed in the boats of that era, all of them had one thing in
common: sails. The boat the watchmakers would create, to
be distinctively Swiss, would not have sails, yet would be
capable of crossing the great ocean faster than any sailing
vessel. When the watchmakers announced their intentions,
the boatmakers of Europe ridiculed them. First of all, Switzerland had no ocean port, and therefore had no tradition–much
less a need of boat-building. How could they hope to construct
a seaworthy vessel if they had never in all their history made
such a craft, even one that *had* sails. The watchmakers-turned-
boatmakers became the great joke of Europe for several years.

*Hello-o, she sing-songed impatiently, but Guido would not be
distracted from his distraction. Yoo-hoo, she said.*

The boat the watchmakers designed was long and sleek and rode low in the waters of Lake Lucerne. It cruised from one shore of the lake to another, continually, and without benefit of sails or oars. The captain steered the boat from a bridge that had the shape of a Swiss chalet. The people from nearby towns came to witness the watchmakers' boat glide swiftly and silently from shore to shore, the bearded captain puffing on his pipe from a balcony of his chalet. The people were mystified but also proud of the genius of their watchmakers.

Jealous foreigners also came to see the miraculous boat, but dismissed it as a fake—since it had neither sails nor oars. Its so-called *secret,* they said, once it was discovered, would bring shame and perhaps the condemnation of the church down on the heads of the watchmakers.

The secret of the boat was its springs. The watchmakers, who knew a lot about watch springs, had made springs fifty feet in diameter. There were ten springs in all, long bands of steel compressed into tight coils by horse-driven ratcheting machines. The horses worked for days, cranking the springs tight. The springs, through a series of shafts and step-up gears, turned the screw that moved the boat through the waves of Lake Lucerne, the only sound issuing from its hull, some thought, was the sound of a ticking clock.

*Her voice, from far away: Faster. I'm peaking.*

The watchmakers estimated that the boat, on a single winding of the springs, could travel as much as three-hundred leagues, or nine-hundred miles. Then, when the springs had spent their pent-up power, the horses, which were stabled on the ship, would once again turn the ratcheting mechanism, restoring the springs to their original potential.

The ship was dismantled and carried across the mountains and down to the Mediterranean Sea where, reassembled, it astonished the world with its mastless beauty. When the sleek

Swiss boat slid silently out of its harbor, easily passing the great sailing vessels of France and Spain, the people watching from shore crossed themselves and whispered prayers of deliverance for surely this strange, sea-going vessel was a device of the devil. But when it was made known by the jubilant watchmakers that the ship was powered by giant watch springs, the mood of the people changed from one of foreboding to one of great rejoicing, for a new era of boat-making had arrived and would bless the great royal families of Europe with the wealth of new empires.

*Here it is here it is here it is O God here it is!*

But then the unforseeable happened. On the boat's maiden voyage to the New World, its great springs failed. The watch-makers knew everything there was to know about the design and manufacture of springs and gearing mechanisms, but they knew nothing about the corrosive effects of salt water. The tests on Lake Lucerne had been lengthy and detailed, but the clear cold mountain air of Switzerland was not like the dense salt air of the ocean. And when the springs froze, caked with green oxidation, the boat, which was named the Lucerne, stopped dead in the water and foundered helplessly in the unforgiving sea. The disaster happened off the Lesser Antilles, in the hurricane season of 1659.

This was the most useful part of the story because it still had the power to depress Guido. And depression, even mild depression, had an anesthetizing effect. His rising pleasure dropped precipitously; he felt nothing, even though Seraghina was now lifting to meet his thrusts with an abandon approaching seizure. Her constant coaching—which delighted him—degenerated to alto grunts.

It was time to quit the story, although it had several more mind-distracting episodes. He let himself go, becoming as athletic as he could, and when he came he also grunted. Then, as he became aware again of the knot of hot pain under his testicles, deep in the soft tissues of the perineum, his grunts rose in pitch.

He rolled off Seraghina, screaming.

"My God, what *is* it?" she said.

"Shipwreck," he said, between clenched teeth.

# Thirty-nine

SHIPWRECK?" SHE SAID. "WHAT ARE YOU TALKING ABOUT?"

"Prostate," he said, hunching over now, as if to protect the hot coals nesting in his lower abdomen, under the pubic bone.

"Come into the bathroom," she said.

She filled the tub with hot water, had Guido get in.

"Jesus," he said, "you could boil lobsters in here."

"Try to relax," she said. She reached down into the water, lifted his testicles, and massaged his perineum.

"Mother of God," he said, closing his eyes.

She went to the medicine chest and found a bottle of Tylenol-3. She gave Guido two pills and a glass of water. "The codeine should help," she said.

She drained the tub and filled it with cold water. Guido looked at her with begging eyes. "Sitz treatment," she said. "Goes back to ancient times."

He shivered in the cold water.

"Can you pee?" she said.

"I don't think so."

"When you feel you can, then do it. Right in the tub."

The hot and cold treatment went on for an hour. By that time the codeine had kicked in. The pain became spotty, then fell off to an occasional knife-twist. Guido's bladder let go.

"Thank Christ," he said, sighing.

"Thank nurse, too," she said.

He kissed the fingers, one by one, of her miracle-working hand. He stood up out of the cold water, trembling, and kissed her mouth.

"Whoa," she said. "We just put out one fire, let's not start another."

"I've got my second wind."

"Don't be an overachiever."

They got dressed and went into the kitchen where she made coffee. The remains of dinner–veal scaloppini and angel hair pasta–were still on the table. She gave a steaming cup of coffee to Guido, then went to check on her grandson, Steven, who was still asleep in his room.

When she came back Guido said, "I'm sorry."

"For what?"

"For my degenerate physical condition."

"Don't be. I had a good time. But you'd better get medical treatment. Let's hope that little bugger is only suffering from some circumstantial hypertrophy."

"Scare me a little, why don't you."

"Whatever works. I'm serious about this. It could be something you don't want to ignore."

Her house was a 1930s California-style bungalow with a screened porch looking out on the street. They took their coffee there and sat in an old canvas glider. Guido reached for her hand just as she was reaching for his. They both laughed at this, but their accidental touch was galvanic–real electricity passed between them–and they were both suddenly self-conscious and afraid.

"I don't want to say it," Guido said. "It's too early to say it, and even if I said it I'm not sure it could mean anything." The fear was pure and unappeasable. Like a child's fear of night creatures.

She understood. "Love," she said. "I don't know what it means, either. I love you right now, this October. I hope it's a long October."

"Maybe we'll have November, too."

"That's the scary part, expecting contract renewals."

They set their cups down on the wide sill under the screen and kissed. It was a sweet kiss, involving only the lips. But then they began to work at it, and it seemed as if they were overruling smart talk. *Fuck renewals,* Guido thought. *Fuck October, too. Fuck November. There is no October or November. No year, no month, no week, no day. Just marks on a blank wall. There is only this traveling moment, this verb that's grabbed us up and is now hauling us away. Love. A lunatic stomp-ass wild horse of a verb.* He hoped for a long ride.

"I feel good about this," he said.

"It's chemical," she said.

Guido slumped down in the swing. Smart talk again. He didn't want that.

"Everything is chemical," she continued. "But that doesn't explain anything away. I hate dismissive explanations."

"Chemistry is good," Guido said, but now he was thinking of Figgis's bombs distilled from aspirins. To bomb. To love. Verbs of change. Verbs of travel. Rapid transit verbs.

"Chemistry *is* good," she said. "The earth and moon are chemical. The sun is chemical. Christ's blood is chemical. God in his deep-space hidey hole is chemical."

"The church might argue with you on that one."

"Let them argue. I've got science on my side."

They talked for a while like teenagers about science and religion and mystery. Then they remembered they were adults—too old to be anything more than mildly depressed at the vast desert of human ignorance, their own ignorance a grain of sand in that appalling wasteland. They laughed at themselves, with genuine merriment. Seraghina went into the kitchen to refill their coffee cups.

When she came back, Guido said, "I've been thinking about your crime scene. Dubrinsky and Xenedes. Didn't the pathologist think there were some problems with it?"

"Such as?"

"Semen. Or the lack of it. You didn't mention semen." He remembered telling Figgis that there had been semen, but that was a small fib to shore up an argument.

She sipped her coffee. "No big deal. Dubrinsky was no kid. He was fifty-five. Some of your older guys don't come, or they come blanks—puffs of air. Has to do with endocrinology. More chemistry. In this case, the lack of chemistry."

"Then there's the notebooks," Guido said.

"What notebooks?"

"That's what I mean. *What* notebooks? The crime scene people didn't report any notebooks, or any other lecture material, did they? Dubrinsky and Xenedes were supposed to be on their way to Pomona to give a scientific symposium."

She studied his face in the near dark. "What are you saying?"

"I'm saying it wasn't murder-suicide. It was murder-murder. But anomalies don't prove anything. Especially if the case has been conveniently put to bed."

"There was another anomaly," Seraghina said. "Xenedes had two broken fingers, one on each hand, along with wrist and ankle bruises. But no one made a big deal out of it. The ME said bondage games are making a comeback this year. He predicts more scopophilia, ninnie-splitting, exhibitionism, and ablutophilia for next year. His terminology, not mine. It's his pass-time, trend prediction in the dark hobbies."

Guido smiled, then thought about what happened to Xenedes. "Fuck. They held him down with a finger-lock while someone kicked a jackhandle up his ass. The poor bastard."

"You seem to know something the police don't," Seraghina said.

Guido thought about that. "Maybe not. In any case, I can't prove it. I called Pomona. They said Dubrinksy canceled the symposium the day before his death. Which of course is bullshit. They were on a goddamned *mission*. The bad guys have covered their asses with lead-lined boilerplate. But I'm not wrong."

"Mission? What kind of mission? What's all this got to do with the price of rice in China?"

Guido laughed. "That's *good*. But it's not China, it's Singapore. And it's not rice, it's hi-tech stuff."

"I guess you think you're making sense. Who *are* the bad guys, Guido? Who would want to murder a couple of professors? And *why?*"

"Three professors. You're forgetting Gregory Inverness," he said, but now he knew he was deliberately misleading her. He knew the Global Visions people had nothing to do with Inverness's murder.

He felt stupid, airing his thoughts. If he aired one, he'd have to air them all. He didn't want to do that. For her sake, and for his.

"Forgive me if I'm being dense, Guido," Seraghina said, "but wasn't Inverness killed by a student? Are you saying there's a larger conspiracy here? A connection between all three? That doesn't make any sense. Why did they create an elaborate murder-suicide scenario for Dubrinsky and

286

Xenedes, then just pound Inverness's head into pâté with a big rock? Does that seem reasonable to you?"

"I've got this out-of-control mouth," Guido said. "I'm sorry I brought it up."

"No, I want to hear it. Why were these people killed, the way you see it?"

"I hate conspiracy theories," he said. "I hear the word conspiracy and I grab my earplugs."

"You started it, sugar," she said.

Guido took a deep breath. "Some other time. Okay?" If he allowed himself to keep babbling, he'd have to explain, among other things, why he was now living in a cheap motel on the far side of town.

They went back into the house. Steven was vocalizing in his sleep. A mix of whimpering and resolute scolding. The furry night creatures were getting out of hand. Seraghina went into his room to tuck him in again. Guido heard the soothing rise and fall of her voice, the limitless generosity in it, the comfort it gave, and he thought of October. They had October, and maybe November. And if they had that much, maybe they had the rest. And that was, as Seraghina said, the scary part.

Guido went into the bedroom. The sheets were pulled loose—naked mattress was showing. The blankets were piled up on the floor. Evidence of tropical storm Aphrodite. He sat on the bed and twiddled his thumbs. When she did not return after five minutes, he opened her night table drawer out of aimless curiosity. It glinted silver, a .357 magnum. He hefted it, saw that the cylinder was loaded with hollowpoints. He thought of Carma, thanked the celestial powers that she did not own a gun like this.

"It belongs to Mitch," Seraghina said. She was standing in the doorway, Steven in her arms. "But he wanted me to keep it. Lots of break-ins on this end of town."

Guido put the gun back. Steven looked at him, his dark eyes wide, glassy with sleep. He pointed a little pink finger at Guido, his cherubic lips mouthing *bang*.

# Forty

THE KOZEE KORNER WAS A DEPRESSION-ERA auto court, complete with a carport for the Mercedes. The motel was Triple-A rated in its day, but the highway that fronted it had long since been usurped by the Interstate. The businesses on this highway were all in various states of collapse, except for the strip joints, porn palaces, and used car lots. Guido's room had a small refrigerator which he'd stocked with a case of Tsingtao and a liter of Herradura Gold.

He'd left a message with Trimmer Swenson's secretary that he would be gone for a few days–his aunt Ronda, hospitalized with emphysema in Phoenix, had asked him to visit her. The secretary, recognizing the lie, said, "Aunt Ronda in Phoenix, huh?" Guido, realizing Phoenix was too close by, said, "Make that Baltimore. Aunt Ronda, hospitalized in Baltimore, in case anyone is interested enough to ask. Okay?"

His room smelled of tobacco and disinfectant. The astringent disinfectant only enhanced the slightly rancid essence of historical sex. The permanently sagging bedsprings had been beaten into submission by ten-thousand desperate trysts. The TV set was an old Zenith vacuum-tube number from the early sixties. The color and tint were spectral and heads at the top of the screen tended to balloon hydrocephalically, but it worked well enough.

The Gideon Bible in the nightstand was as fresh and crisp as it was when put there, fifty or sixty years ago. There was a bookmark in it. Guido opened it to the marked page and saw, underlined in savage red ink: *For you say, 'I am rich, I have prospered, and I need nothing;' not knowing that you are wretched, pitiable, poor, blind, and naked.* In the margin next to this passage, was a crookedly lettered but brutally emphatic

### HAH!

There was another book in the nightstand, a pamphlet. The title, in bold, money-green letters, was *Wealth Without Guilt.* Guido thumbed through it. Again, a passage was underlined, this time in a faint and unconvincing hand: *God Himself wants you to prosper. Why would He want you to be poor and miserable? It just wouldn't make sense, would it? The Heavenly Father wants you to own that condo on Waikiki, that villa on the Amalfi coast, that ski lodge in Sun Valley. In fact, he wants nothing more than your immediate wealth and prosperity! It is a personal insult to Him, and needlessly self-denigrating, to think otherwise.*

oh I'm sure

the dissenter wrote, in a pale blue, apologetic print that lacked all conviction.

Under both the Gideon and the pamphlet was a skin magazine, page after page of moderately attractive naked women, reclining with their legs opened as wide as pelvic architecture allowed. No ink on these pages, just a suspicious, paper-hardening stain here and there.

289

Guido had registered under the name Carson Motley. In this room, he *felt* like Carson Motley. It was the kind of motel room someone named Carson Motley would be attracted to. Carson Motley was the sort who would have underlined passages in a Gideon Bible one minute, then thumbed through a girlie magazine the next. Guido had slipped into the homely name as easily as Carson Motley would have slipped into a pair of old carpet slippers.

Naked and slightly drunk, Guido examined himself before a wavy full-length mirror that had been mounted on the bathroom door. The flawed mirror gave him thin geriatric legs, a melony gut, and a moony face: Carson Motley.

*Carson Motley, hustling cheap burial insurance on the road, found himself in another hick town that was well-stocked with old suckers who would be made to realize they had insufficient burial plans.*

Guido's imagination had the power to give him the heebie-jebies sometimes. He opened another Tsingtao and watched the mid-afternoon newsbreak. A young woman with avocado hair and a wide forehead sallow as a whitewashed plank, read a weather bulletin. Large, unseasonal thunderstorms were going to besiege La Siberia later in the day. Moist air from the Pacific coast of Mexico was moving into the region, where it would encounter a mass of cool, stable air. "Get your Halloween shopping done early!" said the young woman. "It's going to get real dampish out there, folks!" Her face under the exaggerated forehead was compressed into a bundle of affable lines. To Guido she looked like a cross between a Munchkin and a Martian.

Freaks, Guido thought. We are all freaks-in-process.

It was a Kozee Korner rule.

Step into these sour come-crusted chambers and feel the warping magic.

290

# Forty-one

O N THE OTHER HAND, HE WAS IN LOVE. That exempted him from freakdom, didn't it? Loving and being loved took away the boils and warts and webs of scar tissue that callused your soul. It was right there, in the Gideon, underlined in fierce red ink: *You are all fair my love, there is no flaw in you.* But the freak had his doubts. His comment in the margin was printed in resolute block letters, as if he didn't believe the free movements of his hand could adequately express his proud faithlessness:

## NO FLAW MY FUCKED ASS

Wind sent plumes of tan dust in quirky rooster-tails down the wide street that was no longer a major east-west American highway but a shabby avenue of dissolute yearning.

Thunder rumbled in the heavy sky. Guido read in a National Geographic once that there were rivers in the atmosphere that carry as much water from the equator to the poles as the Amazon carries to the Atlantic.

He plugged in his word processor and stared at the gray screen. He decided his new book would be called *Crackpots*. It would begin: "Carson Motley's anger was a god that demanded constant sacrifice. He felt good when he was full of rage and he felt better when he satisfied that rage."

He got dressed and walked to a convenience store two blocks down the street of nefarious enterprise and bought a bottle of lime juice and a cardboard shaker of salt.

A little man in a green suit approached him in the store's parking lot. The man wore no shirt under his stained and tattered coat. The skin of his thin chest was translucent with ruined health. "Sometimes when I come to, I find myself dancing," he said. "It's sort of weird." The little man had tufts of black hair growing on his battered nose.

"It's an affliction," Guido said.

"Yes, it could well be something like that," the man said.

Guido turned to leave. The little man caught his arm. "I need another minute of your time," he said.

"No can do," Guido said, shaking himself free.

"You can, you just don't want to."

"Have it your way."

Just before he reached the door of his motel room, the cloud let go. In a matter of seconds he was soaked. He went inside, found the ice bucket, then filled it from the ice machine next to the motel office. He carried the ice back to his room, locked and chained the door, got undressed again. He made himself a margarita in a plastic cup and took the drink into the shower with him.

"I am very much in love," he reminded himself. "I am exempt from freakdom."

Thinking of Seraghina–her PC muscles, her Kegels, the slopes and curves of her body, her earthy bouquet of aromas– aroused him. He was tempted to appease the great god Pud, but then remembered his trickster prostate and dropped the idea.

Unappeased lust equals rage: the warrior's rule. "Carson Motley's anger was a god that demanded constant sacrifice. It felt good to be full of rage and it felt better to satisfy that rage. But Carson had discipline. He knew how to conserve his forces, he knew when and where to strike. He would not stroke himself into a lull of false indifference."

Guido had another drink, got dressed again, and drove in the downpour to Martin Gassaway's house. Alana Falcon-

292

burg's Saab Turbo was parked in front. Guido snugged his low-riding Mercedes against her back bumper, hesitated before shutting off the ignition, then decided to re-park in the next block.

He walked in the rain back to the Gassaway place. The rain-washed mansions of this neighborhood were monuments to the well-reasoned life. Guido imagined harmonious families inside, enjoying each other's company in tastefully furnished living rooms—maids clearing the dinner dishes, the men of the houses planning new and rewarding business strategies, the women content with their needlework or the latest newsletter from their community service club. He knew better— but the houses themselves seemed like arguments in wood and stone for this blue-sky ideal. The geometrically precise landscaping was insistent. Grounds like these could not belong to people with chaotic lives.

When he climbed up the Gassaway porch, this impression of order and sanity was affirmed by the sound of classical music: an attractive contralto voice, accompanied by a pianist. Guido rang the doorbell, then rang it again, but the music did not stop.

He tried the door. It wasn't locked. He pushed it open and stepped inside. Marty Gassaway was at the Yamaha grand, and Alana Falconburg was by his side singing German *lieder*. They were in a transported state and didn't seem to notice Guido. Alana was wearing patent leather heels and a black strapless dress, and Gassaway was in a tux. They were ready for an occasion of some kind.

Guido sat down on a sofa upholstered in white silk damask. A six-foot tall *ficus benjaminus* stood regally in its clay pot at one end of the sofa. The Borzoi-mix, Isolde, snaked out from behind the tree and slid her narrow head between Guido's legs. Gassaway looked over his shoulder at Guido and said, "You like Schubert, Tarkenen?"

"Who doesn't," Guido said.

Alana had a professionally trained voice, rich and vibrant, and Gassaway seemed to play the piano with some skill. Guido, musically ignorant, allowed himself to fall under the music's gloomy spell. He leaned back into the sofa and listened. Isolde took this as an invitation. She nuzzled his crotch with grateful ardor. Alana's moving voice saturated the room with sentimental grief:

> *"Lebe wohl, du liebe Freund?*
> *Wenn dies lied dein Herz ergreft,*
> *Freund Schatten naher schweift*
> *Meiner seelen Saiten streift,*
> *Lebe wohl, du liebe Freund. . . ."*

Gassaway stopped playing abruptly and turned to face Guido. "What do you want?" he said. "No, let me guess. You've reconsidered your position and now you'd like payment? I'm not ungenerous, Guido. You did us a great favor. Really. I owe you, my man. How much do you want?"

"Not a fucking dime, Marty," Guido said.

"The man's a colorful déclassé saint, don't you think, Allie?" Gassaway said, turning back to the keyboard. He hunched down, studying the keys.

Alana smiled at Guido. It was an uncertain smile. Gassaway played a thunderous arpeggio that made the windows vibrate. Isolde extended her long nervous tongue, gave Guido's crotch a shy lick.

"Haven't you caught on to this creep yet, Alana?" Guido said.

Gassaway pushed away from the piano and stood up. "Oh, heavens," he said. "I believe our crime-writing colleague has come to think poorly of me. Is it because I've accepted the chairmanship of the new Department of Dream Architecture? Preposterous title, I agree. But we all have to make a living, do we not? The salary they've offered me is next to scandalous, Guido. You should look into it. Why don't you send me your vita, along with a letter of application. I think we'd work well together."

Alana looked at Gassaway with some amazement. "Martin, you're not serious! You've a distinguished academic record. Any university would be *lucky* to get you. You can't possibly think of staying on here, after what they've done to our department!"

"I've got the white man blues," Gassaway warbled, stabbing his fingers into the piano keys, striking a blues chord and then another. "Alana doesn't know what we're up against," he said to Guido. "Middle-aged white men are definitely passé, Allie. We don't get the top jobs anymore. We are in*fected* with colonialist mentality. Surely you've heard the charges. They've marginalized me, Allie."

"He's in bed with killers, Alana," Guido said. "The thing is, he feels right at home."

"You see," Gassaway said, "this is the trouble with hacks, they think in foggy-brained clichés. Do you have any idea of what you're talking about, Tarkenen?"

Guido pushed Isolde away and stood up. "I think so," he said. "Global Visions is what you might call a ruthless company."

"Quaint," Gassaway said. "Make a list for me, would you, of international companies that are sensitive and caring. I think you missed the part about the industrial revolution in your high school history class, Guido. Have you heard the term Robber Baron? I think the paradigm for corporate behavior was established some time ago."

"And that makes it okay for them to kill people?"

Gassaway stood up. The tux seemed a size too small. His thick neck looked red hot from razor burns. "Always a pleasure to chat with you, Guido, but Allie and I have a function to attend. Vice-Chancellor Cribbs is receiving the CEO tonight. Should be a wingding. No expense spared."

"What do you mean, '*kill* people'?" Alana said.

"Seems to be a pastime around here," Guido said. A toilet flushed upstairs, a door opened and closed, the floorboards creaked. "Gregory Inverness, for instance."

"What about Inverness?" Gassaway said. He stepped toward Guido.

"You killed him, you prick," Guido said.

Gassaway laughed. A quick laugh, too thin and metallic to pass for merriment. "Come on, Allie. Let's go. Tarkenen's obviously been pickling his brains again. I can smell you from here, you stupid barfly."

"There weren't any tapes, right?" Guido said. "Just the one Inverness had. Maybe Lotty had a copy of it. There was no break-in, and you wrote the threatening note from the bad guys in the mythical green Lincoln. You wanted the tape because you knew it would point the finger in the right direction. You were even smart enough to tell me that up front."

"Correct me if I'm wrong, Guido, but I think Gregory's killer is in the state psychiatric facility for the criminally insane."

"You got lucky. Freddy Marantz is a head-case, an obvious high-profile choice. But he's also a ninety-pound weakling, Marty. He couldn't have beat Inverness's skull to pulp with a thirty-pound boulder. You, on the other hand, can bench press damn near three-hundred pounds. One of your girlfriends told me that."

"Fine. That puts all the weightlifters in La Siberia under suspicion."

"You tossed Freddy's apartment, but didn't find the tape. A pro would have found it easily. That made me think."

"That's your trouble. You shouldn't try to think. In your case it could lead to cerebral hemorrhage. Why don't you just go home and write yourself a nice little batch of clichés. I don't have time for this nonsense."

"Oh God," Alana said. Both Guido and Gassaway turned to her. She looked pale. "You told me, just last night. Oh, Martin, it was so strange. I mean, when you said that. Said if anyone came between us, you'd . . . *kill* them. I mean, you laughed when you said it. But it was your *eyes*. Something in them didn't laugh."

Guido said: "'Could Orphelin kill for love? Orphelin asks himself that a dozen times a day. And the answer is invariably the same. . . . Love and death are linked in the unending dance . . . what's Orphelin's is Orphelin's, today, yesterday and tomorrow.' You killed Inverness because he took something from you."

"I am *com*plimented, Guido!" Gassaway said. "You've read my little romance! I am touched, I am overjoyed!"

"Don't write home about it, Marty. I only read that passage. It's crappy writing, by the way. But it says a lot about the pompous fraud who wrote it."

Gassaway hit Guido. It was a long-armed punch that started behind his right hip, telegraphed seconds in advance. Even so, Guido was too slow to slip it. It caught him high on the cheek and he went down.

"You moronic guinea," Gassaway said. "You come into my house, make wild accusations, frighten Allie, and then you malign my work!" He picked Guido up by his lapels and threw him against the piano.

Pain whiplashed through his body, but he was able to stand up and assume a defensive position. Gassaway stepped through Guido's ineffective punches and picked him up off the floor. He threw him across the room. Guido landed on Isolde, who screamed in surprise then slithered under the piano. Gassaway wandered around the room, looking for something. Guido couldn't breathe—the wind had been knocked out of him. Gassaway found what he wanted, a square of marble with an inscribed copper plate attached to it.

"Oh my God, Martin, no!" Alana said. She launched herself across his path. He shoved her aside. Guido tried to roll away, but Gassaway straddled him. He raised the heavy plaque—an award from the Henry James Society—then hesitated.

"I want you to see it coming, Guido," he said. "I want you to have a little time to think about what this excellent piece of Italian marble is going to do to your skull and its pathetic contents."

Alana threw herself on Gassaway again, this time managing to make him lose his balance. "Please, Martin, stop this!" she said. He grabbed at her with his free hand, caught her dress, peeled it off her breasts, managed to right himself.

"It's between me and him, Allie," he said. "Be a good girl and sit down. Sorry about your dress. I think Lotty's got a sewing kit. We have enough time to fix it up before the shindig at the Provost's."

"He's nuts," Guido said.

The plaque came down hard into the floor inches from Guido's ear, denting the inlaid oak. An intentional miss. "Exciting, isn't it?" Gassaway said. He raised the piece of marble again.

Somewhere a gun went off. Guido, his eyes shut against the coming permanent darkness, was startled in spite of the situation. Gassaway stood up, holding his bloody left arm. Lotty Gassaway was on the stairs. She was wearing a chenille bathrobe and her hair looked as if she hadn't combed or brushed it in days. She had a large-bore Derringer in her hand. The bullet had broken Gassaway's left arm at the elbow.

"You killed Greggy," she said. "I loved him and you couldn't stand it, you son of a bitch."

Gassaway waved at her with his good hand, as if waving to an acquaintance. "Wait, wait," he said, affable and suave in spite of his wound. "I love you, Lotty. I could never hurt you. If I did anything, it was for you, dear, out of love for *you.*"

The man is spreading bullshit on his own grave, Guido thought.

Alana, sitting on the floor next to the sofa, her breasts exposed and quivering, stared at her bleeding lover as if only now understanding what she had been keeping company with. Her mouth was moving but no sound came out. Guido rolled away from Gassaway and the line of fire.

"Love?" Lotty Gassaway said. "You want to explain what this *love* of yours is, Martin? Please, I'd really like to know."

Gassaway started to say something else, but Lotty fired the Derringer again. "Never mind," she said.

The second bullet cut a red line against Gassaway's fleshy neck–a graze wound. Gassaway slapped at his neck as if stung by a wasp, then staggered toward Lotty, smiling now, as if all this was an unfortunate misunderstanding easily cleared up.

Lotty's Derringer was empty. She pulled a handful of bullets out of her robe pocked, spilling most of them on the floor. She re-loaded the stubby, double-barreled pistol and raised it again. When Gassaway was within a few feet feet of her, she fired.

The bullet entered Gassaway's skull just over the left eye. It exited through the back of his head, showering the white sofa and Alana's fine white breasts with chunky red debris.

# Forty-two

A LANA SAT CROSS-LEGGED ON THE FLOOR, unconcerned that the top of her dress was gathered around her waist. She picked the spatter of Gassaway's brains and skull from her breasts. She didn't seem to be in a hurry. Her hair had caught fragments of Gassaway, too, but Guido didn't think she needed to be told that now.

Lotty stood at the foot of the stairs, the gun lowered. She was a tall woman, almost gaunt. Among the dark sheenless moguls of her neglected hair were white patches of blight. "You know what bothered him most about the tape?" she said. "It wasn't the sex. It was when Greggy and I were holding hands and looking into each other's eyes. He had a tantrum over that. He went wild."

Guido helped Alana to her feet. She was calm but unsteady. He went to the entryway closet and found a safari jacket and put it around her shoulders. "Are you going to be all right?" he said.

"Is Martin dead?"

Guido buttoned the jacket—one of Gassaway's—so that it covered her like a poncho. "He's dead," he said. "He's all the way dead."

"I'm not crying," Alana said, dreamily. "I don't understand why I'm not crying."

Guido put his arm around her shoulders. "Shock," he said. "You're in shock."

"I don't think I am, actually," she said.

Lotty laid the Derringer on the newel post of the banister. "Let's go into the kitchen," she said. "I'm so sorry about all this." Her apology was a reflex—the patrician remembering her breeding. She smiled, then laughed. "You think your life is going to be so perfect, and then it isn't."

They followed her into the kitchen. Lotty put a kettle of water on the stove. "Now then," she said, a plucky, take-charge lilt in her voice. "We should all have a cup of brisk Earl Grey." She touched Alana's hand. "I know this must be difficult for you, dear," she said. "Martin made things difficult for most of his women. It was a kind of hobby with him. One of his students attempted suicide when he broke off with her. He used to tell me how trying it was to be so attractive to women. He said it was his burden."

The kettle rattled and steam shot up from the whistling spout. Lotty poured boiling water into a tea pot. "He was a pig," she said. "Just a pig. I'm glad he's dead." She leaned against the stove for a moment, her back to Alana and Guido. Her body, under the chenille robe, quaked. She fought to control it.

"It was self-defense," Guido said. "I mean, he was going to kill me. You did it to defend me."

"Actually I didn't," Lotty said. "I'm sorry, but I wasn't thinking of you at all. When you confirmed what I'd been thinking for days—that he killed Greggy—then I only wanted to kill him, not save you."

"Even so, you did stop him from bashing my head in," Guido said. "The police will see it that way."

"Frankly, I don't care how they see it," Lotty said. "Martin should have been suffocated in his crib."

She turned from the stove abruptly. "Sandwiches!" she said, cheerfully. "I'm utterly famished. I've got a good wurst in the fridge. There's some slaw, too. Are you two hungry?"

# Forty-three

THE POLICE: BORED AND CASUALLY OMINOUS men, blank-faced or smiling faintly, the death of a well-to-do professor at the hands of his betrayed wife, his side-piece present in a ripped dress—pure miniseries material.

Milt Capoletti and Eddie Thorsen were there—the detectives Guido had seen in the cafe after Figgis bombed the air conditioning plant. Capoletti with his blue yam nose leaky under viral assault, Thorsen with nose flat as hammered bronze, his nostrils twin nailholes under his stony eyes. Both owned the impersonal gaze of men who severely narrow and intensify their focus in order to challenge the obvious. Guido recalled something else about them, something the waitress had said: they were a tag-team who liked to bust heads.

A half dozen uniforms were also present, men who took their style from TV—pointedly unaffected by blood and gore, finding small jokes among the bloodslicks and sprayed brains. One of them video-taped the scene in scrupulous detail, vacuuming images into his camcorder. He dwelled on the tea cups and sandwich remains on the kitchen table as if fascinated.

Let's see, Capoletti had said, wiping his nose with a snot-crimped handkerchief. You ate sandwiches after the incident? And Lotty, without hesitation, replied, We were hungry, officer. Capoletti studied her face. Yeah, brawling and killing works up the old appetite, he said. Brains on the floor makes me want to put on the old feed bag.

It lasted hours, the questions asked and re-asked. The ME, Seraghina's boss, a rotund jocular man with thick, black-rimmed glasses and well-oiled, Lord Fauntleroy hair, seemed more amused than the police. He joked as he took Gassaway's temperature rectally. "Whoa, looky *here*. This old boy is cooling off faster than a short-changed whore."

He was a man with a bent toward pedagogy: "This cooling is happening, you see," he said to a young uniformed officer who was looking on, "because he's losing heat by conduction from the center of his body outward to the skin, and then by loss of surface heat through ordinary radiation and convection. Why it's happening so fast, I can't say. Blame the rainy day. Sometimes bread dough won't rise on a rainy day."

Examining Gassaway's head wound, he said, "Something of a gadget, this .44 Derringer. I mean, it's not a weapon I would choose, but it performed, did it not? It got the job done."

He nudged Gassaway's blood-stiffened hair away from the entry wound. "I think we are going to find some extremely handsome inner-table beveling at the entry site when we de-glove the skull. No doubt there'll be some very agreeable exit beveling as well. This has all the earmarks of a first-rate textbook wound. The little lady made neat work of it, didn't she? Dropped the old dog in his philandering tracks." The ME loved his job.

Outside, the storm had tied the sky into angry black knots. Lightning made the lights ripple; thunder rattled the house. Guido now hurt all over, the pain delayed by adrenaline. He asked permission to go to the bathroom. Detective Capoletti granted it after studying Guido for a moment with eyes that held most of humanity under suspicion. "Don't I know you from somewhere?" he said.

Guido shook his head. "I doubt it," he said.

"Swear I've seen you someplace recent," Capoletti said.

303

Guido shrugged, shook his head. Capoletti's impaling eyes held him a moment longer then released him.

It took Guido minutes to generate his arcless stream. When he did it was neon pink. He stared at the clouded water, trying to recall if he'd eaten beets recently, knowing he had not. He zipped up and went back into the kitchen.

"The Ptomaine Cafe," Capoletti said, snapping his fingers. "You were in there when me and Eddie were trying to get that cheap horse's ass to take the tickets he ordered."

"Oh, sure. I remember," Guido said.

Capoletti dug in his jacket pocket. He brought out a crumpled ticket. "How about you? You want to buy a Police Association benefit ticket. You could win a set of golf clubs. Twenty bucks."

Guido took out his wallet and gave Capoletti a twenty. The detective handed Guido the ticket. "Thanks," he said. "Damn near makes my quota."

The preliminary investigation ended. Lotty, handcuffed, was led to a police car. "You know what the Mexicans call handcuffs?" the ME said to a young officer. *"Esposas!* The Spanish word for wife! Does that tell you something, young man? Does that add to your fledgling store of wisdom?"

Guido and Alana were told to stay in town, that someone from the district attorney's office would be contacting them. The ambulance that took Gassaway to the crime lab roared away in a riot of strobe lights and sirens. Isolde, trembling and moaning, was led away on a short leash by a uniformed officer. The house was sealed with yellow tape printed with "Crime Scene—Do Not Cross" warnings, and Guido and Alana found themselves alone in the rain.

"I'll drive you to your car," she said.

Guido knew he was bleeding in his pants, but he was beginning to feel somewhat detached, even from his fear. "Okay," he said. "Thanks. I'd appreciate that."

Her car wouldn't start. She worked the key in the ignition and kicked the accelerator pedal until the heel of her shoe, already damaged in the scuffle, broke off. The Saab made polite protests–small gasps and flutters–but would not start.

"My car's not far from here," Guido said. "We can take it."

They got out into the downpour and strobing sky. Alana limped ahead. Guido, also limping, caught up with her. When they got to the Mercedes they were soaked.

Guido unlocked it, got in behind the wheel. Alana strapped herself into the bucket seat next to him. The car started right up, roaring, but Guido didn't put it into gear. He leaned his head on the steering wheel.

"What's wrong?" Alana said.

"I think I'm passing out," Guido said.

# Forty-four

ALANA SWITCHED ON THE OVERHEAD LIGHT. "What is it?" she said. Guido sat back in the seat and made a face. He thought it was a smile.

"I don't know. I'm bleeding. Maybe internally, too."

"*Too?* Get out—can you? I'll drive you to the hospital."

They managed to trade places. Alana kicked off her shoes, hiked up her dress, and slipped the Mercedes into gear. The quick-revving car fish-tailed away from the curb, then traveled sideways half a block before Alana managed to straighten it. "I'll take you to La Siberia General. It's closest, I think," she said.

"Don't kill us on the way," Guido said. He closed his eyes, pictured gasoline explosions, good German sheet metal accordioned, rubber burning darkly.

The electrical storm had knocked out a power station. The streetlights weren't working. Traffic lights blinked feeble yellow.

"I think I'm lost," Alana said. The car was hydroplaning in a whitewater runoff. The churning front wheels raised tall Japanese fans of opaque water.

"Straight ahead," Guido said.

"No, I'm lost." She pulled the car over, turned on the overhead light again. "Is there a map in the glove compartment?"

Guido doubted low-riders needed maps. He looked anyway. No map, but scraps of paper. Someone's old grocery list. Gas station receipts. A well-made reefer, thick as a thumb—missed by Wolfgang Schnur's clean-up crew, or stashed there and forgotten by one of them. "You want this?" he said to Alana.

She took it, lit it with the dashboard lighter. Handed it to Guido. It had been a while–ten years, fifteen? He'd quit weed for the same health reasons he'd quit cigarettes but had taken up with tobacco again, the more addictive drug. But weed had analgesic properties and so he sucked down an immoderate volume of the harsh smoke, forgetting to carburate. The pain of his coughing fit made him think he had a broken rib or a cracked sternum. Alana took back the joint, ignoring his gasp of pain, sucked hard enough to make the tip crackle. A tiny wildfire edged up the tight ZigZag cylinder. Then it was her turn to lean her forehead on the steering wheel.

"You all right?" Guido said.

Her shoulders rose and fell. She made some wet noises. "Oh, the *shit*," she sobbed. "Oh, the rotten *shit*," her voice scraping against a thickening remorse.

Guido took the fat joint out of her hand, touched her shoulder. "Do you want me to drive? I think I can."

"He was a great lay," she said, bitterly. "Really great. Why am I thinking of that *now?* The son of a bitch. He called me Allie. No one's ever called me Allie. I liked it, made me feel . . . I don't know–*rural,* maybe. Said his wife didn't grasp subtlety. Said he needed a woman like me. The asshole. I'm not *stupid.* Do I *look* stupid? I graduated summa cum laude. I did post-doctoral work at the Sorbonne. But I *am* stupid. I fell for his line of shit like some kind of freshman sorority girl just in from the farm. The fuckhead. I'm forty years old tomorrow. Forty!"

"Happy birthday," Guido said. "Could we go now?"

"You'd think a forty-year-old with my credentials would have one fucking iota of goddamned sense."

Guido shrugged—compassionately, he thought. Sense, like the extra Y chromosome, might be rare. Might even be myth.

"I'm crying," she said, calmer now. "I'm sitting here in the middle of nowhere, in a weird car with Jesus Christ on the hood, and *crying.*"

The sky opened a bit. Moon and stars and the winking red light of a passenger plane slipped through a large vent in the spent clouds. Then the streetlights came on. Boulevard neon flickered and burst into ecstatic dance. A cowgirl twirled a rope, an Indian waved hello, and between them, *Enrique's Comida Corrida*. The plucky world of men and women, of fast food and speedy machines, was making a big comeback.

*We are definitely in the middle of somewhere,* Guido thought. He felt elated. He wanted to hug Alana; decided he liked her. Perhaps admired her.

*Reefer madness,* he thought.

# Forty-five

THEY WERE REGARDED WITH CONTEMPT by the poor and homeless who waited with customary stoicism for emergency medical services. Alana in safari jacket and evening gown and broken shoe, her hair tangled and still matted here and there with blood even though it had been rain-soaked. Guido hobbled along beside her, rocked with pain and vertigo, his pants mapped with bloody urine. He held on to Alana, the two of them swerving and limping through the waiting room toward the receptionist like married rummies on a whimsical promenade.

"This man needs attention immediately," Alana said.

The receptionist looked up. "Right," she said. "So do half the people in this room. Please take a seat, we'll get to you."

"You don't understand," Alana said. "He may be dying."

Guido stared at Alana.

The receptionist glanced up from her logbook, her broad nose twitching. "I smell wacky 'backy," she said. She was a stout middle-aged woman with a helmet of red hair that looked bulletproof. She had seen and smelled and heard most of what humanity was capable of producing and was weary of it but not impressed. She lived by necessity in an unshakable state of bored skepticism.

"He's bleeding internally, and externally," Alana said. "He *has* insurance."

The receptionist raised a doubting eyebrow. "A rare bird," she said.

"He's a professor at La Siberia Tech. Fully covered."

"You should take him to Blueblood Memorial then," the stout woman said.

"Pardon *me?*"

"Prince Wilhelm Memorial," the receptionist said, backing down a bit. "We have nicknames for some of these places."

"I don't care what you have," Alana said. "This man is in critical condition. This is a hospital, isn't it? He needs a doctor now, this instant. I can't drive him to Prince Wilhelm."

Alana did not take crap. Guido decided he really did admire her, reefer madness or not.

The woman was willing to continue the duel—she'd had plenty of practice—but Guido slipped out of Alana's grasp and hit the floor with enough impact to turn a few heads in the waiting room.

He woke on a gurney, an IV drip taped to his arm. Bowls of light passed overhead. *UFOs,* Guido thought. A squadron of monotonous aliens in single file: ceiling lights—moving as the gurney moved. A humming male attendant pushed it from behind.

The double-doors of an elevator opened and the attendant muscled the gurney into it. "Where am I going?" Guido said.

"To O.R. nineteen," the attendant said. "It's a hellatious night. We hardly ever use nineteen. Bad lighting. Half a dozen headshot cases came in since my supper break, plus a bunch of brain-scramblers—head-on collisions. The citizens don't know how to drive on wet streets. Every neurosurgeon in town is here. Even the great Peabody, the man who unstuck the Siamese twins who were head-connected. It's like one big drill-and-stitch party, man."

The IV had something good in it. Morphine, Guido decided. He felt comfortable and relaxed as he was rolled into operating room nineteen where the lights cast strange shadows. The

310

surgery team picked him up off the gurney and laid him down on the operating table. A man who looked overworked to the point of collapse, his face unnaturally pink with hypertension, bent down to him. "I'm Heck Furness, urology," he wheezed. "I talked to you earlier."

Guido blinked. He had no memory of talking to this urologist, a slump-shouldered man with red-rimmed eyes and mealy nose webbed with violet veins, a nose that had been to war. He could have passed for a Hammer and Tong wino.

"We're going to do a prostatectomy. That thing giving you all the misery is big as a summer squash. You can carve a face on it for Halloween, scare the dirt out of the rug rats. Listen up, that fall you took seriously aggravated your condition."

"Fall?" Guido said.

"The lady who came in with you—she said you fell down a flight of stairs. You flopped again in the waiting room. In any case, the renegade gland has to go."

Guido smelled bourbon. Sweat slicked Heck Furness's fluorescent forehead. The gin blossoms on his nose looked like a roadmap to hell.

"Have no fear, " Furness said. "I've done a thousand prostatectomies. I could do you with my feet. Listen up, we use the latest technique here. I'll be working in a bloodless field, that way I'll be able to see prezactly what to cut and what not to cut. This procedure won't leave you incontinent or impotent. In the old days we used to fly blind, most always uncoupling the nerves that let you pee when you want—the same nerves responsible for pumping up Mr. Johnson for show time. This, to understate the case, compromised the quality of life for the patient. But listen up now—those *were* the dark ages, brother."

"Have you been drinking?" Guido said.

Heck Furness smiled. His dry lips peeled back exposing glistening brown teeth. His dark breath reached Guido's face.

311

He showed Guido his right hand, then his left. "Rock fucking steady, my man," he said. "I could thread a needle in boxing gloves."

"I don't remember. . . ." Guido tried to recall if he'd given anyone permission to operate. Maybe Alana had, posing as a family member. Maybe emergency surgery had different rules. Maybe—he thought of Global Visions, of Hollingworth Li, of possible treachery. He tried to sit up. Latexed hands pressed him down.

"Listen up," Heck Furness said. "We're going to give you an epidural anesthetic. You'll be partially awake during the procedure. You won't feel zilch, but you'll be in a twilight consciousness. It's sort of pleasant, you wait and see."

"Here we go," said the anesthesiologist.

"Wait," Guido heard himself say, his voice suddenly far away, as if coming through a mile of garden hose.

The dark closed in around him like warm mud. He felt himself drawn down, buoyant but sinking. He heard a fly buzz. Heard himself snore. His eyelids felt weighted. He opened them anyway, saw the lighted medical ceiling, was aware of the apparatus covering his mouth, then was not aware of it. He heard the regular beep of the heart monitor. And through it all, the crisp and rhythmic voices of the operating team, led by urologist Heck Furness. ("Retractor now. Clamp please. The Metzenbaum, please. Suck it up, Gordy, I can't see the striated sphincter.")

The fly walked up his cheek. Or was it a roach. He couldn't speak. Didn't know what to say. Anyway, it wasn't his place to speak up: operating room rules. He closed his eyes, dreamed a little. Dreamed an ocean flecked with whitecaps. A lifeboat made its way toward him. Twelve men, six of them rowing. Lost at sea, but not disheartened. They sang a sea chanty, one of them crushing chords out of a ragged concertina between huge weathered hands. Vanished then in gauzy fog, the singing voices muted.

Guido rotated away from himself. He fell out of his body as if falling out of bed. The fly, old and heavy, a summer fly in October dotage, groomed its bulbous head. It was on the ceiling, next to a tray of lights. He reached a hand toward it, but the wizened fly walked contemptuously out of range. Guido closed his eyes and the warm dark mud embraced him again, a homely comfort. His breath caught on his soft palate, like a quartering wind in the skysail of a square-rigger, producing a grumbling snore. Heck Furness drawled friendly commands; the heart monitor ticked.

Guido let himself float—a gaseous entity, an amorphous volume of ectoplasm. This gave him vertigo, but the view was splendid. From the ceiling he saw the red trench in his lower abdomen, running from umbilicus to pubis, the trench held wide by large gleaming clamps. The trench was as substantial as his grandmother's gravy boat. (*"Ai cuidado, cuidado,"* the surgeon said, "here's the neuro-vascular bundle—*implore a Jesús* for this professor, Araceli, lest the randy *vato* his ladyfriend remembers so fondly becomes but a tormenting memory.")

The back wall of operating room nineteen opened to the sea, the horizon bearded with silver fog. A four-masted bark—topsails, topgallants, and royals bellied out in the broad belt of the tradewinds—made its way toward Guido. Its jibs and spankers fluttered and snapped with uncontained excitement—a dream with high production values; but more than a dream in its detail and effect. The ship loomed large and Guido heard the lap and wash of seawater, the muscular groan of great timbers. He noticed some damage—torn sail, lengths of mast gone. Then saw her name, in tall gothic lettering on the side, up by the bow: *Emperor Moth*. His father signaled him aboard.

313

He followed the hard-varnished deck: he was a small current of air.

"Guido," his father said. He sat in a chair, the same leather recliner he always sat in to read the papers or watch TV. The winds calmed and the great sails hung limp as laundry.

"Hi, Daddy," Guido said. Years peeled off his voice like rust from an iron hull.

"We've just come out of a bad storm—lost some foresail, plus half the foremast. A piece of the aftermast came romping down and pulped the old captain against the wheelhouse. Don't think he'll make it."

Elmo Tarkenen invited Guido to sit on his lap. Guido was bigger and older than his father, but did not feel foolish. "I've been at sea a long time, son," he said.

"I know," Guido said.

"We've seen many strange things—some terrible, some beautiful, some both."

"Tell me, Daddy."

"A city in Cathay, inhabited by creatures that were half-men, half-lion. A city of thunderous poets, and delicate magicians with fine and tawny hair."

"I'm sorry I doubted you, Daddy," Guido said.

Elmo Tarkenen waved Guido's apology away. "Do you hear that singing?" he said.

Guido listened. A man's voice, thin as hammered gold, rose from below deck.

"The first mate got tore up on a split davit. Looked about as bad as you on that operating table." Both father and son looked down at Guido and the elliptical trench that ran red from navel to pubes. "We snagged a bottlenose dolphin and drained its blood," the father continued, "then rigged up some tubing. Ran dolphin blood into the first mate's veins. Now all he does is lie in his bunk and sing like that. Sometimes the singing attracts a good wind, sometimes it becalms. No way of telling which."

Elmo Tarkenen eyed his son with the squint of an old salt. "You believe me, son? You believe it happened?"

Guido nodded. "Yes, Daddy. I believe you. I hear the first mate singing."

The ship groaned as recalled wind rammed the sails. "Got to be going, son," Elmo Tarkenen said.

Guido watched the *Emperor Moth* move away through choppy seas, carried by wind summoned by the dolphin blood of the singing first mate. His father, still in his recliner, his back to Guido, lifted his pale hand and waved.

The heart monitor skipped and sped. Heck Furness glanced at it.

# Forty-six

His ACCUMULATED MAIL SAT IN A PILE on his kitchen table. Alice Dark had brought it in for him while he was in the hospital. She had visited him there with loaves of homemade bread and foil-wrapped plates of *riso e broccoli,* ("Make you bowel move, Mista' Tarka,") *pesce affogato,* ("Fish make you heal nice,") and for his morale, a nice rum *tortoni*—foods not on the hospital's approved menu. Guido ate it gratefully. Seraghina visited in the evenings but insulated herself from him with a rigidly maintained distance and clothes that would make a Carmelite nun feel unglamorous. They were afraid to share a warm glance while the stitches were still fresh.

Under the usual bills and fliers, a note from Figgis, postmarked Bajomitío, Mexico:

Guido,

I've got myself a little casita here on the south end of Bajo. I'll be commuting to and from school each day. Not a bad drive except for bridge traffic. I heard of your medical difficulties. My sympathies, old man. Hope you can soon see to pee and screw on cue. The bastards hurt me, amigo, but didn't turn me in. Go figure. Looks like we won the war. Posthumous thanks to Solly and Lex. I dug up the remaining six packs of Aussie beer and dumped them in the Rio, also the ones in your basement. I support the international land mine reclamation act. My renegade days are over. I want to create, not destroy. See you at the office.

Guido had heard some of the news while still in the hospital. Global Visions had backed out of its agreement with the regents of La Siberia Tech, having decided to build their own research and development facility in mainland China. "Economic realities" was the reason given for this change of plans.

An unrelated story reported a "gift" worth billions was given to the world over the internet by Professors Solomon Dubrinsky and Lex Xenedes. Shortly after their deaths, the original nanowiring research was "published" on the Science Exchange Website, putting it squarely in the public domain. It was available to all researchers worldwide now, with no obligation on anyone's part to pay royalties. Solly Dubrinsky had programmed the university's mainframe via his office terminal to dump the nanowiring research material into the net the day after the Pomona symposium. It was insurance: if for some reason the symposium didn't happen, the nanowiring secrets would be disseminated regardless. Vice Chancellor Cribbs was furious, but helpless. Dubrinsky and Xenedes outfoxed the Global Visions people, saving the university in the process, though it had cost them their lives.

There was a letter from Sid Mullen:

Guido,

News of your renegade prostate reached N.Y. Jesus. But you're okay, right? I'm thinking that maybe you should do a non-fiction book on the prostate. Title: *To Pee or Not to Pee.* Seriously, all men over the age of 40 live in a state of prostate anxiety. It's what—the number three killer now? Prostate cancer I mean. Something like that.Hey, I'm too scared to get the PSA test. This is a universal fear. And where there's fear there's a *publishing opportunity.* Look at all the books Mad Cow Disease generated, and all of them big sellers. Think about it. We are talking six figures, my man. We are talking talkshow fever.

The operation was a week behind him now. He had good drugs for residual pain. Bladder control wasn't perfect yet, but his arc was magnificent—the vigorous golden arc of a teenager. He sent a bottle of ten-year-old George Dickel to Heck Furness with a note of heartfelt thanks. If urologist Furness needed a drink or two before he operated, then Guido felt obligated to make a contribution to medical science.

The phone rang.

"I pray for you as well as them," she said.

*Oh shit,* Guido thought. "Carma?"

"I pray for them all."

Guido didn't hang up.

"I've got one of them here. I am praying for him, for his soul. Whatever's left of it."

"Who, Carma?"

He heard her breathe. Long and slow, as if the autonomic systems of the body itself were regulating its oxygen intake.

"You betray us," she said. "It's a reflex with you. You give us what you think we want, which is also what we think we want, but the truth is it isn't what either of us want."

"I see," Guido said.

"In that way you betray yourself, too. But you don't have anything to give in the first place—this thing you think we want, and we think we want, *does not exist.*"

Guido didn't respond. He heard something in the background, maybe a man sobbing.

"Ask me what I'm talking about, Professor," she said.

318

"Okay."

"Love. We can't find it. So we take the next best thing. We take the lie instead."

*"She's going to kill me!"* the sobbing man said. Guido almost recognized the voice.

"Who are you going to kill, Carma?" Guido said.

"It's for his own sake. He's confessed. He's clear of his lies, now. His soul is purged and ready—all he has to do is finish my ironing."

"I'm coming over," Guido said.

He called Milt Capoletti. The detective was not at his desk. Guido left a message. Then he drove to 101 Howard.

The front door was not locked. Guido stepped inside, listened. Nothing. Maybe her victim had stupidly finished her ironing instead of making it last. Then he heard her warn against scorch. The man released a chuckling sob.

Guido walked quietly down the hall to Carma's ironing/workout room. He pushed open the door a few inches. Vice Chancellor Cribbs, steam iron in hand, stood naked at the ironing board. Carma sat on her weight bench, a pistol aimed at his back. It wasn't her little purse gun. It was a very large, nickel-plated .45 automatic.

"Efraim said he loved me," she said to Guido without glancing up—she'd been expecting him. "But he's as bankrupt as all the others, isn't he?"

"Not a reason to kill him though, is it?" Guido said, without conviction. It was probably the single universal reason for murder, the one most understandable. He looked at the trembling Vice Chancellor. Why did these creeps go after poor Carma? Then he remembered his own tacky overtures and felt a momentary twinge of sympathy for Efraim Cribbs. It passed.

319

A greater question nagged Guido. How did slime like Cribbs rise to positions of importance? Just by being willing to make stepladders out of the warm, pulsing bodies of ordinary human beings? Of course. Wasn't this the tried and true secret of success?

"Thank God you're here, Tarkenen," Cribbs said. "Tell her, tell her she can't *think* that way."

"You can't think that way, Carma," Guido said. "Only people like Cribbs and his cronies can think that way. Ask Sol Dubrinsky and Lex Xenedes."

Cribbs looked at Guido. He was a skinny man with a pampered pot belly. Naked, he lost patriarchal authority. Ironing tired him. He was not accustomed to physical work. His hand shook as much from fatigue as from fear. "I had nothing to do with that," he said. "Not personally."

"Tell me about it," Guido said. He winked at Cribbs, as if to convey the idea that this was just a clever stall.

"We—they—hired people to do it," Cribbs said. "It wasn't my idea—how could it? I'm a civilized man. I value my colleagues! But, in this case there were billions, literally *billions,* at stake. That kind of money makes its own rules. Surely you can *see* that, Tarkenen. Money—for its own understandable self-protection—often requires unpleasant actions, actions that I had no personal involvement with."

Carma looked from Cribbs to Guido and back again, confused.

"Shut up," she said. "He said he wanted to be with me. He said he was going to leave his wife. He lied. But I don't care about that. Or about any of his other lies. I care about the biggest lie, the lie we both told ourselves."

"'Most of the many women he had known had been picked for their lack of self-esteem,'" Guido quoted. It was a line Dr.

Burnaby had once pinned him to the wall with, a line from a short story by a famous east coast writer.

*"What?"* Carma and Cribbs said simultaneously.

"Don't kill him, Carma," Guido said. "He really isn't worth it. I've got a better idea."

Carma frowned, lowered the gun slightly. "What are you saying?"

"Make him put his head in the toilet. His head is full of shit anyway."

"I'll do it, I'll *do* it," Cribbs said. "Yes, it *is* the better way! Tarkenen's right!"

*Don't be so fucking willing,* Guido said with his eyes. *Make her think you've got something at stake, like* pride.

"Get into the bathroom," Carma said.

Carma rammed the .45 into Cribbs' narrow back, pushed him out into the hall and toward the bathroom.

"Get on your knees," she said.

Cribbs knelt slowly, his bony joints crackling. He even opened the toilet lid.

"Put your head in it," she said. "All the way."

"Thank you, thank you," Cribbs said, his gratefully repentant voice hollow against the wet porcelain.

"Not good enough," Carma said, recognizing that Cribbs had no dignity to lose. She pressed the cold steel of the .45 against his ass. "Be afraid, you stink bug. At least be afraid."

Provost Cribbs retched. Guido pushed the flush lever.

# Forty-seven

D ETECTIVE CAPOLETTI CAME ALONE. His partner, Eddie
Thorsen, was out with the flu. Guido let the big detective
in. "What seems to be the problem here?" Capoletti said, his
dark, nostrils flared with suspicion. He'd just had lunch and
was working his cheese-white tongue around his teeth, sucking
out bits of bread, prosciutto and provolone. Gas eruptions
ballooned his cheeks which he expelled as thoughtful sighs.
He wouldn't have responded to something like this–some
vague crap about a possible assault–a patrol car already in
the area could have covered it, but he was in the mood for a
drive to a part of La Siberia he liked, an area he was thinking
of moving to.

"Dr. Cribbs wants to make a statement," Guido said.

Cribbs, wearing only boxer shorts, was sitting on a hassock,
shaking and blubbering. Capoletti studied him, doubt turning
to disgust. He looked at Carma, sitting, somewhat rigidly, on
the sofa. "And who might this charming young lady be?" he
said to Guido, a lascivious parody of etiquette.

"This is her apartment," Guido said.

Detective Capoletti's eyes narrowed as he put a scenario
together. "Uh-huh," he said. "And, if you don't mind my
repeating myself, just what seems to be the problem here?"

"Dr. Cribbs has some things he wants to get off his chest,"
Guido said.

The detective sat heavily on the sofa next to Carma. "Knows
where Jimmy Hoffa is, does he?" he said to her–jocular,
flirtatious–but Carma didn't respond. She sat quietly, staring
at her hands. Guido went into the kitchen and got a glass of

water. Doctor's orders: keep the system hydrated. Pee a lot, rather than too little. Then he left by the back door. Enough excitement for one day—besides, his presence wasn't needed, it only added confusion to the scene. He walked around to the side of the duplex, then out to the street. He got into his low-riding Mercedes, and, leaving a patch of smoking rubber behind, drove home.

Cribbs—hysterically glad to be alive—bared his soul to Detective Capoletti. Capoletti took notes, skeptical at first, even amused. Then, as the details became too convincing to dismiss, he began to write with urgency. He frowned, licked the tip of his pencil now and then, but he couldn't keep up. He halted the Vice Chancellor's rambling breakdown to get a tape recorder out of his car, wondering why *he* had to be the one to hear this. What if some local honchos were involved? What if the La Siberia power grid was up to its collective hemorrhoids in this mess? A thing like this had to have its own growth hormones. It could turn mole hills into mountains. It was also an infection that spread like gonorrhea. Pretty soon everybody's dick starts leaking bloody pus. Big dicks first—dicks with money, dicks with forty-dollar haircuts and Armani suits—then the little dicks, convenient dicks, dicks with no juice. But the big dicks had the penicillin of money. They could lawyer their way out of it and sail away on their golden parachutes, while the two-bit grifters and grafters did the hard time.

Everyone knew the mayor walked through life with his hand out, looking for grease. He lived like God on his thirty-k salary. The Chief of Detectives, who made only a little more than the mayor, owned a condo in Cancun and a ski-cabin in Big Bear. Capoletti, on the other hand, lived in a four-plex with his wife and three kids and drove a twenty-year old Chevy

Citation. He took his family once a year to Disneyland on his vacations, and wound up taking another year to pay down the plastic. Milt Capoletti was honest by default: nobody needed him, except nickel-and-dime guys like the owner of the Ptomaine Cafe. And even they didn't *need* him. Milt Capoletti had made it his business over the years to make the small time chiselers *think* they needed him. It got him a few perks: sometimes he made his quota on Police Association benefit tickets.

He often wondered about Eddie Thorsen. Eddie pocketed some drop money once, claimed the bag man, a walking rectum, had flushed it down a public toilet. No investigation by the Rat Squad. The thought crossed Capoletti's mind more than once that Eddie split the roll–ten grand in all–with the Chief. Not something anyone wanted to pursue. And no one did. Not even the rats in IAD. Now this incredible shit. If half of what this college administrator said was true, Capoletti knew he'd better sit on it or be ready to trade his badge for a one-way ticket to Buttfuck, Idaho. Because nobody with serious juice was going down because of a confession elicited by Milton Capoletti. Capoletti would be the one to get his stones handed to him in a Glad Bag.

Cribbs, rat-faced with fear–a fear his carefully groomed persona never suspected it was capable of, a fear that took on a life and language of its own–gibbered the story in disjointed parcels to the reddening and increasingly reluctant ear of Detective Capoletti. With the tape recorder running, Capoletti stared at Cribbs who was shaking as if he'd just been pulled out of the North Atlantic in December.

"Okay, okay," Capoletti said after he'd heard enough. "I'm going out to my vehicle to call an EMS van for you. I think you're in shock."

He'd pocketed the .45 he'd found on the toilet tank, after a cursory look around the apartment, and put it in the car. What was up with *that?* The muscle-bound broad expect to be attacked on her shitter? He sat for a few minutes wondering what to do next. Maybe Cribbs flipped his toupee and his incredible confession was some kind of paranoid fairy tale. The guy, sitting there in his boxers, was acting like he was tripping on a whole sheet of microdots—eyes wild, spitting on himself, talking crazy shit a mile a minute. Screwy fucking academic types. Didn't matter if they were professors or administrators, they just weren't like ordinary citizens. Thought they farted perfume and pissed mouthwash. And this Guido character, what was he all about? A professor? He didn't look like any professor Capoletti ever saw. He looked a lot like a worn-out copy of his cousin, Vince Marcellino, the barber. Not too smart, like Vince. How smart could he be, eating lunch in the Ptomaine? How did he tie in with Cribbs and the iron lady?

And why should Milton A. Capoletti give a fat steaming shit?

The iron lady—Cribbs' side-piece, Capoletti figured. Walking around in tight shorts and tee-shirt, no brassiere, tits flying up like launched Scuds, hard bulging ass, strong brown thighs, calves that could saw your neck off. Jesus, he could use a piece of that. He liked women who kept in shape. His old lady, Marie, didn't give day-old cat shit anymore about her appearance. He'd had a female partner once—a beaver with a badge. She kept in shape but she looked like Richard Nixon. Even had a five-o'clock shadow. Tempted him, sometimes, especially when Marie was on the rag, but he couldn't get past that Tricky Dicky face. Marie was still pretty, if you disregarded everything from the first chin down, but sex for her was just another household duty, like mopping out the shitters or hanging diapers on the line. They hardly ever screwed at night. For one thing, they didn't like to miss their favorite TV shows. Then there was always the hassle of getting the brats down. Little Angelo, a mama's boy, was the biggest headache. By the time they got to bed they were ready to sleep. Some mornings, when he felt gism oozing out his pores, he'd beg for it. In those humiliating moments, Marie could break his balls with some stimulating comment like, "Oh Milton, you're only piss-stiff. Go to the bathroom and take a leak, you'll be all right."

For instance, this morning. He woke up with a hard-on you could strike a kitchen match on. Rolled over toward Marie, hickeyed her tit, pushed her fat legs open, worked a finger in up to the first knuckle, and that was as far as he got. Little Angelo started squalling in the nursery, and Marie was up like a shot–thankful, Capoletti knew–for the excuse. Saved by the yell. He waited a while, thinking she *might* come back, knowing that his dick was doing the thinking, then cursed and got out of the bed. In the shower he was still sporting a rock hard choad which he refused, out of principle, to take down by hand. There were better ways to cheat the census.

It was that goddamned White Table Queen squash. Marie had served it the night before, along with pork steaks and home fries. But it was the squash that did this to him, he knew that for a fact. Every time she microwaved White Table Queen squash he woke up the next day with a hard-on that belonged in the hard-on hall of fame. Not that it got him any respect. When she did cooperate it was always with a reluctance you could slab with a chainsaw. She'd take a deep breath, then sigh, *"Okay,* Milton, get it *over* with, you know I've got things to *do."* No appreciation at all for the towering titanium salami that could deflect bullets.

326

Milton Capoletti's Philosophy: Life was a river of shit you had to swim across. So he didn't need to be tying anvils to his feet mid-stream. He ripped the pages he'd written out of his notebook, rewound the tape and erased it. He thought: *Fuck it. Let the crazy son of a bitch tell his story to someone else.* Milt Capoletti had enough trouble keeping his head above the brown river. This lousy world loved to see people like him sink.

He put in the call to the EMS crew then went back into the house thinking of the iron lady. He felt his dick surge a bit as a fantasy took root in his brain: He'd get Cribbs packed off to the psycho ward in the EMS van, then he'd make a move on her. ("Ever ride in a cop car?" "Want to talk on the radio?" "I see you like guns. Want to go out to the range and ventilate some silhouettes with my Baretta?") He'd have to be on his toes, though—she seemed a little strange. Maybe she was just depressed about her boyfriend's crack up. Jesus, what a piss-poor excuse for a boyfriend. Maybe she was ready for a legitimate, card-carrying member of the male sex.

He stopped before letting himself back into the house so that he could get his dick under control. Goddamned White Table Queen squash. He ought to freeze-dry it, put it in capsules, and sell it door to door. Capoletti's Rock Cock Tonic. Smiling broadly, he pushed open the door.

*What the fuck,* he thought. *Couldn't they put their sex games on hold?* The iron lady was on top, her knees pinning Cribbs' skinny arms. *I could get off on that,* Capoletti thought, stirred up again. The boyfriend was bawling and saying *no—don't—please.* And she was jamming something into his face, like she was force feeding him handfuls of her shit. Had to be some kind of dominatrix thing, the disobedient boy getting his daily dose of discipline. *Cute,* Capoletti thought. *But this girl needs her whiskers split by an honest to Christ police officer of the studly persuasion.*

He sat on the sofa and lit a cigarette, prepared to enjoy the obedience clinic. What the hell, it was one of the perks of the job. Live entertainment. Then he saw the thing in her hand. He didn't want to believe it.

Sitting there, still infused with sexual itchings, he watched his career whirlpool down the toilet. He could visualize the headlines already:

## Cop With Big Boner Watches While Nutcase Lady Whacks College Geek.

He reached for his 9 millimeter Baretta, but by the time he got it out Carma had fired her purse gun three times into the forehead of Efraim Cribbs.

# Forty-eight

IT WAS ONE OF THOSE ENAMELED, LATE-AUTUMN skies that only the high desert can arrange. The air was clear and stable enough to allow starlight to thread down through the rich blue canopy. Guido went back to school through the arroyo after having had a sandwich and a club soda at The Lost Cause. He stopped now and then to admire the late afternoon sky. He believed he could see pinholes of starlight winking on and off, like lighthouse beacons scattered light-years across the universe. Guideposts in the outer chaos.

Which reminded him of a story his father had told him about a lighthouse named Philanoir, in Saint George's Channel. The *Emperor Moth,* having lost its rudder and masts in a north Atlantic storm, and leaking badly, drifted helplessly in a hard current toward a mass of rocks that rose up out of the coastal waters of Ireland like the dark gables of a sunken mansion. The men knew they'd had it, but the captain told them not to despair. Not for nothing had his ship been named the *Emperor Moth.* In a large compartment below deck, unknown to all but the captain, there were a thousand glass cages filled with the ship's namesakes: emperor moths. Each cage held a thousand of the large, exotic creatures.

The captain had his men carry the cages to the deck where they were stacked in sail-like arrangements. The glass sails faced Philanoir's beam and one million emperor moths flew passionately against the forward walls of their cages, producing a driving impetus that carried the ship away from the rocks and toward the sweeping fan of light under which the crippled ship was safely beached twelve hours later. It was one of the most preposterous of Elmo Tarkenen's stories, but it was Guido's favorite. The physics of this rescue, even to a five-year-old, was suspect. But the notion of a million fluttering desires generating enough force to carry a drifting ship away from disaster was beguiling.

He could easily visualize the story, but was never able to place his father in it. What was Elmo Tarkenen's role? Was he the captain? The navigator? One of the anonymous deck hands? A polymorphous presence that swam or flew alongside the *Emperor Moth* and its desperate crew? His father never included himself in the dramatic action. It didn't matter. The story was the thing, not the teller. The teller was the expendable vessel.

"You got a cigarette, Jim?"

It was the bearded bum in cardboard shoes. Guido gave him an unopened pack of Pall Malls. He decided to quit smoking, too. Heck Furness had told him his boozing days were over. "Hard drink fouls up the plumbing, Guido," he'd said. "I think you've had enough misery in that area of the anatomy. Stick to a glass of wine at dinner."

He continued on his way. A warm breeze funneled through the arroyo, finding voice in the pampas grass and mesquite and ocotillo. The ebb and surge of wind seethed like the breathing of a tired old man. This ancient lung of the planet, dry and fibrous with flora, wheezed and thrummed. The arroyo had been breathing like this for thousands of years, and would continue for thousands more.

Guido walked past the Renault Dauphin, inhabited by the adjunct professor. It now had bright yellow curtains in the windows. A small optimistic yard surrounded it, fenced with the wood from discarded packing crates. The adjunct professor was inside, typing at the keyboard of a lap-top computer. He looked upbeat, less ravaged by poverty and anger. Guido

330

waved at him. The man looked up, a pencil in his teeth. "Hey," he said, removing the pencil. "How you doing, doctor?"

Guido shrugged. "Better," he said.

"I finally got it," the man said. "I was lost but now I'm found."

"Oh? How so?"

"I got my angle. It's going to get me the Stevens Chair at Princeton, or maybe the Vittorini Chair in Milan. Implosionism. It's been there all along. Fucking implosionism, man."

"Implosionism?"

"From macro-identities to micro-identities. From micro-identities to the previously undetected sub-class of anti-identity entities. These are what I call proto-linguistic subsigns. Right there in every paragraph, sentence, word, morpheme, and phoneme. It all reduces to quantum scream. Maybe I should call it quantumism. My point? All literature, the whole catalog, from Bantu ghost stories to Jane Austen to Mickey Spillaine, is one grand howl of pain. That's all it is. I can find the howl in Nancy fucking Drew."

"I hear you," Guido said.

"Quantumism. My niche, man. I got my fucking *niche.*"

"God bless," Guido said, and continued on his way.

A woman jogged toward him. He stepped out of her way. As she passed, he said, "Carma!" She stopped, turned to face him. She had her kangaroo pack strapped on, but didn't unzip it. Guido fought a disorienting rush of déjà vu. He saw himself, lying in the dry dirt, begging for his life. Heard the shot that scored his shoulder. Saw her mini-revolver, felt it cold on his temple. He broke a sweat, but she only smiled at him, jogging in place. Had the last few weeks been an illusion, time dilated in some inner-Einsteinian space, the mind's final slight of hand? Had he been here all along, learning how to die?

"Who's Carma?" she said.

Guido saw his mistake. She was a runner and a lifter, a cross-trainer, but it was not Carma. Carma, after all, was in the state psychiatric facility.

"Sorry," he said. "I thought you were someone else."

"Better luck next time," she said, her smile open, free, uncompromised by slights, real or imagined.

It was a splendid day, and the world was full of splendid people. He reached into his jacket pocket and took out his new toy, a cellular phone. He dialed the city Crime Lab, asked for Seraghina.

They had slept together the previous night, the first time since his operation, and it had been fine. No sex, but the impulses and longings were intact, pulling at stitches, restored libido worrying the healing meat.

When she picked up the phone he said the difficult word, the commitment word, the cruelest four-letter word in the language. He said it again. The word caught in his throat, came out rough-edged and grainy.

"I know," she said. "I love you, too."

A bird flew past. Guido saw the red chevrons under its wings. He and the bird exchanged a microsecond glance. "Damn," he said. "I feel jinxed, saying it." Her voice made him sad and horny, happy and chaste. She pulled strings that were anchored in his marrow.

"It's stronger than any jinx. It's really ours, Guido," she said. "At least for now. For November. Maybe longer."

"Maybe forever," he said.

"Whoa. Stay real, hon. It's our only hope."

"I'm trying to." He wanted to tell her something, but didn't know exactly what it was. "I want to make amends," he said.

"Amends? There's nothing to mend, sugar."

"There's always something to mend."

He sat down on a flat stone. The breeze kicked up. It made the sound of expelled breath, the earth's long sigh.

He gestured with the cell phone, an inclusive sweep that represented the circle of his life—past, present, and future. He wanted her to understand something he did not fully understand himself. He thought he could sit on this stone for a thousand years and still not find the words for it. "There's always something to mend," he said again.

He thought of Kirsten, how he'd loved her and lost her. He wanted to make amends for that. He would not make Seraghina an appendage, whether they had November or thirty Novembers. He would not build invisible walls between them.

And he knew he was going to put *The Milksop Strangler* on hold. Something else needed mending first. Cash Holub would groan, but his next novel would be *The Voyages of the Emperor Moth*. It would begin:

*Mermaids rose out of the jade green sea, their breasts wreathed in kelp. They swam to my shipwrecked father, singing Elmo, Elmo, tell us your story. Tell us what you know of the hard, dry world. Tell it well, Elmo, and we will tell you how love is kept and how it is lost.*

333